Shakedown Cruise

A.M. PETERSON

The Adventures of Yacht Boy

"Shakedown Cruise"
The Adventures of Yacht Boy
By A. M. Peterson

Copyright ©2022 Anne Marie Peterson.

All rights reserved. No part of this publication may be reproduced, distributed, or transmitted in any form or by any means, including photocopying, recording, or other electronic or mechanical methods, without the prior written permission of the publisher, except in the case of brief quotations embodied in critical reviews and certain other noncommercial uses permitted by copyright law.

Any references to historical events, real people, or real places are used fictitiously. Names, characters, and places are products of the author's imagination and/or created to ensure privacy for the individuals who are used as examples.

Book design created by Anne Marie Peterson
Cover artwork and illustrations by Jon Tocchini
Edited by Liza Gershman of Gershman Creative Agency
Interior Design, Prepress, and Hardcover Book Jacket by Kailash Black

Printed and distributed by Amazon, in the United States of America.
First paperback, hardback, and eBook editions released May 2022.
For permission requests, email: publisher@youngnavigatorbooks.com
Subject Line: Permissions Relationships Manager
Young Navigator Books LLC
www.YoungNavigatorBooks.com

ISBN: 978-1-956986-00-6 (paperback)
ISBN: 978-1-956986-01-3 (hardback)
ISBN: 978-1-956986-02-0 (eBook)

Fiction
DRA Guided Reading Level: 40-70
Scholastic Guided Reading Level: M-Z
Lexile®Levels: 740-1070L
Word Count: 82,576
Grade: 8-12 (ages 12-18)

YOUNG
NAVIGATOR
★ BOOKS ★

Contents

Dedication 1

Author's Note 3

Quote 5

Chapter One – *Casting Off* 7

Chapter Two – *First Crossings* 27

Chapter Three – *Rescue Operations* 85

Chapter Four – *Going for A Spin* 103

Chapter Five – *Season of Giving* 121

Chapter Six – *Surprises* 149

Chapter Seven – *Geronimo!* 175

Chapter Eight – *Body Surfing* 203

Chapter Nine – *Antigua Nice!* 217

Chapter Ten – *Power Touring* 245

Chapter Eleven – *New Year's Eve* 271

Chapter Twelve – *Showtime!* 287

Glossary 297

List of Characters for Shakedown Cruise 316

Acknowledgments 318

Colophon 321

Biographies 325

To my dear son, Adrian
You are the Captain of your Life
The waves are not doing anything to you
The waves are inside you
Be One with the waves
to create the experience you desire.
XOX

Author's Note

A family tradition to tell stories and read books to one another has long been a part of my family. When Adrian, my son, learned to read at a very early age I stopped reading aloud to him. At age 7 he suddenly and stubbornly refused to read. Hence, at age 7, I began to read aloud to him again, so he maintained contact with the many ways of self-expression, communication of ideas, and a connection with the collective consciousness.

One evening, around age 9, he asked for me to tell him a story to help him fall asleep. That story became The Adventures of Yacht Boy, starring none other than my son, Adrian.

Although these stories are 99% pure fiction, some liberties from my real relationship with my son pepper my writing here and there. At one time, Adrian thought that calling his mom and dad Abercrombie and Fitch was funny. I was Abercrombie, by the way, because it rhymed with mommie in his head at the time.

And so it was, that every night I crafted a new chapter in his imaginary life aboard an Italian designed 66m custom built superyacht, that I reflected on my history with boats and envisioned all types of adventures that were suitable for an intelligent, highly sensitive, mostly confident, and sometimes anxious pre-teen with innate leadership ability to embark on.

My present author intention is to create a series of books (this being the first) that reveal the fine capabilities of young people when adults trust in their giftedness and the joys of adventuring around the world.

In my youth, I was a sea scout on San Francisco Bay. I spent over a decade being busy with boats, including skippering two youth programs for a short stint. I've been around many different types of boats and even a few luxury yachts but have never owned anything more than an inflatable swimming pool raft, at this writing.

No matter what age you are, swimming is an essential life skill. Take lessons and learn to be friends with water, especially the sea, which can reveal so much about your inner character, fears, and strengths.

Every opportunity to be on a boat or work on repairing watercraft of any kind is a valuable experience offering problem-solving skills, as no two outings or problems on a boat are ever the same.

If I have any advice for you, my beloved reader, it is this: recognize what self-judgments are and retrain yourself to stop making them. Learn ways to cultivate your inner guidance, stay connected to Nature, trust your instincts, and go for your dreams. You have all that it takes to be amazing, creating the life you intend by staying connected to your inner guidance and charting your own path in life. Just remember to use your inner loving voice as your navigator to solve problems from love, not fear.

Smooth sailing always,
Anne Marie Peterson
Los Angeles, CA USA

"Believe me, my young friend, there is nothing - absolutely nothing - half so much worth doing as simply messing about in boats."

- Kenneth Grahame,
Author "The Wind In the Willows" 1908

Chapter One
Casting Off

Superyacht Marina
Fort Lauderdale, Florida USA
Atlantic Ocean

Adrian Abercrombie stepped down from the black SUV that brought him and his family from the airport to the superyacht harbor in Fort Lauderdale. He was both excited and had some trepidation. The anxiety of not knowing the future was making him edgy. He had given up so much in the past few months in preparation for what was supposed to be, according to his mom and dad, the greatest adventure of his life, but he wasn't so sure.

He had never been aboard nor lived on a superyacht. He'd seen videos of them online, looked at specifications that were complex drawings of the design and interior of the yacht, but it meant nothing to him. This adventure at sea was almost eating him up on the inside, and it was hard for him to distinguish the difference between anxiety and anticipation at this point.

When he first heard about the adventure, he wasn't so sure it was going to be fun, exciting, or even interesting to him. Who wants to live on a boat? Seriously. What kid in their right mind wants to give up their school friends, teammates, house, and online gaming for a year at sea? No one in his age group, that's who.

Instead of being enthusiastic for the unknown, he took a grumbly approach to everything over the last few months. He showed his resistance to his mom when she asked him to pack his suitcases, games, books, and other things that she thought would be good to have on his journey. The list his mom gave him of things to pack was full of items that he didn't think he wanted or needed except his swimsuit, some shorts, and tee-shirts, but knowing his mom, she would look through his packed items to make sure he had everything she knew he truly needed for a great trip.

He remembered his mom telling him he had 1 week to find everything and make it all fit in two large suitcases and to leave them in the living room. At that time, he tried to negotiate with his mom for the items he wanted to bring. With some reluctance, she purchased the night vision goggles to motivate him as a reward. Most items he already owned, but the rest he would have to earn, like the satellite phone, metal detector and remote-controlled boats.

For weeks he pondered difficult questions like:

How was he going to have friends if he wasn't in school?

How was he going to have sports if he wasn't in school?

Who would he talk to?

Why did his mom have to include him and make him give up his life for some fantasy of hers to live at sea? ... He found that he was angry at his mom's plan to live on board a yacht for an entire year. He did not want to be homeschooled, sea-schooled, or whatever you call it.

To prepare Adrian for this life on the water, his mom had

A.M. Peterson

Mom's List of things to Pack

Day backpack
Portable fishing pole
Navy suit/tux
Ties
Dress shoes, belts
Small notebook and pen
Camera/Tripod
Sunscreen
Deodorant
Swimsuit
Clothes for all seasons
Shoes for all seasons
Dress shirts
Underwear
Socks
Jacket for cold weather
Phone/Charger
Comb/Toothbrush

Adrian's List of Things to Pack

Night vision goggles
Pocket knife
Walkie Talkie with headset
Cargo pants with multiple pockets with zippers
Flashlight and red lens covers
Waterproof Velcro wallet
Drone with camera for video
Satellite phone
Scuba mask and snorkel
Lobster tickle stick
RC controlled cars, boats and planes
Lighter and fire starter Mag-bar
Hi-powered binoculars
Fishing spear
Water guns
Compass
Solar cell battery charger/adapters
Underwater metal detector
Laptop, charger and case

enrolled him in swim lessons, which was a good thing as he was able to refine his strokes and kicks. He loved being in a pool and racing to the opposite wall with any kid who would accept the challenge. Jumping off the high dive was super cool, too, but the lifeguards didn't always let him do that if there were too many people in the deep end of the pool. One thing was for sure...this was a necessary life skill, but he was glad to have gotten the lessons behind him.

Many of his friends had moved away over the last year and he was feeling disconnected by the time he got on his parent's private jet to fly to Florida to get onboard their first motor yacht. He was bummed that many parents changed jobs, got divorced and forced change on his friends. Now it was his turn. He couldn't wait to grow up and control his own life. Why did it seem like it was taking so long?!

The driver opened the side door of the SUV and a blast of hot, humid air hit his face. He was still a bit taken aback by the weather in Florida. In Los Angeles, the weather was often hot and dry, with a cool breeze off the Pacific ocean. He gulped a bit and jumped down. Several young men dressed in white and navy uniforms, who had come from the yacht, greeted them in the parking lot and began to help move their luggage.

"Hey," he said looking up at the tall dark-skinned man who put out a big hand to shake.

"Hey, yourself, young man," his smile revealed perfect white teeth in his smiling Caribbean face. He was all muscles and Adrian couldn't help but stare for an extra second. "We're so happy to meet you and your family. Come on, young man, let's lead the way.

"I'm Jimmy Williams, First Officer. By the way, and before you ask me, I'm from Jamaica." He laughed and Adrian instantly liked the sound. Jimmy's voice had a pleasant rhythm, and within an instant, he was intrigued by this man in his crisp white uniform shirt with the anchor and three bars on the shoulders.

"I'm Adrian," he shared back. And remembering his manners, added, "Nice to meet you, too."

They walked past the main office of the new marina and after a few steps he asked, "Where is the yacht?"

"Ah. You'll see her in just a moment when we pass dat big delivery van on your left." Jimmy thrust his chin off to the left as his hands were pulling two large luggage bags on wheels behind him. "It's hiding your view."

"Why do you call the yacht a 'her'? How do you know that it is female?" Adrian asked inquisitively.

Jimmy threw back his head and laughed a loud, throaty laugh. "You'll find out soon enough, my friend."

Within a few steps Adrian could see many superyachts tied to the docks in the harbor. He saw the name M/Y Arabella on one of the top side panels of a yacht close by and his jaw dropped. It was much bigger than he imagined. He took a deep breath and stared at the size of the boat. "Oh, my god. It's huge!" he exclaimed. "We're going on that?!!"

Jimmy caught the look of disbelief and amazement on Adrian's face and smiled. "Yes, my friend, that is your new home for the next year, I believe." He paused when they reached a gate that needed a key-code and once it opened, he let Adrian inside. "After you!"

Adrian almost tripped on the gangplank going down to the docks to sea level. His neck was craning upwards to see where the multiple decks ended. He looked down to assess the environment his feet were in to regain his balance and memorize the direction he was going. Then let out a low whistle of appreciation under his breath. "Wow."

"Yeah, wow is right!" said Jimmy. "That's what I said the first time I saw it. Wait until you see the inside. You ain't never seen anything like it in your life." Jimmy pulled the luggage towards a gangplank leading up to the main deck of the super yacht named after his older and only sister, Arabella. He kicked off his boat shoes and placed them in a basket, indicating to Adrian that he should do the same. "Go on up! Someone will offer you a refreshing towel to wipe your face, neck, and hands; just use it and give it to one of the stews. A stew is a steward. You can ask them for just about anything."

Adrian looked back at where the rest of the family was, and they were just now entering the private gate to the superyacht dock. With a firm grip, he hitched his backpack up and thought to himself, "Well, it's now or never." And marched up the sun warmed smooth teak planks unconsciously holding his breath.

Just as Jimmy said, he was offered a refreshing, ice-cold towel and said, "Thanks. I'm Adrian, by the way."

The lady who gave him the finger towel, a damp hand-cloth to clean hands, was very nice and smiled a lot. Her name was Gabriella. The lady who took the towel on a different tray was named Jane. Both ladies spoke English, yet sounded different, so he asked where they were from. Gabriella was from South Africa and Jane was from Australia. Both had brown hair and were very tan. "They seemed nice," he thought to himself with assurance.

His anxiety was lessening as he met people and realized the crew aboard were friendly towards him.

"Welcome aboard, Master Adrian," boomed a deep voice to his right. Adrian turned to see a medium height broad-shouldered man with a dark red beard and short cropped brown hair. His broad, freckled round face bore a slight smile, but his tawny eyes were serious. His right hand was extended for a welcome greeting. On automatic, Adrian extended his and felt the powerful grip of someone he thought was the Captain of the yacht. He had gold stripes and a propeller on his epaulets.

"Hello," he cautiously greeted this big serious looking man whose hand could have swallowed his hand whole. In a tentative voice he asked, "are you the captain?"

Chuckling a bit, this man pulled his grin off to the left side of his face and said, "No, Mate. I'm the Chief Engineer, Peter Ferguson. You can call me Pete."

Breathing a sigh of relief that he wasn't in a make-wrong for guessing incorrectly, he smiled and said, "Nice to meet you, Pete. And...uh, where are you from? You sound American." Adrian leaned to his left and studied this barrel-chested man who could have been an arm wrestler. He smiled a bit as he waited for an answer.

"I am. Born and bred in the San Francisco Bay Area. Even went to the California Maritime Academy." Pete looked pleased with himself for having been to CMA.

A soft and lyrical Scandinavian voice from behind Adrian almost made him jump. "Don't mind this blaggard. He'll be tellin' ya he was a pirate next, and his parrot speaks five languages at the level of a kindergartener." The gentleman who spoke was wiry, with gray hair and had a classic captain's cap on his head. His epaulets had four gold bars like Pete, but instead of a propeller, he had an anchor.

Pete threw back his head and laughed so loud, Adrian cringed. "Aye, aye, Captain. Just give me enough time and I'll have this young scallywag workin' with me in the engine room with a pet monkey."

The captain had pale blue eyes with quite the twinkle in them and Adrian was quite taken by them. He put out his hand, "Captain Gunnar Johnson, at your command."

"Hi, Captain. I'm Adrian." They shook hands. Adrian looked sideways over at Pete and grinned a bit. He felt he could make a little joke between the three of them. "Should I be worried about this guy, Captain? Is he sus?" Adrian crossed his arms over his chest and in a rather theatrical manner looked Pete up and down.

"Sus?" asked the captain, a little confused.

"Yeah," said Adrian with a grin, "you know, Captain...suspect. Suspicious."

"Aye," responded the captain with a knowing smile. "He's sus alright."

Something inside Adrian made him feel good about their little introduction. He liked both guys right away.

The captain changed the subject and asked Adrian, "Have you been shown to your cabin?"

"No, not yet." Adrian looked over his shoulder where his family was gathered around the big salon on the main deck and shaking hands with everyone. "I think maybe I ought to rejoin my family and see what the plan is for the next hour."

Putting a hand on Adrian's shoulder, Pete steered him back to his family and announced, "This is the man of the hour! Master Adrian!"

"Sheesh," Adrian said under his breath to Pete as he threw him a furious look. "Tone it down a bit."

Pete and the crew laughed. "Hi, Adrian!" was spoken from every crew at the same time. Jimmy gallantly stepped forward and said, "Come on, I'll rescue you from all these intros. You can meet everyone later. It's too hard to memorize thirteen names and faces. You just have to remember mine, since I'm going to be assigned to you as your steward...a.k.a. your new best friend."

"Ah. I see. I've been assigned a BFF onboard, too?" Adrian scowled at his mom. This felt like her doing. Of course, she would have made sure that everyone had someone to watch out for them and then some.

"Hey! Hey!" Jimmy urged, quick to cut him off. "Don't jump to conclusions and judge your mom. This is how it is on yachts. Every crew member is assigned to a cabin to serve the guest and make sure they have everything they need to have a good experience. Your mom had nothin' to do with me being the one assigned to you."

"Oh." Adrian felt a bit abashed and lowered his head some to hide his embarrassment. He noticed of late that he was blaming his mom quite a bit for his life circumstances, which wasn't fair, and he realized it made him feel like a victim. "Sorry about that," he mumbled.

"No problem, man. We' good." Jimmy pointed to his backpack and asked if he wanted him to carry it. Adrian shook his head no. His most important stuff was in his backpack, and he wasn't going to let anyone, not even his new BFF touch his stuff. "OK, then, come. Let's find your cabin."

Jimmy pointed upwards and shared that his parents' private apartment also known as the "owner's cabin" was one deck up. He and his sister Arabella Grace were on the main deck. They each had their own room or "cabin." Jimmy entered the first cabin on the right side of the well-lit hallway. "And here we go! Yours is the starboard cabin on the main deck. Your sister is in the port cabin across the passageway." He held the door open for Adrian to enter before him. Once again, Adrian's mouth fell open in disbelief at the spacious and luxurious cabin that was all his.

The first thing he noticed were two bunk beds that hung down from the ceiling for friends to sleep over. His bed was a queen size bed covered in pillows and looked extra inviting. He wanted to throw himself on top and check how soft it was. Two large floor-to-ceiling windows looked out onto the dock, and he knew that when he was at sea, it would be the ocean he could view. A desk and massive TV were off to the side with a small table and squishy poufs for sitting on.

Jimmy, as his tour guide, opened the door to the bathroom *en suite* so he could take it all in. Adrian's eyes popped out when he saw the marble walls and sink, walk-in glass shower with jets and a huge rain shower head mounted in the ceiling. "Dang." He let out his second low whistle of the day and stood turning circles in the oversized bathroom. "My bathroom back home didn't look this nice. Don't get me wrong, it was nice, but this is capital letters N-I-C-E!"

"It's something, eh?" Jimmy asked with a knowing smile. "I'd say you are going to enjoy life aboard the Arabella. Wait until you meet our chef! I hope you love to eat!" He winked at Adrian and turned to bring the suitcases deeper into his cabin.

"Oh. My. Gawd." Adrian began, "I love to eat! Are you kidding me? I think I was born to eat! Now, I'm hungry just thinking about it." He left the bathroom and set his backpack on the desk in his room. Pausing to place a protective hand on his bag, he asked, "Do me a favor, Jimmy?"

"Sure. Anything. What is it?"

"Don't touch my backpack, okay?" Adrian asked as nicely as he could. He just wanted some privacy about his stuff and no one to touch it. He didn't mean any offense, and it appeared that Jimmy's nod shared he understood one hundred percent.

"Roger that, Adrian," he acknowledged and brought in the last bag. "Why don't you go explore the yacht and I will start putting away your clothes and such for you. I'll be putting the suitcases in a storage area below decks, so if there is anything you hid in the pockets or lining that you need, tell me now." He winked at Adrian with a big grin. "I was a boy, once, too. I was always hiding something."

Adrian smiled and denied that there was anything in the luggage that he needed. He patted his backpack, "I got everything I need in here."

Jimmy nodded and held the door for Adrian to leave the cabin. "See you later!"

Adrian went across the passageway to his sister Grace's room and knocked once. He heard his mom and tried the handle to go in. His sister's room was similar, except it was two twin beds dressed in an expert touch. Everything else was similar in both layout and design. He had to admit, the cabins were beautiful. He would give them seven-star ratings.

"Hey," he greeted the three gals. Gabriella, the soft-spoken lady who was Grace's assigned stewardess returned his casual greeting with her own accented one. "Hey, yourself."

"Are you settled into your cabin, sweetheart?" his mom asked. "We're just getting Grace settled in and then we are going upstairs to our cabin to meet your dad and get a bit organized."

"OK. Cool." Adrian was fiddling with the iPad he found on the nightstand and eyeballing the remote control that looked identical to one in his room.

"That's for the window shades," Gabriella announced, "setting an alarm, and contacting the crew, among other things."

"I see that!" Adrian kind of half laughed as the shades started to come down on the two windows at the exact moment she informed him of its function. "Wow, that is so cool!"

"Adrian," Grace said with a bossy attitude, "just leave it alone, will you? I didn't ask you to come in here and start messing with my things."

"Wah, wah, wah, wah, wah…" he mocked her and placed the iPad back down. "I'm not messing with your things. OK?" He turned to leave. "And one more thing…you're not allowed to come into my cabin, you hear me?" His mom sighed and shooed him out of his sister's cabin. He left but not before his mom stuck her head around the door and said in a warning voice, "Adrian…knock it off. We're here to relax and have fun."

Rolling his eyes, because he didn't want to express in an authentic manner what he was really thinking inside, which he knew was a sign that he wasn't standing in his power, he sighed and suppressed his feelings about his sister. His mom hated him and Grace rolling their eyes for any reason. From her perspective she believed he wasn't having an authentic conversation with his sister. He agreed it was a shortcut to sharing his judgment of Grace, and he could do it while she was talking without having to open his mouth. *Maybe I am being lazy. And I guess I don't really want to tell her what I really think because I don't believe she would listen or change for me. She always treated me like I'm a little boy. And in my opinion, she is spoiled.* She was four years older than him, so it was hard to connect sometimes. Her big thing in life was getting a boyfriend and her driver's license. And it wasn't like she would be driving anywhere over the next year. He had better things to do.

Wandering towards the back of the yacht, he went down the stairs he found aft of the TV lounge outside his cabin, he opened various doors and looked inside other cabins that were similar to his and Grace's. There were four total underneath his and his sister's cabins on the lower deck just at the waterline. His parent's cabin made seven. That meant the yacht could have a total of fourteen guests. His mom had wanted to have her siblings and their spouses onboard for family trips, so she had thought to get a yacht that could have everyone all at once.

He went back up the staircase three flights, which led him to the bridge deck. A quick look aft revealed a spacious deck with a dining table and chairs with some chaise lounges for sunbathing. He turned and wandered down a passageway towards the bow. A small sign on a wooden door revealed the captain's cabin was to the port side just before the bridge where the captain steered the yacht.

Hearing two familiar male voices, he made his way towards them with some hesitation. He made eye contact with Pete and then the captain, who he asked if it was okay to come into the wheelhouse also known as the bridge. He didn't know if he was interrupting a private conversation or if this area was off limits.

He couldn't wait to see this part of the yacht with all its fancy electronics, computers, and monitors. With a hearty and reassuring 'aye' he leapt into the brain center of the superyacht. Pete and the Captain continued their conversation while Adrian looked around the wheelhouse.

He was blown away at the command center before him. This was better than any gaming room or gaming chairs he'd ever seen. Monitors were lined up across the front of the bridge with scanners, radar, GPS, electrical systems, radio communication devices and so much more than he could take in, at that moment.

He ran his hand along the smooth navigation desk he found off to the side of the bridge. The table held paper charts under an acrylic sheet hinged to the table along the back wall of the bridge. He lifted the heavy lid up to reveal more nautical charts, navigation tools and pencils. He closed it softly and went to stand at the wheel. With a light touch, his fingers ran over the varnished wheel. It was amazing that such a small wheel could command a 66m yacht. He saw levers and joysticks for navigating the water-jet propulsion system under the hull and he was sure he was going to have a thousand questions in the days to come.

Pete had left and it was just him and the captain. "This is cool stuff," he marveled. "Wow. I can't even imagine what it all does."

"Well," shared the captain, "I'm sure in the days to come you can join me here on the bridge and I can start teaching you about what each of these gizmos do."

"I'd like that," Adrian replied sincerely. Looking forward he asked, "are those windshield wipers?"

"They sure are."

"But...you're so high up...and there is an overhang. What do you need those for?" Adrian was a bit perplexed as he considered each of the windows that created a massive windshield for the captain.

"In high or stormy seas, we can get quite a bit of salt spray up here." The captain reported this to Adrian with an even voice knowing it could be quite alarming to a first-time sailor. "And when it rains, and the wind is blowing, or we are driving into the rain, it can be blinding."

Adrian knit his brows together in thought. "And how often do you have to use them?"

"Not very," the captain reassured him. "Come on, there is a party to attend. Let's take the lift." Exiting the wheelhouse together, they chatted about Adrian's life back home as they walked to and entered the chrome and glass elevator. The Captain pushed the button for the main deck and the glass doors opened in one smooth mechanical movement. "I hope you enjoy yourself today, Adrian. Do try to meet all the crew. I'm going to say hello to a few people your parents invited aboard, and I'll see you later."

They parted ways in the middle of the main deck lounge where a private party was in full swing. His family's yacht broker and insurance agent were enjoying drinks and appetizer type foods along with some of their staff. The crew stood discreetly in the wings, and two of the crew were bartending. He realized it was close to lunchtime and walked outside to the food table. He loved bite-size foods and just about anything one could eat with their fingers. The table was flooded with an assortment of food from one end to the other. Was this what life onboard was going to be like every day? He sure hoped so!

Taking a fine bone china plate with a gold band and decorative anchor on the edge, he began to fill his plate with crab cakes, sushi rolls, an interesting vegetarian Asian concoction wrapped in rice paper, and a petite French tart with custard, and topped with blueberries for dessert. Popping a perfect piece of a dragon roll into his mouth he munched away while walking over to the top step near the port railing. He looked over the stern deck below him. Filled almost to the brim was a large pool with a glass wall. It was just like the pictures. He was definitely going to check that bad boy out later.

Stuffing another roll into his mouth he looked across the water to see what the horizon held. Nothing but blue skies and fluffy white clouds. The harbor was crowded with yachts of all sizes, some of which were being cleaned or worked on by crew.

Turning back to face the party crowd, he looked to see where everyone was and what they were up to. His sister was on her phone talking to her best friend and looking at her nail polish. His mom was talking with the British guy who brokered the boat deal. His dad appeared to be engaged in interesting conversation with the marine lawyer who managed the contracts, and the three marine engineers who did the inspections on the boat. All boring.

He stuffed a crab cake in his mouth and moaned with pleasure at how good it was and launched himself off the step to go back and get more.

At the table, he piled three more crab cakes on his plate and two more dragon sushi rolls. He needed to meet the chef. This food was amazing. And if there was one thing Adrian loved more than anything else, it was food. Especially good food.

Wandering over to Jimmy at the bar, he excused himself for interrupting to ask if he could meet the chef.

Jimmy wiped his hands on a bartending towel and folded it before setting it down. "Sure thing!"

They walked through the main salon, zigzagged past the lift, went through a door on their left, turned right down a passageway that led forward and through another door before they arrived in the galley. "Chef Zak! Meet your latest admirer! Master Adrian."

Chef Zak, dressed in a white chef's coat with the name M/Y

Arabella embroidered on the left breast area and a black chef's cap on his head, looked up and wiped his hands on a towel. Coming around the center island workstation that was several meters long, he shook Adrian's hand. "Nice to meet you, Adrian. Are you having a good time so far?"

"Yeah, I guess so." Adrian shrugged and brushed off the chef's social niceties to get to the main point of conversation he wanted to have with the chef. "I...uh, well, I wanted to meet you. I just, uh, well, I just had your crab cakes, and they were super amazing. I mean, they were THE best I've ever had in my life! I have to know how to make them." Adrian, once he got his courage up, got all of that out with some dramatic hand gestures.

With the slightest tilt, Zak bowed his head. "Thank you! I'm so glad you enjoyed them."

"Enjoyed them?" Adrian asked in mock disbelief, "I loved them!"

Zak and Jimmy chuckled while sharing a glance. "Like I said," Jimmy began with a smile, "your latest fan."

"Tell me, Adrian," Zak started, "do you like to cook?"

"I love to cook. I've been cooking and baking since I was like, um, you know..." he waved his left hand in the past, "like six years old. And I've been watching videos online for years to learn how to make things. I'm probably a food-a-holic."

The men laughed and Zak leaned back on the counter behind him. His face was a study in both serious contemplation and curiosity. "Adrian," he asked in an inviting tone, "Would you be interested in helping out in the kitchen here and there, to learn some new stuff?"

Adrian straightened up and blinked his eyes twice with incredulity. "You're asking me to help out here?" He was stirred up with the potentials and possibilities and excitement flooded his whole being. "Seriously?"

"Dead serious." He put out his hand to shake on the deal and Adrian jumped forward to shake it. His eagerness made the men smile.

"Deal." Adrian paused long enough to say to both guys, "this sea adventure just got waaaay better."

"Well, that settles it then." Jimmy pronounced with a twinkle in his eye for Zak, "you report for kitchen duty at 4AM tomorrow morning."

"Wait. What?" Adrian looked downright confused. "You are joking with me, right?"

Zak laughed and took a dish towel and flogged Jimmy with it lightly. "Go on, man, you're going to give this kid a heart attack before we even leave the dock." Turning to Adrian, he said, "No. Just enjoy yourself. I'll keep you posted about what I am making and then you can pick and choose what you want to learn and just swing by the galley ahead of time."

"Whew." His relief was visible. In a flash that surprised the men, he grabbed the towel from Zak and rolled it a few times and advanced on Jimmy who laughed and started to back away.

"I think I heard the Captain callin' me. Gotta dash, Master Adrian, see you around." Jimmy leaped out of the way of Adrian's flick of the towel at his legs.

Adrian handed the towel back to Zak. "Jimmy seems cool, so far," he shared.

Zak nodded in agreement. "We all love Jimmy. He's got a good head on his shoulders and a great personality. We all agreed that he should be your cabin steward, although it is most unusual for the first officer to act as a stew because of his rank and experience. He's also trained in small boat handling, is a jet ski and water ski instructor, lifeguard, and a few other certifications…

like SCUBA. You could get certified while onboard."

"Wow!" Adrian was blown away by all that talent. He had never done any of those things before. "I hope I get to be as good as him."

"Oh, you will. That's the whole point of connecting the two of you." Zak stuffed the towel into a basket that was for galley laundry and observed Adrian watching him. "We take towel hygiene seriously around here. I touched it, you touched it, Jimmy's leg touched it and we've shaken hands, you were eating finger foods... so it now must be washed because bacteria could be on it. So, when you are in the galley, every precaution is taken to keep your family and the crew healthy."

"Roger that," Adrian agreed. He watched Zak wash his hands at the sink like a doctor preparing for surgery and pull out a fresh towel from a drawer where several dozen were rolled tight and stuffed inside. He made a mental note about where they were stored since he planned on coming into the galley quite often.

"You like chocolate chip cookies?" Zak pulled a large metal tin down from the top shelf of a cupboard. "This here is my secret stash."

"Who doesn't?" Adrian asked with a smile as he reached inside the tin and helped himself to a golden cookie bursting with dark chocolate chips.

"Well, I don't know anyone who doesn't. And these are made with all organic ingredients and dark chocolate I special ordered from Belgium." He watched Adrian sink his teeth into the cookie as he walked towards the commercial size stainless-steel paneled fridge. "Milk?"

"Yes, please!" Adrian affirmed with a big nod of his head.

Within seconds he was chugging a glass of ice-cold milk and he closed his eyes with pleasure. "OMG. That's all I got right now.

OMG." He fist bumped Zak, walked over to the sink to place his empty lunch plate and glass in it, thanked him and left the galley saying over his shoulder, "Thanks, man. I'll see you around."

Before they cast off, two of the crew began draining the swimming pool for the voyage ahead. The captain called a meeting with all hands on deck and discussed safety and emergency procedures for man-overboard, fire, accident, and security protocols at sea and in port. The Abercrombie family practiced putting on life jackets and listened to how to get in and out of the small power boats stored on board. They walked through the main salon and passageways to cabins and identified and observed locations of fire alarms and where first aid kits were placed throughout the yacht. Satisfied with their knowledge, the captain dismissed everyone and returned to the bridge.

After the mandatory meeting, Adrian hung out in his cabin to have some space away from everyone. There was no one at the party he needed to talk to.

He had a sudden realization that he was now on a very large boat with seventeen people for the next year. There were some deckhands and stewards he still had not met. He was glad Jimmy was his steward and Zak was his chef. That was two major scores for the day. He hoped this meant this year-long family journey aboard the motor yacht Arabella was going to be good. He thought about pulling out his laptop to jump online and see if his friends were on but instead closed his eyes for just a few seconds to take it all in.

Chapter Two
First Crossings

Nassau, New Providence Island
The Commonwealth of The Bahamas
North Atlantic Ocean

Adrian woke up with a start and jumped to his feet with a rush of anxiety. He took in the cabin and quickly settled down when he realized where he was. It came back in a flash that he was now living fulltime, with his family, aboard *M/Y Arabella*. Drawing a deep breath, he moved to place his backpack in a dressing room closet. After a quick trip to the bathroom, also known as "the head," on a boat of any size, he left his cabin to go exploring.

He found his mom and dad enjoying a bottle of champagne on the main deck and waved hello before heading up two flights of stairs to the most interesting place he could think of: the bridge. "Hi, Captain. I hope I am not interrupting anything." Adrian remained in the doorway hinting at requesting permission to enter the bridge. The captain waved him in. With deep focus, he was looking at a monitor and one of the crew he hadn't met was to his side. This young man caught his eye and smiled.

"Hello, Adrian. I'm Bryce Fraser. I'm the resident IT specialist and electrical engineer." He put out his fist to do knuckles behind the captain's back, which Adrian met with his own.

"Hey." Adrian perked up at the words IT specialist. He loved all things computers and the internet. He was glad to meet someone working in this area of expertise.

Bryce continued. "We're just looking at the digital charts for the waters we are crossing to make sure we are in the deepest section when we travel through the Bahamas. Want to have a look?"

"OK." Adrian moved in between the men as Bryce took a half-step to the side. He reached in and pointed to the screen. "That red dot is us. See the top? That's north. We're headed east southeast, so the dot shows us moving slightly down and away from Fort Lauderdale. See that land mass on the left, or west? That's all Florida that we are passing and leaving behind us. See the island in the right-hand corner? That's New Providence Island and the city of Nassau, the capital of the Bahamas."

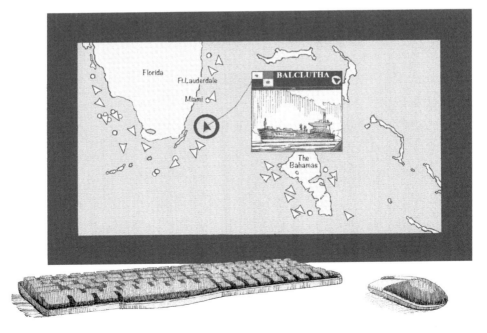

Nodding his head that he understood, he pointed to the screen and asked if the other dots were other boats.

"Yes, other vessels. We can click on them and get their name and position." He used his finger to touch the screen and double tapped one of the dots. "See? This one is a shipping container named *Balclutha* registered to Panama. Pick one and see where it is from."

Adrian double tapped a yellow dot and up came a box of information. "Uhh, okay...this one appears to be the motor yacht *Endless Summer* registered in the Bahamas." He paused as he determined the data relating to the boat on the screen. "Cool!"

He angled his head to look at Bryce and asked, "What do these other monitors do? One has an obvious electrical panel on it, and another has a weather map with radar. And are they Macs or PCs?"

Bryce smiled with his lips pursed and straightened up from the console table he was leaning on with his forearms. The captain injected a comment before he let Bryce answer, "Adrian, Bryce is our computer guru, and he will talk for hours on end about computers. If you give him an inch, he will take a mile." The captain smiled with fondness at Bryce, placed a fatherly hand on his shoulder and then added, "I've known Bryce all my life. He's my nephew, and he is like a son to me. My sister adopted and raised him. We count on him for all things computers around here, so add him to your cell phone before you leave the bridge."

"Nice." Adrian liked the easy-going relationship the captain had with Bryce. He wished his dad treated him the same way. Warm and loving, not stressful and judgmental.

"So, yeah, Adrian, we can talk shop anytime," Bryce invited. "And to answer your question, as you may have noticed all the cabins have iPads running the features because they are easy to use for guests, but we run all the ship systems on PCs."

"Are you using Linux or Microsoft?" Adrian inquired. He and his dad had built a few computers from scratch using each of those systems and he admired each system for their inherent features but also capabilities.

"All these systems were designed for Microsoft so that the user interface would be familiar for most users. On my own personal machine..."

"You use Linux." Adrian finished his sentence for him.

"Indeed, I do!"

"Me, too."

"I see we have lots in common and loads to talk about." Bryce said in a friendly manner. "But right now, I got wires to trace and pull down in the engine room. Let's catch up soon."

"Sounds good. Thanks." They fist bumped again and Bryce disappeared through the open door.

"Adrian, would you like to steer?" the captain asked. "Stand right here and face forward. I'll be right here beside you." He moved his body away from the helm so Adrian could move into the position of helmsman.

"OK." Trying his best to hide his considerable hesitancy, Adrian took the wheel in his hands, and instantly felt growing anxiety in his body. He was afraid he would do something wrong, like run aground in shallow water or hit something underwater and put a hole in the ship and cause everyone to be unhappy. He hated when he did something wrong. "What if I hit something?"

"Adrian!" the captain chided with zero judgment in his voice, "do you see anything in front of or beside you? No. Did you not see the deep water we are in?" He pointed to the depth sounder which presented new and slightly varying numbers in the hundreds of feet.

"Alright," Adrian breathed out his fear. "It's just that sometimes things don't always go the way I want them to...you know, and then my parents get mad at me. Well, mostly my dad. I'm pretty sure he thinks I'm stupid."

"Well, I do not for one second think you are stupid!" The captain added some emphasis to his words to imply that he was a bit horrified that Adrian's dad would for a single moment consider his super bright child to be less than intelligent. "And I don't think your father thinks that is true about you either. Maybe it is time for a course correction. You know, think about it from a different perspective."

"Yeah, well..." he began, "every time I don't do something right or on time, he yells at me. And it always has the energy of 'you're an idiot' or 'don't be stupid' in the tone. How am I not supposed to think otherwise?" Adrian's face looked sullen as he steered the ship without moving the wheel. "Am I doing this right?"

"Yep!" The captain grinned. "Just keep us on this course of 125 degrees magnetic so we can motor past the Bimini Islands of the Bahamas to starboard. Use this monitor to track your course." He pointed to the black framed computer monitor just in front of the helm.

"You know," the captain began with a kind tone, "sometimes parents sense the full potential in their children and unconsciously create high expectations. Parents might not know that they have expectations of their kids to express intelligence in all aspects of life all the time, but because they want the best for their kids, they can express this hope unconsciously. And when someone isn't living their full potential, the parents or teachers or elders might believe demanding the kid to live the potential is how to go about correcting their course in life. And last time I checked, no one likes demanding energy sent in their direction." He paused and let that sink in before continuing. "Any idea why demanding improvement isn't as effective as guiding that improvement like I guide this crew and this ship?"

Adrian thought about it in his own life and considered his relationship with his parents. *Why would my dad demand I be smart when I am smart?* He felt a little lost in the conversation. *Does my dad think I am forgetting to be smart? Or is he afraid I am not smart enough?* "I have this experience sometimes with my parents and sense you know better than I do, but I think it has to do with fear inside my dad that he isn't doing enough to help me be the best I can be in life, even though he obviously is. I have a feeling this trip will turn out better than I expected. Already I'm learning all kinds of new stuff!"

"Correct," the captain confirmed. "Fear is a powerful instigator. When people begin to fear that their needs are not going to be met, they start making demands on people. I suspect most people who are very intelligent fear the possibility of their own stupidity. They fear being wrong or being considered stupid, which may lead them to needing to be right all the time or being perfect so no one can point out that they are wrong or stupid."

"Yep, I know someone like that....that sounds like me and my dad."

The captain chuckled and added, "I was driven by perfectionism in my youth. The first time I crashed a small boat against a pier, I thought my world was over. After that, I decided living with perfectionism was too stressful and spent years undoing my need to do everything perfectly. Don't get me wrong, the accident was dangerous, but I learned to calm my reactive mind to bad situations so I can have clarity of mind and solve my problem from a peaceful mind not a fear-driven anxious one."

"I can't imagine a person gets to be captain by being dumb or sloppy," Adrian shared with caution. "How do you find balance?"

"Good question." The captain paused and considered it and checked one of the monitors for a reading while he came up with his answer. He took a breath and tilted his head to look up at the intersection of the windshield and the ceiling. "Ease and flow versus push and force.

"When I am pushing to make something perfect, I am forcing something to happen because I have fear behind it. I am now quick to notice if I am pushing to get it right from fear of not being on time, or a fear of being judged by the owners or colleagues, or fears stemming from a need for safety because the sea can be more powerful than us. The pushing causes mistakes, and I now hear my voice change when I am pushing or forcing something, and demanding energy definitely creeps in. This vocal change alerts my brain to the fact that I need to slow down and relax in order to make good safety decisions."

"How do you switch it off and do, what was it?"

"Ease and flow are on the other side of the coin of push and force." The captain raised his left index finger to pause the conversation and took a brief moment to answer a crew question over his walkie-talkie. Back to Adrian, he continued. "OK. I find that when I don't come from fear, but trust, I end up having faith in myself and the crew when facing a situation that requires problem solving. Granted, I have years of experience to draw upon and all the collective wisdom of the people around me. Ease just happens automatically and solutions just flow. Does that make sense?"

"I think so." Adrian mulled the words over in his head. "Experience helps. Knowing you can do something successfully does help, too."

"True. But you can have ease and flow while you are learning, too. Like right now."

"Right now?"

"While you are learning to drive this yacht, you have me with all my knowledge partnering with you." The captain smiled and turned to face him, "Don't you have trust and faith in me to support you driving the yacht to our destination, even though you have never driven before?"

Adrian stood still at the helm contemplating the captain's words. He wasn't comfortable being responsible for this 216.6' yacht that cost nearly a hundred million dollars. If he damaged it, he was in big trouble. "Are you sure I'm doing it right? This is not ease and flow for me. It creates stress in me because I've never done this before." He was so frustrated with himself for asking, but he always felt this underlying need to be doing everything right. He just feared doing things wrong. It often killed his joy being caught up in perfectionism. His problem was always present, and he never seemed to know a life without it. Perfectionism just left him wondering what punishment was around the corner when he got things wrong. Needing to be right all the time sucked. Big time.

"Relax, Adrian, you are doing great. Make a choice to trust yourself in this experience with me here beside you. I will not allow you to fail." He laughed and put a hand on Adrian's shoulder, "my insurance would go up and your parents would replace me!"

"Seriously though, let go of the idea of success and failure and ease and flow will commence. Success and failure is a minefield to navigate, in my humble opinion, and creates pressure, stress and denies a person of being present in the moment because fear is present in both elements. And if fear is your motivator, you will do everything to avoid the thing you fear and miss the value of the experience you are in."

"OK. Sorry."

"What do you believe you need to apologize for?" the captain asked with compassion in his voice without taking his eyes off the monitor in front of him that he was programming for their next course change by the looks of it.

"I dunno. I guess I…" his voice trailed off as he took a moment to reflect, "I just felt bad for asking for reassurance."

"Hey, let it go. You don't need me to tell you that you are doing good." The captain straightened up to look ahead. "You are the captain of your life and no one else. When you start reassuring yourself that you are doing well, you start noticing how you are doing things right instead of looking for how you are doing things wrong." He smiled at Adrian. "Are you ready to turn the wheel slightly to starboard by a few degrees?"

"I think so." Adrian took stock of what the captain said and feeling more positive, he asserted, "Sure! How much do I turn this wheel without flipping her over on her ear?"

The captain chuckled. "Thank goodness we have stabilizers on the bottom of this ship, so that is not going to happen, but a tight turn would not be good for this yacht and everyone in it."

He reached over to handle the wheel with Adrian and gently moved it an inch or two and held it in place as the boat began to turn a few degrees to starboard. He used his free hand to point to the monitor. "See how the compass is changing?" The numbers moved from 125 degrees to 127 degrees and when the digital compass reached 130 degrees, the captain straightened the helm and left it with Adrian. "Hold this course."

Although he got tired standing at the helm for over an hour, he maintained his position. Soon, Adrian could see the shape of land on the horizon in the distance and the effort became interesting. "Those are the Bahama Islands up ahead?"

"Yes. That's right. And it gets shallow in places because this is an archipelago with a few atolls here and there. Archipelagos are—" the captain could not complete his sentence as Adrian interjected the description.

"—tens or hundreds of coral islands, and atolls are coral islands that grow out of the sea. But what created those higher spots?" Adrian pointed to the slight elevation on the horizon.

"Coral, over millions of years, along with seashells and other creatures made what I believe are limestone hills. I would wager that those are all limestone." The captain paused as he gave thought to the subject, then added, "Google it, and report back to me what you learn. I can't imagine it being volcanic or anything else, and certainly those hills can't be more than 60 feet high above the sea."

"Oh, by the way," Adrian began, "I've been meaning to ask: how long have we been on the road and how long before we get there?"

"First," the captain began in a friendly but educational tone, "we're at sea, not on land, so we say underway. We've been underway for over six hours and we're traveling at about 10 nautical miles per hour. We've got a couple nautical miles to go."

Adrian almost cringed at being corrected, but he knew better than to go into any more self-judgments about being wrong around the captain. He sensed the captain was not judging him one bit. He breathed out his make-wrong and answered, "Roger that. Underway. Gotcha. So..." he did some quick math in his head. He calculated that by traveling at ten nautical miles per hour, he would cover five nautical miles in half the time or thirty minutes. Half of five would be two and a half nautical miles in 15 minutes. "So...about 10 to 15 more minutes until we reach Nassau?"

The captain gave an affirmative nod. "That's right. We're going to dock and let the Port of Entry Customs and Immigration know that we are here. They will send an officer to our boat. Then we must present our paperwork for the boat and all people aboard. Each country we visit requires you to pay a fee to dock, obtain a tourist visa or immigration card to stay and you must announce the length of your stay, show identification, list all the firearms and ammunition you carry on board and add things like pets and vaccination cards. You can always extend or shorten your stay, if necessary, but those are the basics. Technically, only the captain is to deal with the officer they send out, but they know me, and you may accompany me if you like." He glanced over at Adrian and sized him up.

"Please change into a collared shirt and wear some boat shoes. Always present yourself in a proper manner when dealing with authorities. It shows respect and tells them how you want to be treated. OK?"

"OK, Captain. I can be ready by the time the boat is secured," he promised, giving a thumbs up.

Reaching over the console, the captain picked up the telephone handle for the radio, punched in the number 16 and called over the airwaves for the port master. "Motor yacht *Arabella* to Nassau Harbor port master's office. Motor yacht *Arabella* to Nassau Harbor port master's office. Over."

The speaker crackled and a male voice replied, "Nassau Harbor Port Master's office to motor yacht *Arabella*. Switching to channel 9. Over."

"Wilco," the captain replied and typed in the number 9 on the keypad. Once the channel switch went through, without skipping a beat he said, "Motor yacht *Arabella* to Nassau Customs and Immigration, seeking entry and berthing, over."

"Roger that. This is the Port Master, what is your length?"

"66 meters. Over."

"OK, we have space. Pull into the north end of the super yacht dock and take the first available berth next to motor yacht *Infinity*. Over."

"Wilco." The captain hung up the handset to the radio and took the helm. He put in an earbud that had a coil of wire behind his ear that led to a walkie talkie on his hip. He reached back and touched a button to talk to the crew. "Place the quarantine flag out. Stand by to berth. All fenders out. We're taking the end berth on the north end. Prepare the bow anchor and ground lines. We are stern tying as per usual. Motor yacht *Infinity* will be to starboard. Over.'

Quarantine? Puzzled, because Adrian could not hear the replies from the crew, he took a step backwards to step towards the open door to look outside. The captain had slowed the boat down over the last nautical mile or so and they were creeping towards the harbor in such a way that there was no wake being produced by the yacht, which would have rocked a few boats. Now the captain was jockeying this huge boat to thread a needle through multiple boats and reverse the engines to back into the dock. He noticed the wind was behind them, slowing the boat down a bit. Heck, the height of their boat would block the breeze on a small building it was so tall.

He came back inside to watch the captain navigate the boat using both the directions from his crew over the earpiece and the video camera views projected on his monitors. Twice he stepped out onto the wing to use a set of joysticks to be precise with the amount of engine power and water jets he was using to thrust the boat sideways, forward, and back. Adrian stayed as quiet as he could while this complicated maneuver was going on.

Back inside the wheelhouse, he saw the captain was listening to someone on the radio that resulted in several buttons being pressed and monitors touched. He saw the throttle in the zero position and gears in neutral. "We did it!" The captain turned to smile at Adrian. "We're docked! Welcome to Nassau!" He gave Adrian a high-five and sent him off to change.

Adrian rushed down two flights to his cabin and changed into a white polo shirt tucked neatly into navy-blue shorts with a woven canvas belt to match. When he looked at himself in the full-length mirror, he declared to his reflection, "Oh, wow," and he laughed to himself. He looked like a paid member of the crew in a uniform without the *M/Y Arabella* embroidered on the left breast area. His brand-new deck shoes were brown leather over his bare feet. He ran his hand through his hair to freshen up.

Without making a sound, he ran on with a light spring in his step through the passageway through the main deck and pulled up to the crew gathered around the bar. "Hey."

"Hey, right back. We heard you helped get the boat here." Gabriella was smiling at him. She was quite playful in her personality, and he liked that. "We didn't know we were going to have such experienced yachties onboard. And you even look like one of us!"

Adrian felt uncomfortable with this teasing and attention and felt compelled to correct her estimation of his qualifications. "I'm not experienced. The captain was letting me drive for a short bit. That's all."

"It's all good." Jane chimed in. "We're happy you are getting to do stuff on the boat. You look like you are going ashore, but you know you can't until Customs and Immigration give us permission."

"Yeah, well, the captain invited me to present our documentation with him," he admitted.

"Wow. That's impressive. The captain never lets anyone be present with him when the customs and immigration officer comes to the yacht; it's not allowed by law when we are under the yellow flag." Gabriella looked at Jane. "Huh." It was more of a statement than a question.

"Yeah, wow." Jane added, "I've never seen this before, Adrian."

Adrian shrugged. He didn't know why the captain invited him, but he was glad he did. He wandered over to the stern to watch Jimmy and another guy get the passerelle out of its cubby hole to bridge the space between the yacht and the dock so everyone could get on and off the yacht without falling into the water.

He watched Jimmy operate a device on a heavy cable that was attached to the hydraulic motor of the passerelle. Like a simple freight elevator operation, there was a green button for go, a red button for stop and an on and off button. The movement was slow and steady. He was mesmerized with the slow exit of the telescoping pieces that were nestled inside the largest part of the teak and stainless-steel bridge, which was attached to the stern wall of the pool club deck. At the narrowest end, there were several caster wheels that turned in all directions. That helped with the odd and unusual movements of the sea. This narrow bridge from ship to shore floated up and down with the yacht but never left the deck of the dock.

Jimmy put down the remote-control box and started lifting stainless steel fence railings into the holes of the passerelle. This gave people a handrail to hold while walking the narrow plank to shore. Within minutes it was completed between the two men, and they were checking the stern lines that tied the yacht to the shore. Satisfied they came back aboard, and Jimmy turned to introduce his deckhand. "Adrian, have you met our infamous deckhand and crew bosun, Brian Kelly, yet?"

"No. Hi Brian, nice to meet you." Adrian stuck out his hand to introduce himself properly. Brian took his hand and shook it. "What's a bosun?"

"A crew leader." He paused and after taking in Adrian's neat attire he observed, "You're ready to go ashore, I see." Brian mused with some sort of European accent that sounded vaguely like his granny's. "Have you been in the Bahamas before?"

"No, first time." Adrian replied then, because he felt unsure of what to add to the conversation, he shared, "I'm going to meet the port master with the captain in a few minutes."

"Well, now!" Brian let out a low whistle. "That's not an everyday event, is it now, Jimmy? I don't think that's allowed, is it?"

"No way, mon." Jimmy's Jamaican accent was full on now. He and Brian had an easy-going friendship by the looks of it.

"Have you guys known each other for a long time? Like, did you work together for a long time?" Adrian asked, full of curiosity.

"Yeah, me and Brian go way, way back." Jimmy laughed, "You might need a time machine to go as far back as we go."

"That's right, mate." Brian laughed and put his arm around Jimmy's shoulder. "This man here pulled me out of a pub one night in a small town near Cork, when I was a rotten teenager, and he saved my life. I probably owe him my life. But that is another story for another time. Especially when the captain is not around."

"Did I just hear my name?" The captain had approached behind Brian and Jimmy and Adrian's eyes furtively darted back and forth between the crew to see how they were going to react in case the captain had overheard the conversation.

"Well, sir, in a way, sir." Jimmy, with great haste, responded to cover up the awkwardness of the conversation. "When the Captain is not around, we are usually in charge. Isn't that right, Captain?"

The captain looked suspicious. Turning to Adrian he whispered, "That sounded so sus."

Adrian clamped his lips together in an effort not to smile. The captain gave the men a candid look and said, "Carry on. Adrian and I will be finished with our meeting soon. Let's get the boat washed before the sun goes down. The owners are meeting friends tonight and bringing them back to the yacht. Oh, and one last thing; get the Bahamian courtesy flag ready to be flown when I give the signal." He arched his head back to view the yellow quarantine flag and nodded his approval.

"Aye, aye sir." Jimmy and Brian responded in unison and as the captain turned his back on them, they both winked at Adrian. "Have fun!"

Adrian grinned and turned to follow the captain down the passerelle. It was the first time he had ever crossed from sea to land on a passerelle.

They stood on the quay, which was solid concrete and paralleled the dock, and he asked about flying the Bahamian flag on the boat. "Captain, I'm wondering why you asked the guys to get the Bahamian flag ready to fly. Aren't we Americans? Don't we fly the American flag on our boat? And what is with the quarantine flag? We're not sick or diseased."

"Well, we are not officially permitted to be here until the harbormaster gives us the a-okay. We must fly the yellow Q flag to let everyone know that we are in quarantine and waiting for permission to disembark. It's a formality. A country wants to make sure everyone that comes ashore is healthy and not going to spread diseases to their country." He paused while that piece of info was digested by Adrian. "Remember how the Spanish sailors brought smallpox and other diseases to the islands and the Americas when they first arrived?

"When we are in another country, we fly a small flag of the nation in which we are operating our vessel off the stern flagstaff. Sailboats fly it from the starboard spreaders, which is about halfway up the mast." He looked around the harbor and found a sailboat to illustrate his point. "Look there. See the small flag under the starboard spreader? And side note, if they had two masts on their sailboat, it would be flown on the forward mast." Adrian squinted in the direction of the sailboat and nodded his head.

"It's considered a sign of respect and shows that you recognize that you are in their waters now. It means they have jurisdiction over your vessel while you are in their territory."

"Oh. That's interesting." Adrian mulled that over in his head. "So, if something happens, like two boats crashing, their laws apply?"

"Yeah, something like that." The captain changed the subject as he spied a tall man in a crisp white officer's uniform walking brusquely towards them. "I have a surprise for you. I want you to meet my longtime friend Adrian Thompson." The captain held out his hand to his friend and they embraced each other with their opposite arm.

Adrian Thompson was a Caribbean man who spoke in a somewhat English accent mixed with an island sound which resulted in a quality that was both quite formal and pleasant. He exuded friendship and Adrian liked him immediately when he greeted him with a cheerful, "Hello, young man, welcome to the Bahamas. I've heard everything about you from my friend the Captain! I hear we have the same name!" In an instant, he felt like he was on vacation instead of a year at sea. Adrian stuck his hand out to shake and said, "Thank you, it's nice to meet you. I don't often meet people named Adrian."

"I know. That's why I asked the Captain to break the law and bring you here. We're going to keep this little escapade to ourselves now, won't we? I don't want to get no one here in trouble."

He winked at the Captain, "You see, the Captain and I have had plenty of adventure in our lives when we were on an explorer ship in the north Atlantic ocean. We broke a few too many rules in our day to stay alive or to just have fun. Today, we are having fun, but also because it is educational for you to see how ship traffic gets permission to come into the Bahama's at a port of entry."

With a touch of formality, the captain brought Thompson aboard the stern and all three of them sat at a small table and comfortable chairs. Ice cold air-conditioning flowed down from ceiling vents. The captain opened the thick leather satchel he had brought with him and began to present their papers. He showed proof of vessel registration, handed over a stack of passports, and a list of required items.

The men chatted about local stuff for a few minutes then the inspector turned his attention on Adrian. "So, my friend, you know that technically you were not allowed off the boat during quarantine, right?" Adrian nodded his comprehension. "So, we are going to call the crew now and have them raise the flag quickly so that you can leave the yacht and go exploring this beautiful island." He laughed while the captain radioed the crew from his walkie-talkie. "Now you are all free to move about the country!" He stamped his seal on multiple papers and handed them all back to the captain, who handed him a check to pay for entry and berthing.

"I'll see you around, Adrian. Welcome to the Bahamas." The big officer stood up and reached across the table to shake his hand. "You need anything, you go to my office over there and ask me, okay?"

"Yes, sir." Adrian replied. "Thank you! Maybe you can come back and see more of our boat sometime." He turned to look for permission from the captain.

"Yes, yes, of course, Adrian." He turned to his friend and invited to come aboard anytime. "On official business, naturally." He winked at his friend and they both roared with laughter. *Clearly there is a story behind their meaning of official business*, Adrian thought. Thompson turned to leave the stern via the passerelle.

Thompson paused and shook his right forefinger near his temple as if he remembered something. "Gunnar, one more thing. I wanted to mention that there are notifications being sent to all port authorities and harbor masters that antiquity thefts are on the rise in the Caribbean."

"Why is that?" Adrian asked Thompson with surprise and deep curiosity.

"I suspect several things. One reason is that digital equipment for locating treasure is becoming very advanced and affordable, making it easier to analyze the seafloor and beaches. And two," he gave a brief shake of his head, "It is becoming easier to acquire antiquities through internet black markets and smugglers are getting more and more clever about how they move the goods."

"Anything I ought to know beyond this?" Captain Gunnar asked with sincerity. "We're keeping to the most trafficked areas with low risk for pirates and other nefarious people. Our insurance company keeps us informed of problems with pirates, and we can't go into those areas because if anything happens the insurance won't pay."

"Roger that. I don't have any proof of this, but I think the treasure hunters are organized like drug dealers. I think it has to be a multi-level operation with small-time treasure hunters bringing goods to dealers, who bring the valuables to distributors with contacts for buyers." He turned to Adrian who was listening carefully to every word. "It's always been this way, but something about the scale to which this market is moving, I think it has become a well-oiled machine, if you know what I mean."

"Thanks for the heads-up, my friend. It's good to know." He shook hands with his friend and said goodbye.

After Thompson left, Adrian saw most of the crew hosing down windows, bulwarks, and decks to get the salt water off. It was hot and humid, and the sun was close to setting. It had taken the whole afternoon to arrive in Nassau.

Adrian felt a little lost for something to do. The captain had headed back to his office to put the passports in the safe along with the other papers. The crew were busy. His family members were nowhere to be seen. He looked around the dock for a moment and seeing nothing obvious to do, he turned around and headed to the galley to see what was for dinner.

In the galley, Zak and two other crew he hadn't met yet were busy prepping plates and food. Another crew member was busy at the sink. Adrian read their signals that maybe he shouldn't be there. Zak caught his eye and said, "Yeah, man, we're a bit busy right now. We're in the dinner rush. I'd get ready for dinner if I were you. We're serving in 20-minutes."

"Oh. I didn't know. Thanks." He backed out of the galley and wandered upstairs to the topmost observation deck over fifty feet above the water to watch the sun set behind another island in the distance. The Bahamas looked interesting, and the water was where all the action seemed to be. Ambling down the portside stairs two flights to his parent's cabin, he knocked to learn if they were ready for dinner. "Come in!" his mom called.

"Hi, Mom!"

"Hey, Adrian, how was your first day at sea? You seemed kind of busy with Captain Gunnar today. Everything go well?" His mom was always asking how things were for him. In her professional life, she had helped people deal with fear, anxiety, and other family problems. When she saw problems developing in him, she was quick to talk things over with him so he could reframe his thinking.

One time his mom noticed that he was always calling his ideas *trash* and she helped him let go of his belief that his ideas were bad without first knowing if that was true or false. He discovered that he feared his ideas would be judged so he judged his ideas before they could be rejected by anyone. Underneath that fear was another idea that he didn't like to be judged by people, especially his parents.

His mom had helped him see that he was rejecting his ideas to try to prevent feeling the pain of being judged. She taught him to deal with his feelings so that *if* he got judged, he could label the feeling he felt inside like anger or sadness and breathe that feeling out to support himself. Recognizing that he was choosing to feel victimized by people's judgments, he decided not to react to and just observe, without making any judgments on the people judging his ideas. That was when he had the epiphany that people were judging because of their own fear. And very soon after he started to believe in his ideas and stopped calling them trash.

"Yeah. I had a good day, mom." He looked around for his dad. "Where's dad?"

"He should be out of the shower in a minute. He took a nap and missed docking. We're just getting ready to have dinner, then go out to meet some friends." She was putting a fancy earring in her ear. Her sundress was aqua blue, and she looked happy. He was glad. They chatted for a few minutes longer about what he got to do today.

His dad came out from his walk-in dressing room dressed in golden brown linen pants and a white linen shirt. He looked fresh and young. He felt like he was seeing his dad for the first time. "Dad, you look good. Relaxed, even."

The compliment made his dad smile and pull his shoulders back a bit with pride. "Thanks, son! I feel pretty good. It was nice to start our journey and land here in these turquoise waters. Don't you think so?"

"I do!" Adrian enthused. "I can't wait to hit the beach tomorrow. Do we have plans?" he asked excitedly, hoping the answer was yes. He knew his family loved going to the beach. And knowing his mom so well, she would want to hit the water as soon as possible.

"I think tomorrow the captain wants to bring us to a private beach where they filmed a movie." His mom sounded excited, too.

"OK," Dad announced in his let's-wrap-this-up tone of voice while strapping on a gold watch to his left wrist, "we better head down to dinner. It's served in 2-minutes." On the way to the dinner table, he knocked on Grace's door to collect her, and they all walked in as a family and sat down to eat. *It is beginning to feel different*, Adrian thought, *in just one day, we're finally acting like a family again by eating together.*

The next morning, Adrian woke up as the sun came up over the horizon. He looked at his waterproof watch on his bedside table and got up. He wanted to go to the gym before breakfast. He was committed to staying in shape while living away from the soccer field, basketball, and tennis courts over the next year. He threw on some shorts and a tank top and left his cabin so as not to wake his sister or disturb the crew.

He was confident that he knew the layout of the yacht and pretty much had memorized where everything was on each level from the technical drawings the builders provided his family. The gym was on the lower deck, so he slipped down a staircase from the main deck in the yacht's stern quarter.

To his delight he discovered there was a rowing machine, a treadmill, an elliptical orbiter and weights galore! He decided to warm up on the treadmill and ran a comfortable 10-minute mile. He opted to run another mile when something caught his eye... *holy smokes!* There was an elaborate sound speaker system to play music built into the room. There were high quality speakers in the walls and ceiling. The designers thought of everything! He stopped the treadmill and leaped off the moving platform to head straight for the iPad laying on a side table. He found a list of music channels that he could play while working out and got a playlist going. Now his workout would be done to his favorite classic rock.

He grabbed a hand towel from a basket and wiped the sweat off his face and neck, then sat down on the rowing machine. After a few minutes of rowing, he let the handle recoil to the starting position and got up. He was curious about the other doors in the room and figured one had to be the sauna and the other a bathroom.

The first door he opened was the sauna and next to it was a day head. The door aft of the staircase he came down led to a steam room and an *"experience shower"* with multiple showerheads and jets --for after spending time hot steaming or using the dry sauna. On the opposite wall there were doors to another day head and dive equipment and other water toy storage. That storage space was close to the same size as the gym.

A full-length mirror allowed him to work on isolating muscles in his arms and legs with a balanced posture. It was easy to lean and get twisted while working with weights and he appreciated the mirror as he concentrated on his lifts. He remembered being nine years old and starting with a four-pound weight. Smiling to himself at how long ago that sounded, he picked up a twenty-pound weight and started doing curls with his forearm.

Fifteen minutes later he threw his sweaty towel into an empty basket for laundry and turned off the music. He left the gym and headed to his cabin to put on swim trunks. As he looked at the double bunks next to his bed, he felt a wave of longing to have some friends enjoy all this with him. But who? Everyone was in school, and Winter Break was weeks away. Ignoring his loneliness for the time being, he opened the door and headed back aft.

He climbed into the pool and slipped down deep into the water. The water felt good on his tired muscles. Brian was on watch and waved to him. Adrian closed his eyes, so he didn't have to see the people starting to wander the dock or up on the quay looking down on everyone. He spun around and put his back to the quay and looked up at the yacht. He studied the lines of all four decks above him. The protective glass walls with stainless steel rails looked shiny in the daylight as they wrapped the edges of the decks. During the night, he knew that the night crew had been busy detailing the ship by washing windows and tidying up. They also refilled the pool so it would be ready for their stay at this marina. He still couldn't fathom how much work this yacht entailed, and he surmised he was about to find out.

When the skin on his fingers began to wrinkle, he got out and grabbed a fresh towel off the nearest chaise lounge. He wiped his face and headed back to his cabin leaving a trail of water behind him. He was ready for a huge breakfast and an all you can eat pastry bar. "Oh, yeah," he thought to himself, "I could eat half a dozen chocolate croissants right now. Chef Zak, don't let me down!"

His sister was the first to come out to eat and join him at the breakfast buffet. She had her swimsuit on and a pair of shorts to cover. She filled her plate with a little of everything except the bread or pastries. "What are you having, Adrian?"

"As many chocolate croissants as I can eat." He grinned from the lounge, licking his fingers of flaky pastry and dark chocolate.

"Oh, come on," she complained, "I hate that you can eat all that sugar and not pay a price!"

Adrian laughed, "Yeah, well, work out in the gym with me each morning and you can." He jumped up off the sofa and met her at the table. Looking around he grabbed a plate and piled bacon and eggs on it, then smothered his eggs in hot sauce. He loved trying different hot sauces and keeping his endurance or tolerance for spicy heat at maximum capacity.

"Dang, man," Grace started in on him after he drenched his eggs with habanero sauce, "how do you not suffer from all that burn?"

"Easy. I'm used to it." He picked up a small table basket lined with a napkin of fresh yeast bread slices, butter and fruit preserves and walked back to the table. "What are you drinking?"

"Just water. I want to hydrate. I think coffee is probably not good for my brain." She lifted her glass of ice water with lemon slices in it and sipped it. "I think it also gives me acne, but I'm not sure."

"Mmm." Adrian answered through a mouthful of fresh baked fresh bread. Grace was always into holistic and nutritious living. Sometimes he was interested in what she shared, but most of the time, it was all about what it did to her skin, brain or metabolism.

"Did you hear we are going to swim with pigs and pet nurse sharks?" Grace dropped that bombshell across the table with an air of calm while forking some scrambled eggs and sausage.

"What?!" Adrian sat up straight and leaned forward with interest. "When?!"

"In a few days, I think. And there is an underwater cave we are going to visit, too." She chewed her food in between soundbites.

"Anything else I should know about?" Adrian asked with impatience. *Why am I the last to know?*

"Mmm." Grace added while swallowing a sip of water. "Yeah, to get to the cave ... you have to swim underwater and hold your breath for a long time but when you come up inside it, you can breathe, and it is massive inside."

"Are you serious?!" Adrian was on the edge of his seat. This sounded amazing to his ears. He hadn't been so sure there was anything interesting for boys to do on these islands, which seemed like they were designed for adults to go shopping, then to dinner, drinks, and nightclubbing...none of which interested him. Besides, he was too young. "Who told you this?"

"Perkins, the cute deckhand." She smiled her wicked smile that Adrian knew too well. She knew flirting with the crew was off limits. He hated when she got all interested in a certain boy. It ruined everything. All she was interested in were the boys in her life. She didn't even make time for her brother, who was a boy.

"I haven't met him yet." He almost asked her to introduce him but didn't want this Perkins dude to have extra interaction with his sister if it helped his case. "I think I saw him on the bow managing the bow anchor and groundlines when we pulled in."

"Yeah, he does foredeck." She tossed her long dark blond hair over her shoulder and nibbled a ripe strawberry. "Here come mom and dad."

"Hey, kids!" Their mom greeted them in a cheery fashion and sat down across from Adrian. "Enjoying your morning?" She glanced at her daughter and down at her plate, then over to Adrian. "What's good?"

"The chocolate croissants." Adrian replied with a grin.

"Naturally." His mom replied with a sideways shake of her head. "Adrian, you and your dad have been blessed with a great metabolism!"

"Yeah, that may be so, but I worked out in the gym this morning before all of you were awake so I could enjoy a few croissants."

"A few?!!" His mom leaned forward with her mouth open in shock at her son's appetite for sweets, and her eyebrows knit together. "Just how many did you eat!"

"Four." He sat back with a Cheshire cat grin of pure satisfaction on his face. "I would have eaten five, but I wanted to leave a couple for dad."

"Someone say my name?" His dad pulled out a chair and sat down with two plates. One for him and one for mom. Jane came over and served espresso drinks to his parents. She politely asked if anyone would like anything else.

"I'm good, thanks," Adrian replied with a smile. Turning to his dad he asked, "Hey, dad, what's the plan for today? I heard we are going to swim with sharks or something in a few days."

"Correct." His dad wiped flaky pieces of croissant off his chin and brushed his shirt clean of crumbs. "Wow, these are amazing!"

"Totally," Adrian agreed with enthusiasm. "Zak's the best!"

"Well, our captain said that he wants to bring us to Exuma Island at the weekend. We will take the yacht as it's over seventy nautical miles away and we'll use the tender to zip around the island to have fun in different locations."

"What is a tender?" Grace asked with piqued interest.

"It's our yacht's super-fast small boat that will carry us to shore. It's 27.5 feet long, has an inboard diesel engine with water jets on it," his dad paused, "We'll have Captain Gunnar and a crew member escorting us."

"Cool!" both kids said at once. "I can't wait!" Adrian added with exuberance for a new island to explore.

"Shall we go ashore and check out the pirate museum? I read good reviews about it." His dad looked at his dive watch, "And meet back here in 30 minutes?"

Georgetown, Exuma Cays
The Commonwealth of The Bahamas
North Atlantic Ocean

The days passed pleasantly on Nassau, as they explored multiple beaches, local islands, went to dolphin shows, water and adventure parks, historic places with landmarks and enjoyed transitioning from city to vacation life.

Moving the boat from Nassau to Exuma Cays was a relaxing and uneventful trip. At a cruising speed of 10kn they reached their destination of Staniel Cay in eight hours' time. They passed other yachts and fishing boats during the day and by sunset they arrived at Staniel Cay to anchor in the bay with several other yachts.

The six day-trippers were up before 0800 hours, and Captain Gunnar and Jimmy joined them for breakfast to review plans and what to bring. Raffa and Francesco had climbed into the boat tender garage on the main deck earlier, to lower the tender into the water. It was tied off the yacht's stern by the time the group met up within an hour.

Adrian loved riding in their tender, especially in the seat next to the driver so he could watch and learn. The V-shaped hull was white with a navy-blue stripe on the exterior, with painted letters spelling out *T/T Arabella*. The captain answered the family's question about the two letter Ts in front of the name *Arabella* and he explained that it was an industry standard and identifier that meant "tender to" and the superyacht's name. The tender was top of the line and exciting to ride in.

T/T Arabella skimmed the water at around 30 knots with no effort from the powerful engine. Adrian loved facing into the wind and feeling the mist of salt spray on his face, which wasn't often, because of the high freeboard. The decks were made of teak, like the *M/Y Arabella,* and the digital dashboard was high tech and impressive. He couldn't wait to start learning how to operate and drive this tender.

The short ride from the yacht to the beach took mere minutes. Right away, Adrian spotted some golden-brown spotted pigs under a tree and three swimming in the water. "I see them!" He shouted to his family as his heartbeat quickened and he wondered if the pigs would hurt him. He was standing up now to get a better view. While Adrian was focused on the shore, Jimmy had tossed an anchor out the stern and let the anchor line out and tied it off on a stern cleat.

Earlier, the captain had reassured him that the pigs were harmless and loved people. Chef Zak had given him a bag of old

but viable vegetables from the galley fridge to feed them. *I sure hope they don't bite,* he thought.

The captain cut the engine and eased the tender through the shallow water onto the soft white sand. Jimmy leaped off the bow of the boat and walked up to the nearest tree and tied a bowline knot around the trunk, securing the tender from drifting off to sea. Declining the need for the flip out bow-steps to the beach, the family jumped over the sides into the knee-high water. Jimmy pushed the bow out and the captain took up the slack of the stern line anchor to pull the boat off the sand.

"Hey, guys, wait up." Dad was walking towards them in flip flops and swim trunks. He held a water-proof video camera in his hand. "I want to get some video of you meeting the pigs for the first time and feeding them."

"OK, Dad." Adrian stopped and waited for his dad to catch up. With tremendous excitement, he pointed to the two grown pigs trotting towards him and his father. "Oh, wow, look, Dad, they're running towards us! What do we do?" Adrian grabbed his dad's arm with a small amount of panic.

"Relax, Adrian," his dad reassured him with a chuckle. "I know it's not every day that pigs come running up to you, but they are not attack pigs...and they are curious about what you have in the bag."

"Oh!" Adrian laughed a shaky laugh. He wasn't sure he liked wild animals coming at him. He wanted to be brave, but sometimes he wasn't so sure about wild animals. He was a city boy who was just getting his sea legs, and now he was being challenged to be confident on an island inhabited by pigs. "OK, what do I do?"

"Why not get a carrot out of the bag and throw it into the sea so they follow it. Then you can walk into the water and be with them."

Adrian reached into the bag and took out a small carrot which he broke in two. He threw one half into the wave lapping on shore and a gray pig turned quickly and aimed for it. He took it up in his mouth and came ashore to eat it.

Adrian reached for more vegetables and pulled apart some lettuce for a smaller pig that was at his feet sniffing around. He held it in his thumb and forefinger and dangled it above the pig's head. The pig nosed the lettuce and pulled it down. Another pig, half its size, nosed in to share the prize.

"Wow, Dad, he took it from me!" His dad was grinning from ear to ear. The smaller pig was trying to walk through Adrian's legs. Adrian jumped and squealed, "Aaaaaah!" and ran towards the water with the food bag held high in the air.

"Adrian," his dad began with a calming tone of seriousness, "if I were you, I would either start feeding them quick-style or give me the bag."

"OK, OK, I'll feed them!" Adrian reached into the bag and started feeding the pigs as fast as he could. It was obvious his sister had no interest in feeding them but was walking through the water to get closer to them.

"Let me know when they are done eating so I can come near," Grace shouted, "then they won't want to eat me for lunch!"

"There's no one going to get eaten by a pig today, okay?" His dad was filming the kids in the water. Adrian had a few more pieces of veggies left, and he asked for the bag. "Here, Adrian, switch with me." He handed Adrian the camera and got in the sea with the bag of food scraps.

Adrian wrapped the wrist guard on his right arm and turned on the camera. "OK, dad! I'm filming!"

His dad held pieces of food in his hand and the pigs came up to him and ate out of his hand. He scratched the heads of the pigs and moved in and out through them playfully.

"Oh man, that was amazing!" Adrian exclaimed when his dad emptied the bag and stuffed it in his swim trunk pocket with the Velcro lock. "I got lots of video."

"Thanks, buddy!" His dad was happy and wiping his hands on his trunks. "They are quite something and I've never seen anything like this in all my life."

"Dad, I want to go back in the water and try swimming with them, okay?" He returned the camera to his dad and walked into the water. His sister was further out but watching. "Come on over, Grace!"

Grace inched closer and watched Adrian move around and through the pigs. He did a gentle breaststroke through several pigs who were doing piggy-paddle like dogs, in the shallow water. She saw nothing happened to her brother, so she entered the area where they were most prevalent. "Hey, they're leaving me alone!" she declared with happiness in every word.

"Yeah," Adrian chimed in, "pigs are smart animals!"

Back in the tender, the captain brought them to other areas north of the island. The tender was proving to be tons of fun, perhaps even more so for the captain who confessed that he likes to go fast and even own fast cars.

While looking in the shallows for nurse sharks. He found an area with a dozen or so milling around in the warm shallow waters. Adrian was beginning to realize the captain could be trusted. He was not as nervous as he thought he would have been getting in the water with sharks.

The captain floated the tender into a shallow lagoon and let the kids hop overboard. Adrian and Grace stroked the back of several large sharks and smiled from ear to ear. The skin felt amazing and smooth. The sharks were warm and soft. They didn't seem to mind being touched by humans.

Their mom and dad put their cameras down and jumped overboard to join them. The four of them were grinning and enjoying the lagoon activity. There were all sizes of nurse sharks and the companion fish that lived in community with them. Adrian's mom and dad sat down in the shallow water and let the baby sharks swim around and over them. They looked at each other with love in their smiles. They were being a family again, doing things together and having fun without the stresses modern life brought to their door.

Adrian walked through the water to his mom and dad grinning. "I never once thought I would get in the water with sharks! This is amazing!"

"Isn't it, though?" His mom beamed up at him. "And me neither!"

"These sharks certainly are unusual." His dad pushed his dark sunglasses up on his nose and leaned back on his hands. "They are very docile unless threatened. I read that they hunt at night and like stingrays."

"Yeah, the captain was telling me that they have like 30 to 40 babies at a time," his mom added. "I think he said that the older the shark, the less spotted they are. I guess they fade with time."

"I saw one that was like 12 or 14 feet long!" Adrian exclaimed.

"I don't think they get any bigger than that," his dad shared. "You're lucky. You saw a big one, an adult."

"Well, I think we ought to get a move on if we are to see that cave and then go to lunch," his mom suggested as she stood up and began to wade through the swirling sharks to the tender. Adrian, Grace, and his dad followed her and climbed up via the bow, using the steps that unfolded off the boat forward into the water. Jimmy handed each of them a beach towel to dry off and suggested they grab water from the cooler to stay hydrated.

"Out here, in the hot sun," he began, "even though you are in the water and staying cool and refreshed, you can still get dehydrated because the sun makes you sweat and the salt pulls water from your skin."

"Good call!" his dad, the scientist, praised him. "Now that you mention it, I could drink some water."

Jimmy and the captain got the boat squared away while the family drank water and talked about the sharks. The captain fired up the engine and backed away from the sharks, making sure to keep the propeller in neutral as much as possible until they were in deeper water. He didn't wish to harm any of the sea life with a turning blade.

"Does anyone want to eat a snack?" Jimmy asked. "I brought a cooler with grapes and orange slices, but maybe you will want to save those for after swimming?"

Everyone agreed that they were good, and they looked forward to the next destination of the day.

Heading back towards the *Arabella*, they drove past it and

headed southeast around Staniel Island to find the cay where the James Bond movie *Thunderball* was filmed. Slowing down, the captain navigated to what looked like a cliff with a bunch of wet rocks. "It's over there," he pointed to a cluster of rocks and Jimmy dropped the anchor from the bow, careful to avoid the coral and place it in sand. "It's slightly past high tide right now, so it is somewhat hidden. The tide is moving out, so you will have to mind any current leaving the cave when you try to go in."

"Go in where?" Adrian repeated, not sure what he was supposed to be looking for. "Where's the cave?"

"Under the water, just inside that cluster of rocks," the captain clarified, pointing his finger at the wall of rock while Adrian leaned in to align with his index finger and gauge the dive spot. "You have to snorkel up to the cliff, take in a deep breath, dive under and swim through the coral tunnel to get inside."

"Uhh," Grace began in disbelief, "just how long does one have to hold their breath?"

"Not long. But if I were you, I wouldn't start breathing out until you get through the tunnel and see daylight." The captain turned to look each person in the eye. "Who's game?"

Adrian looked at his mom and dad, who looked back at him before looking at their daughter Grace. Grace, a naturally good swimmer, had put on fins, mask, and snorkel. She had a pair of neoprene gloves on her lap to protect her hands from rocks or coral. "What?" She asked incredulously, noting their surprise that she had geared up so fast without waiting for their consensus. "I'm going. Anyone else?"

"I think we can all do it," mom said with confidence. "Mask up everyone! The Abercrombies are going in!"

Within minutes, they were in the water and following Grace towards the wall. It always amazed Adrian that his sister could be fearless sometimes and at other times a total wimp. He couldn't predict what she was going to do in certain situations.

The power of the fins gave him confidence that he could kick like heck to get through the tunnel and with his powerful breaststroke, he could pull himself forward. They took a moment to assess the cliff a few feet from the cave opening, which they had not spotted yet.

"Remember, head for the light," the captain shouted to them with a laugh, as he motioned with his hand for them to keep going.

Adrian took a deep breath through his snorkel and dove down to see if he knew where he was going. He saw the opening and returned to the surface. *I can do this*, he thought, *I've got this*.

He released the bottom of his mask to get the water out, took a deep breath and then dove down and kicked with all his might. He pulled himself forward and thought his lungs would burst. His ears felt a tiny amount of pressure as he went down deeper to clear the ceiling in the coral rock formations. He saw beautiful aqua blue light and swam forward into the cave and clawed his way to the surface to gulp air.

He lifted his mask so he could see while treading water with his fins. Everyone made it and was smiling and saying wow! He spied a place where he could pull himself out of the water and sit on a rock. He sat back and looked around the cave in awe. When he spoke, the sound of his voice was loud and echoed off the damp walls. Even to him, his voice sounded unnatural and too loud. "Mom, we did it! This place is awesome!"

She smiled back at him and lay on her back looking up at the holes in the ceiling where sunlight was streaming through. It was calm inside the cave since they were the only people in it.

Stalactites were growing down from the cave ceiling. Sunlight streamed through the openings in the ceiling and illuminated the blue pool. Sunlight refracted sparkles bounced off the water and lit the walls and ceiling. Tropical fish swam inside this indoor pool that was quite significant in size.

His dad was snorkeling around the cave looking down at the bottom and exploring the cavern walls which were greenish and glowing from the sea. *That was the scientist in him*, he thought as he watched his dad take in the environment. Grace had joined him and was pointing out things to look at.

Wanting to take his mother's perspective on the cave, he left his mask around his neck and slipped off the rock to swim to the middle. Flipping over onto his back, he floated nearby and looked up at the patch of sky.

The skylight, as he called it, was irregular and he thought about whether he or any of his friends could jump down forty feet or so into the water without hurting themselves. It would be quite the dare! He wasn't sure he was ready for that kind of action.

The famous Thunderball Grotto cave was an interesting experience, but he was through with it. He let his mom know he was leaving the cave and, with her own thumbs up she followed him out.

Soon all four of them were treading water near the entrance and talking about how cool it was to have gone in. All agreed that they wouldn't have missed it for the world. They decided to snorkel along the rocks before returning to the tender as the tropical fish, colorful corals and sea life clinging to the rocks were prolific and worth exploring.

When they got back in the tender, they thanked the captain for such an interesting experience.

"I'm really digging The Bahamas!" Adrian declared as he stretched out in the hot sun and asked Jimmy, "Hey, any chance I can have those orange slices, and could you peel the grapes?"

Jimmy laughed and said, "Sure, but you can peel those grapes yourself. That's where I draw the line!"

While Jimmy rummaged in the food storage box, Adrian reflected on the underwater cave. *That cave would make the perfect pirate's hideout. I bet it was used for treasure once upon a time.* Turning to the captain he asked, "Do you think that cave was used by pirates?"

"I'm fairly sure it was the first time it was discovered," the captain began, "Until it became too popular. Then it would be useless as a hiding place."

"I read somewhere that some guy found an engagement ring with his metal detector in this cave," his mom shared, "That must have hurt to lose such a sentimental piece."

"That's cringe worthy," Grace said, "I'd be beside myself with guilt if I lost my fiancé's ring! Note to self: No jewelry while snorkeling!"

While everyone enjoyed ice cold fruit, the captain navigated around the island and brought the boat into a small marina. The captain suggested they all eat at a particular restaurant where he knew Adrian could get a platter of the freshest seafood. Seafood was Adrian's favorite food and there was nothing he liked more than a wide variety of the sea's offerings.

They sat outdoors at a table and watched people and boats pass by. This particular remote island was on slow speed, relaxing and mellow. It was unlike Nassau; in fact, it was the exact opposite.

The captain suggested that they stroll to work off lunch. The marina neighborhood was too small to call it a town. An hour of walking around was more than enough.

His dad asked him what he wanted to do when his mom and sister headed into the nearest beach store to look at sarongs, postcards and beach jewelry. Since he wasn't sure, he suggested

they take a systematic approach to the area and walk down one street, make a U-turn and come back on the other side.

"Sounds logical," his dad said, and they began their journey of looking at a variety of buildings both residential and commercial. There was a super relaxed atmosphere to this tropical beach town and when they came to a small store selling hot coffee, his dad and he shared a high-five.

Opening the glass door, they entered the shop and smelled the sweet smell of fresh baked goods and coffee. His dad group-texted his mom, Jimmy, and the captain to inquire if any of them wanted a coffee. All of them said yes.

While his dad was busy buying cookies, Adrian looked at a cork bulletin board on the bakery wall. Local advertisements for services were posted and to the right one poster got Adrian's attention. It was a wanted poster for information on four men suspected of violating salvage laws by stealing and dealing in antiquities taken from shipwrecks in the Caribbean. He took a photo of it with his cell phone. *I wonder how these people work. How can four people get around and do all of the heists without getting caught?*

He helped his dad carry the coffees back to the marina where they cut their walk short to deliver coffee. Adrian offered buttery cookies with sprinkles to everyone and soon they were hanging out in the shade of some palm trees sitting on benches and boulders talking about life in general.

"Dad, how do treasure hunters work?" Adrian asked. "I get that someone does the diving, but then does that same person also sell what they find and if so, to whom?"

"I suspect that today it's organized crime." His dad looked out to sea and took a sip of coffee. "I suppose there is someone who is like an art dealer. Someone who has contacts with wealthy people, who is willing to look the other way and ignore the law and run the black-market.

"Then you have the distributor, who knows the dealer and the divers. You could call this person the middle-man." He paused and looked at his wife and daughter, "Or middle-woman!

"And the diving team, of course. They have to run underwater operations on a grand scale, spend weeks and months at sea using magnetometers which is a fancy word for a high-tech metal detector they drag behind the boat looking for anomalies in the magnetic field. They could use sonar and other digital photography equipment to map the seafloor, too. I guess you could search by low flying airplane or helicopter. But what do I know?" He laughed, "I'd be the type to just look over the side of the boat!"

"But how do the divers know what's valuable?" Adrian drilled deeper into the conversation, "Would someone need a background in history or archeology?"

"I'm sure it helps," his dad concurred, "But if a ship shows up and it looks as old as President Lincoln, I'd stake money on it, that anything you could pull off it would be of interest to collectors of the American Civil War era."

"And if it looks as old as Columbus," Captain Gunnar injected, "You are talking about Spanish Armada history, and it is extremely valuable!" Adrian's dad and the captain laughed together, which made his mother smirk. He and Grace looked at each other confused at how bizarre adults can be sometimes.

The captain added, "The treasure hunting bug has infected many people. I wouldn't recommend you go down that road, son, or you will find yourself living on hopium."

"Hopium?" Grace asked.

"The addiction to false hope," the captain supplied. "Hopium can make a person's mind unstable as they get caught up in their potential fame or greatness and it intoxicates and spurs them on to chase the unimaginable. Treasure hunters can be an odd breed. Very charismatic and inspired, but just don't get caught up in their tales of potential riches."

"Is it illegal to take treasure out of the sea?" Adrian asked.

"Yes, and if you are caught, you will be prosecuted by the country that lays claim to their ship and all artifacts." Captain Gunnar gave a slight shake of his head, "There were men who sold Spanish treasure they found in Bimini, and Spain got wind of it and extradited them out of the United States for prosecution in Spain. They had to return all the money, the goods and received jail time, too."

"Wow. That's pretty serious," Adrian stated. "How did Spain even find out? Did they post their findings on social media?"

"I don't know, but I can tell you this," the captain's tone was dead serious, "If you or Grace ever find anything, you come to me immediately, okay?"

"OK," Grace and Adrian said in unison.

They ambled back to their high-speed tender at an easy pace and headed back to the yacht. Adrian still hadn't quite adjusted to calling it home, yet, and one day he hoped it would feel like home.

When he got back to his cabin, he pulled out his laptop and started digging like a digital warrior on treasure hunting in the Caribbean Sea. Story after story revealed many treasure hunters defrauded their investors and it landed them in jail. *I wonder what makes people so greedy.* He saw several corporations that were organized to take investment money and he saw that they did pay dividends on the recovery of treasure, but those companies were far and few in between. *I wonder if the guy doing the hunting believes it really is his treasure when he finds it since he did all the work, and then decides he should be the one that wins the gold?*

Closing his laptop, when he got the text that dinner was ready, he walked up to the owner's deck with his head full of questions and very few answers. Placing his napkin across his lap when he sat down across from his mom and dad next to Grace he asked, "I've been thinking..."

"Oh, no," Grace exclaimed, "Not again! The last time you had a thought I thought we'd never hear the end of it."

"Give it up," he chided his sister as Gabriella and Jane presented the first course of the meal. "Thank you."

"No worries, mate," Jane replied with her smooth Australian accent. "Did you have fun today?"

"Yeah, it was awesome! Riding in the tender is the best. I love how fast it goes!"

"Aw, that's wonderful," she gave him a private wink and headed towards the passageway to return to the galley.

"Dad, I was curious about these companies that do treasure hunting and pay dividends. What do you know?"

"Hang on. Let me invite the captain in to discuss this with us. I think he knows more than I do." His dad signaled to Gabrielle who opened the mic on her walkie-talkie and spoke softly to the captain. Minutes later he entered the deck.

"How can I help?" Captain Gunnar stood at ease in his daily uniform of a white polo shirt embroidered with *M/Y Arabella* on the left breast and navy dress shorts. His hands were held loosely behind his back, as he waited for the questions.

Adrian's dad briefed him, and he nodded his understanding. "Right. So, here's the thing, Adrian: most treasure hunters know that it's a job. They know they have skills but lack the funds for equipment, maritime lawyers, expert knowledge of antiquities, and other expenses. The first and most important aspect of going after treasure is the law.

"The moment you leave the land you leave the law of the land and then you come under maritime law. The laws are tricky to navigate. First, you must consider what country you are sailing under. If you are on a boat registered to Panama, you are under Panamanian law. Now, consider the water you are in. Are you 12 miles off the coast of America? If yes, America's maritime laws apply. Then you have economic zones that extend up to 200 miles off America's coast. Sometimes, the countries next to America have to share some of those zones because they overlap. Mexico and Canada share some space, so it helps if they share common maritime laws.

"This is important because you need a maritime lawyer

to negotiate the salvage laws of all those entities and spaces. Just because you live in the U.S. doesn't mean those laws apply because you are U.S. citizens. Your parents registered their yacht in the Cayman Islands for complex financial benefits, but just know that we sail under Cayman Island laws on this yacht. Are you with me so far?"

Heads nodded yes, so the captain continued, "Let's say you and Grace dive off an island where we anchor, and you see something that turns out to be an old ship's cannon encrusted with barnacles and coral. Exciting, right?" His eyes twinkled and he looked over at Mr. Abercrombie and winked. "Is it yours?"

"Finders keepers, right?" Adrian's grin was meant to elicit confirmation, but the captain shook his head no. "I know if I found it, I'd want to bring it up and clean it and put it somewhere like our front lawn!"

"Oh, dear me, no!" his mother exclaimed with a hand over her heart at the very thought. "When you have your own house, you can decorate it any which way you like!"

"I think that's a cool idea," his father said, looking at his wife with surprise. "Don't you think it sends a very clear message?"

Laughing, the captain continued, "Here's the problem, Master Adrian: let's say that cannon is attached to a ship that is claimed property from Spain saying it is part of the country's national heritage. They have a legal claim to it, even though it is underwater."

"Bummer." Adrian leaned back in his chair and sighed with his shoulders slumping.

"If your car with valuables in it rolled into a lake because you didn't set the parking brake, wouldn't you want to put a sign on a post on the beach that says 'Do Not Salvage. Property of Adrian Abercrombie.' -until you could raise enough money to get your car out of the lake?"

"Yes, Captain, I would. I'd make sure my sign was set in concrete and waterproof." He smiled, "Point made. But what do the countries have to do with anything? Are you saying that if I bring up that cannon, I'd have to tell Spain?"

"Affirmative. Under maritime salvage laws and depending on the international agreements in place for ownership of sunken treasure, you have to notify the authorities immediately...which is why I was so emphatic about you informing me immediately if you find anything, because if you take something and word gets out, you can be arrested for theft."

"Yikes," Grace whispered for Adrian to hear without moving her lips. He uttered an "uh-huh" loud enough for her ears.

"I've only hit the highlights, but it is very complicated, and cases take a long time to go through courts because all the applicable laws have to be sorted out and charges made by country." He took a breath and moved his hands to his hips. "So why do people organize to hunt and retrieve treasure as a corporation?"

"Well," began Grace, "it has to be profitable on some level."

"It is," confirmed the captain. "Oftentimes, these corporations do the searching, and when they find something they present it to the courts and begin negotiating to bring up the treasure with the country that claims it. I don't know of one country in the world that has its own multimillion dollar salvage operation for their claims. I would imagine a percentage of the gold and silver bullions, which are pure form metals shaped like bars or bricks, would be considered part of the hunter's payment, but coins and art objects go to museums and auctions to create revenue for the country."

"OK, so if we find treasure, we tell you, mark the map, form a corporation, get a maritime lawyer and raise venture capital, sell stocks in our company, promise dividends and retire rich. Did I cover everything?" Adrian grinned. "I want to find treasure!

Who doesn't want that?!"

His parents looked at the captain and all three shook their heads in disbelief. "Adrian," his mother began, "trust me when I say: you do not want to spend your life dealing with legal entanglements!"

"Listen to your mother," the captain urged with a hint of a smile. "Besides, you'll spend more time looking over your shoulder in paranoia, worrying about someone hacking your email, or accessing your notes and charts on the treasure location than if you just lived your life and enjoyed it."

"We'll see," Adrian said somewhat aloof. "I have a feeling that I am the type to find treasure. Just sayin'..."

"That's what we're afraid of!" his father said with a rue laugh. "Thank you captain. I think our young lawyer here has it all figured out." The men laughed and shook hands before the captain departed for his office.

Georgetown to Long Island
The Commonwealth of The Bahamas (East)
North Atlantic Ocean

The captain was waiting for ideal wind conditions to move M/Y Arabella to another island. After a week of playing in the water with some of the water toys, diving on ship and airplane wrecks, and birdwatching to explore other fun islands, like the one with the giant rock iguanas, it was time to move on. Flat seas and a light breeze from the southeast promised good passage south. Adrian was allowed to pull up the large, oversized fenders as they pulled away from the dock where they had stayed the last two nights in Georgetown, the capital of Great Exuma Island. He dragged them to the stern where the crew deflated, rolled them up and stored them away.

Almost ninety minutes later, when *M/Y Arabella* crossed the demarcation line on the earth for the Tropic of Cancer, the crew blew the horn for fun so the Abercrombies would know they had reached a milestone in their travels.

The distance from Georgetown to Clarence Town was almost sixty nautical miles and traveling at a speed of fourteen knots, they arrived about four and a half hours later. Anchoring outside the entrance to the Harbor, the crew prepared the tender for a visit to Dean's Blue Hole after lunch, the world's second deepest sea water hole.

The Abercrombies had visited many of the blue holes the Bahamas offered, but this one was supposed to be the most phenomenal of them all. Everyone was excited and anticipation ran high. Adrian and Grace were both nervous and looking forward to scuba diving in the deepest known salt water blue hole that reaches depths of six-hundred and sixty-three feet.

Brian, being a bit of a prankster, told Grace that if she got too close, she could be sucked in. And for two seconds she believed him, which got everyone laughing. "You're lucky my mom raised me not to play *'I'll get you back'*, Mr. Brian, because I am tempted!" Grace smiled at him in such a way that he knew she would if she dared and he quickly replied, "It's ok, Miss Grace, I'll be there to save ye, if anything happens. But just the same, I think you should relax because I heard they turned off the vacuum last month."

Jimmy reminded them that they needed to take advantage of the incoming high tide to access the beach and hole for diving, otherwise they shouldn't be accessing the hole from the sea and should have taken the road. All hastened to the stern to board the tender and they set off.

Jimmy took his time to navigate the extremely shallow depths with the depth sounder posting going at very slow speeds so as not to touch coral or rocks underwater. Adrian sat on the bow and scouted the pathway for him, using his eye to spot depths based on colors. He signaled with his hand to move left and right when going forward was dangerous. The v-hulled boat drew a little over a meter below the waterline and with high tide, the water level was on average four to five feet. It was doable but not advisable. The wind and tide could change and create difficult conditions leaving the cove because of the reef. On the plus side, the tender had no exposed rotating parts or protrusions under the keel since it was jet propelled diesel engine technology. If necessary, they could fly across a sand bar at speed depending on the distance to deeper water. The distance to the shore was only going to get shallower until they ran aground.

Once safely inside the protected cove, Jimmy steered to starboard and headed directly for the freediving platform anchored in the middle of the blue hole. Creamy white limestone cliffs with pocked arms surrounded the cove with low green shrubbery covering the top. The entire scene was calm and awesome to take in.

Dean's Blue Hole, named after the landowner, is the most notable underwater sinkhole and a favorite with free divers who hold their breath down to one-hundred and twenty meters and back to the surface. Jimmy had been giving them both lessons in diving and both were now certified in the basics. Today they would be entering a hole that was a vertical cave dive containing all sizes and species of local fish, including dolphins. Today's dive would bring them to eighty feet deep, the most they had ever dove.

The tropical sun beat down on the tender as she skimmed

across the water at twenty knots. Jimmy and Brian were guiding the family today and anticipation mounted.

He navigated the tender to a spot where he gave the signal to drop anchor in the shallow sandy bottom, then he turned off the engine. The lagoon tucked deep in the corner of the cove was quiet and warm. There wasn't a hint of a breeze behind the cliff.

"You feelin' the jitters today, Adrian?" Jimmy cracked after turning off the engine. "You and your sister have done plenty o' dives in the last week. This should be a piece of cake."

"I'm just a little anxious," Adrian confessed, his face asking Jimmy to understand his concern. "It's a steep drop off, and the bottom is a long way down. And there is nowhere to go if there is a shark. I read that they have been seen in the hole. But you know, you can't believe everything you read on the internet!"

"Yeah, mon, I don't think we have ta worry about sharks here. Dey like der space." Jimmy smiled a reassuring smile and continued to pull on the sleeves of his short sleeve wetsuit.

"Hey, Jimmy, you said this is the second deepest hole. Where's the world's deepest?" Adrian asked while slipping his mask over his head and pulling it under his chin while he adjusted the snorkel in the side strap.

"China. It's called the Dragon's Hole." Jimmy replied while securing his buoyancy-controlled device (BCD) vest that would hold his tanks and dive accessories. "It's somet'ing like six hundred and sixty feet deep, but I've never been."

"Dang, that's deep." Adrian put his flippers on over his neoprene dive booties and moved to sit on the edge of the boat like he was riding a horse. They were in such shallow water, he would have landed like a turtle on his back if he did the typical fall backwards move into the water with his tank on.

"OK! Let's go!" Brian got everyone moving to adjust masks and breathing devices into their mouths.

One by one, the family and crew slipped over the boat sides with their tanks on their backs and stood next to the tender and adjusted their masks.

The water was super clear with visibility to perhaps thirty meters. The visible difference between the mouth of the hole, which was a hundred feet across and the surrounding beach area was stunning. Pale blue water over white sand, three feet deep and perfect for wading out to the ledge instantly changed to a viridian blue green, teal color that would challenge any artist to capture it's unique luminosity.

"OK, folks, here's the plan." Brian called everyone to attention. "Jimmy is going to dive with Grace and Adrian. I will dive with Mr. and Mrs. A." He turned to check in on their gear with a glance. "We're going to go down slowly to a depth of eighty feet with proper stops going and coming. Then when I or Jimmy give the signal, we are going to slowly come up resting every fifteen feet, so no one gets the bends.

"At about the sixty-foot mark, it's going to get really big inside, like three-hundred feet across. If your granny uses a hot water bottle in bed you know the shape of this sinkhole. It may get very dark and there is no reason to freak out. We all have flashlights to inspect the walls and underside of the ledge.

"There is also an ascent line here, attached to that floating dock in the middle of the pool." Brian continued. "If you get disoriented, look for it. The line from the mouth of the hole will focus the light on it.

"Who's the air hog here?" Brian asked with a big grin. "'Fess up now." He waited and Adrian tentatively volunteered his hand.

"Well, I might be. Sometimes I get a little anxious and I start breathing fast, which I know wastes my air supply."

"No problem," Brian assured him with a neutral tone, "You and your dive partners check your air gauge more often, ok? We don't want you running out of air down there." Adrian and Grace nodded their heads that they understood. "Remember, one third to go down, one third to explore and begin ascent and one third of your air for reserve."

"We good?" Jimmy asked, sounding pumped up for the dive. Everyone gave the okay sign with their fingers and he said, "Let's go!"

"Wait!" Adrian nearly shouted. Everyone stood up and faced him. "Sorry, guys, but could someone get a video with my camera of me falling off the edge into the deep blue?"

"Adrian!" His mom's voice said it all. She wanted to get going.

"I'll do it, Mrs. A. Why don't you three get going." Jimmy urged. "Grace, you want me to get one of you, too?"

"Yes! Please!" Grace enthused. "That sounds super cool! How 'bout I go first and then I'll swim over to the vertical wall and hang out at the surface with my snorkel?"

"Cool, I'll stay out of your video and wait until you're clear." Adrian walked backwards until he was a good ten feet away from the gaping edge of the hole.

Jimmy positioned himself about ten feet under the surface and ran the camera. Grace walked in and walked straight off the edge and free fell to about fifteen feet straight as an arrow going down and then swam over to the wall as promised. A shower of sand fell off the ledge down into the sea's gaping mouth like an underwater waterfall. Adrian saw her snorkel exit the water and he walked to the ledge and spread eagle fell face forward soaring off the ledge with every muscle keeping his body rigid. He fell face forward and when he realized he was about twenty feet down, he slowed and cleared his ears and waited for his sister and Jimmy to join him.

Passing the camera to Adrian with extreme care, he gave him a nod and the okay sign to convey that the video was good. Pleased, Adrian gave him an enthusiastic okay sign back. He signed *thank you* by placing the palm of his hand on his chest below his breathing regulator and extended it towards Jimmy.

They stopped at fifteen feet and checked their buoyancy. Satisfied with their neutrality in the water, together they dove down at a rate of one foot per second and then paused to take in the vast cavern that spread in all directions. Adrian looked at his depth gauge and it read seventy-five feet. His air usage seemed to be ok. He nodded at Grace and Jimmy who also checked their gauges. Okay signs from all dive partners and Jimmy pointed to the wall which disappeared below them into deep dark blue water. Remembering he had his camera, he took pictures of Grace and Jimmy, some fish that darted along the wall and up at the irregular circle of light that came through the surface.

Grace pointed at the ledge and with her flashlight on, dove under it and looked at the underside and back paddling, she came back into the center and shook her head as if to say, "nothing to see there." They explored the wall and observed fish and corals while gradually making their way up.

Jimmy checked Adrian's air gauge and pointed to his dive watch and upwards. Time to go. He looked at the gauge and saw that he was almost at half his tank. His depth was fifty feet. Grace saw him moving up and joined him. Jimmy gave them the slowdown sign and tapped his watch. All of them held their dive computers in one hand and kicked upwards while releasing air from their BCDs. Pacing themselves at a rate of thirty feet per minute to prevent the nitrogen gasses getting trapped in their blood and soft tissues, they swam up towards the sunlight that streamed down.

Every twenty feet Jimmy checked their computers. Adrian was running the lowest on air. They reached fifteen feet below the surface and held onto the centrally placed ascent rope to wait five minutes. Adrian took more photos of them hanging out and when Jimmy gave the signal, they released the rest of the air from their BCDs, raised a hand up above their heads to make sure they didn't hit anything or anyone and slowly came to the surface.

Ripping off his regulator, he shouted, "Woo hoo!! That was awesome!" He kicked his way over to the ledge and crawled out onto it. "We did it!"

"Woo hoo!" Grace shouted and punched the air. "What a blast!" Treading water, she asked Jimmy if she could drop her gear in the boat and just snorkel around.

"Yeah, sure, no problem. You feel fine?" Jimmy inquired, to be sure as he moved in that direction, too. They sloshed through the shallow water and stood up to unclip their weight belts and vest. Jimmy had Adrian hold his gear while he climbed over the stern swim platform and reached down for the equipment. Free of the bulky gear, the teens turned around and swam back towards the blue hole to see their parents just exiting the water.

"Mom, dad! Wasn't that the coolest thing ever?" Grace asked while standing up on the ledge next to her parents and Brian who were exiting the hole. "What took so long?"

"What was your rush?" Her dad countered with a smile. "We had a perfect dive."

"Wait. What?" Confused, she tilted her head and said, "I don't get it. We rushed?"

"We didn't take too long. We maximized our air by being peaceful and meditative down there. I'm guessing one of you ran your air down early." Her dad stood up and started making his way to the tender. "But then again, we have adult lungs, more diving experience and probably are looking for a less athletic experience…you know," he grinned and put his thumbs and middle fingers together and closed his eyes, "Just be One with the whole underwater Universe."

"Oh…" Grace nodded her understanding.

"Honey, how was your dive?" Her mom touched her arm. "Did you have fun?"

"I loved it. It was so beautiful down there." She stood up and inched towards the underwater ledge, "Go drop your gear and come snorkel. I'm not ready to leave yet."

"We've got to make the tide, though."

"I know." She turned and dove over the ledge and swirled around like a mermaid to clear the hair off her face and swam on a gradual line towards the surface. Taking another breath, she headed for the vertical wall where she saw her brother's neon green snorkel sticking out of the water. With some powerful strokes of her fins, she swam another fifty feet and caught up with him.

Adrian popped up and removed his snorkel to speak, "Hey! Check out these fish. There's hundreds of them. I saw sergeant majors, blue tangs, and I think tarpon."

They snorkeled along the wall and then came up to check on the adults. Spinning around they caught sight of them, and they were waving and calling them back. "OK!" they shouted in unison and headed for the boat.

Their mom pushed bottles of water on them when they got in the boat. "Drink up. Diving is very dehydrating, and your bodies need to continue healing the effects of being down deep."

Brian hauled up the anchor and with his polarized sunglasses read the water depths for Jimmy to navigate out of the inlet. They crawled along at a snail's pace to make sure they didn't scratch the coral or hurt the boat.

Small waves were crashing on the reef that was fairly quiet when they entered. Adrian tried to get a glimpse of Jimmy's face to see what he thought of the situation. Brian was timing the waves and making Jimmy wait for his call to slip through the reef. He pointed to an opening, "I think that is the best way through. It's super narrow but it's the only exit I can see. The surf is coming in because of the wind, which changed direction and the tide is at slack water."

"Roger that." Jimmy considered his options along the reef. He, too, watched the surf line. "I think if I go through there, I will go where there is less white water."

"That's what I'm thinking." Brian agreed.

"I'm going to go at speed through that slot, ok? You might want to sit down in the boat, Bri."

"Roger that." He dropped down on a seat on the bow. No one spoke, while the crew studied the waves. Without much warning, Jimmy opened the throttle when he saw a wave coming in and rammed the bow of the boat through the opening. The incoming swell lifted the boat higher by a foot and they cleared the reef. A massive smile broke out across Jimmy's face and Adrian stopped holding his breath.

"Nothin' like a good escape through a reef, eh?"

Adrian's parents did not look so happy. They exchanged a look.

Jimmy looked at his depth sounder. "Ay, we had four point two five feet under us when we came through."

Brian smiled and said, "Well, now, where would ye be if it weren't for the luck o' the Irish?"

"It's all you, man!" Jimmy agreed, "You all right back there, Mr. and Mrs. A?"

"We're fine," Adrian's dad declared. "It was a bit tense there. I don't think we are used to cutting things this close."

"Roger that. Let me assure you that you have nothing to worry about, Mr. A." Jimmy said with a calm and sincere face, "I never would put any of us or this boat in danger. However, if we had left any later, we might have been camping on the beach tonight."

"Dad, that was seriously like an amusement park ride just now," Grace defended Jimmy. Turning to him and Brian she said, "Just so you know, I wasn't worried for one second."

"T'anks, Miss Grace." Brian saluted her and turned back forward. "Pass me my walkie-talkie from that storage box, Adrian, will ya? I'm gonna let the captain know we're on our way back."

Jimmy opened the throttle, and the tender flew across the water back to the yacht, which had swung on her anchor with the wind direction change. Waves formed and created chop that they bounced off of. Adrian and Brian exchanged a grin as the wind flowed through their hair and dried their bodies. He glanced back at his sister and parents who were grinning. This boat was definitely more fun than the superyacht. *This is the life!*

As soon as the tender was lifted into the garage, they weighed anchor and set a course for Turks and Caicos southeast of their location. Within minutes they were passing Clarence Town and a large explorer yacht over two hundred and fifty feet long close by the harbor holding its position with just the engines.

Modern and muscular looking with a gold toned paint job on the hull with cream color on the superstructure, black tinted windows gave it a dynamic and intense look. The yacht went by the name *Orion*.

Physically fit men in black polo shirts and khaki shorts lined the decks in preparation of something. They all wore dark sunglasses and big black watches, had earbuds and walkie-talkies and looked very cool to his eye. Adrian stood on the port promenade deck along the main deck and watched the glistening yacht stationary in the water. It did not appear to be aground, nor under anchor. He couldn't tell if the men were looking at him through their sunglasses as he was looking at them. As they stood by the large customizable davit crane being lowered to the deck, he picked one of the guys watching them pass to starboard off their yacht, to throw a friendly wave to and received a curt nod in return.

He took his cellphone out of his backpack, which he had brought with him in the tender and took pictures and videos of the yacht for his collection of cool looking vessels. This one had a slight military feel to it with the decks stacked forward and stubby bow shape for icy waters. The hydraulic crane was being folded to the deck and looked more powerful than the tenders needed...*but what do I know?* Adrian walked to the stern to continue watching the explorer vessel which had an extensive deck with a touch-and-go helicopter landing pad and assorted water toys and tenders on the stern. The personal watercraft toys were being cleaned by another crew member after use, so the seawater didn't create salt spots. They had a landing craft he would love to ride on and see how it worked. With every nautical mile the *Arabella* made forward, the golden yacht got smaller and smaller in the distance. He turned away from the view and headed to his cabin to shower and change for dinner.

Chapter Three
Rescue Operations

Turks and Caicos Islands
United Kingdom Overseas Territory
Northern Atlantic Ocean; Northern End of West Indies

Within an hour they had placed several miles between themselves and the northern Bahamas as they headed southeast to Turks and Caicos Islands, a British Overseas Territory. The captain set the autopilot for a Southeast by East course for most of their time at sea since leaving the Bahamas, since the Gulf Current and wind would cause their course to drift northwest.

One of the things that Adrian enjoyed was keeping track of all the different wildlife he saw underwater. The crew pointed out a coffee table size book of fish and corals of the Caribbean that he used to identify many of the different species. He started using his notebook to record his sightings underwater. Little by little, he was starting to recognize certain types of fish, like Blue Tangs with their stunning electric purple blue color, green Moray Eels, and Queen Parrotfish with their pouty lips and aqua blue colors. He loved the hyperactive Sergeant Majors with their black and white regimented stripes on yellow, who would pop to the surface for a puffed cheese treat or other bright orange chip.

Over the last week he and his family got lessons on how to use the over and underwater scooters called Seabobs®. These electric portable winged propulsion toys brought loads of enjoyment to Adrian and Grace while snorkeling. These water toys could propel a person up to eight and a half miles per hour under the water. When they went under water, they wore dive masks and fins. Most days they circled the yacht at anchor and raced each other between buoys and played water tag. Jimmy was always around on a jet ski to make sure nothing happened to them.

Jimmy explained to the family that on occasion swarms of jellyfish would appear out of nowhere, carried by the currents. Jellyfish were not a problem over the last week, but just in case someone got a sting, Jimmy was there to help. He also said that a special swimming pool made with a framework of inflatable edges and a box made of fine fabric mesh could be placed in the water for them and their guests to swim if jellyfish were ever a problem. Adrian thought that sounded very interesting and he would love to see that someday.

Every time the yacht's tender came out, Jimmy taught Adrian more about how to operate it. Adrian joked that he would have his boating license before his driver's license, and he agreed. With a couple hours of daylight left, he wandered out of the main cabin to look out over the stern.

One of the deckhands that had been previously on night watch, found Adrian looking at the frothy wake. "*Ciao, Adriano, il capitano* wants to see you." Francesco, a friendly Italian guy and his cousin Roberto had been working the 8PM to 6AM shift and sleeping during the day. Raffa, the other Italian deckhand and Brian, the Irish guy, were now pulling the night watch.

"*Grazie, Francesco*!" Adrian replied with gratitude in his limited Italian. He turned and headed up four flights of stairs to the bridge. "*Ciao, Capitano!*"

"Oh, hello, Adrian. I see Francesco found you." The captain smiled back at Adrian. "Here." He handed Adrian a small walkie-talkie and earbud with a curly wire attached secret service style. "This is now your equipment. You have access to all conversations with me and the crew. It's not a toy, but I expect that you know that already. You must be responsible with it at all times. If the responsibility ever gets to be too much, you may choose to return it to me or Jimmy. We all agreed that you are quite helpful at times, and it would be good to have you know what we are up to and to find you to pitch in."

"Wow! Captain, I don't know what to say!" Adrian already had the earbud in his right ear and was plugging in the wire to the radio. The captain turned to look out to sea so Adrian wouldn't catch the smile of amusement on his lips. He regained composure and looked over to Adrian to see if it was already in place and he was touching the button to speak.

"Testing my radio. This is Adrian. Over." He spoke in a super clear and brief manner.

The captain listened to the crew letting Adrian know they heard him. He looked at Adrian's glowing face that registered the pleasure of belonging to the crew.

Looking forward and squinting at the horizon, the captain pointed to something in the distance and asked Adrian if he could see it.

"Yeah…," he started to say, "hang on. Let me get the binoculars on it." He dashed over to the where the binoculars were stored and put them to his eyes. Adjusting the focus, he squinted at the horizon. "Holy smokes, Captain, someone's sailboat mast with mainsail is in the water, and they are on their starboard side. Here!" He passed the binoculars to the captain and allowed him to assess the situation.

"Yep..." the captain agreed and put down the binoculars in front of Adrian. "Keep your eyes on the boat at all times and report any new information. Maybe stand on the port wing for a clear view and let me know if you see people, smoke, debris...anything." The captain called over the walkie-talkie to Jimmy and Brian to standby to launch the yacht's tender and other emergency equipment. Then his next call was to the Turks and Caicos search and rescue on Grand Turk Island on channel 16, which is reserved for emergencies.

"Motor yacht *Arabella* to search and rescue Grand Turks. Motor yacht *Arabella* to search and rescue Grand Turks. Possible Mayday. Over." The captain spoke in clear, short, clipped bursts. He released the radio send button as soon as he finished talking. He repeated the request a second time when there was no response. Soon a voice came over the radio.

"SRR Team on Grand Turks responding. What's your emergency and position?"

"This is the captain of the motor yacht *Arabella* reporting a visual on a sailboat on her starboard side in the water and responding. We're about 2 nautical miles and 10 minutes from her location. Over."

"Message received. What are your coordinates and course? Over."

The captain gave the latitude and longitude of the *Arabella*'s position, their speed and direction of travel with an estimate of arrival.

SRR Team responded with a question, "Can you assist with rescue and medical if necessary?"

"Affirmative. Over." Next, the captain heard the SRR Team put a request to any vessels in the area to respond. Keep us updated. Over."

"Wilco." The Captain turned to Adrian. "Adrian! Anything to report?"

"Yes!" Adrian responded with urgency in his voice, "I see a person on the keel holding the port side gunnel of the sailboat. I think I see them gesturing to someone inside to get out. No life jacket on. Can't see the other person yet." He kept the binoculars on the opening of the sailboat hoping to see them. "Captain! It's two men! I can see them now!"

The captain picked up the phone and reported to the SSR Team the additional information. Then he turned to Adrian and asked if he could read the name on the stern of the vessel.

"I think it is *Tyche*, but I can't say for sure." Adrian was squinting hard to make out the strange lettering. "It's painted in funny writing and it's partly in the water. Definitely from Florida."

"Spell, please."

"Tango-Yankee-Charlie-Hotel-Echo." Adrian took his eyes off the binoculars and turned to the captain for further instruction. He was making notes.

"Roger that. Thank you for memorizing the phonetic alphabet." The captain nodded and then told him to run down to help Jimmy and Brian get the guys out of the water. As he raced down the stairs with adrenaline flowing through him, he overheard the captain on his earpiece telling the guys to grab extra life jackets and make sure Adrian wears one. The yacht slowed as it got within a hundred yards northeast of the sinking sailboat and remained neutral, idling in the ocean as the crew used the hydraulic davits to lower the v-hulled tender into the sea.

The water was choppy and there were 7-9 knots of wind out of the southeast. Jimmy drove while Brian and Adrian discussed the plan for rescuing the sailors over the walkie-talkie's open mic. All three wore life vests with E.P.I.R.B. beacons and whistles. They were high-end life vests intended for serious sailors recreational or professional. They didn't inflate until they got wet, or one pulled the cord to turn on the signal manually, so they were comfortable to wear during action.

The tender reached the sailboat in mere minutes and circled it with caution while assessing the situation. It was not obvious what had happened. Adrian had his cell phone camera out and was taking pictures while Jimmy stood at the helm and talked to the one in the boat gathering stuff into a duffle bag. Brian was talking with the guy on the keel.

Jimmy ordered the guy on the keel to catch the life vest and put it on immediately. It was not the specialized life vest that the crew of the *Arabella* were wearing, but it was coast guard approved. Brian threw it over to the guy on the keel who caught it and put it on. Adrian switched to video to record conversations after he heard the captain suggest it over the walkie-talkie.

Brian asked him what his name was and who else was on board to which he replied, "Mike Nichols, from Miami, Florida. He's Jonathan McCready, from Hollywood, Florida, and the boat owner. Can I come aboard?"

"Yeah." Brian reached out a hand to steady the tender against the keel and Mike slid in and took a seat.

"I can't tell you how happy I am to see you guys." He seemed a bit shaken and his skin was like chicken skin, pale, waxy and covered in raised bumps from being cold and wet. "I thought we were going to die out here."

"Would you like a blanket?" Adrian asked him with concern in his voice.

"Yeah. You got one?"

Adrian set his phone down with the camera lens side up while he pulled a mylar blanket out from a first aid kit he had grabbed from the bar near the pool club in the back of the yacht. He opened the Ziploc® bag it was stored in because the guy's hands were shaking from being exposed to the water and wind. He suspected some mild hypothermia.

He helped wrap the blanket around Mike then helped him back into his life vest. Next, he asked, "How long have you been in the water?"

"Maybe a couple hours, maybe three? I couldn't get Jon out. He kept looking for stuff to rescue."

"Like what?" Adrian asked with innocence.

"Our passports, wallets, cellphones ... and some other stuff." Mike was wiping his nose which was dripping water and mucous.

"So, you've been on the keel in the wind and waves, and he's been inside in the water for three hours?" Adrian spoke so the captain got everything. "Why weren't you wearing a life jacket?"

"Well, they were stowed under the stern lazarette with our dive equipment and once we went over, something jammed the hatch hinge, and we couldn't get it open. Even the life ring is in there." Mike looked miserable.

"Where were you heading?" Adrian asked.

"Well, we were supposed to be headed home to Florida yesterday." Mike ran a hand across his balding head. "But we decided to detour from Samana Cay back to Plana Cays so we got a late start."

Adrian and the captain had been talking about Samana Cay earlier in the day when they sailed past it and how it is uninhabited now and thought to be the place Christopher Columbus first made landfall back in 1492.

"May I ask where you were sailing from?" Adrian smiled a

sheepish smile and explained his question, "I've never been on a boat rescue mission and I'm so curious about what happened. And I'm sorry you are having a bad day."

Mike smiled at him. He understood and he was almost glad the young man was taking his mind off the events of the day. "Yeah. We left Plana and were sailing close hauled on a port tack passing along Crooked Islands. We had been diving near Plana Cays all week. We made it around the corner at Castle Island…" his voice trailed off as if he had just regretted talking. Waving a hand to dismiss his effort to share, he shook his head wearily and said, "Anyways…"

Adrian's mom had taught him that any time someone used the word "anyways" it was a subtle way of saying "disregard everything that I just said before I said *anyways*." *Why would Mike want me to forget everything he just said?*

Glad he was still recording with his phone, although he wasn't sure with the wind and additional voices how much could be picked up by his phone's microphone.

Jimmy had the tender in neutral and allowed the wind and tide to allow them to float alongside the cockpit, which was submerged in the water as the boat lay on her starboard side. Brian held the tender off so it would not rub against the sailboat.

Adrian continued to take pictures of everything he could see with discretion. It was difficult to zoom in and get images of the cabin. Jimmy was telling the man inside he had one minute to get out. His voice spoke volumes…*or else!*

Jonathan was saying over and over, "I'm coming, I'm coming. Give me a second." He was slogging through the water making the boat move in an odd manner in the water.

"You have 30 seconds!" Jimmy commanded. Adrian shivered. He'd never heard Jimmy be authoritative, and it was impressive. Jon

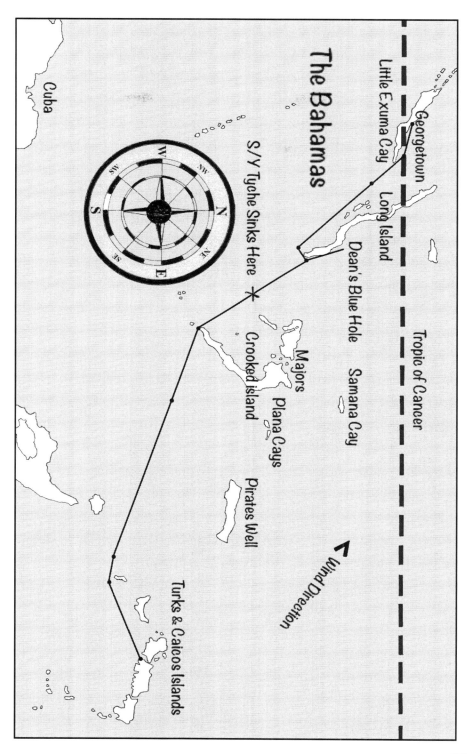

must have heard it, too, for he exited the sinking boat and climbed over the port railing to the keel. This forced Jimmy to maneuver the tender around the bow. Adrian was glad as he videotaped the boat from stem to stern, including the sail in the water.

He didn't see a hole in the bottom of the boat, but maybe it was on the other side. Something seemed off. Why was the sail on the starboard side, the sinking side, if they had turned the point and were headed northwest? Given the wind direction, the sail should have been on the port side for going with the wind on a downwind reach. Maybe he was thinking about it wrong. He wasn't the most experienced sailor, but he'd been on a sailboat a few times, and he'd learned how to tack and jibe.

Jon clambered into the tender holding a large duffle bag and wouldn't part with it. He kept making sure it was zipped up tight. He looked over at Brian and gave him a particular look. Adrian didn't quite understand the look's meaning to its fullest extent, but Brian did and dropped his head and went back to shivering.

"How did your boat sink?" Adrian asked Jon. Jon took in Adrian and his earnest eyes.

"Jerks sabotaged it." He seemed beyond angry and in a dark mood. Adrian figured he would have been, too, if his boat had sunk.

"Wow." Adrian's eyes got big as he looked at Jon and with deep sincerity asked, "Do you know who would have done that to you?"

"Yeah, I have a suspicion it was a hunter," he growled. He was starting to chill out in the wind. His hands were wrinkled from being in the water and Adrian offered him a mylar blanket, too, but he realized that Jimmy was in high speed to get the men back to the yacht, so he tucked it back in the first aid kit. Within a minute the tender was alongside and Pete, Bryce, and Raffa were at the stern swim platform under the pool club area to assist.

Moments later, Adrian was aboard while Brian drove the tender to the garage area. He ran up to help with the hydraulic davit to lift it out of the water. Standing back from the edge of the garage to make room for the boat to be hauled in, he lowered the hoisting hook and bridle to Brian and waited for him to attach it to the tender.

Pete, Bryce and Raffa escorted Jonathan and Mike into the gym where they had them strip down and go into the sauna to get warm. Someone had already turned on the sauna to get it warm and the guys were happy to get warmed up after being cold and wet for hours. Then they showered. Jane had brought robes and hot tea for the men while they were in the shower, and then departed for the galley.

Adrian heard the captain call him over the walkie-talkie to report to the bridge. "Be right with you, Captain. I'm hauling in the tender with Brian. Give me five. Over." He waited for Brian to step out of the tender and check the chocks that held the tender secure in the garage and headed up top. Brian handed him the first aid kit to return to the bar. "Both tenders have first aid kits stowed near the helm. It is mandatory equipment to pass inspection by US Coast Guard standards." He smiled. "But good thinking. Keep it up."

"Roger that, Brian. Thanks." Adrian turned and raced up to the bridge.

"Hi, Captain!" Adrian was a touch out of breath by the time he reached the captain. The captain was checking the monitors and when everything looked good, he turned to Adrian.

"Well done, son!" the captain congratulated him. "You were professional, kind, helped us get loads of information we might not have had if you hadn't asked them what happened when you did."

Adrian beamed with the praise. "I'm sorry they lost their boat, but they are safe now."

"Maybe." The captain's response made Adrian straighten up and knit his brows.

"What do you mean?"

"The owner of the sailboat said he thought his boat was sabotaged. That means that whoever did this to them may still be trying to hurt them." The captain's voice was serious. "Because you made important discoveries to their story, I was able to make a call over my satellite phone, and keep their story off the public radio channel, to the authorities in Port of Providenciales. They will want to question these men when we bring them ashore."

"Oh." *That is sobering.* Adrian asked, "Captain, one more thing…the boat owner, Jonathan McCready, he was frantic trying to get and find stuff on the boat to take with him. He won't let that duffle bag he took off the boat leave his hand. It's heavy, too, by the looks of it."

"Thanks, Adrian. I'll look into it….so to speak." He smiled at his own joke and Adrian smiled back.

"Did you just make a joke, Captain?" Adrian asked with some bravado and a straight face.

"Ah, go on with you!" The captain laughed out loud and picked up the radio handset to call a marina that could take their yacht for the night. Adrian threw him a salute and headed to his cabin to change.

On the way down he met Jimmy. "Hey, mon, you got your phone on you?" He held out his hand, "Let me take it."

"Yeah." Adrian fished it out of his pocket and handed it to Jimmy. "There's video and photos."

"Thanks, mon. I'll get it all back to you by dinner." He tipped his hand in a slight salute to Adrian as he raced down to the crew quarters where his laptop was in his cabin.

He dropped the first aid kit off behind the bar and returned to his cabin. The sun was low in the sky and Adrian sighed even though he was full of energy. The whole incident happened so fast, and he was still feeling pumped from all the action. He turned into his cabin, stripped down, and took his second shower of the day. The golden-brown scum off the keel was under his nails and had dried on his knuckles. Just touching the sailboat's keel and hull to hold the tender off it for a few seconds was enough for him to feel dirty.

As fast as he could, he dressed for dinner and ran his hand through his short hair. At least he didn't have to wear shoes on board. That might be the single most awesome thing about living on board a yacht. He entered the main deck and headed for the bar on the port side. He asked Jane for something sparkling and wet. She laughed and made him a fancy non-alcoholic refreshing water cocktail and brought it to him.

Adrian had heard the captain ask Jimmy, Pete and Brian to command the vessel while he spoke with the two extra men onboard. His parents and the men were sitting with the captain. The men were drinking hot tea and talking with the captain who was recording the meeting on a small digital recorder. He saw Adrian and beckoned him over with a quick come here motion of his hand. He took a seat at the table next to his mom, across from the men.

The captain asked a multitude of questions about how the boat sank and both professed to not knowing.

Adrian's brows pinched together in thought. *I know they know the answer. Why aren't they saying anything? I even think they know the jerks who did it.*

Gabriella entered the salon where they sat and handed a folder to the captain and whispered in his ear. The captain glanced through the images printed from a color printer on photo paper and glanced up at the men.

"Gentlemen," he began, as serious as can be, "there are gunshot holes in your mainsail. Care to explain that?"

"Wha….? What are you talking about?!" Jon's vocal pitch went up to high to be considered normal and he sat up straighter. He was flustered and his blood pressure rose several points as he started ranting hotly about it not being his fault and being sabotaged by pirates. Adrian felt a bit alarmed at the sudden change of character in him and stiffened. His mom, sensing his fear, reached over and placed a calming hand on his arm and squeezed it gently to reassure him that he was safe.

We wouldn't be in waters with pirates because the insurance company would have told us not to go here. They are lying. Adrian fidgeted in his chair wanting to speak but held his voice.

The captain pushed one of the photos that Adrian had taken, under McCready's nose. He picked it up and looked at it then looked at Mike and threw it on the table.

"Can I see that?" Adrian asked with curiosity. He didn't notice the gunshot holes on the sail that was underwater when he was out there, but maybe he caught it on his camera. And maybe Jimmy had seen it, too. His dad reached for it and after a brief glance, slid it across the table to him and his mom to study. After a moment, his eyes met his mom's and they both raised their eyebrows a fraction of an inch to indicate shock and surprise. His mom pushed it back into the table.

"Did my boat sink, or can it be salvaged?" Jon asked after a long pause.

"It's drifting. It may sink." The captain was very neutral when he spoke.

"Great," Jon sounded depressed and disappointed. Like a man who had lost everything.

The captain stood up and radioed for Raffa and Francesco to

escort the two men to the crew's quarters for a meal and a space to rest. After the men and crew left, the captain made sure they were out of earshot before speaking.

"I suspect these guys are casual operators and treasure hunters. I think they stepped on someone's toes. Like...someone in the big leagues, because this sailboat is not a typical treasure hunting vessel." He paused and put his hands on the top of a chair to lean on it as he brought his head closer to his listeners. "Your son did a tremendous job today rescuing and interviewing these two. He is proving to be a first-rate sailor, even if he's only been out to sea for a couple weeks. His maturity and ability to be responsible are more than I anticipated from someone his age." He paused while Adrian's mom put an arm around her son and gave him a squeeze.

His dad leaned over the table, smiled and shared, "Well done, son."

"I plan on keeping Adrian out of this possible criminal case from this point forward, although I think these two guys are mostly victims not perpetrators and way in over their heads on something nefarious. Adrian's photo and video documentation of the...shall we say...crime scene," the captain put air-quotes around the last two words he spoke, "was valuable and will be most helpful to the T&C authorities, maybe even the men's insurance company, if they are lucky. And like a good attorney, he asked great questions out there in the boat!"

Adrian glowed from the inside out. He just did what he thought was the right thing to do and followed his instinct. It was nice to hear, but as the Captain said on the first day they met, he was the captain of his life now, not someone else. "Well, thanks, Captain. I was just happy to break up the day with a little excitement!"

The captain left and Grace strolled in. Mom, Dad and Adrian were rehashing the story in excited voices. Grace asked, "What? What did I miss?" The three of them looked at each other and just laughed and laughed.

"Grace," Adrian started with a shake of his head, "you need to get out more!"

After dinner, Jimmy caught up with Adrian and brought him to the crew quarters. He ushered him inside his cabin and sat him down at his laptop. "Check it out, young man, you de big hero of the show today!"

He went through the photos and zoomed in on the cabin that he couldn't see into while he was on the tender, but on the monitor the photographic images were zoomed in and it revealed clear plastic boxes that were sealed in plastic with stuff in them floating on the interior. "They may have been moving drugs, Adrian. And the captain is going to check their bag now. I mean look! Look at that photo!" His excitement was palpable as he looked through the photos and saw how clear the images were and the only sign of damage was on the sail.

"I guess whoever shot the sail, shot the side of the boat, only we couldn't see it because it was underwater." Adrian surmised.

"Yep. And now they will go after that boat and seize it as evidence."

"Were you scared of them?" Adrian asked with respect, as the realization of who and what they were up to landed on his brain.

"Me?" Jimmy laughed out loud. He pulled up his lower leg to reveal a taser and diving knife. He shared, "Brian and I both brought a little friend along just in case. And their greeting party was armed, too, just in case they got funny on us."

He laughed as Adrian's eyes got big and his mouth opened in a silent gasp as he realized the crew were carrying small taser guns and knives. He continued on, changing his tone to be more serious, "Look, my friend. We have to be real out here. We cannot carry guns by law out here or we get impounded by the port authorities. Dese waters are full of pirates, smugglers and other nefarious people who believe dat is de only way to get their needs met by participating in illegal activities. You know what I mean?"

"I guess so." He didn't like the sound of Jimmy's truth. He had been working for years with his mom to see the good in the world, heal the world of bad thinking, including his own and now... He wondered what was going to happen to those two men. "Will they go to jail?"

"Possibly. It depends on what their story is and what the magistrate has to say." Turning off his computer monitor, Jimmy waved him out of his cabin and shut the door and locked it. "Here's your phone back. And do you have any idea how difficult it would have been for Brian and me to get photos like you did? Impossible. De guys wouldn't have liked it. I guess because you are a kid, you were not taken so seriously, and they behaved nicely with us rather dan put you in harm's way. With dese people, it can go either way. But we sure are glad you were with us today."

"Well, it was quite the adventure! See you later, Jimmy. And thanks." Adrian gave him a fist pump and left through a connecting door and went out to the back deck. It was dark and the sea filled a great expanse. They had covered a lot of territory today and it was starting to land what he had experienced. He yawned and looked at his wristwatch. It was not yet his normal time to go to sleep, and although he had had a long day he needed to process his day. *Perhaps a short walk on the decks to check out the yachts will help me wind down from the day's excitement.*

He went up to the upper deck and gave his parents big hugs. "Thanks for, well, you know...your support today. It felt nice."

"Oh, you are so welcome. We love you and are very proud of you." His mom and dad wished him a good night's rest and he wandered down the stairs to the main deck to the stern where he found Grace sitting at the bar with a book and sparkling water.

"Hey," he said and kept walking to his cabin where he dreamt through the night of the leader he knew he could be.

Chapter Four
Going for A Spin

Providenciales "Provo" Island
Turks and Caicos Islands, British Overseas Territory
Atlantic Ocean

Adrian woke up early and discovered the yacht was docked in a new marina on the north side of the collective group of islands called Turks and Caicos on an island called Providenciales. The bright sun came through his windows and filled his cabin. He stretched and got up to go workout in the gym.

An hour later, with an Electric Light Orchestra song in his head, he hummed to himself as he showered and got ready to leave the boat. During his workout, his parents had slipped a note under his door that stated they were having breakfast ashore and leaving at 8:30AM. Mom had written, "PS: Dress nice."

Carrying his deck shoes in his left hand, he ambled down the passageway to the rear of the main deck where he found his family waiting for him. His mom smiled and said, "you look so handsome, Adrian! That orange color looks great with your golden tan." She kissed his head and gave him a squeeze. "I see you already got your workout in."

"Yeah," he smiled as he patted his stomach's abs with affection, "I'm not letting these babies get weak over a year away from sports."

"Don't you see what you are doing out here as sports?" his mom asked with a twinkle in her eye. "You paddleboard, swim, dive, run on beaches, kayak and all, I might add, in competition with your sister and dad."

He just smiled. "Not the same mom. A guy needs his friends and a team to play competitive sports. You know that."

"Do you really need the competition? Can't you just have fun and let go of having winners and losers?"

"Aw, come on, mom. You know what I mean. I want the challenge that going against another player offers." Adrian felt a bit exasperated with his mom. She always brought up the problems with living in a thought system called duality and what it created, like winners and losers, or good and bad. He didn't know why the world was set up the way it was. It just was. "Can we talk about something else?"

"Sure! What do you say we head over to the big resort and have breakfast? We heard it's wonderful."

"I'm here, let's go!" Adrian led his family down the passerelle and up the dock. At the front of the marina, they hired a car to take them over to Long Bay Beach where they dined together and talked about recent events. His dad filled everyone in on the latest from the captain.

"Both men were brought to the police station and arrested. The duffle bag held drugs and minor antiquities that they had taken from some island or shipwreck. A team of divers and a tugboat are working on retrieving any other drugs on board and possible valuable artifacts." He paused and added, "they won't be going anywhere soon. I suspect they will be tried here and transferred

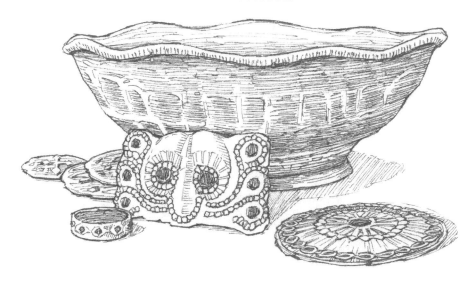

to a prison in the Virgin Islands suitable for American citizens."

"Whoa. They had drugs on board our yacht?!" Adrian gasped. "Did the captain know?"

"He sure did. He pulled rank on them and notified them that they were under his jurisdiction on board his ship and took possession of the bag as evidence, searched it, and popped it all into a plastic garbage bag and moved it to the safe until the authorities could take it ashore."

"I wish I had been there for that." Adrian lamented with a hint of disappointment. "The captain sure can be a tough guy when he needs to be."

"So, what are we doing today?" Grace asked. "I was hoping to spend some time shopping. Mom, you want to go with me?"

"Sure, babe. I think we can do that." Turning to her husband she asked, "What about you and Adrian? Any plans?"

His dad turned to him and asked, "What do you think about getting a fly-fishing lesson?"

"Count me in!" Adrian enthused with his eyes shining bright for a moment, before they dimmed. "But isn't it a bit late in the day for fishing?"

"Yes, but not for lessons. I noticed there is an outfit back at the marina that takes people out and teaches them." His dad raised his eyebrows in a questioning fashion for a long second, seeking input. "What do you say?"

"Only one way to find out." He smiled. He loved fishing but didn't ever catch anything. He hoped his luck would change soon.

"That settles it." His dad took one last sip of his coffee, removed his napkin off his lap, dabbed his lips and put it on the table to the left of his plate. He pushed back his chair and asked his family, "Shall we go then?"

"Yes!" the other three replied in unison.

The ladies stayed at the resort where they had eaten brunch to shop the boutiques, while the men went through the lobby to hail a taxi back to the marina.

They set up an appointment for an hour later and returned to the *Arabella* to get changed. Forty-five minutes later they were walking back down the passerelle to the marina office in long shorts, long sleeve tee-shirts for sun protection and water sandals. They also wore baseball hats and sunglasses, and in their backpacks they had their high-tech life jackets, snacks, water, and cameras.

A tall Caribbean man greeted them at the front doors of the marina's office. "Are you Adrian?" He smiled and reached out a hand to shake. "I'm Big Wayne. I'm here to teach you how to fly-fish."

Adrian reached out his hand and shook Big Wayne's hand. "Nice to meet you. Where's Lil Wayne?" he quipped.

Big Wayne laughed and said, "That's my son. He's at home at his grandmother paintin' da fence." He turned to shake hands with Adrian's dad. "He's quick, that son of yours."

"Oh, you have no idea," his dad replied with a chuckle, putting an affectionate hand on his shoulder.

"I have five sons. All are named Wayne. Only the first born

goes by Wayne. They're all clever!" he laughed and added "like their mother!"

Adrian gasped. "You named all your sons Wayne?"

"Sure." Big Wayne smiled with pride, "it's a tradition."

"But what if you had a daughter? Would you have named her Wayne, too?"

"Hahahaha! No," he responded, "It's never happened before, so I don't know. Maybe Jayne –spelled with a Y?"

Adrian grinned. "Maybe."

"Let's go. The boat's this way." Big Wayne led the way to a gate on a dock for smaller yachts and held the security door open for them to walk through. "Everything is on the boat. Straight ahead on the right."

A white and gray painted Action Craft fly-fishing boat was tied to the dock with the remaining bow and stern lines flemished in a tight clock-coil on the warm dock planks. The new boat glistened in the sun. A single superfast Mercury outboard engine hanging off the stern powered the boat with 300 horsepower. He couldn't wait to hear the noise of the outboard engine at full throttle. The 24' boat had compartments everywhere Adrian looked. Over the driver's console was a black rig with a shade awning and rack that held several fishing rods.

"Where is everything?" he asked with growing curiosity. "Don't we need tackle boxes, bait and other stuff if we catch something?"

Big Wayne held up his right index finger and said, "Ah! Wait until you see my magic boat! It holds everything!"

He hopped aboard and indicated they should follow. He walked to the bow and began opening all the hatches built into the bow's deck flooring which revealed cooler-type storage with water, fully plumbed for keeping fish fresh. He showed them how some of the hatches flipped up to offer seating and create backrests for passengers. Under the steering wheel was a hatch that opened and formed a table for tying lines and attaching flies and bait. Inside the compartment were half a dozen cubby holes with clear plastic boxes that organized colorful flies, hooks, weights, additional feathers and more. Adrian was fascinated at how organized the boat was in terms of its thoughtful layout.

And it went on and on, as Big Wayne, fulfilling the role of boat salesperson, opened hatches in the stern to reveal live bait coolers with circulating water pumps. When the last hatch was opened and its function revealed, Adrian exclaimed in genuine amazement, "Wow, this boat is amazing!"

"It is! It handles the flats so smoothly and if the water gets rough, *no problem mon*, as we like to say in the Caribbean." He laughed in Adrian's direction. "OK, young man, prepare to cast off the bowline. Dad, take the stern line and we'll get out of here and go fish."

Big Wayne drove the boat fast. Adrian and his dad kept high-fiving each other over the centerline of the stern where they sat in the port and starboard seats respectively. Big grins plastered their faces as they headed away from Iguana Island and Mangrove Cay to a secret fishing place Big Wayne loved to take people. Adrian's hair was blown backward by the wind that whipped up from the speed they were traveling across the water. He was glad he stuffed his ball cap in his backpack and tightened the security string on his polarized sunglasses, so they didn't blow off his face. The 300 horsepower outboard lived up to its reputation and provided a huge amount of power from Adrian's perspective. If it were any more, they'd be flying out of the water and skipping over the top of it.

After about 30-minutes, Big Wayne slowed down and navigated over some coral where Adrian could see the bottom. There were fish everywhere he looked. And no people in sight, nor any other boats. It was quiet and peaceful now that they had come to a stop. The equatorial sun was also hot overhead.

"OK, guys. Here's the t'ing." Big Wayne began. "Fish like quiet. They spook easily. So, walk softly. Talk softly and carry a big fishing pole!"

"Roger that." Adrian nodded his head in agreement.

Big Wayne hoisted a fishing pole out of the rack over his head. "First, you need to rig up your rod. These poles are all saltwater poles, and the handle end is thicker in case you need to fight with a big fish. For fishing anything over ten pounds, use a number 9 or 10 weight rod.

"This neon green line floats. It's called a *fly line*. This piece in the middle is your *leader line* and one end is thicker than the other end, which is where you tie on a *tippet*. And at the very end of your tippet, you tie a fly on your line.

"You need a good reel to bring your fly line back in. The reel is your muscle that makes the fish tired. It has to be fast and strong."

"How do you know where the fish are biting?" Adrian asked him, changing the conversation.

"Good question!" Big Wayne answered while he tied a colorful fly to the end of a monofilament tippet line. "You could look for birds diving into the water eating small bait fish. Or look for fins and tails breaking the surface. Or watch for ripples in the water where the fish are eating insects. You can also find fish under mangroves.

"And…if you know what the tides are doing," he continued, as he locked the lid on a plastic box and put it back in the shelving before him, "you know that the big fish come in to eat the little shellfish and crabs in the shallow waters when the tide is coming in. When the tide is going out, the tide sometimes washes small fish and crabs out to slightly deeper water and that is where you find the bigger fish waiting with their hungry mouths wide open."

Stepping away from the center console, he stood in the middle of the space behind the driver's seat and began to demonstrate to his two guests how to hold the rod. "Today we play cat and mouse. The fish is the cat, and the mouse is the fly. You want the cat to pounce on the mouse, yes? And so, it is with de big fish. We want him to go after de fly.

"Are you ready to crack the whip and tease de fish?" he smiled down at Adrian. "You know the hands of the clock, Adrian? Well, you point the tip of the rod at 10 and bring it back to 2." He moved the rod between 10 and 2 in smooth back and forth gestures and released the line. They all watched it sail forward through the air effortlessly and land several yards from the boat on top of the water. He rewound the line on the reel with a uniform speed and ease of a pro who had done this thousands of times.

"The motion will help you keep your line from getting tangled. This heavier line will give you all the momentum you need. No tiny fishing weights necessary. The line is heavy enough that it will fly off the reel when you let it go. Here." He placed the rod in Adrian's hands and showed him how to hold his fingers on the line while he moved between 10 and 2.

He stood back and commanded Adrian to let it rip after two or three smooth whips of the rod forwards and back. The first time he let go of the line too soon. The second time, he forced it too far forward and it flew out into the water just in front of the boat. The third time, he hit the tip of the pole on the overhead awning. With shoulders slumped and a dejected sigh, his face reflected his lack of joy. "I can't get it." He complained. "I'm terrible at this."

"Adrian," Big Wayne started with a fatherly tone, "Did you know Michael Jordan, the greatest American basketball player ever, missed over 9,000 baskets? It's true. He also missed 26 shots that could have helped his team win the game. He's still practicing and playing ball. Mr. Jordan did not stop trying to throw a basketball after 3 failed attempts."

"Wow, he did?" Adrian's dad asked, with the lift of a disbelieving eyebrow. "That's incredible. How many did he make?"

"Over 12,000." Big Wayne shook his head. "And that is just the ones recorded during a game. I can't imagine…"

"OK! OK!" Adrian injected impatiently. "I get it. Let me try again." He took the rod firmly in his right hand. He locked his wrist to brace the stock end with the reel against his forearm. He began swinging it between 9 and 3 and then corrected himself. He kept looking at his rod as it went back, and he observed that twisting his head was throwing off the motion. Frustrated, he looked down at his feet to recenter his mind and let go of the previous failed attempts and breathed out his frustration and self-judgment that he wasn't getting it right.

Feeling reset, he took a deep breath and looked across the water, then up at his pole at his 2 o'clock position and began moving his pole forward and back. He released it and the fly flew across the water expertly and landed.

"Woohoo! I did it! I got it!" he cried out loud with obvious happiness. "Do I just start reeling it back in now?" He looked at Big Wayne for guidance.

"Yes." Soon the line was back in, and the reel was full. "Try again."

Adrian kept casting. He didn't give up. He messed up an equal number of times as he got right. "Wow. This really is harder than it looks." He acknowledged his present truth without judging it and was therefore quite peaceful with his experience.

Big Wayne had put his dad on the bow of the boat. He was standing on the cushy gray carpet pads that covered the hatches. He was balanced and casting in the opposite direction than Adrian. That's what happens when you have two right-handed people on board. Each fisherman needs space to the outside of their right arm to swing the fishing line.

His dad was struggling with it, too. He could hear his dad often muttering, "Rats," "Shucks," and "Dang-nabbit" every time his cast failed to land on the water any meaningful distance away. Adrian smiled to himself. He wasn't the only one making self-judgments about his fly-fishing attempts.

Suddenly there was a tug on his line while he was reeling it in. "I got something!" he yelled with glee. "I got a fish!"

Big Wayne came over to his side and wrapped his long arm around Adrian's right side to guide his efforts in reeling in and working the fish. "Easy now. Easy. Just let the fish get tired. You've got this." He pulled the neon green line onto the floor of the boat behind Adrian, so it wouldn't get tangled. "Keep reeling in. Keep reeling in."

Soon a silver-colored fish was flipping and flapping in the water alongside the boat. His dad had set his rod in a holder and had whipped out his phone to take video and pictures. "Woohoo! Good job, Adrian! You did it."

Big Wayne grabbed a fish net for Adrian to scoop it up out of the water. He held Adrian's fishing pole while he caught his fish in the net and landed him onto the boat. Adrian took the end of the line and held up the fish which was flipping now in the vertical position. "Oh my gosh! He's huge! Dad, look!" He held up his prize fish while his dad took pictures.

"Let's measure him before we throw him back." Big Wayne pointed to the edge of the boat and Adrian laid his fish's nose to the zero on the ruler. Looking at where the tail landed on the ruler, he cried out, "It's 14 inches!"

"That's a good size bonefish. It's almost an adult." Big Wayne had a pair of pliers in his hand. "Are you ready to release him now and get him back in the water?" He passed the pliers to Adrian who clamped them on the backside of the hook and reversed out the hook.

"OK! Here goes nothing!" he shouted to his dad on camera, and he counted backwards, "3, 2...1!" And the fish slipped into the water and wriggled away. "Oh man! That was Ah-maz-ing! *Amazing*!" He got high-fives from Big Wayne and his dad. "Wow. My first fish." His eyes were ablaze with the excitement of it all.

He sat down on the starboard quarter seat and watched his dad. "You're done for the day?" asked Big Wayne.

"Naw. Just takin' a break." He reached for his backpack in a storage compartment and pulled out his water bottle. Taking a big, long swig, he could smell the sunblock, salt water and fish smells on his fingers. "I can't believe my luck!"

"Why not?" Big Wayne asked, "You're on my magic boat. We always lucky on this t'ing."

"By the way, what's the name of your boat, Big Wayne?" Adrian asked. He hadn't had a chance to look at the sides or stern when he got to the dock.

"*Serendipity*."

His dad chuckled. "Big Wayne, that is the perfect name for your boat. We can all use a little serendipity in our lives." He picked up his fishing pole and tried a few more casts before calling it a day.

Big Wayne put away the rods in the rack and fired up the engine. He looked back over his shoulder to make sure that Adrian and his dad were sitting down before he floored the engine. "Hang on!" He yelled, as he pulled a fast and tight circle, and the centrifugal forces caused the guys to be held to their seats at a fierce angle. They were laughing their heads off at how powerless they felt to move against the g-forces of the outboard engine. Big Wayne laughed, too. He knew hot-dogging his motor was only for

special people. These were his kind of people. He gave them one more spin and then straightened out his boat and headed back to the marina.

They helped dock the boat, with Adrian tying the bowline to the cleat on the floating dock. His dad adjusted the stern line and ran the excess back to the middle cleat of the boat where he had seen it tied as a spring line to protect against surge in the marina.

His dad paid and tipped Big Wayne and expressed his sincere gratitude for such a terrific day on the water. "You really provided a great service today. That was loads of fun! We both had a great time."

"Yeah," chimed in Adrian, "you're a good teacher. And I loved when you started doing donuts in the water with the boat! That was awesome!"

"It was great to have you both aboard my magic boat." He shook both their hands and added, "Come back again soon. Any time you are in TCI, let me know and we'll go fly fishing again. And next time, dad catches a fish! OK?" He winked at Adrian's dad.

"Bye!" Adrian waved to him as they turned to walk up the ramp to the marina gate to return to the *Arabella*.

"Dad, that was so much fun! Let's do it again sometime."

"I agree. That was a blast. He was a lot of fun, too." His dad smiled and looked over at his son. "I'm so happy you caught your first fish! We'll have to show your mom and Grace the photos."

"And the captain!" Adrian added. "I told him I never catch anything. My unlucky streak is over!"

"I would definitely say so," his dad agreed with a happy look on his face.

They reached the passerelle and unhooked the no trespassing sign that read, "Only Owners and Crew Allowed" and passed through to the yacht's main deck. His dad looked at his dive watch and shared that it was a few minutes to cocktail and appetizer hour. He suggested they clean up and meet back on the upper deck. His dad made a dad joke calling it "Happytizer Hour!"

"Daa-ad!" Adrian groaned at his dad-joke. "OK," Adrian acknowledged the plan, "I'll check in on Grace and let her know. I'm guessing they are back. And I'll let Chef Zak know where to send the stews."

His dad gave a thumbs up and headed for the owner's cabin upstairs.

Adrian popped into the busy galley and burst out with his big news, "Zak! I caught my first fish today! It was 14 inches long and probably weighed about four pounds!!"

"Wow! That's incredible!" Zak expressed his happiness for Adrian but was busy prepping for the dinner meal and didn't quite make eye contact. "Did you take photos, I hope?"

"Yep! My dad took some. I'll show you later when I get them on my phone." Seeing that Zak and his *sous chef* Jean-Marie were not able to talk, he chose to leave them alone to concentrate. "See ya later! Oh! And we're going to do Happy Hour on my parent's private deck upstairs."

"Roger that. *Merci*, Adrian." Jean-Marie said in her delightful French accent, "And I'm happy for your first fish!"

He gave her a thumbs up and disappeared over to his cabin to freshen up.

After dinner, while looking across the swimming pool in the stern, he asked Grace if she wanted to walk the dock with him. They both liked to look at the variety of boats, large and small, and see the registration countries and names. The marina was full, but the superyacht dock was quiet. Generators hummed and LED lights shone down in all colors around the waterlines of the yachts creating an enchanting scene. Soft

laughter from a party on a deck over his head to his right caused him to look up, but he couldn't see anyone.

They stepped down onto the dock and put their shoes on. "Let's start over here and walk to the end, then turn around and go down the other side. Sound good?" Grace suggested.

Nodding his approval, they took off. Grace was looking at the yacht moored next to them while Adrian was paying attention to what was going on down the dock. Two men were attempting to lug a large duffle bag towards a yacht. By the looks of it, it was very heavy and twice they set it down to give themselves a rest.

"Wow, this yacht is from Cyprus!" Grace was excited to find a country she hadn't seen before on the stern of a yacht. *"M/Y Artemis.* I love the name!" Realizing her brother was not paying attention, she pushed his shoulder to get him to look at her. "Dude! Check out this yacht and its logo. It's cool, right?"

"Uh-huh. Yeah. It's nice." He glanced at the iconic female Grecian figure whose skirt was pulled up into a bow and arrow. "Check those guys out, Grace. What do you think?"

"They should have used a dock dolly to cart it down to their yacht!" she snorted through her nose with an imperious tone. "Clearly they overestimated the distance they thought they could carry a heavy bag."

"They are being so careful with it." Adrian began walking towards them keeping one eye on them and one eye on the yachts. A third man came down a passerelle and took the front section of the bag and helped them haul it up into a yacht walking backwards. *What could be so heavy? Dive equipment?*

"Ooh! Look at this staircase, Adrian! That's so cool!" Grace distracted him to look at a sweeping stern staircase and he could not have cared less. "I love the way the lighting is worked into each step."

Adrian picked up the pace to walk down closer to where the men were last seen, and Grace followed. No one was guarding the passerelle and the privacy chain was hanging. The yacht was named *Neptune* and registered in Monaco, a small country in the Mediterranean Sea known for being a tax haven for the ultra-rich and famous.

Male voices walking towards the stern made Adrian say to Grace, "Come on, let's not be caught staring."

"What's your trip?" she scowled at him and looked up as two men leaned over the railing look down at the two teens. "Oh, hello! I like your yacht's logo and how it's lit up."

"Hallo!" The crew member returned her pleasant greeting as he stepped down the passerelle to clip the chain in place that prevented trespassing. "Having a nice night?"

"Yep! Just taking in all the yachts before curfew." She laughed, waved and began walking towards the end of the dock where two more yachts were moored. Adrian smiled and without looking gave the guys a straight-arm half wave that never made it higher than his shoulder level as he followed his sister. *What the heck were they hauling this late at night that was so heavy they didn't use a cart or dolly?* They stood at the end of the row and looked out across the water and up at the sky. It was a perfect night.

"They didn't pass our stern." Adrian said all of a sudden. "We would have seen or heard them."

"What?" Grace was confused, "Are you fixated on those guys with the bag? Why don't you just go ask them?"

"Nah. My brain just likes puzzles. You said why don't they just use a dock-dolly, and they underestimated the weight. I think they left a yacht and carried it a couple boats over. Who's next to us again?"

"*Artemis* and on the other side is *Moonriver*." Grace looked at him awaiting an explanation.

"I dunno. It was odd." He shook his head and said, "Come on, let's walk back."

As they passed *Neptune*, the crew member was standing watching them like a hawk.

"On watch tonight?" Grace asked with a hint of coyness.

"You know it, luv!" he replied with his thick British accent and a harsh laugh. "No rest for the wicked!"

Adrian felt a shiver and rubbed his arms as if chilled. "Well, enjoy your watch. Good night!" He waved and kept walking. Grace waved and caught up with him.

"What the heck, Adrian? You're acting so funny."

"I guess it's just been a long day or two," he confessed, "I think I'm going to turn in and go to bed."

"Oh, alright."

Adrian looked up at *Artemis* as they passed by it and saw a crewman on night watch looking the direction they had come from. *Those two are connected. I wonder how.* He and Grace each gave a short wave to the crewman as they passed, which was common courtesy among crew and neighbors. The night watchman nodded and turned to walk the deck.

Dropping their shoes on the mat, they walked barefoot up the passerelle without making a sound. The neighbors had gone inside, and many lights were dimmed, or window shades drawn for privacy. They didn't see their own crew on night watch as they said good night and went into their opposing cabins.

Chapter Five
Season of Giving

Puerto Rico
Unincorporated United States Territory
Northeastern Caribbean Sea

Back at sea, the captain set a new course for Old San Juan in Puerto Rico. They took a compass heading of south by southeast. They passed a large island occupied by two countries, namely Haiti and Dominican Republic to the west. The *Arabella* traveled 374 nautical miles in less than 40-hours. They had left on a Monday morning and arrived by sundown on Tuesday.

Adrian realized that he hadn't played any video games since he left Fort Lauderdale and was a bit surprised when he realized that he had survived these past weeks without online games or even game apps on his phone. He idly picked up his phone and thought about calling a friend but changed his mind. Last night, his dad had forwarded the photos of their fly-fishing trip with some happy emoticons, and he'd downloaded them to his phone. Picking the best one, he sent an email to a small group of his closest friends about his first catch and said, "Wish you were here to go fishing with me" before sending it out.

He wasn't great at writing letters or emails, as he preferred video calling. Thoughts of his friends frequented his mind, and he was surprised that several weeks had already passed, and it was almost Christmas. He could not believe that so much time had passed, and he wondered what his friends would be doing for the holidays back home in the States.

The yacht was going to be in the Caribbean all winter before making a transatlantic crossing in the spring to be in the Mediterranean Sea for the months of May through late October. This was to avoid hurricane season in the tropical regions and cold driving rain and winds in "The Med" over the winter. Everything pertaining to vacationers closed in The Med after peak season in August-September, so it wasn't the most interesting time to be there.

He hadn't thought much about what his family planned to do for their first Christmas at sea. He wasn't even sure they would have a gift exchange. His family certainly didn't need gifts, nor did his parents expect or want one. Everything was being taken care of for them and by their financial resources. He thought instead about what he could do for the crew and the captain.

He texted his mom:

> Adrian: **Hey, what are we doing for the crew for Christmas?**
> Mom: **No idea. Let's discuss**
> Adrian: **Can we throw them a party?**
> Mom: **Sure. Why not? Let's take them to dinner**
> Adrian: **What about gifts?**
> Mom: **Leave that to me**
> Adrian: **Where are you right now?**
> Mom: **My deck. Come up**
> Adrian: **See you soon**

He left his cabin and hiked the portside staircase to his parent's cabin, walked through it and out onto her deck. She was reclining on a large, cushioned chaise lounge that was easily 10 feet across. His mom was cool. She picked her battles with him. Her main thing was that he release his fears and create solutions based in love. It wasn't always easy, but with her help, he did his best to avoid solving his problems inside more fear, which he was known to do on many occasions and cost him a few friendships. Nowadays, he had more authentic conversations with friends that didn't include demands, ultimatums and suppressing his emotions when he got upset or anxious. And his friendships deepened when he listened to their perspective more and stopped insisting that his perspective was the best.

One of the last times he remembered gaming online with his closest friends who had moved across the country, his mom heard him yelling directions at them about how to play the game. His mom had put a note in front of him that read: "You're badgering them. Stop making them wrong. Slow down and take their perspective." Later he found out that his best friend was on the brink of ending their friendship because he always insisted they play a certain way. He was glad his mom had interrupted him although at the time he thought she was being a know-it-all. "I want to get gifts for the crew, too." He jumped right into the subject of Christmas and added, "I just don't know what to get."

"Well, start by letting go of 'don't know' so you open your heart and mind to knowing. Your inner guidance will share with you, if you *open* to it, what to get or make each person."

"OK, right, I forgot." Taking a deep breath, he let it go and said, *"I let go of not knowing and open to know what to get the crew."* He asked next, "What's the plan for tomorrow?"

"There is quite a bit of history in Old San Juan. It is one of two of the oldest cities in the Western Hemisphere. I believe it dates to the year 1521. Your dad and I thought we might start at Fort San Cristobal on the east side and work our way around to the southside where there are shops, restaurants and other touristy stuff that you and Grace might enjoy."

"Shopping sounds interesting," he mused aloud. "Where are we supposed to be on Christmas Day?"

"Well, months ago the captain told us we had to pick a Christmas destination island before we left Los Angeles, so I picked Antigua in the West Indies. He said that Christmas is the busy time of year and getting a berth is difficult. He has reserved one in Falmouth and English Harbour. We have two weeks to cover roughly 260 nautical miles. There are plenty of islands we can visit along the way. Let's figure out what we want to do between now and then."

"I did want to explore Puerto Rico, somewhat, before we left. I heard there are waterfalls we can go to. Is that true, mom?"

"Yes, but they are hours away in the mountains." She looked thoughtful for a moment and then suggested, "You know, you are going to visit many waterfalls on different islands over the next several weeks. Can you wait?"

"I guess so." He pondered his next move. "How about visiting caves? There's one in the central northern area about 100 km from here. I think it would take an hour or so to get there."

"You can do that with your dad. I have no interest in seeing caves." His mom laughed at the thought. "I'll leave that to you. I'd rather go to an art gallery or museum full of light and beauty."

"Caves can be beautiful," he countered. "What about your friends who live in Carolina, just a few minutes east of here? Are they coming to visit us?"

"Oh, my gosh, yes! I promised to text them. They are supposed to visit us tomorrow morning to have brunch on board." His mom reached for her phone to text them a reminder and the marina gate info.

"Isn't he a guitar player or something?"

"Yes. He's amazing." She picked up her phone again and asked that Pepe bring his guitar. "Thanks for reminding me."

Grace arrived and they got up and sat down at the dining table on the owner's deck.

Zak and Jean-Marie had prepared an assortment of classical Puerto Rican cuisine from flavorful chicken and pork *empanada* appetizers to *balacitos* a salty fried cod fritter, and *tostones* –little bite-sized bowls made from mashed plantains filled with meat and topped with onion, cilantro, and tomatoes. For dinner there was fresh caught fish, with side dishes of *mofongo* created from mashed plantains and flavored with garlic and fried pork skins; rice with small pigeon beans, green olives and *sofrito* --a sauce made from tomato paste, olive oil, onions, garlic, herbs, and peppers.

Later, Jane brought up *flan e queso* made with cream cheese and caramelized sugar and tiny *tres leches* "three milks cake" for dessert. Everyone was stuffed by the time they finished their desert.

Adrian was moving his dessert fork through the last drops of the *tres leche* cake on his plate when he had an inspiration to bake a cake for the crew for Christmas. He would have to talk Zak into allowing him time and space to bake in his galley when it was convenient to him.

After his workout the next day, Adrian went for a walk along the harbor. The rule his parents and the captain gave him was that he could walk locally and not roam too far, meaning walkie-talkie radio distance. It didn't appear to be a touristy area at all, but it was interesting. The biggest yachts had to park their boats in an area that was close to the cruise ship ports. The area had hospitals, libraries, museums, and government buildings. It had the flavor of important business, but with all the fast-food businesses mixed in with kitchen supply, sporting goods, and other retail stores it felt confusing.

He turned around and was back to the yacht by 10:30AM to freshen up for receiving their family friends Ana Maria and Pepe.

He went up to the bridge to see if anyone was around and found Bryce pulling apart the main console. He had moved two monitors off the top and stacked them on the ledge of the windshield. "Oh, hello, Adrian. Could you hand me that roll of black electrical tape?" He reached his hand out while keeping an eye on the colorful wires he was keeping separate with his left hand. Adrian placed the roll in his outstretched hand and stood by.

"Whatcha doin'?"

"I'm installing a new, and rather small piece of equipment. It monitors various systems on board and transmits that data to the onboard server and the electrical system monitor. I thought I'd try it out. It has its own battery backup and can hold data if this system goes offline, it can tell me which system I can be disappointed with."

"Ah. Sounds important!"

"Let's hope I never need it!" Bryce laughed. "Hey, I heard we're going to be in Antigua for Christmas. Are you excited?"

"Sort of." Adrian admitted to the electrical engineer. "I fear this Christmas will be totally boring since it's just us. No offense to the crew."

"None taken." He cut a piece of black tape between his teeth and set the roll down. He proceeded to wrap a few wires together and finished up by screwing the back plate of the console back together.

Adrian continued his musings aloud, "Our family has some very nice friends that live down there that are like family. We are hoping to have a big party onboard with some of them, but I think it will be after the holidays since they manage hotels and resorts. It's their busiest time."

"Thanks, buddy." Bryce said when Adrian took his power screwdriver from him and returned it to his open box. Then he added with great confidence, "You'll have a good time in Antigua. Everybody does."

"Hey, is everyone going to be here for Christmas and Christmas Eve, or will some people go home?"

"I'm not sure. I hope we are all together for Christmas, but yachties don't have much say in when they get time off, especially during the busy season." He dusted off the top of the console and returned the monitors to their place. There was no evidence that anything had changed.

"I hope we are all together, too," Adrian admitted with a measure of sincerity, "It wouldn't feel the same without everyone here."

They left the wheelhouse and wandered down to the galley to see if Zak was there and if there was any leftover *tres leche* cake. They walked into what appeared to be an informal meeting of the crew and an empty, sticky glass cake plate.

"Wow." Adrian looked in the dish as if hoping it would magically come back. "Nothing but crumbs."

"*Si, è uno dei preferiti,*" Raffa revealed as he lifted his plate up to his mouth to sweep in the last crumbs on his plate. "Zak knows to make a lot of it. Our other preferred choice is chocolate cake."

Zak walked in and started shooing everyone out of his galley. "Come on, we have guests arriving any minute now. Out! Out! Out!"

The crew scattered like ants and disappeared in a matter of seconds. "Can I bring anything up, Zak?" Adrian offered.

"I think we are good, right now, Adrian." He wiped the island countertop with a kitchen towel and some disinfectant spray. "Anything on your mind?"

"Um, yeah..." Adrian began. "May I please use the galley to bake a cake for the crew...for Christmas. And if yes, can you please keep it a secret? I want to surprise them."

Zak stood up straight from wiping the island top and put the back of his right wrist on his hip. He was still holding the towel. "I think that is a marvelous idea and I think they would love it!"

Adrian's face brightened and he asked, "When would be a good time? Afternoon on Christmas Eve?"

"Let me think about it as we will probably be underway. We can simplify the menu for that day so you can use the galley." He looked up to the ceiling as he sorted his thoughts out. "It's very doable."

"Cool!" He thanked Zak and headed out through the galley door that led to the main deck so he could wait for their guests. He was going to bake a cake for the crew! Now, he had to figure out what to get the captain. *If only I had some ideas*...he wished.

Pepe and Ana Maria, native Puerto Ricans, offered to show Adrian's family around after brunch. After they finished eating, Pepe took out his guitar and began to strum Spanish style music that was very hypnotic and beautiful. The world got quiet around the yacht as others strained their ears to hear his playing. Passersby on the dock slowed down to enjoy his playing, crew from the neighboring yachts on port and starboard and their guests lingered over the ship's rails to listen in and be swept away by the dulcet strains of his Latin music.

Pepe seemed lost in the music and so was his audience. Adrian was captivated like everyone else. Pepe finished playing and closed his eyes and held his guitar with reverence. When he opened them, he seemed rather surprised to find an audience spellbound all around him. Enthusiastic clapping from all directions broke the spell as his playing ended, and as the crowd disbursed, the master guitarist bowed his head accepting the praise with grace. He touched his lips and raised his fingers to the heavens. Lowering his guitar to its case, he closed it shut and took a deep breath. Brightly, he asked, "Where to first?"

Adrian was captivated by Ana Maria and her highly caffeinated outlook on life. She was hyper and giggly, and never spoke less than a million miles an hour. She loved and lived life at high speed. He was mesmerized on a whole new level. He'd never met anyone like her. She was older than his mom but acted like she was in her mid-twenties. She was like a bunny with batteries in her that never stopped.

She got all six of their party crammed into a mini-van taxi to start touring the old fort. She had them laughing and managing the lack of personal space in the van. Everything she did brought fun and laughter to the world around her. He often caught Pepe looking at her with love and knew that they were a special couple. He knew they did not have children but had been married for a very long time. He wondered if one day he would look at someone special that way, too.

Ana Maria whirled them around the town for the best coffees and pastries, the best ice creams, appetizer and *tapas* bar, best beach, history lessons and interesting architecture. She was full of interesting facts about the place and the day passed quickly.

Adrian's dad suggested they go back to the yacht and relax over some drinks. Ana Maria was the first to vote in favor of returning. "Let's throw a party! Let's throw on the disco lights and dance the night away!"

When the yacht was first commissioned, and Adrian had reviewed the plans and notes by the designer and architect, he was embarrassed by all the disco accessories planned for the yacht's main deck bar area. He had scoffed at the idea of a disco onboard.

The entire main deck bar area converted to a nightclub, complete with state-of-the-art digital DJ mixing equipment and speaker system, lights, strobes, disco ball –the works! He couldn't imagine ever wanting to use that place for a disco, but now he felt a bit different towards the space. He wanted to see Ana Maria having fun in that space. She alone might be able to change his mind.

Jimmy, Gabriella, and Jane were notified by his dad via text, to set up the disco area and by the time they arrived, there were strobe lights, fog, music and drinks all set up for a party. All lit up, it looked inviting and amazing. Jimmy was working the music and doing a masterful job repeating beats and making the place come alive with the sounds of a throbbing Caribbean party.

Ana Maria hit the dance floor with Grace and his mom, and they started dancing, twirling, and laughing. Ana Maria reached out to Adrian to dance, and he met her on the dance floor with a show of teenage boy reluctance. She pantomimed across the dance floor to Jimmy "robot dance" and he switched gears without anyone noticing and next thing Adrian knew, he and his family were laughing and making the most hilarious robot moves ever, especially his dad. He burst out laughing after a few minutes. He couldn't believe he was acting like a robot on a dance floor that he previously thought was ridiculous.

Jimmy put on some other fun popular songs, and they all continued to have fun, spinning, jumping, hip-hopping, and trying to outdo each other for funniest moves. The time just flew by.

Ana Maria started fanning herself and begged to take a break. They all left the dance floor and joined Pepe and his dad around a table. Gabriella and Jane brought over a tray of cool drinks and asked Ana Maria what she would like to enjoy. Soon they were all talking about their travels through different Atlantic and

Caribbean countries. Before long, they stood up and gave hugs all around and said goodnight. Adrian promised to keep in touch via email with stories and photos of his adventures.

With a feeling of contentment, he and Grace wandered down to bed. "Good night, Grace."

"Good night, Adrian. See you tomorrow." Her cabin door closed before his. He could hear the generators, but otherwise the yacht was quiet, and the music was off.

He felt like he did back in their old home when they had a family party, and everyone had a great time. The feelings were of warmth, close friendship, came with an emotional high, and were unforgettable. Just like today. *Maybe...just maybe*, he thought as he threw his clothes of the day on the chair in his cabin, *one day this big ole boat could feel like a home to me*.

In the days that followed, they flowed one into the other as they explored Puerto Rico, moved on to St. Thomas in the U.S. Virgin Islands, then on to St. John's and made day trips into the British Virgin Islands of Tortola and Virgin Gorda. The snorkeling was amazing, and Adrian took lots of underwater video to make a long version movie for his friends back home.

The captain wanted Adrian to explore Saba and give him his opinion of the tiny island. They anchored out and woke up to a bright, sunny, tropical winter day of 85 degrees off the steep volcanic sides of Saba, an island owned by the Netherlands, nestled in the northern region of the Lesser Antilles.

"What's with Saba? I don't see a single beach from here," Adrian asked the captain. "What do you know about it?"

The captain gazed through the windshield and studied the island. "She is a jewel...the Unspoiled Queen of the Caribbean. She has a different energy to the other islands. I can't explain it, nor can I explain some of the strange sounds or experiences

I and others have around the island." The captain had grown a goatee and was stroking it with this right hand as he tried to express his thoughts about Saba. "I find it intriguing and mysterious. However, no one else on the crew has ever experienced it, so I wondered if perhaps you might."

A bit perplexed but willing to tune into the island and see if there was anything to the captain's story, he agreed.

"It looks like a volcano," Adrian commented thoughtfully. "Is it?" He picked up the binoculars and gazed at the island.

"It is a potentially active volcano, and it will give us months of notice before it is active," he assured Adrian, "therefore, we have nothing to worry about."

"Well, it certainly looks imposing with those cliffs," Adrian noted to the captain. "I bet there is some awesome underwater snorkeling at the base. Are we going to go there now?"

"We are! You had best change into a swimsuit so you can kayak or paddleboard over with Jimmy and the gang." The captain sounded like his normal self again and shooed Adrian off to go have fun before they headed to St. Kitts and Nevis for the night.

The nice thing about having a boat was the ability to stop the boat and go for a swim whenever you liked, provided the water was not dangerous. Adrian appreciated that the captain made fun stops along the way for him and his family to enjoy different sand bars, cays, atolls, and now an inaccessible from shore rock-and-pebble beach at the base of a steep cliff on the island of Saba. It wasn't much of a beach. It was more like a rocky stretch or shelf that was present only at low tide.

The captain's musings about Saba lingered in his head, and he reflected on what he was referring to. "I wonder what he experienced..." Adrian said aloud as he paddled over to the beach on his stand-up paddle board.

He pulled his board up high on the narrow strip of rocky beach and leaned it and the paddle against the almost vertical cliff. He studied the water and proximity to the board and decided it was far enough away for the time being to risk losing it to the tide. He saw the *Arabella* anchored out in the not too far distance. It was beautiful in the morning sun, glistening white and inviting to the heart of an explorer. He walked over to the end of the beach and looked up at the cliffs. To call it a beach was a stretch. He was grateful for his water shoes as he crunched small rocks and hugged the shoreline. He had an hour to hangout by himself if he wanted. Grace was snorkeling at the opposite end and Brian was on a jet ski keeping her company. Captain Gunnar never let anyone swim alone.

Alone with his thoughts, he sat on a dry rock and leaned back. He felt at peace. He was amazed at how many weeks had slipped by. Reflecting on his time, he didn't miss being in school, or his sporting games, now that he thought about it. He felt like a different person since leaving Los Angeles. Happier, if that was possible. He felt a smile growing inside himself.

He picked up a small rock and threw it at the water lapping the island. It sunk rapidly out of sight.

Minutes ticked by without him noticing.

He was distracted by a fly that landed on his knee and he brushed it off. He picked up another stone and threw it without much energy. He felt so relaxed…so peaceful. He looked at his watch and jumped to his feet. Nearly 90 minutes had passed, and he ran to his paddleboard and started back. Jimmy was hanging out on a jet ski waiting for him. It passed through Adrian's mind that Jimmy would have said something if he was causing a problem by being late.

He caught up to Jimmy and said, "Hey, man, I'm sorry. I lost track of time."

"No worries, mon." Jimmy grinned at him. "Captain told me to let you have your time on the island."

"He did, huh?" Adrian looked at him with curiosity. "I don't know where the time went. I really don't. I just sort of lost track of time after I sat down."

"Yeah, no problems, my friend. I had a relaxin' morning because of it. Let's just go back." Jimmy idled the jet ski nearby and let Adrian paddle on ahead of him.

The crew put the water toys away while Adrian took a quick shower in the gym and toweled off. He rinsed and wrung out his swimsuit and put on a robe and climbed the stairs to his cabin. He saw no one and was glad. He dressed and then laid down on his bed. He wasn't ready to see anyone on board just yet. He closed his eyes and drifted off to sleep although he was not tired.

Later that afternoon, Zak texted Adrian that he could use the kitchen on Christmas Eve. Excited, he went and looked at Zak's cookbooks in the galley while sitting on a tall stool in the corner. He stayed out of the way and made notes on a piece of paper. He would have everything he needed to make a triple chocolate cake for the crew, their other favorite cake. He left a shopping list for Zak before he left the galley.

Falmouth Harbour, Antigua and Barbuda, West Indies
Member of the Commonwealth under Queen Elizabeth II of the United Kingdom
Caribbean Sea

The days passed in the blink of an eye and soon they were pulling into Falmouth Harbour, Antigua, West Indies. Falmouth Bay was gorgeous and blue. Yachts were moored, anchored, and tied to docks. Magnificent island homes dotted the ring of mountains around the bay. His heart skipped a happy beat when he considered the potential for new adventures on the island. Exploring islands was proving interesting since they were all different.

The quarantine flag was flying, and he decided to skip the docking activity and get busy in the galley. He couldn't leave anyway until the captain obtained clearance through the port authority for both Antigua and Barbuda, which meant customs and immigration. Last night, the captain had his entire family do an online declaration, as it speeds up the processing. The captain had shared that they would be docking in a National Park which sounded exciting to him. However, obtaining clearance in this country seemed to take a little more time since cruising permits, entry declarations and port forms were required and there was running back and forth between the different agency offices. And when they would leave these islands, do all the above paperwork in reverse.

Humming to himself, he washed his hands, put on an apron, and pulled out the electric stand mixer in the corner, the paddle attachment, bowls and measuring cups. He opened cabinets and found the dry ingredients. He opened the walk-in fridge and located eggs, pounds of unsalted butter, milk, and cream and placed them with care on the counter next to his recipe and notes.

Adrian knew he needed to work on an organized timeline for optimal results, and he thought all his steps through. The last ingredient he would work with, he knew he needed to make first, which was melted chocolate for his frosting. He found a small saucepan and filled it with water halfway up the sides, then he placed a glass bowl on top and added some bitter-sweet dark baking chocolate to melt. This flavoring had to be cooled to between 70 and 80 degrees before adding it to his Swiss buttercream frosting or it would ruin the texture.

For the cake's thick chocolate *ganache* filling, he filled a saucepan with 1 pint of heavy cream to heat but did not turn it on. He opened a large bar of semi-sweet baking chocolate and measured the amount he needed on a cutting board and began chopping it into small chips with a heavy knife. He swept the broken chocolate into a bowl and set it aside.

Moving to the double ovens, he preheated the lower oven to 350 degrees and took 3 round metal baking pans from the cupboard next to the oven. He greased all the pans with unsalted butter, parchment paper lined them, and greased them again, this time on the paper and dusted them with cocoa powder. He did not want his cakes sticking to the pan!

He inserted the paddle into the stand mixer and locked the bowl in place, then added the butter to soften and cream it. With great scientific care, he measured his white sugar and set it aside while the mixer was running. Cracking his eggs, he dropped them into a bowl for ease of pouring them out when the time came. He grabbed a set of liquid and dry measuring spoons and set them down nearby.

After weighing the flour and cocoa powder, he set it in a sifter and began to sift the salt and baking powder into the light brown colored mix. He poured cold milk into a large measuring cup and left it near the mixer. And last, but not least, he made a single shot of decaf espresso and added it to the milk. Everything was in place, or as his mom would say in French, *mis en place*.

Checking the butter, he discovered it was ready for the sugar, which he poured in a slow, steady steam. With that step done he waited until it was the right color before adding the eggs one at a time. Then he poured in some vanilla.

The convection oven preheat alarm went off and he checked that off his mental list. He started adding flour and espresso-milk to the batter by thirds, alternating wet and dry. Soon he was ready to pour them into the pans.

The bowl was heavier than he thought, and it took two hands to carry it to the island where his pans rested. He grabbed the 8-ounce measure and using it like a cup he ladled chocolate cake batter into the pans. He weighed each pan and adjusted the weight, so they were almost even. Then he tapped them lightly on the counter to get any major air bubbles out. Popping them in the oven, he remembered to set a timer for 25 minutes.

He texted the chef:

Shakedown Cruise — The Adventures of Yacht Boy

Adrian: **Zak, is the oven evenly hot?**
Zak: **You there now? I'll come up**
Adrian: **Thanks**

Zak blew through the galley door and said a loud, "Hey, hey, hey! Look at you, baker man!" He surveyed the total mess on the counters with flour dust, chocolate and butter wrappers, cream carton and eggshells. The cap was still off the vanilla bottle and at risk of being knocked off the counter by a careless elbow. He let out a low whistle. "Dude! You have to start cleaning as you go!"

"Heh!" Adrian chuckled, "You sound like my mom. Don't worry. I'll clean up."

Out of habit, Zak walked to the sink and washed his hands and asked over his shoulder, "How can I help? Oven?"

He walked over to the oven and read the digital readout, briefly turned on the oven light and peeked through the glass door without opening it. "Looks good."

"So, I put the cakes in for 25-minutes, but since it is chocolate, I wanted to be sure the oven didn't run hotter than normal or have a section that runs cooler. Our old gas oven used to do that, and I had to compensate."

"Oh, man, you sound pro!" Zak enthused. "You're in luck. These ovens are some of the best I've ever used. Perfect cooking every time." He opened a drawer and rummaged around in it and came up with a long needle like object with a ring on the top. "Cake tester."

"Ah!" Adrian's eyes lit up. "Thanks, I would not have known where to find that."

"What else can I do?" Zak spotted the chipped chocolate for melting in the bowl. "Ganache?"

"Yep. Want to finish it while I make some Italian buttercream frosting?" Adrian asked with interest. "Oh, and can you find the cooling racks?"

"Roger that!" Zak found everything and began heating cream to add to the chocolate, while Adrian began separating eggs for the frosting. He placed the extra yolks in a glass bowl, covered it and placed it in the fridge.

"Good" Zak approved. He was enjoying observing Adrian and noting his practical knowledge about how to work with the leftover raw eggs and refrigerate them immediately. Chef talked about his galley while he stirred the hot cream into the chocolate and got the two ingredients turned into chocolate silk.

They worked well together and got white sugar and water soft boiled to a syrup for the meringue and Zak suggested he find cold packs to place under the mixer bowl to cool the meringue mixture so he could add butter and melted chocolate. Within minutes the cakes were cooling on racks and the meringue was close to being completed.

"What's your plan for the third chocolate?" Zak asked. "Want some white chocolate stars I made and stored away for a special occasion?"

"Oh, yes, please! That would be fantastic for a Christmas cake." Adrian then admitted, "Actually, I hadn't thought that far ahead, you know, how I was going to get the third chocolate into the cake."

Zak placed the cakes into the fridge to air cool them quickly. Ten minutes later, Adrian began to layer the cakes with cooled ganache and chocolate buttercream. He watched with dismay as his cakes started to slide to one side. "Oh, no!"

Zak rushed to his side and took in the leaning tower of cake. "Well, looks like the cakes need something to stabilize them and hold them together. How about a wooden dowel?"

"Yeah, I've no experience here for troubleshooting a falling cake," Adrian confessed with his disappointment evident.

Zak pulled open a drawer and rummaged through it. "You might need your ganache to be a little bit cooler. Here, try this." He handed a bamboo skewer to Adrian who held it up with a questioning glance.

"What do I do? Just shove it through the middle of the cake?"

"Yep"

Once stable, the cake grew in size as all the layers built up to a considerable size. "Whoa! This thing is huge!" he shared as he spread the last of the buttercream across the top of what appeared to be a ten-inch-wide by six-inch-tall cake. "Oh, my gosh! It's a tower of chocolate! I've never made such a tall cake before!"

"This is your first time making this?" Zak looked confused.

"Yeah!" Adrian confessed. "I've helped my mom many times in the kitchen, and she always explained the steps to me, but this is the first time I did it all by myself."

"Holy Christmas, Yacht Boy!" Zak exclaimed. "I've gone to cooking school and there were people who couldn't bake their way out of a box of cake mix. Dang! You have talent, Yacht Boy."

"Heh-heh-heh," Adrian laughed, shaking his head while looking down at the floor.

"What's so funny?" Zak asked with a half-smile, leaning on the island workspace with one hand, the other on his hip.

"I learned something really great from you and you called me *Yacht Boy*. I must be fitting in!" He grinned so hard his cheeks hurt. "The last argument I gave to my mom about why I didn't want to come on this trip was that I didn't want to turn into a yacht boy."

They laughed together and appreciated the situation. Zak handed a plastic storage box to Adrian and said, "Merry

Christmas, Yacht Boy. Here are your stars."

"Thanks, Zak. Merry Christmas to you, too." Adrian took the box and began placing stars on the cake with an artistic flair. "I couldn't have done it without you."

"Adrian, look. You can cook or bake in my galley anytime but only if..." Adrian straightened up as he heard the *but* and made eye contact with Zak. "You've got to clean this galley as you go along, if you are going to use it. We've got meal prep up next so better get a move on!" Zak gave a high-five to Adrian and left the galley. He saw so many similarities between himself and this young man he had the pleasure of getting to know and work with over the last month. He felt a bit emotional remembering his own youth and his grandfather who taught him how to run the family bakery. *Must be the time of year*, he mused as he lightly went down the stairs to his cabin singing something about figgy pudding.

Adrian surveyed the galley and sighed. His mother hated him experimenting, as she called it since he rarely used a recipe, in her kitchen back home. He knew he made tornadoes in Kansas look tame compared to some of his messes. He literally hated this part. Wishing someone else could do the cleaning, he sighed at the job before him. Upon assessment, he began putting away ingredients to clear space. He washed, dried and put away bowls and pots to get the biggest items cleared out. Loading the dishwasher with the small stuff, he looked around to see if he missed anything and satisfied he turned it on. The last chore, which was the only one he actually found satisfying, was washing the counters. At long last, he threw his apron and the dish towels into the hamper and left the galley the way he found it.

That evening, Adrian invited all the crew, the captain, and his family to take a break and come to the main deck's large dining table for dessert. He had laid out red and green napkins from the bar supply and had a stack of dessert plates and forks. As they stood around the massive dining table for fourteen, he felt a tiny bit sheepish but found the courage inside himself and cleared his throat.

"OK, everyone, can I have your attention?" he began, and everyone went quiet. "I baked you a triple chocolate cake for your Christmas present and I even had a little help from Chef."

"Oh, no!" Zak interrupted him, "I was his *sous chef* at the very end. He gets full credit."

"So, as you can imagine, this was a hard year for me in the beginning..." he swallowed hard, took a breath and started again, "I didn't want to leave my friends, sports programs, you know, the life of a kid, basically.

"I, uhh ... I found all of you to be really friendly, and nice, and that really helped me get through all my fears about living aboard a yacht.

"I wasn't sure what to get 13 people, who I...and don't take this the wrong way." He held up a cautionary hand with an embracing smile, "I feared all of you at first and now, to me, it feels more like friends...well, more like family to me since we're all living under the same roof for over a month. I figured you all like *tres leche* cake, because Chef makes the best *tres leche* as we all know, so I thought I could bake you a triple chocolate cake. You know ... *Tres chocolate* cake!

"I hope you all enjoy it and Merry Christmas!" he ended his long-winded toast with a deep breath and relaxed now that it was over. Not waiting for anyone, he picked up the long cake knife and a serving tool, he cut into the gigantic tower of chocolate, being careful to remove the short bamboo skewer once the first slice came out.

"Merry Christmas, Adrian!" Everyone cheered.

Chef waited until the voices died down a bit and he yelled, "Merry Christmas, Yacht Boy!" And everyone laughed, including Adrian and his mom.

The captain let his crew know that they had 20 minutes to enjoy cake and then back to work. He walked over to Adrian and while eating a plate of cake, he complimented him on his baking. "I had no idea you could bake. You know triple chocolate is my favorite?"

"Oh," Adrian started, looking a bit surprised, "I had no idea. I'm glad it worked out this way. I didn't know what to get you for Christmas. I'm glad the cake was a surprise for you, too, knowing that what they probably wanted most was just a day off!!"

"Yes, it is perfect." He paused for a moment and said, "I haven't exactly seen you around since we left Saba." He looked at Adrian from under his eyebrows while he ate his last bite of cake.

Adrian looked down. He lowered his cake plate and fork and contemplated what to share. "I didn't know what to tell you. It was kind of a nothing event. I went over there and walked to the end of the rocky beach and just sat down. I didn't hear anything." His voice lowered and he looked at the floor. The captain waited.

"Something odd did happen." He announced with a touch of hesitancy, then took a deep breath and continued, "I...I lost track of time. It was like...I was present one moment and the next I was flicking a fly off my knee and then I was lost in time..." he shook his head to clear his thoughts which sounded mixed up and confused even to himself. "I dunno. I came to an odd awareness suddenly and boom! Ninety minutes passed. I jumped up and raced back to the boat. I kinda freaked. Nothing like that has ever happened to me before. Time folded, or disappeared, or bent...I'm not sure. Does that answer your question?"

The captain nodded sagely. He smiled and looked over at Adrian. "Thank you, Adrian."

"For what?" Adrian asked, a bit confused.

"This is a Christmas present of great value to me," the captain assured him. "I had a feeling that the island would speak to you. It doesn't speak to everyone, but you...I had a hunch it would speak to you."

"What does that mean?"

"Did you feel peaceful?"

"Yes."

"Did your soul feel free and relieved of the past?"

"Yes," the light was beginning to dawn on Adrian, and he looked less and less confused. "I did reach an understanding with the past if that is what you mean. It didn't have power over me anymore. I felt more in the present moment."

"Yes," The captain's eyes glowed with pleasure now that Adrian understood. "The past doesn't exist anymore but summoning up your memories is like bringing up your demons. If you do that, you victimize yourself without anyone's help and you get to relive all the pain and suffering. In the end, you miss the present moment and all of its new and fresh opportunities. Be in the now, buddy. Be in the now."

Adrian nodded his head with deeper understanding and smiled over to the captain. "Thanks for, you know, being there for me. I hope I wasn't too much of a pain in the beginning."

"No, you were just scared of your new life and all the new people in it." The captain smiled with compassion, "I know my crew, and I knew they would be a good team for you to learn and grow with. It was up to you to decide that you wanted to enjoy life and be the captain of your life. I'm glad you did."

"Thanks, Captain, me, too."

"You're most welcome!" The captain returned his attention to his empty cake plate and said, "You can make this precise cake for my birthday when the time comes."

"Sure thing!" Adrian then looked at the captain with an inquisitive look and held out his hand for his empty plate. "Seconds?"

"Don't mind if I do!" The captain winked and handed his plate over to Adrian.

Christmas morning, Adrian and Grace met in the passageway and ran up to their parent's cabin as if they had always spent Christmas on board a yacht. "Morning, Mom! Morning, Dad! Merry Christmas!"

"Can't you kids wait until a normal hour to do Christmas?" Adrian's dad rolled over and pulled the cover over his eyes. Grace ripped it off.

"No way, Dad! It's Christmas morning and you know what that

means!" Grace turned a full circle in the middle of the cabin with her arms fully outstretched. "Presents!!"

"Honey, why don't you get your presents and open them?" Adrian's mom instructed him toward the little tree with white lights. His mom was a white-Christmas-tree-light freak. Only white lights were allowed at Christmas.

Grace had used the remote control to turn the tree lights on. Since the cabin window shades were still down, the cabin was cozy and dark. The tree was bright and pretty. Under it sat several boxes.

Grace and Adrian both dove on the pile of gifts and ripped into them. Grace got jewelry, clothing, a purse, and some of her favorite perfume. Adrian discovered two remote controlled boats; a sailboat with real canvas sails and the other one a classic power boat. In another box he found a short fishing spear from his dad. "Hey, Dad, thanks! This is awesome! I love the RC boats and fishing spear. These are more things we can do together!"

His mom had bought him cargo pants in two colors and a long sleeve sun-protector shirt for spending hours fly fishing. "Hey, Mom, these are perfect. Thanks!"

"You're welcome!" his mom answered while she watched them from her pillow. "Can you kids go now? Your father and I want to sleep for another hour or two."

"OK, mom, " Grace answered as she gathered everything in her arms and put it all into a large gift bag she had opened earlier, all for ease of carrying her loot back to her cabin. "Bye, Mom, bye Dad. See ya later!" And in the blink of an eye, she was gone from the cabin.

Adrian had loaded up his gifts and started to leave but hesitated since he knew they wanted to go back to sleep. "Uh, Mom? Dad?" he started.

When they each uttered a drowsy "huh?" and he knew they

were both listening he added, "Sorry for all the grief I gave you earlier in the year. It's turning into the best year of my life....so thank you! And Merry Christmas, Mom and Dad!"

"Merry Christmas, Adrian!" said his dad without turning over. He was smiling and his son heard it in his voice.

"Merry Christmas, Adrian!" his mom said with a smile that he could see and feel as he walked to the cabin door. "We're happy for you...and we love you..." she paused and playfully added, "yacht boy!"

Adrian grinned at the reference as the heavy cabin door closed behind him without a sound. He shook his head slightly and rolled his eyes as her words replayed in his head. He had a happy feeling he was stuck with this nickname for a long, long time.

Chapter Six
Surprises

Pigeon Beach
Falmouth Harbour
Antigua

The island of Antigua was sweltering hot and defied the notion that it was winter in the northern hemisphere. Adrian wiped sweat off his brow and sideburns and cleaned his hand on his shorts. He looked over at his sister Grace and she was wiping her neck.

"Hey, sis, want to go down to Pigeon Beach to cool off?" Adrian suggested while looking at his watch. "It's almost 11 o'clock so we can be back in time for a late lunch, if you want to go for a quick dip."

"Yeah, I would like that," she responded and stood up to go put on her swimsuit and grab a towel. "See you on the dock in 5 minutes?"

Adrian was already headed down the passageway ahead of her, "Yep! Roger that!" They split off into their respective cabins. Minutes later he was headed to the dock with his sister on his heels.

Walking with care down the passerelle, they passed two of the crew talking to some crew members of another yacht. "See ya later! We're going to Pigeon Beach for a bit," Adrian informed them of their plan to swim around the corner at the closest beach. "Oh, and can you let Chef Zak and our parents know that we may be a tiny bit late for lunch?"

Taking off down the road, they found many other people at the beach. Several of their crew had some time off and were relaxing with other crew from visiting yachts.

The water was warm and inviting. Neither waited, they just dived in and reveled in the refreshing water.

"Hey, Grace, do you ever wish you were back home?" Adrian treaded water and felt the swells that came in from the Caribbean Sea lift him up and down before they crashed gently on shore.

Swimming with a lazy breaststroke into the swells, she took her time to answer. "Sometimes. Mostly, I'm just in vacation mode." She paused to look over at her younger brother. "How about you? Do you wish you were back home?"

"Oh, heck no! I'm really digging this unschooling gig idea of mom's with no textbooks, essays or lectures. I do read all of the time, but it feels like it's fun, finally!" Adrian shared with a grin, "I give mom credit for being inventive with how she's schoolin' us."

"It's different being out of school," Grace began, "I'm actually thinking about all kinds of stuff that I normally wouldn't consider, like how to care for the marine environment long term. And, you know, I miss my friends, but I'm so busy, so... not really. Doesn't make sense does it?"

Adrian tried standing up, but the water was deeper than he realized. Bobbing back to the surface he wiped his eyes and shared, "I get it. I do miss being with my friends." He swam up to her and faced the swells and rode them with her. "I thought you weren't missing your friends."

"Well, we talk and text every day, so not really." She looked at him and gave him a typical girl look of exasperation. "You could be doing that, too."

"I guess..." Adrian turned on his back and looked at the palm trees and massive white clouds in an otherwise blue sky. He held his position by doing some elementary backstrokes. "I'm more of an *in person* kinda guy."

Grace splashed water at him for an answer and he turned upright to tread water and return the kind of spray she knew Adrian was going to fire at her in response. "That's no excuse!"

"Oh, yeah?!" He sliced his right hand through the water and doused her face with water. She laughed and returned it fast, and he had to start using both hands to return fire.

"OK!" she yelled with laughter in her voice, "Stop! Stop!"

"Hey, you started it," Adrian responded with one final slice that she averted her head from. "Let's swim out to the buoy!"

They freestyle crawled through the incoming swells for a hundred yards and pulled up to tread water. They knew it was not wise to go too far out because people in dinghies with powerful outboard engines dashed around the harbor with little care of swimmers. The beach looked beautiful from out in the bay. "Check out that bank of dark gray clouds behind the mountains!" Adrian twirled in the water to look in the direction his sister pointed out. "That looks like rain, doesn't it?"

"Yes, it does and it's close." He confirmed. "Although there isn't much wind for those big rain clouds...but it is definitely pouring rain over there and it looks like it's moving this way."

"Maybe it's the calm before the storm?" Grace offered. "Let's swim back. It's probably close to lunch time, and we'll need to shower before we sit down at the table. Come on!" She turned towards the beach and began swimming to shore. Adrian followed her.

Adrian loved storms. He loved the sheer power contained in a weather system to command everything in sight from the wind, pelting rain and gusto that each storm expressed. He noticed that tropical storms could be rather wild near the equator, and it sometimes made him feel unsettled, when he considered hurricane level winds that could send a roof of a building hurtling through the air at speeds nearing one-hundred miles per hour cutting down anything in its path.

He pulled up in the surf line on shore and did his best to leave as much sand behind. Every beach goer had an eye on the sky, and some were picking up blankets, tote bags and picnic baskets to return home or to their yacht. He and Grace slipped on their water sandals and shook out their towels to head back. A strike of lightning cracked in the distance and soon they heard the boom of thunder. "Whoa!" They said in unison towards each other with shock and awe in their eyes.

"I can't recall being in a tropical storm on Christmas Day, do you?" Grace asked as she picked up the pace and followed the beach crowd down the road.

"Nope," Adrian agreed. "This is my first."

The lightning and thunder got louder and louder as people scrambled for cover. The wind picked up without warning, as the sun disappeared behind clouds. The first fat drops of rain splattered the road and they both turned their faces up to the sky to receive the water descending from the heavens.

"Why is there never enough rain to actually give you a sip of water?" Adrian mused aloud. "You would think with all that rain…"

"…some of it would fill up your mouth and actually be satisfying?" she completed his musing.

"Yeah. Always disappointing." He turned back to enter the dock as they began to get drenched. The rain was warm and cleansing.

When they reached the boat, they asked Brian, one of the deckhands for a hose and he met them in the stern and helped them wash all the sand off before they came aboard.

"Yer gettin' me all wet out here!" he teased them as he shot their feet and shoes with a blast of fresh water.

"Sorry, Brian," Grace smiled as she gave him a big smile and raced up the stern steps to the main deck. "Not sorry!" she returned over her shoulder, as Brian looked at Adrian and laughed.

"What a tease!" Brian said with a shake of his head. "All set there, mate?"

"Yep," Adrian returned as he, too, bounced up the stern steps after his sister. "Appreciate the car wash, Brian!" Brian waved his hand up in the air to acknowledge the gratitude and continued to rinse the traces of sand off the stern and dock area before the owners returned to the yacht with their guests.

Grace and Adrian showered and changed amidst claps of thunder and bright flashes of lightning. They both landed in the passageway at almost the same time. "Good timing!" Adrian shared as they walked towards the table set up for lunch. "Any idea where mom and dad are? I thought they were sleeping in?"

Chef Zak personally brought out large plates of lunch for these two hungry teens and asked how their swim was.

"Our swim was great, until we felt and saw the storm coming," Grace said as she accepted a burger and fries and refreshing sparkling water with lime. A small side dish of his homemade garlic dipping sauce for fries sat between their plates and she was busy dipping and eating fries as fast as she could.

Zak walked over to the edge of the main deck where it was still dry, but rain was encroaching on the outermost edge, "Yeah, this will blow over pretty quick. I already see some blue sky beyond the squall."

Adrian looked over and saw some sunlight and blue-sky peeking through the storm. "Any idea where my parents went or when they'll be back?"

Zak startled for a second. For a moment he was taken off-guard by the questions, as he had been sworn to secrecy. He recovered enough to take his eyes off the clouds and rain to give a smooth answer, "Uh, no idea. I just knew they would not be here for lunch."

"Hmm." Adrian munched his burger in silence, without noticing Zak's discomfort with his questions. "Hey, Grace, want to watch a movie after lunch?"

"I guess." She licked her fingers of salt and garlic sauce. "There's not much else to do until the rain passes."

They were semi-engrossed in a high school chick flick that Grace chose, and Adrian agreed to watch with some reluctance. Neither party was enjoying it much, so when they heard multiple voices floating down the passageway from the main deck from where they were sitting outside their cabins in the movie lounge, they looked at each other with questioning looks and Grace paused the movie. Sticking their heads around the corner to see what the big fuss was about by several crew that flew out of the galley door nearby, they jumped up to head aft to discover who had come aboard.

"OMG!" Grace squealed as she opened her arms wide and ran the final yards to full body embrace her girlfriend, Lizzie. "No way! No way!" Her best friend was squealing and jumping up and down with her while all the parents looked on with grins.

"Way!" Lizzie replied with a final big squeeze and separated from Grace to say "hi" to Adrian.

"Hi," he responded with considerable disbelief. Then turned to his parents and Lizzie's folks with a quizzical look. "Wow! Welcome aboard and Merry Christmas, Mr. and Mrs. Sanchez. You are the last people I expected to see onboard today." He was shocked. Neither of his parents had said anything and neither had Grace.

"Did Grace know Lizzie was coming?" he asked his folks.

"Nope," his mom replied. Then she turned him around and pointed through the rain, "you might want to help those twin boys over there with their bags before they turn into drowned rats." He squinted through the rain and his heart exploded with happiness. "Oh, my god, Mom, you're the best." He started to run off but stopped for a half second to look back and said, "you, too, Dad!"

His parents exchanged a pleased and happy look between them at the success of their surprise, as he ran off to help his friends, the Nasif brothers, get out of the rain.

He raced across the passerelle to get to his buddies who were attempting to dash through the rain without anything to shield them. They dragged their carry-on size luggage behind them with their heads ducked.

"Braden, Brody, let me help!" Adrian ran to their side and grabbed a bag from Brody. "Run up the passerelle, Brody. I've got this!" He followed and deposited the bag on the dock at the end of the passerelle where Raffa took it and raced aboard. Turning back, he raced to Braden who had almost made it to the stern and invited him to run up first. He took the bag and handed it over to Perkins, a night shift deckhand who happened to be up and about. Running back down the dock to assist Mrs. Nasif, he took her luggage so her hands would be free to hold the railing on the passerelle. Brian was at his side taking her tote bags and gift bags that were soggy and wet from the rain. Adrian dragged the luggage behind him while she jogged ahead to get out of the rain. Handing it off to Brian who had returned, he trucked over the passerelle and ran to hug his soaking wet and happy friends.

"I can't believe you're here! This is awesome!" Adrian was just as excited as his sister and did his best not to squeal.

Brody took off his glasses and tried to dry them with his shirt, but it only made them worse. "Let me have those, love." Jane, the brunette stewardess appeared from nowhere and gently lifted his glasses from his hands and dried them with a delicate linen napkin. Then dabbed his nose and brow sweetly to remove a smattering of raindrops from his face.

Brody's mouth was slightly agape as he took back his glasses and put them on. "Where did you come from?"

"You mean the galley back there?" she threw a thumb over her uniformed shoulder, "Or my homeland of Australia?" she asked gallantly.

Brody smiled. "I see what you did there. Clever." He gave her an appreciative glance. "Thanks for helping me clean my glasses. It's n-n-nice to see you." He fumbled and stuttered and blushed a bit then corrected himself, "I mean, nice to meet you." Jane smiled, threw him a wink and walked off to help someone else.

For about fifteen minutes everyone chatted and talked about their flights and how things were back home in the States.

"Brody, come on! Let's go to my cabin so you guys can change and then we can do something." Adrian urged him along. Adrian saw him turning circles, looking for all his stuff, and he cut short his visual search by explaining that the crew had already put his suitcase in his cabin. "And, if I know our stewards, they tag teamed and put all your stuff away while we were busy talking."

"Wow," Braden said, "That's cool. I wish we had that kind of service at home. I'd never have to clean my room!"

"Tell me about it," Brody replied with a twinkle in his eye, "I rather like having my glasses polished by a nice Australian lady."

"Hey, guys," Adrian opened the door and ushered them in, "you're welcome to take showers or whatever."

"I don't need a shower, just let me grab some dry clothes."

Braden opened his clothing drawers that Adrian pointed to and pulled out fresh, dry clothes and headed into the bathroom to change.

Brody, stood in the cabin looking around. "I like your room, Adrian. This is neat-o." He walked over to the bunk beds that were neatly made up. A chain suspended the top bunk from the wall near the ceiling. When not in use, it could be raised up and secured with slide bolts to move it out of the way. "Hey, this is cool. I want the top bunk." He threw his pajama shorts up on the pillow to mark his space and a paperback novel he was reading on the plane. Adrian picked it up and read the title. It was the Count of Montecristo.

"Oh, man, I love this book!" he cried out with excitement. "This is one of my all-time faves, Brody! What do you think so far?"

"I like it. I wasn't sure where it was going at first, but when he pulled off his escape, I was hooked." Brody enthused. "Please, don't tell me anything. I don't want any spoilers!"

"OK, I won't." Adrian promised and set the book back down.

Braden burst out of the bathroom in a fresh change of clothing and Brody walked into it. Adrian could hear him saying, "wow," "oooh," and "whoa" as he discovered all the plumbing fixtures. Minutes later he emerged in a dry set of clothing, pointing behind him saying, "that is some shower, Adrian! I am definitely taking a shower tonight with all those jets and things. Dang, man, that is pretty darn cool."

"So, Adrian," Braden began tucking his shirt tails into his navy and red plaid shorts, "how are you doing, you know...with life on board, missing school and friends...?"

"Umm, you know, it's been cool. I sort of feel like I am on a perpetual summer vacation." Adrian acknowledged, "But when I saw you guys on the dock, walking towards us....oh, man, it hit me. I miss you guys and our other buddies. I mean, yeah ... It's been one exciting island trip after another. The crew and captain talk with me all the time, so part of me doesn't notice missing my friends.

"But I was so happy when I saw you..." Adrian put a hand over his heart. "For real, guys. For real."

"Our mom kept it a secret from us." Brody volunteered. "She didn't say anything. She said we were getting on a plane and going to a Caribbean island for Christmas week. I didn't even consider that we might see you."

"Me neither," Braden confessed. "I was just like, oh, we get to go on a beach vacation over Christmas and avoid family."

"No way!" Adrian was excited that his friends had just as big a surprise as him. He liked that his friends were open with him. "That's so cool!"

"Can we see the boat, Adrian, or do we have to wait?" Braden asked inquisitively. "And are there any *rules* we need to know? My mom was worried that we might act funny or something." The boys laughed together. Brody and Braden's mom, having been raised to be very proper, was always reminding them how to be mannerful, so they knew what was expected of them. Adrian knew exactly what they meant, since his mom was very similar.

"Right, like calling the captain *Skip* or something," Brody laughed. "We told our mom to just relax, and we'd let you tell us everything we need to know."

"It's pretty simple, guys..." Adrian started in as he opened the cabin door and stood back to let them file out into the passageway. "No shoes on the boat. Don't be late for dinner. Wear a shirt at all meals. And no loud music or noise before 0700 or after 2200 hours."

"Twenty-two hundred hours?" Brody looked at his friend funny. "What are you talking about?"

"That's ten o'clock at night for you landlubbers," Adrian

replied with a twinkle in his eye and a smile on his lips. "We use the twenty-four-hour clock around here. If it is in the afternoon, just subtract 12 hours." He instructed them before adding, "you'll get used to it. Trust me."

He brought them down into the engine room for a thirty-second tour where Brody, interested in all things digital and mechanical was enthralled with the two massive MTU diesel engines, and an exhaust system that flowed below the water so the passengers on board did not have to smell exhaust while on deck. He loved the shiny bright chrome and clean engine room. "This is amazing!" He had to roar somewhat over the generators as they walked into the next section where he introduced his friends to Pete, the chief engineer and Bryce, the electrician, and computer and internet technologist.

Adrian brought them through the gym where the boys raced to get on workout machines and fired their respective machines up. They test drove the elliptical orbiter, treadmill, and rowing machines before opening cabinets to find yoga mats, blocks, jump ropes, barbells, and many other physical training equipment.

"Wow, Adrian," Brody began, "this must be your favorite space onboard. Am I right?"

"Yeah, you got me." Adrian smiled. "I get up early and work out for an hour every morning." He walked over to the iPad and selected the sound system and hit play on his favorite classic rock workout jam and blasted it.

Braden and Brody's eyes widened and expressed their awe of his life. "Holy cow, Adrian! That's awesome!" Braden exploded with excitement, "What time tomorrow?"

"Crack of dawn, followed by breakfast" Adrian dropped a hint, "you won't want to miss it." Changing the subject he asked, "Are you ready for the rest of the tour?"

"Heck, yeah," Brody affirmed and followed Adrian through the remaining decks, ending the tour on the bridge.

"Knock, knock, Captain Gunnar!" Adrian stuck his head through the door to the bridge, where he found the captain reviewing the logbooks. "Merry Christmas!"

"Oh, hello, there! Merry Christmas, lads," the captain straightened up and put his pencil down to walk over to the boys to shake hands. "You must be Braden" he correctly guessed his friend's name and turned to extend his hand to his slightly shorter, and younger by mere minutes, twin brother with the eyeglasses. "Nice to meet you Brody."

"You, too, Captain!" Brody was in awe of meeting the captain, but not his brother. Braden seemed indifferent and was already looking around to leave the bridge. The captain turned on the windshield wipers to clear the recent rain drops off the glass and both boys turned their attention to the bow at the sudden movement. "Wow, there is quite a bit of space up front, isn't there?"

"Yes, Brody, there is." The captain pointed to the bow and shared what each area contained below decks so they could connect the dots in their mind's eye with the anchor locker they saw earlier on the tour and the location of the crew's quarters and Adrian's parent's apartment or cabin below the bridge. "It's a very well laid out yacht. It's one of the nicest I've ever commanded."

"Neat." Brody was inspecting the computer equipment and Adrian interrupted him to move them back down to the main deck.

"We'll leave you be, Captain." Adrian said, "thanks for taking a minute out. I just wanted to give them a quick look at the bridge. See ya later!"

They all waved goodbye and crammed into the elevator to head down to the main deck. The boys were so excited to ride in a glass elevator on a yacht. They exited the lift with excitement and were full of appreciation for the design of the super yacht.

They passed Grace and Lizzie on their version of the tour. "What are you guys planning to do for the rest of the day?"

"I dunno, Grace." Adrian answered honestly. "We haven't talked much about plans, yet. I think they want to get something to eat first, then figure it out." He started walking backwards towards the passageway to the galley as he threw out a friendly invitation, "Come find us."

Chef Zak looked up from his island workstation. "What can I get you boys?"

The boys looked to Adrian for guidance. Adrian asked them if they had eaten lunch yet. Nothing, yet. Adrian ordered them burgers and fries and Zak stopped them at the door. "You know we're having Christmas dinner in a few hours. How about some snacks to hold your hunger off?"

"OK, yeah," the boys agreed, and they marched out of the galley back to the main deck. The rain had stopped, and they stood at the aftmost edge of the main deck looking around. Yacht crews everywhere were using squeegees to clear raindrops off glass before it dried and left spots.

Braden asked, "It's pretty darn cool that you have your own swimming pool onboard." He was looking down at the stern where a glass walled tub was the main feature of the stern. "Can we get in it later tonight?"

"Sure!" Adrian was excited to share the fun. Wanting clarity about their plans he asked, "You guys are here for a week, right?"

"Yeah," Brody answered, sounding somewhat bummed. "My mom wants to spend New Year's Eve here and then go home because she has a big legal brief to write."

"Cool." Adrian was thrilled to have his pals hanging out for the holidays. His brain was racing with what to do with them first. As for Antigua, he and his sister had only explored the immediate area and Pigeon Beach in the last 24-hours. "We might want to see if the captain has plans for all of us collectively. Let's go find everyone and check in."

"Good idea, Adrian," Braden praised, "you lead the way."

Nelson's Dockyard
English Harbour
Antigua

The boys found their family members, guests and the captain sitting around the large dining table on the owner's deck one flight above. Finding seats, they sat down and joined the conversation about tourist attractions on the island.

"I don't think this rain will last more than another 30-minutes," reported the captain. "The radar and weather channel states this is a brief storm that is passing through and will extinguish itself soon."

"Good!" Adrian's mom exclaimed. "Do you think Shirley Heights will be open tonight for music?"

"Absolutely!" the captain affirmed. "The steel drum band will be playing and the rum drinks flowing." He turned to the group of teenagers before him, "you will enjoy the band, as they are fun, and the music is quite lively. Oh! –and another thing; wear flat closed-toe shoes for walking. It may be a bit muddy up there."

"OK, how do we get there?" Adrian's dad asked the captain. "Taxi?"

"Yes," he said, "I'll have Gabriella arrange for two mini-van taxis to be here at 1700 hours so you can catch the sunset. Meet back here as a group and she will lead you to them by the yacht club. She will accompany you, as she is very familiar with this island and will offer you some local information and point out things of interest. She'll also help you plan other tours on this island, which has several interesting sites to take in.

"In the meantime," the captain continued, "since you have a little over an hour before you must leave, why don't we plan some other days of the week? There is a fantastic beach I want to bring all of you to for a swim. I thought we could do that tomorrow...and go by boat."

Everyone nodded in agreement. In the meantime, it was suggested by the captain that the teens stick together and walk the local area between English Harbour and Falmouth Harbour. "This area was a British Naval base for over 200 years. There are plenty of cannons, parapet walls, and old fort buildings you can climb around on. Nelson's Dockyard has places to explore and shop or eat. Have any of you ever heard of Lord Horatio Nelson?" Looking around at the blank stares of the American teens, he found Adrian's dad's eyes smiling and that of Lizzie's mom. "Well, I'll tell you. He started off as a small and sickly child and went to sea with his mom's brother when he was only 12 years old. By age 20, he was a captain in the royal navy. He went on to become the most famous admiral and sea warrior in British history during the time of the Napoleonic Wars. You do remember Napoleon Bonaparte, yes?"

Brody jumped to his feet and struck a pose. He placed his hand inside an imaginary jacket. "You mean this guy?" Everyone was laughing at his goofball antics.

"Yeah," said the captain with a grin, "that guy. Well, it turned out that ole Nelson lost an eye during one of his battles."

Adrian's dad had placed a hand over his mouth. His eyes were brimming with mirth at this point. The captain noticed it and said, "I believe your dad knows a thing or two about this."

Grace looked over at her dad. "What's so funny, Dad?"

He lowered his hand from his mouth to speak, and he was grinning from ear to ear. "Well, there is this phrase people used to say when something was never going to happen. And it was, 'when Nelson gets his eye back.'" The captain and other adults were all grinning now.

"He also lost his right arm when he got shot by a musket ball." The captain pantomimed a chop to the upper arm. "They had to amputate it. So, the French got his right eye and right arm."

"How did he die?" Adrian asked, fully engaged with the history of a man that began a life at sea younger than he did. "How old was he?"

"A French sniper shot him, and he was mortally wounded. He was maybe 37 years old, I think." The captain paused while the group in front of him took in how young he was when he was shot. "But I think he died quite pleased with himself."

"What do you mean?" asked Lizzie.

"Well, he was an inspirational and impressive leader in the war. He caused the Spanish and French to lose about 20 ships to the British, and fourteen thousand men, half of whom became prisoners of war. So, when he died in the afternoon on the day he was shot, he was pretty certain that his victory over France was complete."

"Oh, that is sad," Lizzie lamented. "Was he married or have children?"

"Yes, and apparently she was quite beautiful and the love of his life! Her name was Emma. Lady Hamilton. They had a daughter named Horatia. And there is something rather interesting about

Lady Hamilton." The captain paused and looked at the girls. "She was incredibly beautiful and was the subject of many oil paintings by an English painter named George Romney. But after Nelson died, she didn't have his protection, shall we say, and ran into debt, spent time in prison for her debts and died at age 50."

"Oh, my goodness, that is tragic!" Mrs. Sanchez exclaimed. "We have no idea or appreciation for how difficult it was for women trying to make it on their own two hundred years ago. It sounds like her daughter was very young when she died."

"Oh, she was," added the captain. "She was almost fourteen years old, when she was suddenly orphaned in the world."

"What did she do?" Braden asked, "was she adopted?"

"No," the captain continued. "She returned to England and took care of young children that were relatives of her father's. Then she married when she was 21 and had 10 children."

"No way!" Grace exclaimed, "She was just a few years older than me. Who gets married that young?"

"People did back then, even at your age," her mom informed her.

"Well, not me." Grace looked at Lizzie who nodded her head in agreement. "I won't even be through with my university studies by age twenty-one."

"Since when are you going to university?" Adrian snorted. "All you're interested in is your phone and latest crush." Braden and Brody snickered, too.

"Am not!" Grace declared hotly. "I'm going to be a marine biologist!"

Adrian, his mom and dad all looked at her with some genuine surprise.

"Good for you, Grace," her dad enthused with pride. "I'm glad to hear it. We always have room for another scientist in this family."

"I'm impressed," Adrian said with genuine respect. "I support that, Grace. You are good at science and math, so I can see you getting into a good school."

"Yeah," Lizzie agreed. "Go for it, girl!"

The captain turned to Lizzie, "what are your plans?"

"Oh, I'll probably major in Spanish, since I'm bilingual," she tossed that out conversationally and it sounded like she wasn't terribly interested in being a Spanish major.

"Horatia, Lord Nelson's daughter, spoke five languages." He shared this trivia with her. "I'm sure it made her quite a refined and educated young woman back in the day. It's always good to know a second language."

"Captain," Braden asked, "what's your second language?"

The captain squirmed a bit and looked over at Adrian's dad for some support. "Actually...French, so to speak." He and Adrian's dad laughed out loud while the rest looked a bit confused. "That's code for sailor mouth."

Adrian smiled and offered some comfort through words, "It's okay, Captain, I think you're in good company!"

Since they were marina guests, they did not have to pay the small entrance fee to get into this historic area. The young sailors walked into English Harbour along Dockyard Way and explored Nelson's Dockyard.

They marveled at the size of the iron anchors on display, and the rusty cannons, which the boys climbed on and leaped off parkour-style.

They made it to the end of the road after a few short minutes of walking. Fort Berkeley, which guarded the entrance to the English Channel, was the true end of the road. The boys counted the number of slots that cannons filled, tried to move a rusty cannon, and considered the powder magazine built in 1811 for its bombproof attributes.

"I'm pretty sure the way this is built into the embankment makes it very bombproof." Braden insisted with his brother. "Look at how thick the walls are."

"I'm pretty sure the way they built bombs back then are no match for how they are built today." Brody argued back with his brother. "This powder house would have sustained some damage from the ammo of that era exploding but I would bet that a modern bomb would decimate this building."

"Maybe." Braden refused to budge on his assessment of the building which had withstood the test of time over two hundred years. "Hopefully, we never find out."

"Well, I wouldn't want to be the guard person on duty, back in the day, when all hell was breaking loose." Brody proffered. "I'd bet most of the soldiers lost their hearing with over two dozen cannons going off. The echo inside the guard house would have caused hearing loss."

"Probably." The boys climbed over the embankment wall to clamber over rocks and stones that led to the sea. The girls were hanging out in the shade of the guard's stone house at the top of the point. "Let's look for treasure." Braden continued and led the other two boys down where they found the usual plastics and stuff that wash ashore at high tide. "There's nothing here," Braden concluded with disappointment. "This place has been picked clean. There's no wartime artifacts to be found."

"Uh, wait a minute..." Adrian was rolling some rocks around and noticed a rough but round gray ball the size of a marble. "I found something." He picked up a galvanized metal looking ball about half an inch around. "Do you think this could be grapeshot from one of the cannons?"

Brody took it from his fingers and rolled it between his thumb and forefinger. "I think so."

"Maybe the captain would know." Braden scrutinized the gray metal ball and finding nothing important or unusual, he handed it back to Adrian who put it in his pants pocket. The captain later identified it for the boys as lead grapeshot and a lucky find since the islands have all been picked clean by treasure hunters over the centuries.

They scurried over the rocks and climbed back up to the girls, who looked at the time and suggested they return to make their taxi ride to Shirley Heights. Together they left the Dockyard, but not before saluting Lord Nelson's name on their way out.

Gabriella was waiting for everyone at the road leading into the yacht club where she had arranged for two mini-van taxis to meet. The afternoon sun was well past the meridian and headed for the horizon. Although she had appeared patient, now she urged them to "Hurry, hurry!"

Their party of eleven caravanned up the hills above English Harbour until they reached Shirley Heights. It seemed everyone else on the island had the same idea to celebrate Christmas Happy Hour and watch the sun go down to some reggae music and tropical drinks.

Gabriella asked them to set alarms on their phones or wrist watches for 1845 hours to return to the yacht for Christmas dinner prepared by Chef Zak and Sous-chef Jean-Marie. Dinner was to include the captain and chief officers, and it was best that no one be late.

Adults got in line for drinks and the five teens wandered as a loose group through the throngs of both islanders and tourists. There were people selling trinkets and souvenirs, people singing and dancing and standing at the cliff's edge to watch the sun go down with cameras poised for both selfies and sunset photos.

Lizzie and Grace decided to dance while the boys remained on the sidelines listening to the bright albeit funky reggae sounds of the steel drums. Adrian spotted his mom and dad and Mrs. Nasif standing in a group listening to the music and sipping rum punch drinks. The Sanchez' were dancing and Gabriella had disappeared out of sight. He wagged his head in the direction of the cliff to his buddies, and they followed him to the edge where they stood side-by-side looking out over the water.

"What're we doin' tomorrow?" Brody asked. "I forgot already."

"We're going to Rendezvous Bay Beach. It's a remote beach on the island that you can only get to by 4-x4, horseback, boats or walking." Adrian informed him. "Captain said we were going to go by tender."

"What's a tender?" Braden asked.

"Smaller boats we take out to shore from the main yacht. We have two." Adrian filled him in. "One is kinda luxurious, I guess you could say, since it is covered, and you don't get wet or dirty. The other one is fast and sporty and for beach trips or errands ashore. Let's just say it's more fun."

"Cool! I can't wait!" Brody announced with excitement.

"Hey, are we ever going to leave the dock and ride around on your yacht?" Braden asked with curiosity.

"I think so," Adrian said, "I'm not sure what all the activities are for the week. Heck, I didn't even know you guys were coming!"

"It's all good." Brody put his arm around Adrian's shoulder. "What matters is that we have a stunning sunset before us, good friends around us and an awesome dinner to celebrate Christmas in just a couple hours."

"Yeah," Adrian put his arm around Braden's shoulders and the three watched the sun go down. "I feel like the Three Musketeers."

"Hahahaha!" Braden laughed and ducked out from under Adrian's arm. Striking a pose he said, *"All for one and one for all, united we stand divided we fall."*

"Oh, my gosh, do you remember in English class what you told the teacher," Adrian began with a disbelieving laugh, *"You are very amiable, no doubt, but you would be charming if you would only depart* ... and the whole class fell silent then laughed their butts off. It seemed so innocent, except she knew you didn't like her." The boys laughed uproariously for a few seconds.

"Yeah," Braden confessed, "she wasn't too keen on me after that. She always seemed to give me a hard time."

"That was a good story." Brody agreed. "Every guy in the class was into that book because we made it fun. Remember that?"

"I never thought I would ever quote literature," Adrian began, "but after that class, it seemed really hilarious to throw down quotes to our classmates like we were challenging each other to a duel. We were a good group of guys."

"Still are." Braden corrected him and looked at Adrian seriously. "We all miss you. You really knew how to get everyone into a game or something."

"Yeah," Brody added, "no one motivates people like the way

you do."

Adrian nodded at receiving the recognition, as he stared out at the setting sun. His voice was low and full of wistful emotion when he next spoke, "I do miss everyone. I guess I can get caught up with everyone when the year at sea is over, but I suspect by the time we get back, everyone will have moved on. We'll see.

"For now..." he lifted his voice into a cheerful tone as his diving watch alarm went off, "we have a five-star feast to go to mates!"

Two hours later everyone was seated at the oval dining room table that seated 14 on the owner's deck. The teens sat at the aft end, with the parents around the opposite end. The captain shared the head of the table with his dad, with Grace and Adrian facing them. The first mate, Jimmy, came in dress uniform like the captain and took a seat near the young men. Also dressed for the occasion was chief engineer Pete, who sat in one of two empty seats between Mr. Sanchez and his daughter Lizzie. The chief stewardess, Gabriella, in her fancy navy dress sat between Lizzie and Pete. When they were all seated, Adrian's dad stood up and waited for everyone's attention.

He raised his wine glass in his right hand, "My wife and I would like to formally welcome you aboard our new home, the *Arabella*, and thank you for making the journey to celebrate Christmas with us. We appreciate your keeping the surprises for Grace and Adrian." He inclined his head to the two mothers who made it all possible.

"Furthermore, I'd like to introduce you to our wonderful captain! -who would like to say a few words in just a moment. But before I turn the table over to him, I'd like to thank our crew for making our time aboard quite effortless. Please relay our gratitude to the entire crew. The transition to the life of a sailor has been made possible by their tireless efforts.

"Finally, I'd like to say that everything in life is better aboard a yacht! If you don't discover this for yourself over the course of a week…" he trailed off and shrugged his shoulders as everyone laughed. "It's true! We eat better, sleep better, and I believe we're nicer people."

Adrian elbowed his sister discretely and muttered under his breath, "That's for sure!" to which she elbowed him back and whispered, "Shhh."

"So, raise your glass to…" he turned to face the captain and extended his fluted glass, "Captain Gunnar for making this trip a reality, and" turning to his son and daughter, "to family, who makes life a richer experience," then he turned to their adult guests, "and good friends to share it with. Merry Christmas everyone! Cheers!"

"Cheers, Dad!" Adrian and Grace raised their mocktail drinks to their dad and smiled in his direction. They had extra reasons to be happy this Christmas.

The captain stood and when everyone went quiet again, he began. "I was offered this job six months before we even left the dock. I was told that there would be a family living aboard with two teenagers." A few people chuckled and he paused. "I had my doubts about how long I would last." Now people openly laughed, especially the young adults at the table.

"But with each passing day, I gained more and more respect for these four people who I have watched become resilient, adaptable and set a new course for themselves each day inside heart-centered consensus. And I've seen this happen most days that we've been on board since we left in November." The table was silent.

"It's not often I see teenagers and their parents agreeing to do what is best for everyone, but a little birdie told me that it was their mom's idea to work at making sure that every big decision was agreed to by each family member so all could be happy with the direction they take together.

"I knew that these parents ..." he looked at Adrian's mom and dad and paused while he considered his next words. Adrian looked at his parents and saw their serious contemplation of the captain's toast. The captain continued, "these parents had such good intentions for their children, noble goals for their education, and deep desire for their children to stand in their strengths and become their own person.

"I've watched each member of this family grow over the weeks. And what I have seen has impressed both myself and my crew." He looked at Adrian and Grace and smiled. Merry Christmas and Cheers!"

"Cheers! Cheers!" The cry went up around the table and the captain winked at Grace and Adrian from all the way down the table. They smiled back with deep affection for the captain and raised their glasses full of sparkling cranberry juice to him. "Merry Christmas, Captain!"

Grace leaned over to Adrian and privately shared in his ear, "He's the best, isn't he?"

Adrian nodded and whispered back, "Yes, the best!" And they clinked their crystal glasses to honor the captain and each other.

Chapter Seven
Geronimo!

Zip Line Adventure Park
Fig Tree Drive
Antigua

A note slipped under the door before the sun came up announcing a change of plans. Two mini-van taxis arrived to take the family to the rainforest for a zipline adventure. There was a sudden cancellation at the adventure park and a big opening became available which meant they could accommodate everyone. The boys cheered and threw on shorts, tee-shirts, and sandals.

After breakfast, they walked down the passerelle to head towards the Yacht Club. Adrian and Grace were casually looking at yachts and pointing out cool features to help them learn a thing or two about superyachts. Grace stopped and waited for Adrian and soon all were gathered in a loose circle around her. "Adrian, isn't that the Neptune you saw those guys drag that bag onto?"

Adrian nodded, "You're right, Grace. Same yacht." He looked around for Artemis. "I don't see the other one."

"What's up guys? What's *Neptune* about?" Braden asked as

they resumed walking out towards the gate. Adrian brought them up to speed on everything from the Bahamas and Thompson's warning, the wanted poster he saw, the strange bag and ended with, "It's probably nothing. But I can't help feeling that something hinky was going on."

"I hear ya," Brody said. "Gotta go with your gut instinct, bro. Tell us more."

"I'll do one better." He fished his cellphone out of his pocket, so his friends and Grace put their heads together to look at all his photos and videos relating to his story.

"What's this cool looking vessel? Check out those crane looking things on the back!" Braden said as he peered into the phone and zoomed it in. "That's pretty awesome, Adrian. I dig this yacht. What's it for?"

"Those are davit cranes, and these types of yachts are explorer yachts and can travel long distances, even go into waters with icebergs or areas where the water might freeze around the boat. They can be used for scientific discovery labs, have submarines on board and other cool robotic stuff for diving."

"So, it could be used for treasure hunting, right?" Lizzie inquired.

Adrian started grinning and looked at Grace. He slapped his forehead and said, "Now, why didn't I think of that?"

"What's this explorer yacht's name?" Lizzie asked Adrian as she handed his phone back.

"*Orion*."

"The hunter," Brody shared.

"Hunter." Adrian repeated the word and tried to recall the recent use of the name. "The Hunter! Grace! Remember McCready said he knew the ones who sabotaged him? He said, 'the hunter' and I thought he meant a treasure hunter. What if he meant an actual guy? Maybe Hunter is the guy who shot his boat!"

A sizzle of electricity went through Adrian as his thoughts began to connect dots surrounding the mystery of stolen antiquities. *I need to set this aside and be with my friends right now. Be in the present moment.* A couple of vans pulled up and the side panel door opened. Changing the subject for himself and the others, he smiled and asked with enthusiasm, "Ok, who's up for ziplining?"

They piled into the vans and wound their way north through the villages of Falmouth and Liberta. The driver made a series of left turns through Liberta until they were on Fig Tree Drive headed west towards the sea. Fig Tree Drive increasingly became very bumpy and both drivers had to slow down or risk hurting their van's suspension system. They had driven past a cricket field and open plains, and sleepy villages. They drove through lush green mountains thick with black pineapples, banana, mango, and papaya trees until they came to a forested area so green and dense that it was unlike any other part of the island. The driver slowed and pulled off the side of the road at an adventure company building announcing their destination.

Bursting with excitement, the teens jumped out of the taxis and confirmed a time to be picked up with their driver after their adventure. The five teens raced to the front entrance, slowed enough to pass through the gate and walked in as a noisy group. They were eager to get outfitted with harnesses, climbing equipment, gloves, and helmets for the journey ahead.

Braden had his video camera mounted to his chest. Brody had his camera on his helmet. Adrian hadn't yet figured out what he was going to do, so he just held it in his hands and took video of his friends taking video. He was pleased that Grace and Lizzie were part of his gang, participating on this adventure together. It just occurred to him that Grace had become more of a friend since this journey had begun and he liked this new relationship he had with her.

The adults were close behind and got their equipment last. The teens went first and listened to all the safety rules and explanations of how the adventure experience was going to go. They were all impatient to get going and, when the guide was satisfied that they knew all the rules, he led them to the first of a dozen climbs and places to experience thrills on steel cables, carabiners, and ropes.

Up ladders, across a swaying rope bridge, walking with ropes and zipping through the tops of trees from wooden platform to platform, everyone had a chance to go first and demonstrate survival. They screamed and laughed and yelled at each other all morning as they took hundreds of photos and videoed every bit of action.

Sweat was pouring off them as the tropical heat and rainforest made for a humid experience. The boys were standing on a platform built around a tree. It was their last run of the morning. "Hey, guys, we have to make a vacation video of all these fun times before we go." Brody mentioned it as they waited for the last zipline to clear. "What do you say we combine all the photos and videos and make a slideshow movie for our last night together?"

"Brody, you're a genius!" Adrian high fived him on the platform thirty or more feet over the ground. "Let's plan a party for the last night together."

"Dude," Braden interjected with a tone of seriousness, "you know how much work that is? I'm here to relax."

"Adrian, we can do it, and leave him out of the credits." Brody turned to urge his brother to move, "Dude, it's your turn. Go." He practically pushed his brother off the platform. When Braden left their earshot, Brody turned to his friend with an idea.

"Adrian, we can do it." Brody enthused and got more excited, "Listen, we can do a little bit each day before we go to bed. What do you say?"

"I say we do it!" Adrian smiled. "Then we'll have this video to always remember the best Christmas ever!"

"Yep!" Brody nodded and pushed up his glasses up his sweaty nose. "Best Christmas ever."

Tired, hot, sweaty, and happy guests came aboard the *Arabella* after swinging through the trees all morning. They sat down on the couches of the main deck. Jane and Gabriella immediately came over to take drink orders. Jimmy and Brian were bartending. The boys had the foresight to walk past the bar and give their drink orders way ahead of everyone else.

"Well, that was fun, but I am exhausted from the heat!" Braden and Brody's mom commented as she took her straw hat off and fanned her face. Her feet were up on the lounge, and she looked done for the day. "I think I'm going to stay here in the air conditioning and read on the boat, then maybe go for a swim."

Mrs. Sanchez agreed with that idea and so did Adrian's mom. "We can go up to my private deck where we can be left alone to relax."

Adrian's Dad and Mr. Sanchez decided to head over to a famous Dockyard hotel and investigate the bars and restaurants.

The young adults weren't sure what to do when Jimmy came over to pass out their cold drinks and overhearing their indecision about how to spend the afternoon, offered several suggestions to them. "You can go over to Antigua's Donkey Sanctuary or visit Betty's Hope Sugar Mill. There is also a place where you can go swim with stingrays." Jimmy smiled that big inviting smile then he turned on his Jamaican accent full force and said, "I bet you all'd like dat one."

"Oooh, I think I'd like that," Adrian responded, savoring the idea for a bit. He took a long draw on his straw and looked over the top of his drink at his buddies. "Wanna go swim with the stingrays?"

"Heck, yeah!" Braden was all for it.

Brody looked a bit nervous, "Isn't that the sea creature that stung that famous Aussie dude in the heart and he died?"

Jimmy replied, since all five youths were eyeing him expectantly, "Well, yes, but the Caribbean and Atlantic stingrays are tame and fed by the local tour operators. I don't think they are going to sting the hand that feeds them, now, do you?"

Grace spoke up, "I don't think we were meant to swim with stingrays and tame them. No one has studied the effects that humans have on these animals, have they?" She challenged him.

"No, Grace, probably not." Jimmy laughed and added, "in vacation land, everyone is out for a buck. In these places, for tourists, they keep things safe, so we don't get a bad reputation. I'm sure they found a way to allow petting without people getting stung. Some of the rays have lost their barbs, I hear."

"Well, that doesn't sound too humane, if we had anything to do with it," Grace stated with emphasis. "How would you like it if your defense mechanism was removed." Jimmy and the boys nodded their heads and looked at each other, not sure what part of them was their defense mechanism. Jimmy's lips twitched as they looked back and forth with no clue.

Brody, who had been googling it pulled his head up from his phone and reported, "there is one study that says stingrays may like being petted by humans. The stingrays came to the hands of the study participants to elicit back rubs. But that's all it says."

"OK," Grace didn't sound convinced. "But all those hands in

the water? --putting bacteria, sunscreen and other stuff like hand lotion, medicated creams or perfumes can't be good for the animals. Even if the saltwater pool used in the study has a filtration system in it."

"True," Jimmy agreed. "Well, you don't have to go swim with them, how about you just go snorkeling down at the beach and look for them in their natural environment?"

"I like that idea much better," Grace declared to the group, "what do you say, Lizzie?"

"I'm in. Sounds good." Lizzie looked half asleep on the mound of pillows tossed upon the oversized sunbathing sofas. "I need a short nap after lunch before we do anything. Or you all could go on without me. I think I have a touch of jet lag or it's the heat. Either way, the beach sounds great!"

Zak and Jean-Marie came out of the galley passageway rolling a cart loaded with tropical fruit salads, piles of sandwiches, plates of cheese and charcuterie, assortments of breads and crackers, and platters of ice-cold lemon bars, candy cane and white chocolate sugar cookies, chocolate dipped butter cookies with Christmas colored sprinkles and seven-layer cookies. Although there was a massive amount of food placed on the table, there was next to nothing leftover when they staggered to their feet to return to their cabins to relax and get changed.

The boys threw themselves on their beds and no one said a word. Adrian closed his eyes for a moment of respite. He heard Brody mumble something and Braden trying to answer. He tried to open his eyes, but sleep came swiftly, and he was out cold.

Shakedown Cruise — The Adventures of Yacht Boy

Rendezvous Bay
Antigua

A knock at the door woke Adrian up. His friends were still napping. He looked at his dive watch and saw that it was after 1500 hours. Opening the door, Jimmy invited him out into the passageway to talk.

"Hey, man, what's up?" Adrian asked, rubbing his eyes as he stretched and yawned without covering his mouth.

"Your bros are asleep in there?" Jimmy asked.

"Yeah, we all just kind of passed out after lunch." Adrian smiled. "It's all good. They may have some jet lag.

"What's up?" he repeated with a bit more of a serious voice, as he noted the sounds of the powerful engines of the yacht were already fired up. The captain was planning to move the boat by the sounds of it.

"We're going to move de boat to Rendezvous Bay Beach around the corner. De Captain said dis docking situation keeps our pool club locked up tight and all you kids need water toys to play, so we thought we would go and drop de anchor dis afternoon." He let that sink in and then asked Adrian if he wanted to help with the dock lines or fenders.

"Always!" Adrian affirmed in a low voice so as not to wake his friends, "Stand by, let me get my walkie-talkie." He grabbed his personal equipment the captain entrusted him with for working the yacht as crew and followed Jimmy to the stern where he handed him the remote control for the passerelle. It was his first time to operate it, but he had watched every time, memorizing the steps so it never got jammed or entangled with stern lines or people.

Jimmy threw two heavy duty yacht braid stern lines onboard and spoke into the walkie-talkie. He walked up the passerelle in several quick steps and said, "Stern lines are clear, Captain. Passerelle being retracted." Then signaled to Adrian to rapidly bring the fancy gangplank in. Adrian hit the retract button and it telescoped back inside itself in a few elegant mechanical folds. It wasn't fast, but it was moving. Within a minute the length was already inside the yacht's stern and folding under itself. Adrian clicked his walkie-talkie and reported in, "Passerelle clear. Over and out."

Jimmy coiled lines and brought them up to a locker, and signaled he was going amidship portside.

Adrian put the remote control away and ran lightly to the starboard side to work a fender. It was imperative to keep it at the fattest part of the yacht and keep it between the two boats. If there was any risk of the fender getting caught, and the line or fender snapping back at the deckhand, he was to let go. At no time was he to try and push off the other vessel. This wasn't a small sailboat that he could use his body as a shock absorber and lever, this was hundreds of tons of weight directed into a small area that could be bone crushing.

Further ahead of him was Bryce, holding a fender line. Jimmy and Gabriella were on the portside working fenders. He loved the clipped, rapid talk that went on over the comm system when they moved the boat as a team. Raffa and Brian appeared to be handling ground lines off the bow. Pete was calling info up from the engine room and the captain was on the helm directing his team.

With the speed of slow-moving molasses, the massive superyacht began to emerge from her berth at the marina. The fenders rolled and squeezed against one of the neighboring yachts, but everything was good. As the ship cleared the other ships and dock, he lifted his fender up off the hull from above the waterline and dragged it back to the stern for stowing away while deflating it.

Opening his cabin door with stealth, he checked on his friends and they were sound asleep. He opened a drawer and removed his polarized sunglasses since they were heading west into the sun. He was ready for anchoring. He slipped out of the cabin and headed to the bridge.

"Hello, Captain!" he said brightly. He only spoke to the captain when he wasn't engaged with serious business. They were already at the mouth of Falmouth Harbour and heading out to sea.

"Stand by Adrian." The captain, in essence, told him to not speak. He was listening to the crew. After a minute, he turned to address Adrian. "OK, we're heading north, and we'll anchor in the bay if there is space. It can be a bit roll-y in there, but I think for one or two nights, we should be good."

"Is everyone on board?" Adrian asked with a sense of alarm. "I thought my dad and Lizzie's were going to the Dockyard and the girls to the beach."

"Yes, they did, but you can take the tender and go get everyone in half an hour."

Adrian's heart skipped a beat. The captain was giving him permission to take the tender and go get his family and guests. "All by myself?"

"No. Take Jimmy and your friends with you, then come right back." The captain didn't want to reveal a smile to Adrian, but it was hard. "You need a deckhand to help you. And I want everyone to wear life jackets."

"Of course." Adrian knew better than to take people out without life jackets. The tender had some life vests stored under seats, but the captain was a cautious and smart man.

"You're taking three and picking up four people."

"Roger that. I'll have eight life jackets with me, that'll be enough for everyone."

The captain nodded and went back to checking his monitors.

"Stand by on anchor." Adrian stepped behind the captain so as not to be a distraction. A couple of minutes later the captain asked him what his plans were with his friends.

"Oh, I'm sure we'll figure it out. I really want to run something by you, Captain." Adrian fidgeted nervously next to him.

"Sure. Fire away," the captain invited.

Adrian ran through all his findings on the yachts, the men and the strange behaviors on the dock back in Turks and Caicos and ended with, "What do you think, Captain? You think they may all be connected, especially the Hunter theory?"

The captain rubbed his jaw as he stood at the helm and considered it all. "There's not enough information or evidence, I don't think, but an investigator might find the link to Hunter interesting."

"I did have another thought," Adrian inserted, "We left Long Island and three hours later from sailing past the *Orion* outside Clarence Town, we encountered McCready and Nichols who said they were in the water for about three hours. There was a crew member cleaning a watercraft in the stern when they pulled in. It could have been used to get close to the sailboat. I have photos and videos of them 'cause I thought *Orion* was such a cool vessel."

"Let me think about it and see who the investigator is. I promise I'll talk with them." He took calls from the engine room and crew and then returned to speaking with Adrian, "I don't want you and your friends investigating this, understand?"

"I understand," Adrian said with his fingers crossed behind his back. Thinking to himself he said, *I'm sorry,* but *I can't promise to stand under you, Captain, especially if I have an opportunity to solve this mystery.* He hoped his telepathy reached the captain, but his confidence wasn't too high. *Thank goodness for sunglasses so he can't see I can't look him straight in the eye.* Adrian did not want to be deceptive with the Captain. He hadn't so far. He didn't like how he was feeling right now, but he wanted to keep his options open. *I don't like being told what I can and can't do.*

A short while later, the captain checked wind direction, water depths and distance from shore to determine where to anchor. He listened in as the captain turned the boat into the wind and dropped anchor and drifted back towards the island. He slipped out of the bridge and walked to the stern of the bridge deck to look east at the sparkling aqua blue-green bay with a perfect curve of white sand on the beach and thought it was truly one of the most beautiful beaches he'd seen in weeks. Luscious palm trees lined the beach creating a paradise.

He left the bridge deck and headed down a flight of stairs to the main deck's bow, to lower himself through a portside hatch to help launch the tender off the port side. Jimmy, Brian, Raffa and Francesco were there sorting through equipment to prep for the hydraulic davits to lift and move the boat over the water. Adrian stayed back out of the way. There were already too many people here in this small area. Raffa was the first to step back when he got the bowline attached and could hold it off to the side where he wouldn't get hit by the moving boat. Francesco took the stern line and moved into the shadows of the space in a similar move.

Brian operated the remote to advance the hydraulic davit outward. Jimmy was sitting in the middle of the boat making sure everything was going well. He tied a fender off the starboard side forward of the beam, and another one aft of the beam.

Jimmy caught his eye, "Are you going to wake up your friends or just come with me?"

"Let me go rouse them. If they sleep too much, they won't sleep tonight and tomorrow they'll all be messed up." Adrian concluded by adding, "Give me a minute and we'll meet you at the stern platform."

He ran up the stairs and opened his cabin door. Braden was awake. He was sitting on the edge of his bunk looking a little strange. "Hey, are you alright man?"

"Yeah, I think so. I feel a little groggy and a little queasy." He stared at the floor. "Man, I'm tired!"

"Do you want to go for a joy ride on the tender?" While he waited for an answer, he reached up and rustled his friend Brody by the leg. He stirred and sat up without bumping his head on the ceiling.

"Are we going now?" Brody asked, rubbing his eyes.

"Yeah, but you gotta move fast. The tender is in the water, and we've got people waiting on a dock."

Braden stood up and said, "OK." Brody slid down off the top bunk and asked Adrian if he needed shoes.

"No, yes, oh, I dunno, just bring them!"

The brothers, working at top speeds, freshened up in the bathroom and headed down the pool club deck steps with Adrian and climbed aboard the tender. Jimmy had purposefully laid out life jackets for the boys to put on. Adrian managed his own. Jimmy gave him the slightest of nods in the direction of the driver's seat and Adrian jumped at the chance to drive. Jimmy had left the engine idling in neutral.

He looked back to check that his friends were sitting down and had life vests on, which they did, and he nodded to Jimmy to catch the stern line from Francesco. He reached out to Raffa, who threw him the bowline, which he threw in its entirety onto the deck of the boat near his feet. Jimmy pulled up the fenders and sat down near Adrian and began to coil the line.

Adrian put the boat in forward and advanced the throttle. He turned the wheel gently to starboard so the boat could immediately ease away from the sides of the yacht and not create damage. As soon as he was several feet away, he gave the engine more gas by pushing the throttle towards the bow and it leapt forward across the waves. Although he had some trepidation and a feeling of anxiousness in his gut, he was grinning from ear to ear. He was glad Jimmy was along for the ride, although part of him felt he didn't quite need him, even for the docking and getting tied off since there were always people willing to catch a line and he could also put the boat in neutral and let it drift alongside a dock, if necessary, while he tied the boat up.

He looked over his shoulder to see his friend's reactions. They were also grinning and having a good time. He sped up the boat a little more. Soon they were flying across the water and pounding the swells. Salt spray was flying off the sides of the V-shaped hull and wind brought it across the side misting the passengers in the stern.

"Don't get the boat too wet, we have more people coming." Jimmy yelled into the wind. He was grinning, too, and reached across to give his young buddy a high five. "Good on ya, *mon*, you da real deal!" Adrian loved when Jimmy's Jamaican accent came through strong. He had observed that the first mate spoke proper English around adults.

As he steered the boat into Falmouth Harbour, he decreased his boat speed so he did not create a wake that would disturb other boats at anchor or at the dock. His eyes scanned all the yachts looking for signs of *Neptune*, *Artemis* and, although it was a long shot, *Orion*. Only *Neptune* was present at the dock.

He pulled up at the marina's temporary guest dock near the main entrance and tied up. He left the motor running, but idle since his dad and Mr. Sanchez were present and ready to come aboard. There was no sign of the girls.

After waiting around for fifteen minutes, Jimmy suggested

Adrian jog over the hill and check the beach to get them. Brody and Braden offered to come, but Adrian knew he would be faster without them. He suggested they check the local road and other areas in the opposite direction and report via cellphone to him, if they were located, and he would relay the message over the walkie-talkie to Jimmy.. The boys agreed to return in 10-minutes to the boat regardless. They split up and went their ways, leaving Jimmy and both dads at the boat.

Walking at a relatively fast clip, the two brothers walked along the waterfront in Falmouth searching both sides of the road. They turned around when they got to the road leading into English Harbour. Looking up and down the road, they didn't see the girls and retraced their steps to the guest dock.

Meanwhile, Adrian jogged up the hill to Pigeon beach in the hot sun. He loved to run and was quite light on his feet, but the high temps and humidity made it hard for anyone to run. Soon he was racing downhill and through the sea grape trees to Pigeon Beach. He walked along the damp shoreline to make good time while scanning faces and the water for the two girls. Reaching the end of the strip of sand, he cut through the trees and headed back. He found the entrance to Windward Beach on the other side of the hill and on a whim, cut down through the sea grapes to this unique beach he had only heard about.

He entered the cove along the cliff and saw the rocky beach stretch out for almost half a mile. It was gorgeous. There were very few people on the beach. And those that were there, were sunbathing naked. Grinning foolishly, he realized he had stumbled into the nude beach. And, best yet there was no sign of the girls here, for which he was grateful.

Adrian stopped for a breather. *Where would they have gone?* he mused to himself. Turning around he walked back through the brush to the main road and back to the dock. He reported back via walkie-talkie to Jimmy that he checked both beaches but no sign of the girls. "Want me to walk down to our previous dock and see if anyone saw them?"

"Not a bad idea," Jimmy answered.

Adrian went through the locked gate for the super yacht dock. He knew he couldn't run on the floating docks, so he walked at the fastest clip he could until he reached the area where they had berthed the *Arabella* the last two nights. When he came into view of *M/Y Neptune*, he slowed and took in all the details he could. Slipping out his cellphone he took a quick pic and put his phone away. *I'm just a kid taking a picture of a cool looking yacht for my vacation photo album. Why do I feel guilty?*

Sitting cross-legged with their backs to him at the end of the dock were Lizzie and his sister in their swimsuits and sarongs drinking sodas surrounded by young men. He hid behind a concrete piling and observed the little dock party and took a sly pic for evidence.

There were three male crew members from another yacht entertaining them. Another young man dropped down off a nearby yacht carrying a bag of cookies to share. Adrian pressed the send button on the walkie-talkie and turned away so no one would hear him. "I've located the missing girls. Drive to the end of our previous berth and come stealthily. Over."

Within minutes the tender floated into view with Jimmy at the helm. Mr. Sanchez and his dad were standing on the port side with bow and stern lines in hand, looking perturbed. The crewmen at the end of the dock caught the lines and tied her off. The girls were on their feet faster than a jumping jack. Adrian began walking the rest of the dock at a snail's pace, so he could take in the whole scene.

The young men said hasty goodbyes and began to disappear

into the yachts they came out of, while the girls hopped over the side of the tender and sat down. Adrian reached the stern line, bent down to untie it, and cast off the line into the back of the boat where Brody caught it.

Adrian leaned over to privately speak with Jimmy and asked, "how do you ground someone while at anchor?" His eyes twinkled with humor.

"You don't. That's why they invented brass!" And they both laughed. The captain had shared with Adrian that in the olden days, when a sailor misbehaved, they had to spend hours polishing brass and it gave them time to think about what they did wrong.

Before reaching the middle of the harbor, Jimmy slowed down and put the boat in neutral to switch places with Adrian so he could drive and bring her alongside *M/Y Arabella*. The weather was perfect for taking a drive and the water was nothing short of spectacular for creating a joy ride for his passengers. With every incoming swell, he drove the boat at a forty-five-degree angle up and guided the bow down the backside of it. Salt water sprayed out the side and cast white foam to the left and right.

Adrian spotted a dolphin dive out of the water off to port and aimed the boat in that direction without slowing down. He kept a straight line out to sea and saw it pop up out of the water again. From behind him he heard Brody shout, "Look! Dolphins!! ... Over there!!"

All eyes were on the spot Brody was pointing out just to the front of the bow of the boat. Two large bottlenose dolphins surfaced to play in the bow wake. Their powerful tails kept up with the boat speed and soon other dolphins joined them. Adrian felt his heart explode with excitement and joy as three more popped up on the starboard side. "Wow! Everyone, look! More, over there!"

Adrian's passengers were leaning over both sides of the boat

watching the dolphins play alongside the boat as they traveled far offshore. Jimmy and Adrian, with their earbuds in, heard the captain call over the walkie-talkie to them, "What's going on out there? Going for a joyride?"

"Dolphins, Captain." Adrian reported. "There's over a dozen of them! You should see this!"

"I am seeing this," the captain replied in a pleasant voice, "I am watching you in the binoculars at this moment."

Adrian chuckled and waved in the direction of the M/Y *Arabella* sitting at anchor in the distance, her elegant white lines and tinted glass windows reflecting the afternoon sunlight. "A few more minutes, Captain, and I'll turn her around. Over."

"Roger that. Over and out."

Jimmy gave Adrian a thumbs up. "Now would be a bad time to do a donut."

Adrian laughed and gave him a thumbs up. He told everyone to hang on and began turning the boat to starboard to head back. The dolphins followed for a short while and then said silent goodbyes as they went on their own way. Everyone was fired up and chatting as he brought the tender to dock off *Arabella*'s stern.

The engine was in neutral and as Adrian gauged the wind and water speed against their forward momentum, he noted that the boat was compatible with approaching the super yacht without risk to any person or equipment. He nudged the gas just a wee bit to acquire more momentum, which helped him head the bow into the wind and waves yet come close enough without touching the docking platform so a bowline could be thrown to Raffa who stood at the corner to receive it.

Jimmy leapt out and took the stern line with him and pulled the boat in closer so guests could embark onto the yacht. The girls leaped out and raced up to Grace's cabin before they had to hear another word about their little tea party at the end of dock. Both dads thanked Adrian and Jimmy and headed up the stern steps. Brody and Brady asked what the plan was for the tender.

"I think we are going to leave it out. Jimmy?" Adrian looked over questioningly at Jimmy and Raffa and both nodded.

Adrian and Raffa threw off the bow and stern lines for Jimmy and threw them into the boat. Jimmy motored the boat at low speed around to the port side and waited for Raffa and Adrian to get out the carbon fiber whips to secure the boat for the night. While Jimmy worked from inside the tender to tie off the boat to the whips, Adrian asked, "Hey, Jimmy, since there's a few hours of daylight left, what do you say we inflate the super slide, and all go for a swim? What do you say?"

"Can do!"

Jimmy and Raffa hauled out a massive pile of white plastic with blue and aqua green stripes that was bundled up and secured with lines. It took two men to move it.

"What the heck is that thing?" Brody asked as he tried to figure it out.

"Oh, you'll see." Raffa teased. "Give us *30-minuti* and we'll give you *30-piedi* or more! You and your brother will be scratching your heads trying to figure out what career to go into so you can afford one of these babies!"

Jimmy was opening a cabinet to take out an air compressor. He grabbed hoses and a bin of white 3/8-inch yacht line and other paraphernalia. "Ready? I think I got everything." Jimmy called to Brian over the walkie-talkie to help them with the slide.

"We'll go change while you get it set up." Adrian announced and beckoned to the boys to follow him. "I'll let everyone know that we have some late afternoon fun in store!"

Brody was still watching the crew over his shoulder as he left the pool club area. He thought maybe it was a horizontal slip and slide type of inflatable toy, he pondered how it would work. *Maybe the motion of the sea swells lifts it up and down...* he thought, *now that would be cool...like a perpetual motion machine!* With eagerness, he climbed the stairs and headed with enthusiasm to Adrian's cabin to change and race back to watch more of the operations to set it up.

Adrian ran up the three flights of teak stairs to the owner's deck where he found all the adults sipping drinks and gabbing away. "Hey, everyone! Special announcement! The crew is setting up a two-story super slide so we can all go swimming before dinner. The water is a perfect 80 degrees Fahrenheit, or 27 degrees Celsius if you prefer, and you are all invited." He didn't wait for any questions or comments, he turned and ran all the way back to his cabin to change into a swimsuit. There were no signs of the boys.

Before he headed back to the pool club on the lower deck, he slipped into the galley to grab a snack. Zak was in the air-conditioned space preparing appetizers and dinner with Jean-Marie. "Hello! How are you?" Adrian walked up to the opposite side of the island, out of their way. He spied the oversized pots on the stove full of water and exclaimed with great anticipation, "Ooo! Are we having lobster for dinner?"

"Yes," Zak said as he continued to work. He wiped his hands on his white apron tied to his middle and asked, "are you looking for a snack? I put a whole tray for you kids on the main deck."

"Ah! You read my mind!" Adrian smiled and started to back away towards the door. "Zak, my friend, you are the BEST!"

Jean-Marie burst out laughing and lifting her knife to point at Zak she said in her French accent, "you know this hungry man so well!"

Zak grinned, "yeah, I do. I was once a teenager with an appetite from the north to the south pole. Why do you think I became a chef?"

"Bye, see you later!" Adrian barely heard the question as he ran through the main deck to find the plate of goodies. His buddies were standing around it, stuffing their faces. Jane was bartending.

"I'll leave a cooler of drinks near the pool club." Jane offered. "You're going to be jumping from up there, right?" She pointed up another level to the owner's deck and winked at Adrian.

"Wait! What?" Brody asked, a bit dumbfounded, wiping crumbs off the corner of his mouth. "We're jumping from up there?" He walked to the edge and looked up over the side then down to the waterline of the yacht. "That's kinda high up, isn't it?"

"That's gotta hurt," Braden said, scratching his scalp over his ear. "I'm not jumping off the side from 30 to 40 feet up."

"Guys, relax. Jane's teasing you." Adrian grinned at her. "We're not doing anything other than climbing an inflatable slide. You'll see." He picked up some Italian focaccia bread with olive oil, sun dried tomatoes, black kalamata olives, rosemary and flakes of sea salt and took a huge bite. "Mmmmmm!"

"I know, right?" Braden picked up a large square of focaccia bread and raised it over to Adrian as a mild salute, "Dude, you are livin' the life. This pizza bread is freaking awesome!" He stood by the table and ate one right after another. Brody and Adrian did similarly, but watching Braden eat was like watching a giant swallow food whole.

"Dang, bro'" Adrian laughed at him, "you sure can put away food like no one else can!"

"Ha!" He wiped his face with a napkin and patted his belly. "OK, guys! I'm refueled. Let's go!"

They fled down the stairs to the platform dock and dove in one right after another into the clear aqua blue waters with rebel yells. A water fight commenced within seconds until Adrian decided to make a beeline for the other side of the yacht. With curiosity, the brothers followed and pulled up short to tread water when they saw the massive three-story super slide attached to the upper deck of the yacht.

"OMG! Dude!" Braden was flabbergasted taking in the size of this adult version of a kid's bouncy house water slide. "This thing is huge!"

"I know! Come on!" Adrian turned back around and swam over to the swim platform. The boys followed and soon they were pulling themselves up on the swim platforms and walking across a towel to dry their feet so they could run up three flights of teak stairs on the port side to reach the owner's deck and climb up the inflatable steps to the top of the slide.

"Brody, do you want to go first?" Adrian offered. It was a generous offer since he loved to go first. "And you have to go feet first and don't hold the sides. Cross your arms over your chest or keep them straight up over your head like you're doing back-float."

"Heck, yeah!" Brody yelled before he grabbed the handrail and began ascending the super slide to the top.

Adrian and Braden watched from either side of the slide where they had a view. Lizzie and Grace had joined them seconds ago and rushed over to see Brody get to the top step.

"OK, guys, here I go!" He took a deep steadying breath, sat down, and crossed his arms over his chest before wiggling his butt over the edge while a white hose streamed water down the slide to reduce friction. As he felt the first prickles of momentum begin, he yelled at the top of his lungs, *"Geronimo!!!!!!"*

The kids at the rails cheered and rushed to be next in line. Brody was in the water yelling up to all watchers, "Guys! That is awesome!"

The adults let the teens play for over an hour and then the dads entered the scene. They had such a blast that they dragged all the women over to the slide and had them go down. Soon everyone was in the water and enjoying the late afternoon sun.

Jimmy, Francesco, Roberto and Raffa each pulled out a bright colored Seabob® and lowered them into the water for the adults to use. Weighing in at 29kg, once the Seabob was in the water, the 64 pounds of pure propulsion was not noticeable and easy to handle.

The adults zipped around the boat at high speeds, doing donuts and figure eights. Several times the dads, wearing protective dive masks on their eyes, dove under the water with them and popped up here and there when they needed a breath of air. Coming back to the floating docks Brian and Francesco had tied off the stern for the assorted water toys they pulled out, Adrian's dad pulled off his mask and exclaimed, "Wow, these toys are intense! I still cannot get over how agile they are on and under the water. It's incredible!"

Francesco nodded with a big smile in his olive-skinned face, "*Si, si, signore*! *Irrefrenabile* ... Irrepressible!" he translated that last word, although it sounded similar. "The hydrodynamic shape makes piloting the Seabob *perfecto*." He reached down to secure the Seabob to the floating dock they had tied onto the stern platform. "È *stimolante, no*?" Adrian's dad agreed that the Seabobs® were inspiring.

Adrian asked if he and the boys could play with the motorized surfboard, but Jimmy deferred until another day. "The water needs to be calmer for beginners, and it is late in the day. Ya gotta be fresh, when you learn, and we want your brothers to have de most fun."

"OK," Adrian conceded. He knew Jimmy was right and while they were not hard to use, getting them out required some time, planning, teaching and it helped to be fresh in mind and body. He just wanted to add more play to the day for his friends. He hung on to the edge of the swim deck and chatted with Jimmy while the rest played. "Hand me a snorkel and mask, will you, Jimmy?"

"Sure thing!" Jimmy wandered over to the storage locker for all things diving. He selected Adrian's favorite mask and snorkel and handed it down to him.

"Thanks!" Adrian dragged the mask headband over the back of his head and pulled the mask over his eyes. He adjusted the snorkel in his mouth and angled it back to where it would stick out of the water and allow him access to air when he was face down in the water. Looking down into the crystal-clear water, he took a sample breath to test it before letting go the side of the platform.

He paddled face down for a few minutes looking at the sea life below him, which wasn't much. It was a sandy bottom and reflected the sunlight. Occasionally, a lone fish swam around the bottom. He saw empty conch shells with some type of algae growing on them. He turned and swam the length of the yacht for a while and then looked at the underside of the yacht's hull.

He saw the starboard side stabilizer midship and towards the stern he saw the jet propulsion side thrusters and two propeller shafts with brass props. The boat's draft sat over 10 feet deep in the water and he knew instinctively diving under it to swim the 36 feet across underwater with a snorkel mask on was not a smart idea. Yet. He came up for air and grabbed a corner of the stern swim platform. Jimmy was standing there keeping an eye on him.

"How's the bottom, Adrian?" he inquired with a light note to his voice. "It need scrubbin' yet?"

"It's all right, I guess." Adrian ripped off the mask and snorkel and handed it back to Jimmy. "It's so interesting to see the depth and breadth of the yacht from underwater. "

"I know." Jimmy agreed. "She's big! I'm glad you didn't go and get any ideas about trying to swim under to the other side."

Adrian laughed, "well, I did think about it, but that's a long distance. I'd have to swim 12 feet under, so I don't scrape my back on the hull. I'd need to practice first, making sure I can swim that distance at that depth before I try."

The big Jamaican man standing over him waggled a finger at him and shook his head. "I really do need to keep my eye on you!"

"Hahaha!" Adrian backstroked away from the platform and smiled up at Jimmy. "What's life without a little challenge now and then?"

"Not on my watch! Speaking of watches…" he glanced at his wrist and took a whistle out of his pocket and blew it loud and long. "Everybody out of the water! … Ev-ree-bod-ee out!"

The last to leave was Brody. "Aww, man, can we do a night swim with all the underwater lights on?" he asked.

"That would be so cool," Adrian agreed. "Can we, Jimmy?"

"Let's discuss it on the way to dinner."

"Oh, yeah, we're having lobster tonight." He turned to Brody,

"Do you like lobster, Brody?"

"Yeah," he said, pulling himself up out of the water. "That's the only thing I can think of right now that could get me out of the water."

With a wave of thanks, the boys turned and marched up the pool side stairs, dripping salt water. One of the crew on night watch would be hosing down every deck while they slept.

Back in the cabin, the boys took turns showering and getting ready for dinner. The sun was casting a golden glow into the room. Braden had picked up the iPad and was playing different songs they all knew and loved at a rather loud but fun volume.

Twenty minutes passed and soon they were ready to leave the cabin for their evening meal. Dinner would be hosted on the owner's deck, so they hiked single file up the starboard stairs that wrapped the elevator, to join the rest of the group.

Zak and Jean-Marie had prepared platters of lobster and many other delights. While all the stewards served, the chef and sou chef chatted with the parents answering questions about the meal. For dessert, the stewards brought out ice-cream sundaes with all the toppings, including more Christmas cookies Jean-Marie had made fresh earlier in the day.

"Hey, Zak?" Adrian threw his voice over to the chef before he left the deck to head back to the galley, "any chance tomorrow night we can do s'mores around the firepit?"

"Are you kidding me?" Brody quickly interrupted, "you also have a fire pit?"

"Yeah, it's that round table looking thing over there," Adrian pointed it out on the stern and Brody turned to look. "The tabletop is just a lid."

"Sure, we can do that," Zak promised with a slight nod. "Just let me know what time."

"Cool!" Brody was excited that they could roast marshmallows and make smores onboard. This trip was turning into one of the best trips ever. It was better than summer camp. He couldn't wait for tomorrow night!

Chapter Eight
Body Surfing

Bright and early, Adrian and his buddies woke up and hit the gym. Jimmy wandered down and asked them if they wanted to try the hydrofoil boards. Adrian's family, in an effort to expand the yacht's water toy collection, had purchased four motorized surfboards with long skegs, and lithium battery operated efoil propulsion systems underneath. The boys' eyes grew wide with excitement at the prospect of fun, and they stood down together off their exercise machines and collectively said, "Heck, yeah! Let's go!"

Jimmy laughed and using the palm of his hand, pumped the air to slow the rush down and said, "Whoa, whoa, whoa. Calm down, I'm not quite ready for you boys. How about you eat breakfast and meet me and Brian down at the pool club in thirty minutes?"

The boys left their respective machines and toweled off their sweat and then headed up the port steps to the main deck's dining table and sat down. The family and guests were already eating and enjoying coffee and fresh juices from the tropical fruits sold on the island.

"Hey, everyone!" Adrian said in a voice loud enough to capture everyone's attention. "The guys and I are going to do the flying surfboards in thirty minutes. Anyone one want to get some video of us?" His dad, while chewing a mouthful of food, simply raised a finger and nodded indicating that he would volunteer.

"Cool. Thanks, Dad." Adrian smiled over to his dad and gave him a thumbs up.

"I want to try them out as well." He lifted his coffee and looked over at Mr. Sanchez and raised an eyebrow. "You coming? They look fun!"

"Don't mind if I do!" He nodded in happy agreement and continued eating.

Jean-Marie, Jane and Gabriella had placed plates of food in front of the three boys who dug into them with impatient forks.

As he munched a thick strip of crunchy bacon, Brody turned to his brother and reminded him to bring his video camera to the pool club. Braden nodded and kept stuffing his face to hurry up. The best he could do was throw a thumbs up in the air without stopping.

One by one they finished breakfast and excused themselves from the table to run down the passageway to Adrian's cabin where they grabbed cameras and headed to the stern deck.

Jimmy had pulled four efoil surfboards out of storage and set them upside down on the floating deck of the spacious inflatable dock he and Brian had attached to the stern swim platform, to create a parking lot for the water toys and general lounging.

Mounted under each of the colorful five-foot-long carbon fiber surfboards that contained a lithium battery for the electric motor that propels it, was a carbon fiber wing, shaped like a fin attached to a 24-inch mast that lifted the surfer when activated by the rider's remote-control device. A remote control for each efoil surfboard lay on each board. Jimmy stood facing the boys with his hands on his hips. He wore a short sleeved, short-pants wetsuit made from neoprene.

"Is anyone else coming?" he asked.

"My dad and Mr. Sanchez, and they should be here any minute," Adrian volunteered. "They needed to get on their swimsuits."

"OK, well let's start with some basics," Jimmy began. Pointed to the pile of lifesaving equipment on the floating deck and he instructed them to, "get a vest and put it on." The boys rushed to don a vest and zip up bright yellow life vests and snap the heavy-duty impact-resistant buckles across the front to make them snug and secure.

Jimmy walked over to them and began adjusting the straps to make them snug but not too tight. "Good. OK, let's discuss the controller next." He had one in his hand with the strap wrapped around his right wrist. "This is how you control your speed." He held up a lithium-ion battery powered, Bluetooth enabled waterproof controller that could bring the surfboard up to 25 miles per hour for over an hour. "Lose this and you are dead in the water."

All heads nodded then turned for a second to notice the two dads quietly entering the space to catch up with the lesson.

"We're not just doing motorized surfing, guys, we're flying." Jimmy scanned the eyes of the boys and saw the level of awesome registering in their eyes. "I just want you to be aware that the faster you go, if you wipe out, it will hurt more than if you are going nice and easy."

"Motorized flying at very low altitude?" Braden ventured with a devil-may-care smile.

"Exactly." Jimmy held up the controller. "This is a smart device. It knows when you have fallen off your board and will stop the board immediately."

Adrian and Brody gave each other a look of anticipation overload, then turned back to give their full attention to Jimmy.

"You guys can skateboard or snowboard, right?" All heads

nodded affirmatively. "OK, so your core muscles are going to help you balance when you stand up, but we are going to start out granny-style."

He hefted a board up and lowered it over the deck platform into the water as if it weighed nothing at all. He lowered himself into the water and demonstrated dragging himself over the board and lying across it on his stomach. "You are going to start on your stomach and get a good feel for the board, how to get on and off it, while holding the controller in your hand. Start slow, then when you are comfortable with the speed, go faster."

"One important thing, before I go," he warned as he floated away from them, "Never aim for the yacht. If you lose control or the motor jams, it will run into the yacht and hurt you, the board, the boat, and possibly other people. Always line up with the yacht and aim for the parking space alongside this floating dock when you return. Slow down and stop just before this platform so you drift close. This makes the safest return. Got it?"

All the boys nodded. "When you stand up, place your weight on your back foot to pop up the nose of the board. As soon as the board pops up, you must shift your weight forward to balance and be a fly-boy.

"If you don't get up and stay up, you may need more juice." He waved the controller in their direction in a slow horizontal motion, indicating that the control was what they needed to solve their speed and balance problems.

"One last thing..." he paused, "where you look, is where you go. If you turn your head in any direction, your body will turn with you and the board will follow.

"Any questions?"

"Yeah," Mr. Sanchez asked, "how do you fall off and how do you stop the board?"

"Good question, sir." Jimmy held up the controller, "you simply let go of the throttle button, and the board comes to a complete stop. Dead in the water, as they say.

"Falling is another matter. You don't want to fall on your board. You want to fall away from your board, or you will hurt yourself. Jump away if you feel yourself falling. Don't try to regain your balance. It's not worth it. Any other questions?" He raised one eyebrow, then turned to get aligned with the front of his flyboard and hit the throttle with a slight pressing motion.

"No? OK! Here I go!"

He moved the board away from the yacht and let his legs drag in the water behind him. He turned a big circle and leaned in for a tighter turn. He sped up and lifted his legs. He slowed down and brought it in. "Now I'm going to show you how to move from your stomach to your knees."

He took off and with quick agile movements, moved to bring his knees under his belly while maintaining his balance. He leaned to the right and completed a circle back. Before he got there, he placed his hands on the board and brought his feet under him and slowly stood up as he passed the aft edge of the swim deck. "OK, who's first?" he yelled as he flew past.

"Braden, you go. Brody went first last time." Adrian was feeling generous since he knew he would have a whole year with these adrenaline inducing boards. Jimmy circled back and jumped off the board just in front of the boys.

Braden jumped in the water and swam to the board to climb on. It was awkward climbing over it with a life vest on, but he managed to pull his weight over the board. When he was positioned and comfortable, Jimmy handed him the controller. He then pushed Braden a few feet ahead of him and got his body out of the way of the underwater foil. "Go man!"

Shakedown Cruise — The Adventures of Yacht Boy

Braden hit the accelerator and shot off with a jumpstart. Startled to the point of laughing, he kept going letting out a loud holler. On his first pass he yelled, "Woooooo hooooo!"

Adrian's dad was filming his effort. Braden swung by the boat a second time and slowed down. "Wow, this is super cool."

Flying across the bay, Brian, riding a gas-powered personal watercraft or PWC, drove up to the yacht and idled twenty feet from the boat observing the playground at the stern of the *Arabella*. He was wearing an orange life vest and red swim trunks, looking exhilarated. Jimmy hauled himself out of the water and began lowering the other motorized surfboards into the water. "Brody, off you go now." He handed Brody a controller and another to Adrian. "Mr. Sanchez, you want the last one?" Jimmy pulled a life vest off the floor and handed it to him. "Here's your controller."

Brody and Adrian were on their stomachs speeding off and Brian followed them. They reunited with Braden and chased each other for a bit before they began practicing the art of balancing on their feet in the standing position to fly over the water. After a few silly attempts, tons of jumping off their boards erratically and loads of giggling, they all found themselves on their feet, screaming at each other across the swells of the bay, before heading towards the back of the yacht where Adrian's dad caught it all on video.

Earlier, Jimmy had launched a second personal watercraft that had been parked in a floating "parking space" between two small floating docks, which he untied and straddled as he backed away from the deck being careful not to touch the yacht or docks. He was also wearing an orange life vest and guiding the boys away from the yacht. He stood up and steered his PWC just ahead and off to the side of the boys. Mr. Sanchez came up in the rear, still on his knees and grinning from ear to ear, with Brian coming up last. They were a quarter mile out in the bay and having a blast.

They rode the boards for almost 40 minutes before their legs got tired and they started heading back to the yacht. Jimmy had them kill their engines several yards away from the yacht and hold off until he cleared them to come in. He secured his PWC to the platform and jumped out. One by one, he called the boys in and took their controller and then hauled the surfboards out and placed them in the center of the floating deck. Just before the last one was hauled in, Mr. Sanchez flew past on his feet in the standing position. Everyone cheered their loudest and Braden whistled an enthusiastic piercing sound that carried across the water.

"Hey, guys, is it our turn yet?" Grace, Lizzie, and the moms were standing in the doorway wearing swimsuits, ready to play.

"Sure thing, ladies." Jimmy had the boys hand them the wet life vests to put on and began giving instructions. Adrian walked over to his dad and held out his hand for the video camera.

"Go on, Dad, grab one and go before the girls drain the battery." Adrian winked. "There's about 20-30 minutes left on these batteries. Go for it!"

His dad grabbed a life vest and lowered a surfboard in the water and took off. Within minutes he was on his feet and flying over the swells with Mr. Sanchez. Adrian ran the camera while they raced each other across the bay and back. Brian was always nearby at a safe distance making sure he was available if they needed him and that other people, if they were to enter the bay, would give them all plenty of space to move around.

Coming back, Adrian saw that his dad and Mr. Sanchez were riding the swells in parallel and then going off the tops and backs of the swells. He hadn't noticed the increase in the swells while out there, but they were getting a little bigger. The girls were going to have some fun.

The moms who were guests switched with the dads, while the

two girls hit the water. Adrian's mom hung back to give them a chance to experience the adrenaline rush of motorized flyboarding. She could do it anytime and often did.

Brian kept close watch on everyone in the water. Jimmy asked the boys what their plan was and asked them to stay put, while he rode the PWC to bring up the rear with the group that was on the water.

Brody began filming alongside Adrian and they didn't talk while they captured both the water, wind and voices that sped by the swim platform. Brian gave a lasso sign to wind it up and head back since they'd been out on the water for about 25 minutes. Jimmy tied up and began helping the ladies up into the yacht and hauling flyboards to the center of the floating platform. Everyone was chatting and hands were animating their experiences as they moved as one large cohesive group upstairs to the sitting area on the main deck where they hung out in the hot Caribbean sun until lunchtime.

Nonsuch Bay
Freetown
Antigua

The captain wanted to move the yacht from anchor. The weather was perfect, but the swells were increasing, and the boat was in an unprotected bay. Adrian heard Pete fire up the engine and asked the boys if they would like to see some of the yacht's operations.

"Lead the way, yacht boy!" Brody stated with enthusiasm. He'd heard the story the night before about his new nickname. Adrian smiled and elbowed him in the ribs.

"Knock it off," he said playfully.

"Aw, the kids are going to love that name when I get back home and tell them!" Braden teased.

"Come on, let's go grab tee-shirts, so we can go into the engine room. I also want to grab my walkie-talkie back in my cabin."

"Roger that," Brody said. Adrian gave him an appreciative look for using the language of mariners.

Back at the cabin, the boys changed out of their swimsuits and donned regular clothing since they would be in a workspace. Adrian put his earpiece in and turned on the walkie-talkie.

"Pete, this is Adrian, come in."

"Pete here. What's up?" Adrian could hear the drone of the twin diesel engines in the background.

"OK to bring my friends down to the engine room right now?"

"Uh, yeah..." he could hear Pete was distracted. "Sure. Come on down for a little bit."

"Roger. Wilco."

The boys headed down a staircase not used by the guests that led to the engine room. Bryce was in the engineering office studying a large binder and consulting two computer monitors. He had noise silencing ear protection on, so he waved to his visitors and returned to concentrating on his task at hand.

Continuing deeper into the engine room, Adrian reached into a wall dispenser of soft neon colored foam ear plugs and handed pairs to each of the boys. "Put these in. You have to wear them." He had to yell over the noise. The boys were all ears and elbows as they jammed green plugs into their heads. The noise was abruptly muted, and they looked down the row at the mirror finished handrails lining the walkway of the engine room where Pete was standing with a clipboard, pen, and flashlight. He had noise canceling ear protection on, and he, too, waved to the boys and held up one finger to indicate he needed more time. "I'm checking for leaks. Show them what you know!"

Adrian gave him a thumbs up and bought the boys around the engine room to point out various systems. He showed them where the oil levels were checked, the remote-control switches for the engine were located, banks of switches for turning on the engine and a variety of monitors.

"There are two generators on board, and we keep one running all the time to get power to the air conditioning system, water pumps, battery chargers, lights, and more. Even washing machines and dishwashers run off one generator." He paused to think about what else to share.

Brody asked in his loud voice, "Do you ever run both at the same time?"

Adrian nodded, "Yes. We run both when there is huge demand on the yacht because everyone is using electrical devices."

"Hey, Adrian," Braden interrupted, "Where are the fuel tanks and how much fuel can this beast hold?"

"I'll answer that in a minute," Adrian yelled back over the

noise, "While we are here, check these white cylinders out!" He pointed over to a nearby area and shared that, "This is a fuel filtration system that takes water and impurities out of the fuel. No matter where we are in the world, we can create cleaner fuel for our engines. Sometimes the fuel in third world countries is too dirty for our engines, so we clean it here.

"We can hold a couple hundred thousand liters of diesel in three tanks and travel around 5,000 nautical miles." Adrian continued, "There is a port, starboard and day tank. The filtered fuel goes into the day tank. Makes sense, right? It's the clean fuel reservoir for the engines to draw from."

The boys nodded. Adrian went on, "sometimes they have to move the fuel around because if one side empties, the boat would be listing to one side." He beckoned them to the next spot.

"Check this out!" Adrian pointed to collections of hoses that were attached to the engine. "These are the oil filters. One of these hoses moves dirty oil into a disposal tank.

"The engines combined have around 5,700 horsepower." Adrian raised his eyebrows for impact. "Think about it. Fifty-seven hundred horses to pull this yacht." The boys were impressed.

He brought them closer to a wall where there were several fuel pumps and showed them where the red button was to turn off the fuel. "These are fuel tank shut off values. If ever there was a fire, this switch will shut off the fuel."

"How do you have fresh water on board? Do you store it in tanks, or...?" Braden's eyes were searching the equipment around him and soon he spotted a water system in a stainless-steel box.

"Over twelve thousand liters of fresh water are stored in tanks and there is a pump system for it. But here," Adrian pointed to the silver-toned box, "this is our water maker."

"How does it do it?" Brody asked.

"Do you have a reverse osmosis water system at home?" Adrian asked.

"No, don't think so."

"Well, this box is attached to a pump that takes in gallons of saltwater and runs it through several filters to remove particulate matter." Adrian pointed out some fat looking pipes attached to the wall that ran behind the box. "Inside those pipes are filters that work by osmosis; only the pure water makes it through the filter, which goes into the storage tank."

"Cool." Both brothers nodded knowingly. "You guys are totally self-sufficient out here. How many liters of fresh water can you make in an hour?"

"Around 250 liters and there are two tanks, so that the weight is evenly distributed."

"Where does the exhaust go?" Braden was looking over the two large engines and it was not obvious where the carbon monoxide was transferred. "Is it sent underwater?"

"Well, first it is filtered in that canister over there," Adrian pointed to a vertical cylinder mounted on brackets and attached to exhaust pipes. "Once it is filtered, to get out the maximum amount of carbon, it gets sent underwater. This way there is little to no smell on deck."

"I see alarm systems and cameras everywhere. Why is that?" Brody asked.

"The captain can observe the engine room by adjusting the camera view at any time, especially if there is a problem and he needs to know what is happening or who is present."

He took in their interest level, and Brody was making funny faces in a shiny convex chrome plate and smirking. "Are we done? You want to go?"

"Yeah." Braden shouted over to Adrian, "Can we get a galley

tour next?"

Adrian smiled. "If you want a snack, Braden, you can have one without needing a tour of the galley, which I know you have already seen."

Braden laughed, "I'm good. I don't need a tour. Let's get a snack."

Chapter Nine
Antigua Nice!

Nonsuch Bay
Freetown
Antigua

The captain drove the yacht at a slow pace around the south side of the island then headed east. The yacht could travel just over 13 knots while cruising, however, today the captain was traveling at a slower speed to make a short-day cruise out of moving anchorages. They turned into Nonsuch Bay and found a place to drop anchor.

The teens wanted to get in the water, so Jimmy and Brian put out the tender, both PWC, standup paddle boards and Seabobs® for them to use, which kept them entertained for hours.

After a BBQ dinner the chef invited the teens to head up to the owner's deck for roasting marshmallows and making smores.

"We need to get our video downloaded, Adrian, and put more time in tonight to make a movie for everyone. Why don't we put in a few hours after s'mores?" Brody asked. His concentration was on rotating a stack of marshmallows on a metal skewer over the gas fire pit. It was smoking, but not quite on fire. He kept pulling it back and blowing off the singed areas, so they never caught fire. With the gentleness of a surgeon, he would squeeze the sweet blistering cylinders to test for doneness.

"Yeah, I agree." Adrian concurred while he twirled his fourth marshmallow. Suddenly he jumped up from his seat as his fluffy treat caught fire, "Oh, no!" Blowing on it with powerful bursts of air, he put it out then back crumpled down into his seat. "I hate it when that happens." He took a napkin and carefully pulled off the black outer shell. "Dang."

He slid the gooey mess onto a graham cracker and topped it with half a chocolate bar and squeezed it all together. "Ahhhh, perfection!" He sunk his teeth into the s'more and sat back with pleasure.

Grace and Lizzie had already eaten theirs and were sitting back talking. "Hey, Adrian, why don't you go get your night vision goggles." Grace leaned forward and leaned on her knees with interest. "We could look for spaceships and life on shore."

"You have night vision goggles?" Brody gushed with deep interest. "Go get them! I want to try them."

"Sure." Five minutes later, Adrian returned with his goggles, which he took a moment to dust off with lint free paper for cleaning lenses. He looked at Grace and said, "Brody goes first, then you can use them." He handed a pair of night vision binoculars to Braden to play with while his brother explored the world around him with the goggles.

Brody put the goggles on and looked at his friends. He started to ooh and ahh at how much detail he could see on the nearby mountain in the dark.

"How do they work, Adrian?" Lizzie asked him with genuine interest. "Is it all heat signature stuff?"

"That's a good question, Lizzie, but no, they don't really work that way. The goggles amplify any residual light and make details more obvious for the person looking through them. The person looking through them can have an expanded range of vision both up and side to side," Adrian explained.

Continuing, he asked his friends, "Did you know that 1 out of 4 rescues happen at night? These goggles are common in helping people do search and rescue on land and at sea. More and more helicopter pilots are using them to locate people and help patients get to hospitals. It's pretty cool technology."

"But how come in the movies we've been shown that thermal signatures are what people are looking for?" Lizzie persisted. "And like, when their eyes see something bright, they freak out like someone stabbed them in the eyes."

"Well, there are different kinds of goggles. What you are describing are thermal imaging night vision goggles." Adrian assured her, "and yes, a bright light would be painful when your iris is dilated to take in more light. These are just basic night vision goggles, but you can still see an incredible amount of detail."

"Brody, can I try those now?" Lizzie asked.

"Yeah, sure!" He pulled them off and handed them to her. She put them on and looked around the bay taking in the details.

"Wow, this is pretty cool," she announced. "I can see people sitting on boats and walking the beach over there…" she pointed to the northeast. She lifted the goggles to compare her normal vision with the goggles. "Oh, my word. I can't see them at all without the goggles."

"Yep, that's right," Adrian smiled. "Pretty darn cool technology." Turning to Braden he asked, "How are you doing over there, Braden? What are you looking at?"

Braden had his eyes on the yacht across the bay that was anchored far off. He was turning the dial between his eyes for greater accuracy. "Uhhh, just some people in a small speedboat with the lights off loading stuff from a yacht…"

Adrian was curious, "How many? Do you think they are going for a night dive?"

"Hard to tell. There's a lot of small stuff being handed from person to person until it gets up to the deck above the water." Brody shrugged and said, "It's hard to see in the dark from this far away. All I can say is there are … two, three, four people and not many lights on in the bigger boat. The small boat is totally dark."

"Hmmm," Curious, Adrian asked for the binoculars and took a look. It was hard to discern what was happening. "The lights out are very odd, but there are many reasons why the lights on the small boat could be out. Let's not jump to conclusions about anything."

Adrian handed the binoculars to Grace for a turn. She looked around the bay and walked to the edge of the yacht and scanned the bow and stern. Brian and Jane were hanging out on the bow talking. "Ooooh. You won't believe who I see having a cozy little chat on the bow."

Lizzie jumped up and ran over to look. She peered around the edge of the yacht and grinned. "Let's go surprise them," she suggested.

"What are you two looking at?" Adrian wanted to know. "Who's up there?"

"Looks like Brian and Jane are hanging out together on the bow, enjoying the stars over Antigua." Grace shared with an air of knowledge.

"Shall we say hi?" Lizzie asked with a slight teasing sound in her voice. "Let them know we can see them?"

"I don't think we should disturb them." Grace continued to lean over the edge to get a better look. Her line of sight was hindered by the tapering of the beam to the bow. "They must be kneeling on the sun cushions. Now he's letting her have a sip of his drink."

Lizzie leaned out and used her left hand to push Grace back a bit so she could see better. "Aww, how cute...they're leaning over the starboard rail, shoulder to shoulder, looking at the anchor line."

The boys snorted through their noses. "They're on watch," Adrian informed them with a touch of scorn. "Quit reading into it."

Grace and Lizzie took down their night vision equipment to exchange a pitiful look which shared their opinion of the boys. "Let's go sit in the pool and leave these ignoramuses to their marshmallows."

"Good idea." Lizzie agreed. And handing over the equipment, the girls left the owner's deck laughing and chatting about onboard romances, which Grace knew were forbidden.

"Well, guys. What do you want to do next?" Adrian asked. He was burning off the residual sugars on the metal skewers. Small amounts of sugar burst into flame and died out just as quick. Black sugars turned into fragile carbon that took their time falling off the skewers. The carbon would be gray colored ash soon. Adrian propped them up against the fire pit to cool.

Brody was stretched out, hands clasped behind his head, ankles crossed. "I dunno. We should get working on the video. We only have a couple nights left."

"You're right," Adrian agreed. "Let's go now. What are you going to do Braden?"

"I dunno." He leaned forward and stared into the fire. "Maybe watch a movie or go bug the girls in the pool." He stood up and stretched. "Do we need to shut off the fire pit or something?"

"I've got it," Adrian said as he flicked a switch to shut off the gas. In an instant, the flames died, and the boys stood up. "Let's go."

Back in his cabin, Braden changed into clean swim trunks and left to hang out with the girls. Brody pulled out his laptop and sat down next to Adrian at his table. "What are we titling this epic movie? –Holiday Adventure in Antigua?"

"Sure. It can be a working title for now. If we come up with something more epic, we can change it."

"How about "Epic Adventure in Antigua"?" Brody proposed. "We've both used the word epic twice. Maybe it is a sign that that word needs to be in there."

"Epic Holiday Adventure in Antigua?" Adrian countered as a suggestion. As he connected his phone to a USB cable and plugged the end into his friend's computer. "Copy my images and video over so you have them. Then I'll copy my other stuff onto a portable hard drive for us to share files. I don't want to put anything on the server."

"Alrighty, got it." Brody began copying the files over into his hard drive, then proceeded to open the recent file he had created two nights ago in a video editing software program. He went into the timeline and created a title page. Then added animation to the words and sound effects. "What's the name of our production company?"

Adrian leaned back and studied the ceiling. His brain was spinning through combos of names for their imaginary video editing company. They liked to create fun names as the film producers and add a logo to the opener just like in the movies. He started rattling off a series of suggestions, some of which made them laugh or groan. None of them seemed right.

Brody was laughing hard at his last suggestions. "No! We are not calling ourselves Passing Winds or Pier Pressure."

"How about Loon-A-Sea Productions?" Adrian's eyes were glistening with tears from laughing so hard at Brody's earlier suggestions of Buoys In The Hood and Yacht Sea. When the two of them got going, they sparked greater and greater creativity and humor from each other.

"OK, how about something along the lines," he coughed twice for humorous emphasis, "of a knot or rope joke? Like ... Knot Working Films, or Knot to Worry Productions?"

"Oh, my gawd," Adrian was laughing so hard he feared he could not squeeze out a new suggestion and be understood, "Why Knot Films?"

"I actually liked Loon-A-Sea Films. Let's use that one."

Adrian agreed and Brody high fived his friend and began creating a logo with the chosen name. "This is so us," he added with a gleeful chuckle. "We can add some of those other suggestions in the credits for laughs."

"Good idea!" Adrian concurred. "People seem to love our credits more than the images."

"Well, it's an area where we get to express our humor more. The rest is just vacation pics and snippets of video."

For the next three hours, Adrian edited images in photoshop and cut out supportive images to overlay on videos to create layers of dimensions and interest while Brody added media to the timeline. He added in photos of him and family at the airport heading to Antigua. "Hey, we have to get pics and videos from family before we start adding in music and do the timing. We're already at a 15-minute show and the week isn't over yet."

"Hang on," Adrian walked over to a storage area and pulled out a new package of thumb drives. "Let me run around now and get everyone to transfer media to me daily from here on out."

Brody swiveled in his seat to face Adrian. "You know, we better back up our own timeline of delivering this. We have New Year's Eve and then we leave the next day. We might want to share this video at breakfast the next morning if we want to include the New Year's Eve pics and videos. Could turn into an all-nighter..."

"It's always worth it." Adrian assured him. "Let's see if Zak will create a New Year's Day breakfast party on the owner's deck, then we can use the pop-up TV to show the video during breakfast. I'll do a private showing for the crew who miss it later."

"OK, we need to really crank on this!" Brody opined. "Get me everyone's content so I can add it in, then I can do the slide transitions up through tonight. Better go now before people call it a night." He looked at his watch and saw it was after midnight. "You know, maybe you should put a sticky note on each thumb drive telling people what you want and just leave them outside their cabin doors, since it is late. I'll text everyone letting them know about the thumb drives."

"Roger that." Adrian left the cabin and began delivering his thumb drives. Grace and Lizzie were up and hanging out with

Braden on the main deck playing their favorite tunes. He asked them to get their media to him and Brody ASAP. All agreed.

He made deliveries on the lower deck and headed up two levels where he found his dad reading when he went up to his parent's cabin. "Hey, Dad," he whispered to not wake up his mom, "can you download yours and mom's pics and videos? Brody and I are making a movie to show on New Year's Day before our guests leave."

His dad nodded and gave him a thumbs up. "Great idea! I have all that video of all of us on the motorized surfboards. There are some very funny ones, too."

He thanked and hugged his dad goodnight and left without a sound.

He detoured up to the bridge and took the binoculars off their mount and walked to the wing to take a quick look at the anchored yacht with the small powerboat tied alongside. He was curious if it was still there. He scanned the waters behind the yacht in case it was trailing the stern instead of being tied alongside. It wasn't there. It was nowhere to be seen. He looked over the yacht and inspected it with care. The lights that were on were normal for anchoring that he could determine. He wished he had his night vision goggles because the bridge's binoculars were not designed for his level of scrutiny. Sighing with some disappointment, he returned the binoculars and left the bridge pulling the door quietly shut behind him.

Unbeknownst to him, the captain was aware of his presence in the bridge and had slipped quietly out of his cabin. Holding back in the shadows he listened until Adrian left and then proceeded to take the binoculars and peer around the bay looking for what Adrian was interested in. He lingered on the anchored yacht closest to them, but did not see anything out of the ordinary and returning inside he tucked the binoculars away and returned to his cabin. *He's aware of something. I need to watch that one like a hawk!*

Braden was in the cabin transferring his data over to Brody's laptop when Adrian walked in. "Hey, dude, that was quick."

"Yeah, the girls should be over in a minute," Braden handed him the unused thumb drive. "I'll just download daily to Brody's machine."

In walked the girls holding their phones. Lizzie handed her phone over to Brody who plugged it in.

Grace asked the group, "What are we doing in the morning?"

"I would like to do some power-touring. What do you say we knock off a whole bunch of touristy things tomorrow?" Brody offered, "I want to get the maximum photos and videos of us on the island doing all kinds of things."

"I could go with that plan," Lizzie agreed. It was followed by plenty of me-toos. "Where do we start?"

While Brody swapped out Grace's phone with Lizzie's, Adrian pulled out a notebook where he had a list of things to do. "If we start at the farthest location, and work our way back to the boat, we would start with the Donkey Sanctuary, then go to Betty's Hope Sugar Plantation, head over to Stingray City and finish up at Devil's Bridge."

"Should we bring snacks or just eat out?" Lizzie asked. "Or both?"

"Both," Adrian shared. "Finding fun places to eat on the islands is always fun and then you get to try the local cuisine. And you get to learn about the island by hanging out with the locals." He pulled out his phone and texted the crew their plans so they would be ready for them in the morning. Zak needed to know they wouldn't be there for lunch and, if he had to guess, dinner, but they would text from the road. They needed a taxi and dedicated driver for the day, which the chief stewardess would arrange. He included the parents in the text so that they were all informed of their plans in the order in which they planned to explore the island as a group. In a private text, he asked his dad for an envelope of cash to handle expenses for his group and a special check.

"What time are we leaving?" Lizzie asked, then without waiting for an answer suggested, "I think we should probably leave around 9 o'clock, right after breakfast, if we want to do a handful of activities."

"OK," Grace yawned, then disconnected her cellphone and grabbed Lizzie's arm, "we're done. See you in the morning."

Donkey Sanctuary
Bethesda
Antigua

Gabrielle, the chief stewardess, organized a mini-van taxi to pick them up at 9AM at a Nonsuch Bay resort with a dock. With a measure of discretion, she handed Adrian a large manilla envelope that his father had prepared for him. There was a note inside that said, "We may meet up with you at Betty's Hope. Text me when you are ready to head over there." Adrian texted his dad and acknowledged the packet and note with a thank you emoticon.

Jimmy and Brian moved the tender last evening, and it sat alongside the *Arabella* held off by a pair of yacht mounted mooring whips. Whips were one of the things that impressed Adrian. They were heavy duty carbon fiber rods that mounted in stainless steel bases or on bulwark hook mounts, that pulled the yacht tender away from the hull by applying continuous variable pressure between the yacht and the tender. Adding a spring line or two kept the smaller boat from moving out of position. He thought they were just brilliant!

The teens had eaten breakfast in haste knowing time was of the essence. They showed up on the stern to step aboard the tender that was going to run them from their anchor spot to shore. It was blazing hot in the sun and the water was glassy from a lack of wind. Everyone was beginning to sweat. As the boat picked up speed, the breeze cooled them off.

A short walk up the beach to the resort driveway led them to their taxi driver. They were a few minutes late, and Gabrielle assured Adrian, who was worrying, that their driver would wait. "Trust me, everyone is on island time."

The van was painted like a Rastafarian record album with Bob Marley's face on the sliding door. The windows were down, and the music playing was reggae. Stickers of all sorts and sizes cover the windows in the back. The driver wore a massive, crocheted hat in red, green, gold, and black stripes. His dreadlocks stuffed deep inside the hat presented quite the picture. His yellow tee-shirt sported the name Antigua. His smile and island voice welcomed them. "Ayyy," he drawled in his island voice, "Antigua nice, right?"

"Yes," enthused Grace and Lizzie with big smiles. "We love it!"

"Lemme get this straight," he began cautiously with a deadpan face, "your stewardess says you gunna see some donkey, visit old Betty, swim with da 'rays and walk the Devil's bridge?"

"Put like that, maybe we should change the plans," Adrian began with a laugh. "But, yeah, that's the plan!"

"OK, mon, shut the door for me, will ya, and we go see some of Jacko's Donkey's."

Braden pulled the door shut and the driver took off. "He lowered his sunglasses and looked over them into the rearview mirror, "I'm Christopher, by the way."

"Hey, Christopher," came the chorus of voices. One by one, they introduced themselves.

"So, you all from da States. States nice." He turned the steering wheel left and headed up the drive to the street. "I've been to Miami and New York City. You been dere, mon?"

Not one of them had been to either city except to fly in and out. Christopher dropped that line of conversation and tried another. "You like reggae?" He reached over and turned up the volume. All the heads and bodies started moving and swaying and Christopher laughed a big, deep laugh. "You kids alright!"

Adrian had chosen to sit up front. His elbow poking out the window as he took in the view from up front. On a whim, he pulled out his cellphone and took some pics of himself and the driver, and the group in the back seats. He stuck his phone out the window and shot a video that captured the music and the journey for their movie. Before long, they turned down an unnamed road and pulled into the sanctuary. A cloud of dust followed the van and hung in the air.

The grounds were both dry and dusty, but the perimeter had a park-like setting with trees and fencing. A concrete pathway for visitors to walk on gently curved through the donkey's homeland. Pens were located every so often and white bathtubs, used for feeding troughs, were spread out over the land. Watering tubs were also placed around for the donkeys to drink.

The sanctuary was just opening when they arrived, and they followed a small group of visitors through the metal gates covered in guidelines.

A young man, wearing a red tee-shirt and black galoshes to

protect his feet and jeans, was passing out horse grooming brushes that fit in one's palm with a strap that secured the brush to the back of the hand. They accepted the brushes and wandered around until they found some donkeys who were willing to get a brushing.

Brody and Adrian took turns videotaping their group grooming donkeys and carrying on. Then they took pics of themselves with the donkeys. Adrian turned on his video camera and winked at Brody. Nodding his understanding, he called over to his brother, "Hey, Braden! That your new girlfriend?" Then he pealed with laughter. Adrian tried his best to keep the camera steady, but he was laughing.

"Don't be an ass," he retorted with a smirk. Everyone groaned. Even the donkey emitted a loud bray in protest.

The young man came over to them and asked how they were doing. He was just a little bit older than them. "I t'ink dis one likes you, sister." He scratched behind the ears of the donkey leaning

into Grace. "You have a callin' with de animals, do ya?"

Grace laughed. "I keep trying to brush her, but she keeps leaning into me and knocking me sideways. I can barely stand up against her."

"Yer doin' great, give her a hug."

Grace stopped to give the donkey a hug, which Adrian and Brody caught on camera. It was sweet.

Lizzie asked, "Where did all the donkeys come from?"

"Well, dey been here for long, long time. But they cause all kinds of damage 'round de island, so someone had de bright idea to round dem up and take care of dem here where they can get and give love without causing problems to cars, crops and people's landscapin'."

"How many are here?" Grace inquired looking around to get an estimate of her own. "Looks like you have at least a hundred."

"Oh, maybe 'hundred an' fifty," he mused aloud. "De come and de go. Circle of life, ya know?"

"Yeah," said Grace with compassion in her voice, "while it seems sad, it's just reality."

"Exactly!" he agreed. He looked at the boys, "You want to fill a tub with water or feed?"

For the next hour, the young group spent their time helping around the sanctuary. They learned about some of the individual donkey's history, who had been adopted, and the different personalities. Before long, they moved over to the kennels for dogs and cats that needed homes. There were even goats on the property.

Adrian looked at his watch and initiated the group heading out. "I'll be there in a minute or two. I've got some business to tend to." He walked over to the main building where the office was located and opened the door.

"Hi," he began, looking at the woman behind the desk. "I'd like to make a donation. Can you help me with that?"

"Oh, sure!" she enthused as she stood up to shake his hand by way of welcome. "Thank you for coming in today. Where you from, young man?"

"Well, California, but we're just here for the holidays." He took off his backpack and unzipped the main section to dig for the large envelope Gabriella handed him earlier. He pulled out a smaller envelope with a check in it and passed it to her. "My family and I would like to show our appreciation for all that you do here on the island, for all the animals in your care. We hope this check helps your organization take care of necessities and builds your dreams."

She took the check and when she saw the amount, she gasped and covered her mouth with her left hand. "Oh, lord, child, that's..." her voice petered out and she was at a loss for words. "You tell your parents that we are so grateful for this donation! It's going to go a long way to help this place." She grabbed him and gave him a big hug. "You made my day, young man!"

Adrian patted her back and pulled away as fast as he could without seeming rude. He felt a bit awkward. "OK, well, uh... thanks again. I've got to go now." And he backed away from her towards the door with haste.

"Oh!" she gushed and waved the check in the air with a little dance in her step, "I just can't get over this! You made my day!"

"Awesome!" he enthused back with a thumbs up and a quick salute, "Bye!"

"Bye!" She was already picking up the phone to make a call by the time he disappeared out the door.

Wiping his forehead, he shouldered his backpack and walked to the minivan while sending a short text to his dad as he promised. He was smiling to himself. He enjoyed this part of the trip, but sometimes you never knew how people were going to react to his family's generosity towards different projects they found in their journeys. One thing was for sure, people loved getting donations, and his parents loved letting him choose who could receive. He also got to deliver the money and witness the direct impact his choice to empower made on a nonprofit. They liked being anonymous with their philanthropy, and that was great. He always shared with them how the money was received, and they always laughed with happiness.

Reaching the van, he opened the front door and hopped in and said, "Take me to see my old aunt Betty, mon!"

"All right, mon." Christopher rejoined, "I'm on it." He backed up and made a U-turn to head back out onto the same road they came in on. "How'd you like those donkeys? Dey all nice and clean now dat you brushed a few of dem?"

Grace voiced her opinion first, "It was wonderful! One donkey just loved me to death. Now I smell like donkey."

"Dese donkeys dusty all da time." Christopher volunteered. "Dey get love from da tourist during peak season and the school kids off season. But dey sure do love ta be brushed."

"You can say that again," said Brody. "I'm glad we saw this. At first, I thought we could pass on it, but seeing my brother with his girlfriend made it all worth it." The girls laughed and Adrian grinned. Braden reached over to give knuckles to his brother's head, which ended up in a tussle in the back seat.

"Brothers." It was a statement made by Christopher as he looked at Adrian. They grinned. "You no got a brother, do you?"

"No. I sometimes wish I did. I don't have a dog either. I really wish I had a dog." Adrian twisted his lips in regret and looked straight ahead. The reggae covered their voices somewhat. Grace and Lizzie were talking. "It's just me."

"Me no got no brother either, but I got many friends to make up for it," he shared. They came to a main road and he dog-legged left at the big intersection. "Ah, we on the main road towards Betty's now." They drove in silence for a bit. He pushed in a CD and Bob Marley's One Love came on and soon they were all waving index fingers in the air and swinging their arms from side to side, in and out of windows. Spirits were high as they entered the dirt road leading to Betty's Hope.

"I don't know if dere is a tour today. Just wander around and take some pictures and read da signs." Christopher advised. "I'll wait here."

Betty's Hope Sugar Mill and Plantation
St. Peter's Parish
Antigua

The teens climbed out and started taking pictures of the plantation that was made up of several ruins of buildings and a stone windmill tower with the sails and rudder. Broken walls and crumbled rocks lay about the place. It felt hundreds of years old.

An Antiguan gentleman getting on in his years greeted them near the windmill. "Mornin'"

"Morning. How are you?" Adrian asked with interest.

"Very well, thank you," he replied. "Would you be interested in a tour today?"

"Oh!" Adrian perked up at the chance. "Yes, sir, we would."

His smile produced hundreds of wrinkles in his face, and he stuck out his hand. "I'm Elroy."

"Adrian. And this is my sister, Grace, her best friend Lizzie from California, and these are my friends who now live on the east coast in the Carolinas." They all shook hands.

"Nice to meet you all. Well, now, let's cover some basics that might be of interest to you." He took a red handkerchief out of his pocket and mopped his brow. "It seems extra hot today, but let's not let that stop us.

"Come along. How much history do you know about this island?" he walked alongside the group as they walked a rock lined dirt pathway towards the mill tower.

"Well, Antigua used to be an English colony but achieved independence back in 1981," offered Lizzie. "I read that you have since had a prime minister but are still under rule of the crown of England."

"We know a little something about Lord Nelson and his wife and daughter," added Braden. "We explored English Harbor Christmas Day and explored the fort at the entrance of the harbor."

"My parents like the Antiguan rum!" Adrian chimed in.

"Mine, too," said Lizzie.

"Yeah, my mom loves the Antiguan rum punch drink," Brody added. "She said they are the best she's ever had."

"Well, Antigua knows a thing or two about rum." He walked for a step then began to talk. "Back in the rum triangle days when the British, Spanish and French wanted rum, they decided to take over many islands back in the 17th century. The English came here and cleared the brush and planted sugar cane. But they needed people to work the plantation. This need for cheap labor, shall we call it, initiated certain amoral human trafficking sea captains to steal Africans from their homeland and sell them as slaves."

Everyone was silent. It was sobering to hear the story of the island's people. He continued, "The original founding family had problems. The owner was the governor and when he died, his wife fled the island when the French came in and occupied it. After the English got it back from the French, the crown awarded the Codrington family ownership for their loyalty to the crown.

"They turned it into a large-scale sugar estate. They were powerful, influential people and this place became the flagship estate in all of Antigua. But it was at the cost of the Africans who were brought here."

"Excuse me," Adrian interrupted when he paused. "How many slaves worked on this particular estate and when did they get emancipated?"

"By 1680 there were just shy of 400 slaves. And in 1834 they were emancipated, but they continued to work the estate." His voice was neutral and carried no judgment about the situation. "There were about 150 sugar mills in Antigua by then and this one had the most innovations in terms of technology."

"How so?" Braden asked.

"Agriculture is hard work, son. Figuring out ways to carry out large scale cultivation, extraction of the cane juice and manufacturing of the sugar and rum required ingenuity and tools."

"Was the windmill part of those innovations?" Braden asked. "I don't recall when windmills were invented, but I know sails have been around forever on boats and oil paintings at the museum show windmills in Holland for hundreds of years."

"Good question. It is my understanding that windmills have been around since the medieval period, but I had a Persian guest here once that shared with me that in Iran, during the 9th century, they had windmills, but it was a horizontal windmill, not a vertical one like we have here."

"Wow," Braden exclaimed, "I'd have to see a picture of a

horizontal windmill; I can't even picture it in my mind!"

"Yeah, me neither," his brother said.

"I think by horizontal," Adrian injected with an air of thoughtfulness, "they mean the sails were attached to a vertical shaft. That would make the sails look like a paddlewheel turned 90 degrees. This windmill has a horizontal-axle, and the sails are attached to something that makes them rotate facing the wind.

He turned and looked apologetically at Elroy, "I don't know the names of the parts of a windmill. Maybe you can help me."

"You're doing great!" Elroy encouraged him. "And I believe you are right about the sails in relation to the axel." He paused and touched his lips with an index finger while he sorted for his next words. "Vanes. Yes, vanes are sails or blades. And the huge post on the outside, or rudder, is used to position the sails into the wind, just like a child's pinwheel toy."

"Makes sense." Grace looked at the massive wooden post leading from the ground to the top of the windmill, which could be turned and positioned to the wind. "Tell us more about the rum triangle."

"Ah, the rum trade." He paused and straightened up and his gaze went to the far horizon. "The three sides of the triangle were New England, where the United States was in its infancy, here, in the West Indies, and the African Gold Coast. Take away one side of the triangle and the whole dang thing collapses.

"The American Colonies were prosperous because our molasses was sent to the colonies to make rum. The rum was shipped over to Africa. The African slaves were shipped here to the West Indies. They traded rum for lives. Over twelve million lives were taken to the," he put air-quotes around his next words, "New World."

"Oh, you know, I think I remember something about this now," Lizzie inserted. "The success of the triangle trade created more demand for resources and then more land was needed for manufacturing, and it impacted the Native American Indians because they ended up having their land stolen from them."

"Wow!" Brody exclaimed, "I didn't know that was a contributing factor. Dang."

"Yeah," Lizzie continued, "buying slaves meant they could grow cotton, for example, and sell it overseas and locally."

"Not to point the finger of blame or anything, but who were the sea captains who started selling slaves from Africa?" Adrian asked.

"If I recall correctly, it was the Portuguese and a few Spanish traders. They took people mainly from West Africa to the American colonies. And that goes back more than four, maybe five hundred years. There is ancient history of slavery in Africa for thousands of years, my friends. This just didn't start a few hundred years ago with a rum triangle."

Heads nodded. They walked a few more yards closer to the mill when they heard a voice back at the gate yell, "Yoo-hoo!"

Everyone turned and saw Adrian's mom waving a big hat in the air to get their attention. Laughing, Adrian yelling, "Coming!" And jogged down to open the gate and welcome them to the tour.

Returning to the group with all the parents, he introduced Elroy. "We were just discussing the rum triangle and the impact it had on the New World."

"Excellent!" his dad enthused. "Did you know triangular trade still exists today?"

"No," Adrian admitted. "Doesn't international trade with cargo ships and airplanes make manufacturing simpler?"

"Well, it sure does, but America still grows cotton and lumber, for example, and we ship it as a raw material to China, and the Chinese manufacturers process it into fabric or something like pencils." His dad laughed. "I still get a chuckle when I stop to think that it is cheaper to grow and chop down trees in America, ship them to China, who mills them into number two pencils, boxes and ships them to retail stores across the world through a distributor. Imagine that!"

"I know of another triangular trade," Mrs. Nasif piped up. "Newfoundland, on the east side of Canada near Nova Scotia would ship salted cod and corn from Boston in ships bound for southern Europe. Then the ships would load up on wine and olive oil in the Mediterranean Sea destined for Britain. Britain would send European resources back to Newfoundland for distribution."

"Very good," Elroy commended her. "Let's go inside now and I'll show you the extractor." Elroy led his group of ten Americans into the stone mill where they saw the large cast iron machinery of the sugar cane extractor. A shaft came down from the ceiling that had a rust-colored horizontal gear turning a massive vertical gear of equal size that turned three rollers. It was simple and powerful.

"It was easy to operate and effective." Elroy began. "Two men would feed the cut sugar cane stalks into the chute, the rollers would crush it and the juice would come out and fall down into the catchment system below this floor. They would run the plants through two or three times to get over eighty percent of the juice out.

"There was a pump that piped the juice to the boiling house." Elroy paused and said, "nothing was ever wasted. They would dry the crushed stalks and later burn them as fuel in the boiler and at the distillery. Although there were only 2 acres of land, every week they collected five and a half thousand gallons of cane juice from two hundred tons of sugar cane stalks. It was a flagship mill for this reason."

"I have a question," Adrian's mom said to Elroy. "Did they

actually make rum here or was it just the processing of the sugar?"

"Oh, they made rum here, too, ma'am," he responded with a smile. "They boil the sugar, water and scum –which is the fermented part of the sugar in big copper boilers. Right there in the distillery house directly out back." He pointed out of the door to the stone buildings.

"There's nothing quite like Antiguan rum, is there?" she smiled at him with a knowing smile.

"No, ma'am, nothing quite like it." Elroy winked in her direction. "Be sure to bring some home with you."

"Oh, we all plan to!" she laughed then realized what she implied and corrected herself to Elroy, "not the children, of course!"

They finished walking around and exploring. Adrian hung back and gave a generous tip to Elroy for the tour, shook his hand and walked back to Christopher's minivan.

"How about some lunch?" his dad asked him. "Any ideas?"

"Let's ask our drivers. And by the way, are you going to Stingray City with us?" Adrian asked back. "It could be fun…"

"I think we could do that. Divide and conquer?" he suggested. They split up and talked with their drivers. They both agreed that the best choices would be in the area of the stingrays. Back in the vans, they followed each other through rolling hills to the area of Willikies on the northeastern side of the island.

Shakedown Cruise — The Adventures of Yacht Boy

Willikies
St. Philip's Parish
Antigua

They found a funky shack to eat lunch and ordered everything on the menu so all could try local food. They invited both drivers to sit with them and share stories of Antigua.

Cedric, the other driver, started sharing about the influences on the island's cuisine. "The Spanish, British and West Africans all brought their flavors to the Caribbean. But before they were here, the Arawak people who were indigenous to the island had crops of corn, sweet potatoes, chili peppers, guavas and other local fruits that were here already. Our food isn't spicy so much as it is flavorful.

"Then Syrians started coming to our country back in the 1930s along with people from India and Lebanon, and even some Chinese came over. So don't be surprised if you see shawarma on a menu somewhere. We're very diverse!"

Christopher added, "And then you got dem Jamaicans and Dominicans who work here and bring der spicy jerk chicken recipes to da island and we boom!" he crashed his hands together and exploded them dramatically to express divine interaction, "you have the perfect combination of food...sweet plantains or sweet potatoes, spicy chicken, savory fungee, salt fish with super sweet black pineapple and mon-oh-mon you eat 'til they have to roll you home." He laughed and leaned in very hush, hush. "I look like Rasta mon, but me no Rasta. I like to eat goat, lamb, beef, chicken, fish..." Everyone laughed at that. "Ah, here we go!" The chef and a server came out carrying a multitude of plates which they put in the middle of the table, initiating a feeding frenzy.

They were a loud and happy group and after trying roti with

curried goat, conch fritters and conch chowder, fungee made with okra and other vegetables, salted fish with tomatoes, onions and garlic, jerk chicken, seasoned rice with black eyed peas, onion, carrot, celery and bell pepper with herbs, and the all-time favorite pepperpot they were full up. Everyone had a cold non-alcoholic ginger beer to wash down lunch.

"Well, I'm stuffed." Mrs. Sanchez said, pushing herself back from the table. "That was an incredible feast! Thank you for bringing us here," she said to Christopher and Cedric. "Great choice!"

"Totally," Mr. Sanchez agreed. "Their conch fritters are some of the best in the world." He was indeed impressed, and it showed.

"You welcome, mon." Christopher stood up and waved them up. "Come on, times a flyin', we got stingrays to feed."

With his left hand working a toothpick in his teeth, and his car keys in his right hand which he raised up to say goodbye to the owner. "Thanks, mon. It was wonderful." The owner, who could be seen through the window to the kitchen was working ultra-fast to get the next meals on tables, nodded and waved back. Everyone followed the drivers out while Adrian and his dad took care of the bill. He calculated a large tip and folded some Eastern Caribbean dollars, also known as EC, and handed it to the server who took good care of them. "Thanks, man."

"Thank you," the server smiled, "a pleasure. Come back again." They waved goodbye to the owner and headed to the taxis.

"I think I ate too much." Adrian complained to his dad, who responded with a remorseful laugh.

"Well, I wish I had room for more of that sweet pineapple. I'll have to ask Zak to pick some up before we leave the island. I don't know if you can get it anywhere else in the Caribbean. We'll have to research that." He put an arm across his son's suntanned shoulders and as they walked to the taxi. "What do you say we experiment with it and make some cocktails and mocktails with it? Could be good with lime and nutmeg, you know."

"Sounds good to me." Adrian responded with a thumbs up to his dad. He and his dad liked to experiment with drinks as science experiments. His dad had a doctorate in biochemistry and mixing drinks was fun for him. "I'll text Zak to pick some up."

Chapter Ten
Power Touring

Stingray City
Willikies
Antigua

The sky was a perfect blue with a few fluffy cumulus clouds. The crystal-clear water was gradations of swimming pool blue. It took everyone's breath away to take in all the shades of blue and green.

Adrian and his dad went into a bright blue building to pay tour guide fees for the ten participants. They would be taking a five-minute boat ride to a shallow sandy area near a coral reef to play with stingrays. Several other tourists were hanging around waiting for the mandatory introduction class. The guidelines were obvious, but some people needed to hear them. Be gentle, avoid touching the tail or the dangerous barb on the tail and watch where you put your feet. The tour operation would have buckets with squid to feed these super friendly sea creatures, and as soon as the boats showed up, the stingrays would appear knowing they would be fed.

The tour guide went over the way you were to get on and off the boat. If you didn't want to get in the water, that was fine, too.

They followed the guide down to the docks and boarded the fiberglass open hulled boats. True enough, they were at the site within five minutes and tying up to a floating dock anchored near a small island. Moments later, Grace and Lizzie were squealing when two giant stingrays came up to them and nuzzled the front of their bodies. The boys faced the water and taking their time, they lowered themselves down the swim ladders, in full awareness of the rays that could be beneath their feet. They waded out to the girls and joined the excitement.

"This is sooooo cool!" Grace exclaimed with joy. "I never knew they could be so tame!"

Brody leaned over to Adrian to privately share, "I thought she was against tourists touching the rays?"

Adrian grinned back with no response. None was required. The tour guide operator had a bucket of squid and invited the teens to take some and feed the stingrays. The water was so clear and warm, and the sand white beneath their feet. They marveled at how docile the stingrays were to every human in the water.

When the squid was depleted, the tour guide invited everyone to snorkel along the beach and coral before heading back. Everyone paired up with a swim buddy and headed to the reef to do some fish spotting.

Their group made their way back to the swim dock and climbed aboard. They were the last people out of the water and looked happy and refreshed.

"That was the best!" Grace exclaimed, "I loved it!"

The parents and teens were beaming with the joy of their experience. Mrs. Nasif looked around at everyone's face and then declared, "This is definitely one of those things that I would tell people not to pass up."

"Oh, I totally agree," Adrian's mom said, "I'd like to go over to Laviscount Island to see the tortoises and exotic animals. Anyone want to join me?"

Laviscount Island
St. Peter's Parish
Antigua

An hour later they were on a tiny island that was a sanctuary for over fifty Giant Aldabra tortoises. Several weighed between 300 and 600 pounds. A sign shared with the group that they may live up to 200 years of age. "Dang, that's a long time," Brody said. "Do you think they live that long because they never rush anywhere? Let's face it, Adrian, they don't do cardio!"

"Yeah, I don't get it. Maybe it is because they are so Zen, know what I mean?"

"Let's go check out the big iguana and parrots." Braden suggested, leading the way. "I think the cages are over this way."

They were trying to get the birds to imitate their human squawks and laughing at their terrible imitations of parrots. "Oh, my gosh, you guys, we sound ridiculous!" Brody laughed, and feeling called to correct his twin, he said, "Braden, not all parrots say cracker."

"Sure, they do," he said with conviction, "watch and learn." He put his face to the cage and said, "Craa-ker. Craa-ker." The colorful blue and green parrot turned its head left and right, listening carefully to Braden. "Craa-ker. Craa-ker."

Nothing happened, but Adrian was getting it all on film. "Oh, come on, you dumb bird," Braden berated the bird, "how come you don't know cracker?!"

Brody was busting up laughing. "I told you. Not all birds say cracker you fool."

"Aw, shut up," Braden told his brother. "What do you know?"

"OK, guys," Adrian cut in, hoping to stop the growing tension from the judgments being hurled back and forth. "Let's head over to the viewing deck." He turned to leave, and the boys followed him not two steps when the parrot squawked, "Cracker. Cracker."

Braden exploded on his younger brother. "Did you hear that?! Did you hear that?! I *knew* he knew the word cracker. It's what everyone says to parrots. How can this bird not know it?" His voice rose to great levels of triumph as he proved his point and beat his chest with a big thump. "I know a thing or two about parrots and people." He was gloating over his brother but now he was happy with being right.

Brody and Adrian were blown away by the bird and walked back to the cage. Brody ran the camera, while Braden invited the bird to say cracker. "Come on bird, say it. Craa-ker. Cracker." Nothing.

"I have an idea." Adrian ventured. "Turn and slowly walk away, Braden. Brody and I will back away, too, as if we are leaving. Let's just see what happens." Before he turned away, Braden said cracker a few more times and then walked away as planned.

"Cracker." The parrot squawked and Brody yelled, "I got it on video! I got it! I can't believe we got it on video!!"

Adrian laughed all the way to the viewing dock where they ate ice cream and waited for their family to reassemble. "Dude, you nailed it." He told Braden. "That was too, too funny."

Grace and Lizzie ambled down to them licking ice cream cones. "What was funny?"

"Oh, you'll find out at breakfast on New Year's Day." Brody informed her.

A.M. Peterson

Devil's Bridge
Willikies Village
Antigua

Back in the two minivans, they headed to the last place on their list of places to see, namely Devil's Bridge. Outside Willikies Village, where the Atlantic Ocean and Caribbean Sea have their intense meeting on the east side of the island, the ocean waves came in with tremendous force, which is what eroded the limestone rock and created the bridge over thousands of years.

Pockmarked and uneven to walk on, salt spray blew through the air as they picked their way to outer edges of the famous landmark. Geysers and blowholes blasted seawater through portions of the limestone, and they paid attention to where they stepped

around those holes. The edge was dangerous, and everyone took great care to stay away from it.

The power of the wind and water was evident everywhere. With each wave that crashed on the bridge, waterfalls of white foaming salt water poured over the edges. The noise was fierce and breathtaking to listen to.

After quite a few photos including one of the whole group taken by Christopher, they wandered back to the road to return to the resort where they started. The afternoon sun was far to the west, and it had been a long day of power-touring.

Adrian called over to his dad, "Want me to text the crew?" He waved his cellphone as if to show how handy it would be for him to take care of it.

"Already did!" his dad smiled. "Jimmy texted back and said

that Raffa and Francesco will come and get us in 15 minutes or so."

"Cool. And I'll take care of Christopher." His dad nodded and headed over to Cedric's van. Adrian hopped back in the front seat with Christopher. "Home again, home again..."

"Jiggety-jig," Christopher finished. He turned up the volume on the reggae and headed to the resort. Everyone was too tired to sing, move or talk. They all sat in a relaxed silence. Everyone lumbered out of their vehicles back at the resort, but Adrian stayed in the front seat.

"What do I owe you, Christopher?" He gave Adrian a number that had been pre negotiated by Gabrielle earlier in the day and it matched what she told him. "Great!" He agreed and counted out some EC bills and added a generous tip of 50%. "Thanks, mon. You're the best."

"You kids were great to be around." He took a business card off the dashboard. "I know you'll be back around one day. Look me up. I'll be your tour guide anytime." They shook hands and said goodbye.

"Later, dude," Christopher said, "Be cool."

Adrian, walking backwards away from the minivan, gave him a thumbs up and a big smile. Then turned to walk down the path to the dock where the tender was loading guests and family all at once. Along the way, his eyes scanned the bay for the anchored yacht he saw last night but it was gone. Within what seemed like a two-minute ride, they were back at the *Arabella*, discussing showers, naps, and happy hour at sunset on the main deck.

Adrian sent the boys to his cabin and used the shower in the gym. He wrapped a fresh white towel around his midriff and stuffed his dirty clothes into his backpack to carry to his cabin. He walked up a flight of stairs and slipped into his air-conditioned cabin without seeing anyone. Braden and Brody were almost complete, and Adrian got dressed and flopped down on his bed. With a big sigh, he put an arm over his forehead and fell asleep. But only for a couple minutes since Brody threw a pillow at him. "Dude, wake up. You can't sleep now. We planned a happy hour with hot wings and limeade." Brody hit him again and he groaned, then swung his feet to the ground.

"Man, I'm tired. We pulled a late night, had an intense day..." he ran his hands through his damp hair to finger comb it, "ugh, I don't want to miss out on chicken wings, though. Zak makes the best. No joke." He pulled to his feet and shuffled to the door.

"And don't forget, we have a movie to make," Brody reminded him, although he was super tired himself. "Maybe we get to bed early, get up early, skip the workout and move straight to the computer?"

"Yeah, we can do that." Adrian agreed as he held the door open for the twins, "we also have to get everyone's daily download." Thinking more about it, he said, "hold the door." Then walked over to his computer, unplugged it, grabbed a USB cable and tucked it all under his arm and left his cabin. "We'll take files off phones during happy hour."

"Roger that." Brody clapped him on the back. "Always thinkin' ahead."

A few short hours later, the entire list of passengers were in bed fast asleep.

Green Island
Nonsuch Bay
Antigua

Bright and early, Brody and Adrian were up and sitting in the main lounge working at the bar. They had their laptops on the bar top and plates of food and espresso drinks at their fingertips. Brody organized while Adrian edited and labeled images. Hours passed and then Brody stretched and stood up, declaring he was done for the time being.

"OK, I think we have a handle on things. I need a break."

"Well, what do you say we go snorkeling or play with the motorized surfboards?" Adrian twirled a few strands of hair while looking up at the ceiling. "We could also take the tender and find a beach and hang out. I'm fairly sure the captain would let me if Jimmy or Brian came along."

"I'm up for that. Where could we go?" Brody asked, his interest piqued. "There's plenty of islands and beaches to the southeast we could explore. I bet the snorkeling would be amazing over there where it is uninhabited and shallow."

"You take our computers back to the cabin and get changed. I'll go find the captain." Adrian stated and turned to seek out the ultimate authority on board the *Arabella*.

The captain wasn't on the bridge, in his office or cabin. He used the intercom to ask his whereabouts and learned he was down in the engine room with Pete. Jogging down the steps two at a time, he bounded through the ship to the lower deck and found the officers engaged in conversation around the electrical panel.

"Excuse me, Captain?" Adrian injected when there was a pause in their conversation, and he was able to make eye contact with the captain. "May I use the small tender to explore the reef just southeast of here? I was thinking maybe Jimmy or Brian could come with us over to Green Island."

The captain nodded and pressed the button on his walkie-talkie and spoke to both Jimmy and Brian to set up the excursion. "You may go, but I want you to study the charts for that area first and take a copy in a waterproof nav bag with you. There are many risks of running aground or damaging the hull over there, so slow speeds are necessary. You can't anchor in the coral, or you will damage it. If you decide to stop and get out, you must beach the boat. You think you boys can manage?"

"Yes, Captain!" Adrian promised. "We'll be really careful. I'll have my walkie-talkie on me as well. I'll make copies of the charts. Good idea!"

Adrian went to the computer in the crew lounge and located the latitude and longitude for the area they were in. He printed the nautical charts for the island that he planned to explore. The depth markings were all over the place. Shallow depths would drop off to considerable depth, which meant corals were growing in the sea and would require sharp eyes and paying attention to the depth sounder.

On the way back to his cabin to change, he knocked on Grace's cabin to ask the girls if they wanted to join him. They did, and he informed them to meet at the pool club dock ASAP.

Jimmy met him and the brothers on the stern deck where they climbed into the tender. He passed the charts in the clear plastic zippered bag to Jimmy and hopped aboard. "Hey, Jimmy. Thanks for coming. I was thinking we could just mess around the island for a while. I'm not sure what's there, but it would be fun to go for a boat ride, you know?"

"No problem!" Jimmy grinned, "you helped me defer some yacht maintenance one more day. Happy to oblige!"

Adrian turned the key and had everyone sit down. He showed them where the life vests were stored. Jimmy had assembled several mesh bags of masks, snorkels, fins, booties, gloves, and a cooler of water behind the driver's seat. Grace and Lizzie hopped in and sat down. Jimmy cast off the bow and Adrian put the boat in reverse. He navigated the boat away from the *Arabella* and then increased the speed. He aimed towards the opening of the bay where it was known to be a deep channel.

There were a dozen or so boats at anchor on the west side of the island along a beautiful white sand beach that appeared to be linear for a hundred yards. He cut the speed by half, so he didn't create a wake and disturb the boats while driving past their anchorage. Next, he drove closer to the shoreline where it was about ten feet deep. Up ahead were a few more boats tucked into a horseshoe shaped cove with a backdrop of greenery. He cut across the cove without entering and began reducing his speed even more, as he was approaching a cluster of visible coral rising above the water.

He had close to four feet of draft, or hull below the waterline. Big rollers entered the bay and broke on the reef just off the island. There was 100 feet of space between the reef and the island. He looked at the low tide markings that showed depths of 3 and 4 feet off the point of land. He could clear it and avoid the reefs and consider the island's wall as a place to snorkel.

He slowed the boat inside the reef he passed and halted the tender just yards from the reef blocking his entrance to another inlet. He paused to sense the motion of the boat in the water. The swells were rocking the boat enough to move it towards the island, which wasn't making this location optimal for anchoring and having a go at snorkeling.

Consulting the charts, he found the depths too shallow to pass over the reef without some risk. He turned south and drove out through a deep channel between the perpendicular reefs and headed out to sea to clear the danger. Navigating around the reef that blocked his path, he found a deeper channel behind it and worked his way through the water in a counterclockwise direction.

"Ooooh!" Grace exclaimed, "it's soooo beautiful in here! And there is no one here!" Lizzie and she jumped up to look at the beautiful turquoise colors of the water and several white sand beaches that had zero visitors. "Our own private beach!"

"Wow, man, this looks good to me," Braden shared as he too turned 180 degrees to take in the scenery. "Pure paradise." Noticing a gap in the coral leading to the sand he shared, "how about over by that beach on your left up ahead? I see a spot you could pull ashore. It's sand all the way up."

Adrian slowed the boat almost a complete stop and let the wind and waves take him in towards the beach. He pointed the bow towards the sand and nudged the engine just a wee bit to accelerate him against the swells that wanted to take him against the island on the starboard beam. Jimmy leapt off the bow and took a line to a tree and tied it off. In a flash of bright colored plastic coming out of the mesh bag, everyone was geared up to snorkel by the time he finished securing the boat, which made him smile.

"Hey, everyone, listen up." Adrian stood up to make himself the center of attention. "Just like we learned in scouting, we swim with buddies for safety reasons. Just because there is no one else in this cove at this moment doesn't mean that someone won't come in while your back is turned, so listen for small engines that might approach and not see you. If one of you leaves the water, your swim buddy leaves with you. Got it?" He smiled when he considered how goofy his friends and sister looked at that moment. "Wait! Don't anyone move! I want a picture of this. Hang on…" He pulled his phone from the waterproof nav bag and clicked a few shots. Jimmy took his phone from him and made sure he was in one of the photos, too.

"One last thing," he warned, "do not touch the coral or anything else if you don't know what it is."

Jimmy cracked, "And no poke de eels in der hidey holes. 'Kay?"

He and Jimmy took some photos of the snorkelers and then joined them. The water was downright refreshing and crystal clear. There were fish everywhere they looked. The absence of people and boats made it a tropical fish paradise and they pointed out all the different fish they saw to one another with excited hand gestures under the water. Little by little, each pair of swimmers found their own place to explore.

The boys were the first to get hungry. They swam back to the boat and climbed aboard. "The girls are across the cove about five hundred feet away. Why don't we drive over and pick them up?"

They all liked that idea and Braden jumped over to untie the boat then push it off the sand as Adrian took his time to reverse the engine. He put the drive and propeller in neutral when he saw Braden wade through the water then swim to the stern to climb in using the swim step. The sand was like powdered sugar and stuck to him everywhere his skin was covered in sunscreen. He'd never experienced such super fine sand. "That powdery sand must be some of the oldest sand in the history of the island. It's so fine."

Jimmy laughed, "Ya. But you know you can only grind a sand or powder so fine." He chuckled and said, "This is off topic, but there is a sayin' in this island ... 'You don't take sand to the beach,' which means you don't take a girl to a party if der are plenty of good-looking girls at the party." He laughed a big Jamaican laugh and the boys grinned.

"Who knew Jimmy knew so much about sand?" Adrian said to his friends and laughed. He moved the engine into neutral as he approached the girls, who were treading water over a deep area away from the coral. After the girls climbed aboard, Adrian maneuvered the boat with a few forward and reverse movements until he was confident he could head through the reefs and back out towards the *Arabella*.

St. John's
The Capital and Key Port
Antigua

The boys worked long hours into the night to produce more of their vacation video and got up late in the morning. Zak allowed them to enter the galley to rummage for fruit and cereal that they could eat. He had put aside several pastries for them and together they munched chocolate croissants and drank fresh squeezed pineapple orange juice standing up around the island workstation.

Putting their dishes in the sink, they left the galley. Even though Adrian knew he could have called up the chef to make them something to eat like a short order chef, he did not want to delay his plans to go into St. Johns to explore. Brody and Braden had expressed a desire to see the capital of Antigua and he did, too. The girls wanted to go shopping. Adrian went back to his cabin and texted Christopher to see if he was free to drive them into St, John's and made plans to meet him back at the resort dock where he picked them up previously. An hour later they were bopping around the minivan to reggae and heading into town.

Christopher told Adrian to text him when they were ready to leave, and he would come back to get them. He pointed out a few areas to check out as he drove up Valley Road toward the Cathedral and museum. As they passed the public market space building, he pointed across the street and said, "Wait for me over there." He pointed out a large parking lot. "I'll drop you at de Cathedral, den walk back towards de water and explore de shops near de cruise ships. Anywhere you walk you will see new things. Antigua nice, you'll see." He wished them fun and drove off.

The kids walked into the old Baroque cathedral and were quick to notice how much it looked like a ship builder had crafted it. A sign shared that it was built on a fossilized reef.

"Do you realize that this reef is above ground on a hill? Just think about that for a second," Brody posed. "How does that even happen? Volcanic activity? Plate shifts? Did water levels drop millions of years ago exposing the reef? What even causes that?"

"Yeah, that's something to think about," Lizzie responded. "And this place was built in 1683 and rebuilt in 1746 and again in 1845. Why so many times? Did hurricanes destroy it or maybe fire?"

"It says here earthquakes leveled the church twice." Adrian was reading an entry online on his phone that shared the reason. "And those dark pitch pine walls are really a building within a building." He lifted his head up from reading on his phone to notice the walls of the cathedral. "The rock walls are one building, an exterior building. This stuff here," he pointed to the beautiful woodwork on all sides including the ceilings and parts of the floor, "is the interior building, and is designed to reinforce the structure for earthquakes. That is so cool!"

After exploring the architecture and taking some photos of angels, statues, and some of the cupolas outside, they left the church yard twenty minutes later and headed down Church Street towards the water. When they got closer to the water, they turned left following signs for the cruise ship quay.

Throngs of people filled the streets. Adrian recognized that it would be easy for them to get separated in the crowds of people. He gathered them close and stopped them to discuss a plan of action. "We all know where to meet Christopher. How about we split up? I know we aren't interested in what you girls want to shop for." The twins grinned at that and shrugged unapologetically at Grace and Lizzie. "So, why don't we check in 90-minutes from now by text?" Grace and Adrian pulled up the timer app on their phones and set it for an hour and a half from that moment.

"Yep, got it." Grace popped her phone back in her purse and linked arms with Lizzie. "Can we go now, Skipper?"

"Hey, I thought his name was Yacht Boy?" Brody asked, confused.

"Bye, guys," Lizzie drawled. "We're outta here!"

As the girls disappeared in the crowd, the boys scanned for things to do. Braden said, "I don't see anything here for us, let's keep walking and see where we end up." They continued down Thames Street until they reached the Heritage Quay Complex and turned into it. Palm trees in planter boxes with flowers decorated the lane and bright colored buildings offered cruisers popular brand name merchandise duty free and cafes places to eat. High above the rooftops of the shops, at the west end of the quay, were the topmost masts of two massive cruise ships in port, which explained the high volume of people in town.

On a red carpet near a shop, they passed a man playing a steel pan drum with a tip jar in front of him. He was dressed for

Carnival, a springtime festival. Next to him was a woman in a scanty looking costume of bright feathers and glittery accessories expressing Carnival through his music.

A block and a half later, they came to a souvenir shop of a little bit of everything imaginable, with goods spilling out onto the sidewalk. A middle-aged Antiguan woman with a yellow customary plaid headscarf was peeling stickers off a piece of wax paper and placing them on trinkets before placing them on a shelf behind the counter. She said welcome to them when they walked in. "Hello," they responded.

Brody picked up a fridge magnet, a tee-shirt and ball cap. Braden found a wooden carving of a dolphin and a coffee mug. Catching his breath in excitement, his eye was caught by the edge of a steel drum under the tablecloth. "Hey, guys! Check this out!" He pulled the large pan out from under the table and held it up. It was painted in a Rastafarian color scheme.

"Ooo, cool! You gonna bring that home?" Brody asked? "That's sweet." He reached onto a nearby table and picked up a wooden spoon decorated with an Antiguan flag. He touched the metal pan, and it rang a sweet note. "It works!"

"I'm so getting this," Braden declared, marching up to the store owner to pay for it.

Adrian was wandering the back of the store when he came across a wooden game board with a bag of stones resting on it. He was intrigued. It had 2 rows of 6 bowls all the same size, like an egg crate, only larger. On the ends were large bowls. He turned it over, but there were no instructions. Picking both pieces up, he carried it to the woman at the front of the store. "Excuse me? Can you explain this to me?"

"Warri." She was very matter of fact as she helped the brothers with their purchases. "It's our national game. You play with two people. If you want to learn, go down de street near de market house. Der are men playing it all day long in the streets and alleys. Dey will show you."

"Awesome idea. I'll buy it!" Adrian placed the long handmade wooden board on her table so he could pay for it. "I'll carry it and put the small bag in my backpack. Oh! And these too." He placed a stack of Antiguan themed postcards on the counter. He liked to send his granny, aunts, uncles, and cousins a card from the place of his latest and greatest adventure. While his wallet was open, and on a hunch, he took a 20 EC bill and tucked it into his pants front pocket. "Thanks again. Have a good afternoon!" She smiled and waved them off before returning to pricing merchandise.

With the game board tucked under his arm, the three boys hiked down the street towards the market Christopher was to pick them up. Sure enough, in many doorways and sitting on wooden crates from the market were men of every age playing Warri. The players never took their eyes off the board. Everyone stood around watching and talking in the rhythmic Antiguan accent of the Caribbean. The boys joined the throng of men and watched without speaking or fidgeting.

"You play?" A man in his late twenties asked, "or just buy you a board?"

"I just bought one and I want to learn how to play." Adrian looked him in the eye. "You play?"

"Since I was knee high!" He laughed a deep chuckle and waved his arm over towards a stack of crates inviting them to follow. "Come here." Pulling crates apart and placing them into a table and chairs configuration, he invited Adrian to place his Warri board on the center crate and sit down. "You have the seeds?"

"One second," Adrian dug through his backpack and pulled out the bag and handed it over. "I'm Adrian, by the way, these are my friends Brody and his brother Braden."

"Nice to meet you, Adrian." He nodded to the brothers and put his hand across the table and shook Adrian's hand, "I'm Remington, but all my friends call me Remy."

He began placing four seeds in each of the 12 scooped out bowls carved into the board. The end receptacles remained empty. Then he pointed to his row in front of him, "my side," he pointed to Adrian's side and said, "your side. Those bowls are called houses or *kru* in Antigua. We move counterclockwise. The goal is to capture 2 or 3 seeds in a bowl at the end of your turn and remove them from the board and put them in the end bowl on your left. You start on your side and pick up a scoop of seeds from any stack and move the seeds one into each bowl until you run out. If you end with two or three in a bowl, you take those. If you create 2 or 3 in succession at the end, you take those. First to get 25 wins. I'll go first."

Picking up the seeds from the third bowl from his left, he began to place one seed into the fourth, fifth, and sixth of his bowls and the first of Adrian's bowls. "Now you go."

Adrian picked up the seeds in his sixth bowl and placed one seed in each of Remy's first four bowls.

Remy nodded and picked up the five seeds in his sixth house. On his side, the third house had one seed and the sixth house was empty. He had added a seed to each of Adrian's five houses.

Scooping the five seeds out of his fourth house, Adrian placed one seed in his fifth and sixth houses and one each in Remy's first, second and third. He picked up the two seeds in Remy's third house. Remy nodded approval.

Remy's big brown hand scooped up the six seeds from his second *kru*, distributing them around the board until he ended in Adrian's second house. Adrian emptied his fifth house into the bowls to his right and into his opponents.

Remy studied the board for a few seconds, then moved his second house, which had one seed to avoid capture. This gave him three seeds in his third, eight in his fourth, seven in his fifth and one in his sixth. He rubbed his hand across his mouth, waiting for Adrian to move.

Adrian emptied his second house, ending up in Remy's second house. A few men had wandered over to see the two playing. It wasn't every day a visitor took the time to learn the game.

"Ayy, Remy," one grizzled old man laughed. "You gonna have to give up your title. I can read this young one."

Remy smirked, "I'm still in the game, Leonard, don't count me out just yet!" He scooped his first house on his left up and deposited seeds until he reached Adrian's second house. Adrian moved a solitary seed from his fifth to his sixth.

Picking up the two seeds out of his second, Remy moved them into larger caches, eliminating any chance of capture by this American challenger. Adrian moved seven around the board from his third house.

Remy took the two seeds from his sixth and captured the single seed in Adrian's second house. The score was tied, two-all.

Taking all nine seeds from his first house, Adrian moved around the board.

Remy took the two seeds from the first house and blocked Adrian from taking him on his next move. Setting up a future capture at the beginning of Remy's row of houses, he took the three seeds in his fourth house and sowed them around.

"You see here," Remy pointed to his fifth house, "I have 12 now. I have to pass that house when I come to and not feed it and drop the seed in the next one." He demonstrated this move to the boys.

Several plays ensued and more people gathered. Remy was

studying his opponent. Adrian, seeing danger in his fourth house, he moved his solo seed to join four others in the fifth. Remy chuckled.

Picking up a solo seed in his fourth, he moved it one. Adrian moved one from his sixth house to Remy's first, where a pile of seeds was growing. "Interesting move," Remy commented, picking up his solo seed in his fourth and dropping in his fifth to join others.

Adrian had three choices. Move one in his first to the second. Move one from his third to his fourth. Or move four from his fifth around to the other side. He went with his first option.

"You sure you never played before?" Remy asked, lifting his smiling eyes up to study Adrian. His eyes squinted long and hard at this young American boy then he his shook his head in disbelief.

"Never seen the board before in my life! Scouts honor!" Adrian raised his right hand in the classic scout's promise with his thumb on his pinky. He grinned up at the larger group of men studying the board. Then he watched Remy unload eight seeds from his first house into the remaining houses on his side and end on his third. He removed four seeds from Adrian's second and third houses. "Nice play."

More moments passed with each player moving seeds and capturing their opponent's seeds. No one spoke.

Eventually, with each side having captured twenty seeds each, Adrian had one seed in each of the four center most houses, and Remy had a seed in his first house, two in his fourth and one in his fifth. He saw the potential that Remy could keep moving single seeds to build up an arsenal and clean his house out in a few moves. But he still had some plays left.

Studying the board, Adrian asked, "Are we just going to keep chasing each other around the board for the next hour?"

"Naw, not at all, my friend." Remy said, "We call this a draw. You have four, I have four. The perfect play." He pointed to the fact that on Adrian's next move he would be without any seeds to play. "There is no game to play when you have no seeds to play. And I can't feed you." He spread his hands wide. "We are equal."

"Yes," said Adrian reaching across to shake hands, "always and forever. And thank you, Remy, that was a fun experience. I like this game."

He felt a hand on his shoulder and a familiar voice ask, "You play Warri?" Turning to look up, he saw Christopher and grinned. "Adrian, my young friend, I hope you beat the pants off this guy!" He greeted his friend with knuckles and grabbed a crate and sat down.

"No, Chris, it was a perfect draw." Remy rubbed his left jaw with his right hand. "He swears he's never played before, but he managed to create a perfect draw with me."

Christopher looked at Adrian with additional respect. "You play the master and create a draw?" He high fived Adrian. "Never played before?" Adrian wagged his head no, as in never. "Dat's

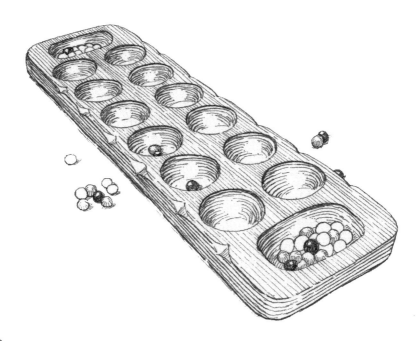

impressive. Dis man have Warri titles to his name. When we be in high school, he take every tournament title."

"A draw is Antigua nice. Thank you, King Remy, for not *gran' slammin'* my American friend and givin' a bad name to our country." Christopher said, putting his hand back on Adrian's shoulder, "he's my best customer! We treat him nice."

Remy laughed, then explained to the boy. "He's talking about a move that would capture all your remaining seeds and you can't continue. But I know better than to play Warri with god." When Adrian looked confused, he clarified and said, "Play Warri with god, then god gives no seeds. It's an old Antiguan expression."

Adrian was all smiles, but he looked at his watch and then at Christopher. "Are you here early?" He reached for his cellphone and saw that the alarm had not gone off, but a few minutes remained. "I better text my sister and see where she is; Stand by." He invited Christopher to play with Remy while the guys watched. He shot her a text and Grace responded that she was still shopping, and could they pick them up at the historic quay named Radcliff? Adrian texted back: yes.

Remy beat his friend Christopher and as the taxi driver stood up to leave, he pointed at Remy and threatened in a playful way, "Dis ain't over yet, my friend, I get you de next time!" While the old high school friends touched knuckles in parting, Adrian packed up his seeds and placed them in his backpack. He shook hands with Remy and thanked him again. Pulling the twenty EC out of his pocket he kept it folded and tucked it into the breast pocket of Remy's collared work shirt and shared, "buy these fans of yours a drink. I think they could use one." Remy grinned, touched the folded bill in his shirt and said, "Thank you, I'll do that! They'll appreciate that." The old men nodded and smiled; by including them, Remy had to accept the money, or he'd never live it down with the old guys.

Climbing into the minivan and placing the Warri board at his feet with his backpack, Adrian texted his sister that they were on their way and to meet on the corner of Nevis and Redcliff. Christopher turned the minivan around and headed up Market Street, and west on Nevis. They spied the girls half a block away and Christopher tooted the horn, while Adrian waved out the window. They slowed down and stopped. Braden opened the sliding door, and the girls dove inside with loads of shopping bags.

"Did you leave anything for anyone else," Brody asked.

"Funny," Grace sassed back, sitting down next to the window. "Whew. That was fun! But it's hot out and I'm thirsty. Did anyone get lunch?"

"Not at all." Adrian next suggested they skip having a late lunch since the time was heading into happy hour, and they could all get something on the boat.

Looking pouty, but knowing he was right, she turned to look out the window. Christopher got the van turned around and drove to a corner market a few blocks away. "Wait here." Five minutes later he had a heavy bag with cold waters and a couple bags of chips. He winked at Adrian. "Best customer, get best Antiguan treatment."

Grinning from ear to ear, and grateful for Christopher's kindness, Adrian took two cold waters and a bag of chips out of the bag and handed one to Christopher. He passed everything else along to the back seat.

He opened his and said, "Cheers!" to his driver. Nothing had tasted so refreshing in so long, Adrian thought to himself, and popped some salty potato chips into his mouth before passing the open bag to Christopher to reach in and help himself.

Back at the boat, everyone yelled goodbye to Christopher who stood atop the slight incline, and once again got a generous tip.

The breeze on the water felt incredible. The brothers suggested they all get a quick swim in before dinner and total consensus happened within a second.

Back on the main deck, Adrian dropped the Warri board and seed bag on a lounge table and continued to his cabin. He passed the captain who was on his way to the galley. "How are you, Captain?"

"Doing fine, Adrian, thank you for asking. How did you find St. John's?"

"I learned how to play Warri today!"

"Wonderful!" the captain enthused. "I'll have to play you sometime. Haven't played it in a while but would enjoy a match with your fine mind."

"You're on!" Adrian started to move off towards his cabin, "see you around captain! I'm trying to get a last-minute swim in before dinner." The captain waved him off and headed towards the galley, while Adrian walked fast to his room.

Chapter Eleven
New Year's Eve

Dickenson Bay
St. John's Parish
Antigua

After putting in several hours of editing on the holiday video, Adrian and Brody crashed after midnight. Even with refreshing swims, good food and air conditioning, all the travel, exercise, tropical heat, and humidity was taxing. Braden spent more and more time with the girls, as the video production got more intense.

While Adrian searched for music that was appropriate with matching lyrics or had just the right mood for their adventures, Brody was busy syncing every frame on the video timeline to the music beat for the portion that represented earlier days spent together. It was time consuming but when it was just right, it was enormously satisfying to see the pictures transition on the beat in perfect timing.

The captain pulled up anchor the next morning after breakfast and they left Nonsuch Bay to continue traveling counterclockwise around the island. Timewise, Adrian and his friends had entered the last twenty-four hours they would have together for some time to come. Adrian suggested they work over breakfast on the main deck so they could take in the passing view of the island.

"Hey, come and check this out." Brody followed Adrian to the port rail where his friend was pointing out rock formations along the island. "Look! That's Devil's Bridge from this side." Both whipped out their cellphones and took pics. "Up ahead is Stingray City, just a few miles up."

"It sure looks different from the sea," Brody commented. "You'd never know what was there, just by looking over the rail of a yacht." They hung out for a bit longer. "Let's go up to the observation deck. We never really spent time up there."

"Sure thing!" The boys closed their laptops on the way to the staircase up three flights to the highest point on the yacht.

"Wow! You can see for miles!" Brody exclaimed with excitement. "We must be forty to fifty feet over the water."

"We are," Adrian smiled and leaned on the railing to appreciate the view. "I love to come up here and watch the horizon and just be alone. It's peaceful. I especially love when sunset hits, and the sea and sky match top and bottom, then it is beyond beautiful!"

He and Brody stood in silence, watching the small islands go by on the east and northeast part of the main island of Antigua. Soon, a large island came into sight, and it had expensive luxury homes on it and what appeared to be a resort. "I looked at the charts yesterday and that's Long Island, and it is exclusive and very private."

"Hey," Brody pointed, "Isn't that *Neptune*? I recognize their superstructure thingy on the top because it looked like a trident. But I could be wrong."

"No, I think you're right." Adrian said as he whipped out his cellphone and took more pictures of the yacht. "I keep wondering how you get antiquities out of the country. Then it occurred to me: Boats and planes. Rich people travel by yachts and private jet. They go through their own immigration check point of sorts. It's not to say that they couldn't be searched at any time, but it wouldn't be hard to leave the island and land on a private airfield somewhere in the States with antiquities...or pass items between boats. Especially once you're close to the US. There are dozens of ways someone could get stuff ashore, especially in Florida where millions of watercraft are using all kinds of waterways."

"True. Someone could jet ski ashore with stuff or bring it to a smaller craft. Or use a tender." Brody squinted over at *Neptune*. "Do you have a high-powered lens?"

"My dad does, but we're moving too fast for me to get it and get back here to take a pic." *Neptune* soon was out of sight as they rounded the island.

"Is there any way you can see where that yacht has been or where it's going. You know, like a website. Have you looked it up to see if it's a yacht for charter or private?"

"No, I haven't, but you just gave me a fantastic idea." Adrian snapped his fingers and smiled at Brody. "Dude, I think I know how we can create a timeline for these yachts! Come with me!"

The captain was adjusting his heading from north to begin turning west due to the coral reefs that grew around Long Island when the boys entered the portside door to the bridge.

"Hello, boys, where's the fire?" The captain smiled at how out of breath they seemed when they only came down from the observation deck. "I saw you on the security cameras. Surely you are not out of breath coming down a single staircase...?"

Adrian laughed, "No! But Captain, guess what?! I just had a great idea and wanted to get your help. Can we use the ship finder app to look up all the names of those superyachts that are suspicious and figure out where they've been and where they are now?

We just passed *Neptune* and Brody thought we might be able to see their history."

With a slight nod and pursed lips that Adrian suspected were itching to express a smile, the captain said, "Not a bad idea, but keep in mind that ship traffic only shows up if their transponder is on, otherwise there is no data. You can use that monitor on the portside to explore the data."

"What's a transponder?" Adrian asked.

"It's an electronic signal emitter between a vessel and a satellite tracker. In this case, the yacht receives a transmission from a satellite and the yacht software responds with their unique signal to say received. This goes on indefinitely until the transponder is turned off. As a ship enters a destination and starting point, the signal goes on continuously and shows the name, type, date, time, and speed of the vessel. The signals are plotted on a nautical chart and can reveal drift, trolling, going in circles and all kinds of info.

"If, as I suspect," the captain continued in a *"don't get your hopes up" tone*, "That anyone who is involved in nefarious activities is not going to have their transponder on…unless they forgot to turn it off while engaged in criminal activities or they need it on for other reasons and cannot hide their position. Have a look and tell me what you find."

From the bridge, they could hear and see airplanes taking off and landing at the VC Bird international airport through the windshield and portside windows. "I can't believe we fly out tomorrow," Brody said in a sad sounding voice. "I wish we could stay longer."

"Yeah, but you can come back." With a few clicks, Adrian brought up the app and found *Neptune*. He touched the past-track button to see the starting location and destination. His heart skipped a beat at all the data he could find on just this one yacht. With Brody leaning in close, he entered *Orion* next and saw their position in the Bahamas. "Captain, any chance you can have your friend Thompson search the *Orion*? They appear to be in his marina right now."

"And what would I tell him?" the captain asked in a somewhat neutral tone of voice. "What reason would he give them?"

"Their position was in the same location as *Tyche* when she went down. He can search for guns...and treasure." Adrian gave his reasons in a reasonable voice for consideration, but he was brimming with enormous excitement. "And I would have him research *Neptune* and *Artemis* because..." His voice faltered and he looked at Brody for help. Brody shrugged his shoulders in a helpless response. "Never mind. I've got nothing to connect those four boats together. But maybe a photo of every crew and passenger of the *Orion* should be shown to McCready and Nickols to see if they recognize the person who shot their boat. Maybe one of them is named Hunter?"

"I agree," the captain nodded. "I will call him when we are anchored."

Adrian let out a breath he didn't realize he was holding. "Thank you, Captain. See you around. We've got a movie to make!"

The crew anchored the *Arabella* in Dickenson's Bay off the coast. Although the bay was seven to eight feet deep all the way to shore, the deep draft of the yacht drew more than the beach area could offer so they stayed offshore in the deeper part of the bay. With the stabilizers, any swell going in or coming out from the island was mitigated.

Spur of the moment plans were being made to attend a New Year's Eve party by the adults on board. Rumors were flying about fireworks. Adults were making plans to go over to the casino and have dinner followed by dancing at a resort. Gabrielle was making notes as fast as she could write and looking a bit nervous at having to get last minute reservations for her party. She stepped off to the side to make contact with several places, while alternate plans were being made.

"What do we get to do?" Braden asked Grace and Lizzie. "No offense, but are we stuck here on the yacht all night?"

"Yeah, good question, Braden." Grace turned and asked her parents, "What about us?"

"Zak thought you all might enjoy a party of your own." Adrian's mom shared. "You can hang out at the beach all day, then come back, change and ..."

"No way," Grace challenged, interrupting her mother. "We are going dancing! There's so many resorts and restaurants on that beach, you know there is going to be a major party scene! I'm not sitting here at anchor listening to half a dozen bands and DJ's making noise. I'll jump over and swim for it if I have to."

There was one thing Adrian admired about his sister, and it was that there was no stopping her when she wanted something. She could be as obstinate as an Antiguan donkey being pulled in a direction it didn't want to go.

"Well," his mom looked for help from his dad. "Honey?"

"What?" His dad looked up from his phone. "Oh, yeah, well ... you can go out, as long as you stick together as a group. I don't want Grace and Lizzie hanging out separate from you boys. If you promise to stick together, and you promise to be back on the beach by oh-dark fifteen to get a lift back to the yacht, you can go."

Adrian saw his mom look at him for more assurance. He nodded his silent understanding. "Look, why don't we have a play day, come back to the yacht, eat dinner, get cleaned up and go back ashore and walk around. If it's not our scene, we take a vote and come back. Majority rules. Agreed?"

With major reluctance, Grace and Lizzie agreed. There would be no more friends visiting the yacht if she didn't follow the guidelines set out for her and her friends. One day she hoped she'd be allowed to go where she wanted.

Braden and Brody turned to Adrian, "You know, we might want to be here on the boat for the fireworks. This could be the best seat in the house."

"I thought of that." Adrian walked over to Gabrielle who was texting someone. She looked up and smiled. "Do you know anything about tonight's fireworks yet? We're wondering if the yacht is the best place to watch them?"

She nodded, "yep, I would plan to be onboard, on the loungers. You'll have the best view of the entire beach. Trust me. You got it nice here."

Thanking her, he walked back and consulted his friends. They walked over to Grace and Lizzie who were sunbathing on the stern. "OK, sounds like we will appreciate being on the yacht for the firework show at 2000 hours. Why don't we go ashore after that for the dancing and people watching? I would only want to walk around in the dark for a couple hours anyways, in all seriousness."

"Fine," Grace agreed and picked up a travel magazine. "But after that, we get our turn on the beach partying. I'm hoping there is a bonfire, and generalized party-style craziness, but don't tell mom."

The boys strolled back into the main lounge out of the sun. "Let's go jet skiing or something."

All day the boys, and later the girls and their parents, enjoyed the inflatable slide, Seabobs®, PWCs and just being lazy in the sun and sea. Around four o'clock they exited the water and enjoyed a freshwater shower by the crew who turned hoses on them. They lounged around the stern with ice cold drinks and some tiny sea food appetizers.

Yachts and power boaters came in to the bay to anchor and take in the party scene all afternoon and into the evening. The bay was alive with parties, lights and small tenders going back and forth.

The crew washed and put away the water toys but kept the tender on the whips for transporting people later. Adrian thought about maybe doing a sunset cruise after the parents were dropped off on the beach to go to dinner ashore, but the moment he smelled Zak's grilling he never mentioned it. Dinner was around the corner!

Zak had prepared a lavish BBQ dinner for the teens. There were tender pork ribs with sweet tangy sauce, burgers, chicken, swordfish, grill-marked corn on the cob, potato salad, coleslaw, mac and cheese, and slushy lemonade to wash it all down.

The chef consulted his group of teens, who were claiming to be stuffed after his delicious BBQ, "I have Texas-style fudge brownies with frosting and peach cobbler with vanilla ice cream for dessert. Would you like to eat dessert after the fireworks just before you go to the beach, or now?"

Five groans went up from the table. "Oh, man, you're killing us!" Brody moaned. "I don't have a square inch of space in me. I vote for after the fireworks." All agreed and Zak smiled. Jean-Marie began removing family-style serving plates from the table.

Grace, feeling festive, turned on the disco ball and began pumping the speakers with music at a loud volume. With her parents away, she took full advantage of the opportunity to blast her favorite tunes. She flipped on the strobes, LED lights and started moving on the dance floor. Lizzie joined her and they started a party of their own. Braden joined them.

Adrian and Brody were still sitting at the table, too stuffed to move. The sun was setting, and dusk washed the beach scene in with warm colors. "I can't believe the year is over," Adrian began, talking over the noise of Grace's music, "can you?" Brody shook his head. He wiped a spot of BBQ sauce off his plate and licked his finger. Jean-Marie came to take his plate and Adrian's. "Thank you, it was delicious!" Brody looked up at her and smiled. "I really enjoyed all the food this week."

"Merci!" Jean-Marie smiled down at him. "I'm glad you like it."

"The food made the trip extra special." She nodded her gratitude. Brody turned to Adrian and placed both hands on his stomach, "I'm going to miss this..."

Adrian laughed and reiterated again, "You can always come back!"

"Count on it!" Brody affirmed.

Lying on their backs on the owner's deck, with Grace's playlist pumping in the air from the deck below, the guys made bets about who would jump to their feet the minute the fireworks started. Lizzie laughed and shared, "you know it's going to be me and Grace! It's such an exciting experience."

When the first burst of light flashed through the sky, it created a stunning experience, and it was the boys that bolted up and wanted to be on their feet for the show. They jumped to the glass-walled deck and stainless-steel railings to take in the visual wonders of the night. The resorts put on a great show. The colorful lights in the distant hotel gardens and beach walks added to the magic of the evening's experience.

Shakedown Cruise — The Adventures of Yacht Boy

One after another, colorful gunpowder exploded in front of them overhead. The sparkles fell from the heavens between the yacht and the beach. It was an ideal location. All five of the teens stayed close at the stern railing watching the sky, shoulder to shoulder, oohing and ahhing. Boom after boom, the fierce sound was magnified across the water creating a dramatic show. Somehow Adrian and his sister were rubbing shoulders in the middle. He said in her ear, "it's a night to remember, isn't it?"

She smiled back a knowing smile and said, "yeah, it sure is," and swung her right hip into his so he went flying into Brody. Laughing, she put her arm around his shoulder pulling him back and gave him a quick hug. "It's an awesome night, bro'!"

Adrian leaned over to catch Braden's eye and gave him a thumbs up, which he returned. He smiled at Lizzie and shared, "I'm glad you came down and spent the holidays with us." She reached behind Grace and touched his back in a gesture of friendship and gratitude. "Me, too!"

Brody was busy with a regular camera and trying to both take pictures and video of the show. "I dunno if I have the f-stop set correctly, but I am taking all kinds of shots."

"Yeah, about that video," Adrian began as he looked at the sky with his friend, "are we going to get that done tonight?" They looked at each other with deep concern, paused, then burst out laughing. "No one knows what we have or don't have. We can throw the rest in, have the computer do auto timing to the slides and call it good."

"I think you're right." Brody said, clicking away. "These are awesome fireworks! I think we are approaching the grand finale!"

Adrian memorized the night. It was beautiful to see the night sky bursting with an overabundance of color and light in the final moments of the show. With no movement under foot from the sea, a gentle moist tropical breeze cooled the air. Perfect stillness hung in the air for a fraction of a magical moment. The sound had barely faded when Braden put his fingers in his mouth and gave an appreciative wolf whistle that reached the beachgoers. Everyone cringed and it broke the spell. "What?" he looked confused and sounded a touch defensive, but was laughing, "it was a good show!" Together they started "woohooing" over the water to share their appreciation of the fireworks. Other boats at anchor tooted horns and smaller boats let airhorns rip the air. It was a party on the water!

"Now!" Adrian commanded, "who's for dessert?" He was left standing at the railing as his four friends turned and ran towards the stairs to get down to the main lounge to meet Zak with his sweet treats.

The girls wore dresses with miniskirts and carried flip flops because they had to get out of the boat and wade ashore. The guys were dressed in loose linen or cotton shirts and dress shorts. They, too, carried their flip flops. Walking along the sand, there were partiers everywhere. The air was throbbing, as every resort or restaurant had a party, and the noise was incredible, but happy sounding. The new year was being brought in by locals and visitors with tremendous energy.

They took their time walking the beach, surveying the land to assess their options. Reaching the end of the beach, they turned and took their sweet time walking north, talking amongst themselves. The sand was lovely and cool on their feet, and the night sky was clear of clouds.

Making a decision together, they turned into the resort at the northern end of the beach and Adrian paid a cover charge to get them into the dance area. He bought everyone drinks to sip on as they moved in and out of the partiers. They toasted each other and sipped while exploring the grounds and checking out the pool area. Grace rushed them back to the dance area and while they scoped out a place to sit, she and Lizzie pushed their cold drinks into the hands of the boys and took off for the center of the dance floor where there was quite a bit of action.

Walking around, the guys found a place to set their drinks and observe the scene. It was loud but fun. Most people seemed to know the popular island songs and reggae hits. He told his buddies he would be right back and wandered over to the DJ, where he found stacks of Caribbean resort music CDs for sale. He bought everyone a CD to remember the trip by.

To their surprise, the night flew by and before they knew it, a countdown had started, so they stood up and rang in the new year with everyone else cheering, hugging and high-fiving each other. Hot and sweaty, but happy to have had their dance experience on the island, the girls wandered over and finished their drinks and thought the CD was a cool gift. "We better head back," Adrian suggested.

"Wait!" Brody stopped them, he asked a passing tourist if he could take several pictures of all five of them and handed him his cellphone. He jogged back to his friends, and they all wrapped arms around their shoulders and posed for the pictures. He thanked the man and wished him a happy new year.

Perkins, the crew member that liked the night watch pulled up in the jet tender. "All set?" He lent a hand to the girls to help them inside the boat. The boys made it no problem. Adrian pushed the bow out and swung himself up over the bow. He gave Perkins a thumbs up who edged the boat in reverse to clear the shallow water of the beach. Adrian kept an eye out for drunk or midnight swimmers, small boats and other watercraft that weren't lit. He signaled okay to Perkins before walking back to a seat next to the driver. A swell rocked the boat and he fell into his seat with a jolt.

Straightening up he laughed. What a way to start the new year!

Brody asked for the final round of photos and videos from the day, and everyone complied. He looked at the number of files everyone took and let out a sigh. He'd have to pick a few and just run with it. "Are we pulling an all-nighter?" He raised an eyebrow to Adrian.

"Oh, heck no!" He snorted at the mere thought of losing sleep to the project. "Share the files and I'll grab a few good ones and we'll call it good."

An hour later they were still working. Brody yawned. "I haven't even packed yet."

"You're packed." Adrian asserted without taking his eyes off his computer. "While we were away, little elves came into my cabin and packed your suitcases and left you an outfit for getting to the airport, and your toothbrush."

"Seriously?" Brody was in awe. "I want to live like this."

"Trust me, it's easy to get used to." Adrian dragged the last file over. Brody took it from the shared hard-drive they were using between them to share files. "What about using one of the songs off the CD that we heard tonight?"

"Already one step ahead of you." Brody passed him the headphones and Adrian watched the final part of the show that included dinner, dessert, fireworks, nightclubbing, and the last pic of the evening. Brody had put a popular Antiguan reggae dancehall hit to end the show and it was upbeat, memorable, and fun all at once, just like the holiday they spent together on the island.

"Here's my list of credits I've been typing up all week," he put it on the drive and Brody cut and pasted it into his show ending, then clicked a couple animation buttons to make it scroll.

Rubbing his eyes, Brody said, "I'll let this text run to the end of the song. There is no rush on this stuff, and we have over a minute of music left." He clicked save and stood up. Pulling off his clothes and dropping them on the floor at the foot of his bed, he climbed to the top bunk and crashed. Minutes later he was snoring softly.

Adrian showered and got into clean, soft knit shorts and turned off the lights. Lying in bed, he started thinking about how he had spent much of last year worrying about life aboard. Over a month had passed so fast that his mind was marveling at the flow state he'd entered, which was so different from his regular routine back home, which was full of push energy and making things happen because he had to make them happen. On the yacht, he flowed with life. He rather liked it and was now feeling more open to whatever the new year had in store.

At the top of his list of important realizations, he liked who he was becoming. He was less anxious, more confident, and looking forward to life, instead of dreading it. While he missed his friends, he didn't think about 'missing out' while he had two good friends with him to celebrate the holidays. *Life is funny*, he thought with an amused awareness, *what I thought I wanted is not what I want now.* And with that, he rolled over on his side and fell asleep.

Chapter Twelve
Showtime!

The boys were woken up with a playful knock on the cabin door. "Happy New Year!" sang their mothers from the other side of the heavy door. "Rise and shine, boys!" They heard the ladies move to Grace's cabin and do an identical greeting before moving to the staircase up to the owner's deck for breakfast.

"Oh, wait!" Adrian jumped up in a flash that was part panic, "Brody, look alive man! We need to get our show on the TV during breakfast!"

Brody slipped down from the top bunk and found the clean clothing that was left for him by his steward. He brushed his teeth and washed his face, then tucked everything else into his suitcase. Braden was right on his brother's heels. Adrian was out the door first with computer equipment under his arms.

Upstairs on the owner's deck, everyone looked tired but relaxed. Faces were smiling, tan and healthy. Mrs. Nasif set her coffee down and said, "I can't wait to see what you and Brody made this time!"

"Me, too!" And they all laughed. "We were up really late this morning to get it all in. I have a feeling Brody is going to sleep on the plane. I think we got three hours of sleep between us."

Brody joined him while his brother sat down and asked Jane for a double shot of espresso latte drink. "Oh, and you better bring those two the same thing."

Adrian plugged Brody's laptop into the TV and added the speaker output to the main system. He had to find all the pieces to make it work, but after a false start, he figured it out. He brought up the Loon-A-Sea Films logo on the screen of the show they produced and turned around to see if everyone was ready. He bumped backwards into Brody and jumped. "Sorry, man, didn't see you there. Ready?"

Chairs moved for better visibility and Adrian hit the play button and stepped back again. This time Brody kept back out of the way. "Fingers crossed…" Brody said loud enough for Adrian to hear. It loaded just fine and began to play.

Their audience laughed at their film production name, loved the zipline and animal photos, seeing the teens hugging their donkeys, but especially Grace's incredible video capture of the dolphins riding the tender's bow wake. They all roared laughing

at the twins and how they teased each other, clapped when the parrot said cracker and much more. Brody had sped up videos of the multiple failed attempts at learning the water toys which was more comical. The moms enjoyed seeing what their children had been doing together on the trip and exclaimed at many of the photos they hadn't seen or known about, like last night's group photo. By the last picture, Grace was both smiling and crying, using her napkin to wipe her eyes. "Dang, guys, this is so good!"

The credits made everyone laugh, since Adrian ran a sidebar list of their production names that didn't make the cut, and they applauded the boys at the end. Adrian and Brody were beaming, bowing to their audience, and promised copies to all. Then they high-fived each other. "Nailed it!" Adrian said loud enough for only Brody, as they disassembled the equipment.

"That's right!" Brody agreed with a big fat grin on his round face while his back was turned to the dinner table. "We can take care of this stuff later, let's eat!"

Grace and Lizzie excused themselves and walked back to their cabin. The captain strolled in and asked if he may join the table, before pulling out a chair and sitting down. Jane brought him a coffee and he turned to Adrian who sat across from him. All eyes were on the captain, and no one spoke.

"Well, boys, I thought you would appreciate an update." His eyes twinkled as the young men before him all sat up straighter and leaned closer.

He took a sip of coffee then turned to the holiday guests and filled them in with some background so they would understand his report, "I have a friend who is a Port Authority in the Bahamas and I reached out to Thompson yesterday afternoon to give him some information that he could share with his network to solve a crime. As you may have heard, we rescued two sailors at sea last week and they were not forthcoming about the ones who sabotaged their vessel.

"Brody and Adrian solved a part of the puzzle in the last twelve hours by connecting the dots between the sailboat that sank and the vessel that may have shot them using our vessel finder app. As a result, the explorer yacht *Orion* has been impounded and all passengers are detained and under investigation.

"Unfortunately, that is all I have on the matter. Now that it is an ongoing investigation, it would be unrealistic to expect more details until arrests have been made."

"Wow." Brody was stunned by the news. His whole being shone with pride. "We may have helped solve a crime. That was never on my bucket list."

"Hahahaha!" Braden laughed, with sarcasm as he hit his brother's shoulder in a playful slap, "You never had a bucket list, bro!"

"Nice. That's good." Adrian let out his breath and sat back in his chair. He added wistfully, "I just wish I could have connected the *Artemis* and *Neptune*. I can't stop thinking they are connected."

"I seem to remember from my high school history class that *Artemis* is the goddess of the hunt," Mrs. Sanchez shared. "Lizzie told me she connected the dots on *Orien* for you on the name Hunter. That surely might be a clue."

"And *Neptune* is the Roman god of the sea. He's the one with the trident for fishing, which I suppose you could interpret as seafood hunting." Mr. Sanchez offered for consideration. "Now you have all three hunters. It could be nothing or it could mean something."

"Wait a second!" Adrian's mom put down her coffee cup with a clatter and put both hands on the table. Turning to Mrs. Sanchez and Mrs. Nasif, she said, "Wasn't that hoity-toity art gallery woman..." she threw her hands up in the air and waved her fingers expressively to pull into her creative mind a new description of the woman she was trying to describe. "You know who I'm talking about! -The dark-haired art collector we met at the Copper and Lumber cafe in English Harbour, who said we could go aboard her yacht and see her private collection...I think she said her yacht is called *Artemis*."

"Oh, yes, her!" Mrs. Nasif snorted with a laugh and rolled her eyes. "I'm pretty sure she tracked you off your yacht smelling opportunity and has a target on your back. She manipulated the conversation at every turn to bring it back to the subject of art."

"Or her dog!" Mrs. Sanchez scoffed. "I think the dog's collar might be worth more than my engagement ring. No offense, honey."

"None taken," her husband replied with a suppressed smirk. "The dog's neck is much bigger than your finger. I'm sure the collar cost more, based on size."

"Yes, her." Adrian's mom turned to face the captain. "She said she was tied up next to us in Turks and Caicos. But I never noticed her or her yacht. Did any of you?"

"Grace and I did one night." Adrian volunteered, leaning forward with growing excitement. "We never saw her, but I think I heard her laughing with some guests. But we think two guys lugged something heavy from her yacht to *Neptune* since they didn't walk past our yacht." He turned to the captain, "When I looked on the vessel finder app I didn't see anything for *Artemis* being here in Antigua. The last position was T&C."

Looking at his mom he asked with a touch of confusion, "She's here in Antigua?"

"Yes!" his mom asserted emphatically, "That's what I'm trying to tell you. Her yacht is sitting moored in English Harbour outside the Copper and Lumber Inn. We sat outside after shopping and had drinks when she came over with her little teacup poodle and we commented on her adorable little dog and that's how she got talking with us."

"I guess she had her transponder off, Captain. What do you think?" Adrian said with a suggestive grin. "Do we have enough info to talk to Thompson now?"

"Maybe," the captain smiled. "You're very persistent, Adrian, I'll give you that, but…I don't think so."

"Mom, can I get a dog?" Adrian asked out of the blue, stunning everyone at the table. "*Artemis* has one!"

"No," his mom laughed. "Enough with the dog request. I told you long ago, a yacht is no place for a dog."

"Yer no fun," he said with a touch of blaming then turned back to the captain. "But back to the business at hand, Captain, we've got proof they've been together in T&C, she is an art dealer, all the boats are named after hunters, and maybe there is a connection between the owners. Thompson could research it, right?"

"Maybe," the captain repeated. "I'll forward your theories to him. Granted, it is an interesting angle, but I believe this part of the mystery may not be solved easily or at all. If I were you, I'd let this part go and drop it. Solving the Tyche incident will be quite significant. You boys make fine detectives."

"Sure, Captain. Roger that." Adrian replied with a smile, hiding his dismay about not being able to connect the other two yachts. "I hear you. There's no evidence, just loads of suspicion."

"Heck, I'm excited to go home and tell everyone what we did," Brody exclaimed with happiness. "It's not every day I get to live like a king for a week and solve mysteries!" Everyone laughed at his enthusiasm.

The captain is right. We found a good piece of the puzzle and may have helped solve a crime. I can be happy with that. So...why then do I feel so...unsatisfied, like something is missing? Breathing out his disappointment he straightened up in his chair and rejoined the thread of conversation.

The captain stood up and thanked the family for their time and wished the Sanchez and Nasif families a smooth trip home.

After breakfast it was recommended that the guests be brought in the big tender to the north quay near the cruise ship dock to catch a ride to the airport. The six guests would ride together, while the Abercrombies stayed on board. Adrian proposed going with Jimmy in the tender to help them connect to Christopher and pay their taxi bill, to which his father agreed.

He texted Christopher to see if he was working and got a yes; for Adrian, anything. He texted the plan and said he would meet him there at the small marina one block south of North Street. Plan A was the east end of the docks; Plan B was the middle where the boats got hauled out.

Just before noon, everyone hugged goodbye and got their port of entry immigration tourist cards to turn in at the airport from the captain. A few last-minute photos and they climbed into the tender and Adrian cast the line off the yacht and brought it inside the boat for safe keeping.

The water was ideal for a jaunt to St. John's, and they took their sweet time to head south to the St. John's port of entry and cruise ship harbor. Adrian scanned the docks for Christopher, saw him and waved like crazy. He waved back and pointed to where Jimmy should bring the boat. Minutes later, Christopher was loading the minivan with luggage.

Lizzie looked at Adrian and gave him a quick hug. "You're not so bad, Adrian."

"Gee, thanks, Lizzie." He smiled. He knew what she meant. He had changed and wasn't so moody and irritable with his sister or her anymore. Everything really was better on board a yacht. "See ya."

Braden and Brody gave manly hugs to their friend and kept it short. They insisted he come to their place next. Adrian wasn't so sure he could get away, but they sure could rejoin the yacht somewhere. They waved down to Jimmy who waved goodbye from the tender, where he kept the engine running at the dock.

"Well, guys, this is it. Keep in touch." He didn't want to get emotional, but he was saying goodbye, yet again. "Text me when you get home. And say hello to the guys for me, okay?"

"Yeah, you got it." Brody said and climbed into the van.

"See ya, Adrian." Braden almost sounded emotional, and he cleared his throat to normalize it then entered the van after his brother. Adrian slammed the sliding door shut. He shook hands with Mr. Sanchez in the front seat. "Maybe next time, sir, we'll get

to spend some time together."

"Oh, I understand." He shared with a happy grin, "but I must say, it was good to hang out with your parents and let all the teenagers hang out together for a week."

Mrs. Sanchez and Mrs. Nasif waved to him and blew him a kiss.

He walked around to Christopher and handed him an envelope with cash in it. Christopher just saluted him and tucked it away in his side door pocket.

"Thanks, man." To which Christopher replied, "Anytime, my American friend, anytime."

Adrian stood back and waved as they pulled out of the marina and headed to the airport. Then he turned away and walked down to the tender.

Without a word to Jimmy, he cast off the bow and stern line. Jimmy brought them out of the harbor under slow speed. Adrian sat down next to him in a comfortable silence. There were no words for a perfect trip with friends, just a good feeling in his whole being.

Jimmy opened the throttle once they cleared the entrance to the harbor and they flew at high speed along the island...just two guys in a fast boat, the sun, and the sea.

Life, as far as Adrian was concerned, was darn near perfect right now. He felt a silly kind of grin coming on and turned to look at Jimmy, who sensed the movement, turned, and grinned back.

Turning away from each other with perfect understanding, they turned in the direction of the M/Y *Arabella*, knowing a new adventure was right around the corner.

To be continued...

Glossary

Aft – this word means at, near or towards the stern, or back of the ship.

Amidship – middle of the ship; or on the midline of the ship. Example, "I was amidship when the main boom swung over suddenly and almost swept me into the sea."

Anchor – a weighted object typically made of metal or concrete and attached to a chain or rope that is lowered to the floor of the sea or lakebed to hold your boat in place, so it does not drift away. There are many designs of anchors, and the most popular have "flukes" that can easily grab into mud, sand, even rocky bottoms to provide reliable strength to hold the boat in place. Anchors are usually stored in a locker and the anchor line is kept neatly coiled and ready to go overboard without getting tangled. On super yachts and ships, only a robust galvanized steel and carbon steel chain is trusted to hold a boat that big.

Antiquities – ancient items that are considered historical treasure.

Beam – this is the middle section of the boat. It is typically the widest part of the entire boat. The beam can be referred to as "port beam" or "starboard beam." For further clarification, and to increase your communication, you can use "forward of the port beam" or "aft the port beam."

Berth – a ship's allotted place at a wharf or dock. The word is also used to describe the bunk or bed that a sailor is assigned to sleep in. To give someone a "wide berth" is to avoid them or stay away from them.

Bow – this is the pointy end of the boat. It is the forward part. It's good to remember that not all bows are pointy. Check out a punt, hydroplaning flat boats, sled boats or blunt nose inflatable if you want to learn more.

Bow line – the rope or line attached to the pointy or front end of the boat that is used to secure it, so it doesn't drift away.

Bowline knot – A strong knot that never jams, even after being placed under extreme tension or pressure or from being wet. Pronounced *bow-luhn*, it's known as the King of Knots.

Bridge – the bridge on a large vessel is the area where the captain commands and controls the ship. The bridge is manned by an officer of the watch. Since the captain also needs to eat and sleep, a second or third in command may be appointed to take control of the vessel. Sometimes the bridge is referred to as the pilothouse or wheelhouse, which is the name for the housing around the helm or steering wheel.

Bulwark – side of a ship above the deck.

Captain – the captain of a vessel, no matter the size, is the ultimate authority onboard. His or her responsibility is to make sure all people aboard are safe, the vessel is safe, and the environment remains safe. All incidents involving the boat are the responsibility of the captain, whether or not they were the source of the problem. Captains are very educated about the workings of vessels, engine and electrical systems, navigating, maritime law, weather and have logged thousands of hours

Compass Heading – the direction a boat is moving. All headings have a numerical value, and any one of the 32-points that are named can be used to describe the heading. Most people navigate by a numerical value. "Keep the boat pointed at 123 degrees or we will miss the channel marker."

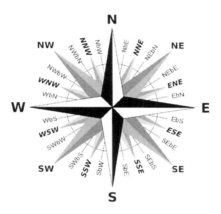

The compass rose, as it is called, is an ancient system for navigating around the earth. The rose refers to the evenly spaced marks around the face of the compass, which represent a unique direction. Each name has a numerical value.

The cardinal points (4) are North, East, South and West. Each point is 90 degrees apart.

The intercardinal points are (4) additional divisions of the four points, namely, Northeast, Southeast, Southwest and Northwest. The cardinal and intercardinal are referred to as the 8 Winds or 8 Principle Winds (meaning the wind directions). Each are 45 degrees from each other.

Shakedown Cruise — The Adventures of Yacht Boy

Each of the named points below are separated by 11.4 degrees on the compass. These 32 points, multiplied by 11 ¼ degrees equal 360 degrees, which is the total number of degrees in a circle.

[32-point compass rose illustration courtesy of Wikipedia Commons, the free media repository; Brosen derivative work: Auanika (talk) - Brosen_windrose.svg]

N - North
NbE - North by East
NNE - North Northeast
NEbN - Northeast by North
NE - Northeast
NbE - Northeast by East
ENE - East Northeast
EbN - East by North
E - East
EbS - East by South
ESE - East Southeast
SEbE – Southeast by East
Southeast
SEbE - Southeast by South
ESE – East S
SbE – South by East
S - South

SbW - South by West
SSW - South Southwest
SWbS – Southwest by South
SW - Southwest
SWbS - Southwest by West
WSW - West Southwest
West by South
W - West
WbN - West by North
WNW - West Northwest
NWbW – Northwest by West
NW - Northwest
NWbN – Northwest by North
NNW – North Northwest
NbW - North by West
N – North (repeat)

Deck – on any boat, the flooring that you walk on is called the deck or decking. On super yachts, teak is the preferred wood for the floor due to its ease of maintenance. See teak definition below. When there are multiple floors or levels on a ship, each level is referred to as a deck. Here are some examples: The "upper deck" is the topmost deck unless it is topped by a "bridge deck" or an "observation deck." The "main deck" is where most of the ship's activity occurs. "Lower deck" has the vessel's engines and bilge pumps, water storage and other mechanical or electrical systems.

Deckhand – a person who serves as crew on a boat that works lines, anchors, sails (if any), fenders, the operation of small boats, maintenance to the boat itself, keeping the boat exterior clean, safe and operational. There may be other job duties that are not listed here and that depends on the type of vessel, the captain, location, and skill level. Overall, these are men and women that help run the vessel.

Dinghy – any small boat (with or without a mast) that serves multiple needs from traveling from shore to ship or between places, racing or pleasure. These small boats can be constructed from wood, metal, rubber (inflatable) or fiberglass. They can be powered by wind (sails), outboard motors or by rowing.

Epaulet – *epaulette* in French. Worn on the shoulder of a yacht crew or captain's uniform, the word comes from *epaule*, which is the word for shoulder in French. Hundreds of years ago, soldiers would tie ribbons to their shoulder to prevent their bayonet or sword belt from slipping. Traditionally, Captains wore two, and lieutenants wore one. The uniform system has evolved in modern times and yacht's use them to communicate rank aboard ships. Symbols and their colors on the epaulet or shoulder boards reveal your job aboard:

   Anchor = Captain, First Officer, and Deckhands

   Propellor = Engineers

Crescent moon = Stewardesses; the historic symbol of the moon refers to food, it was used by Napoleon when he introduced crescent-shaped bread, also known as *croissants*, into the rations for the *Grande Armée*.

Four stripes = Captain or Chief Engineer

Three stripes = First Officer, First engineer, Chief Stewardess or Chef

Two stripes = Bosun, Second Stewardess, Second Engineer

One stripe = Deckhand, Third Stewardess, Third Engineer

E.P.I.R.B. (Emergency Positioning Indicating Radio Beacon) – A personal safety device that activates upon entering the water or manually turned on. It sends a signal which is picked up by satellites and sent to search and rescue teams. Alerts, locates, tracks, and recovers the individual or vessel.

Fenders – inflated plastic or rubber tubes that protect the boat when tied up alongside a dock or other boat. They are tied to the boat and hung over the side where the boat touches another object. They can be small, for a rowboat, or extra-large for a yacht. In ancient days, ropes would be woven intricately to protect a boat. In some scenarios, tugboats use recycled automotive tires to act as fenders.

Flemishing - To "flemish down a line" means that you coil the line on a flat surface, such as a deck or dock by starting with the bitter end (the end part that is not being used) and lay it on the deck in successive circles of line in the manner of a clock spring with the bitter end at the center. It is important to know that right-laid line is laid down clockwise and left-laid line is laid down counterclockwise. This helps the line lay flat, prevent unnecessary knots, trip hazards, and aids in drying the line.

Galley – the kitchen area on a boat where food and drinks are prepared. It can be very tiny and consist of a sink and cutting board on a small boat with a portable stove or BBQ for cooking off the side of the boat, or it can be a full-scale kitchen that could serve a small military on board a ship. Most super yachts have a full array of high-end professional restaurant grade equipment, multiple floor-to-ceiling or walk-in freezers and refrigerators, dishwashers, stacking convection ovens that can hold, for example, several trays of breads, and much more. The galley can be plumbed (piped) for natural gas (propane) or operate completely as an electricity sourced power supply.

Gunnel - the top edge of the hull of a ship or boat. Originally, the structure was the "gun wale" on a sailing warship, a horizontal reinforcing band added at and above the level of a gun deck to offset the stresses created by firing artillery (Wikipedia). The gunnel, now, has more functions on different boats. Sailboats have scupper holes for allowing water to run off the decks built into the gunnel. Cleats can be mounted on the gunnel. Having a raised gunnel along a deck creates a place for a foot to brace one's body against the angle of the vessel when underway. Gunnels can also have padding on small boats to protect the edge. Oarlocks often are inserted into the gunnels or mounted just inside the gunnel.

Head – The toilet or bathroom on board a boat. In olden days, the box for the toilet was built into the bow or "head" of the ship, typically one on port and starboard, and the biological waste matter would drop to the sea. It is believed that the water action from the bow wave would wash the side of the ship. Sailors used these boxes primarily to defecate, preferring to stand at the leeward rails to relieve themselves of urine on the side that the wind wouldn't blow it back on themselves.

Helm – the steering mechanism on a boat. It can be a wheel, which is typical on all powerboats, or it can be a tiller, which is a "long handle or rod" made of wood connected to the rudder which is steered by pulling or pushing it to port or starboard or simply keeping it amidships. On ultra-modern yachts, the helm may be a joystick attached to a computer system, much like a gaming console.

Jet Ski – this is the brand name of a personal watercraft (PWC) manufactured by Kawasaki, a Japanese company, however the term is generically used to denote any type of personal watercraft used for recreational play. It is a gas-powered water toy that one rides on, similar to a motorcycle. All PWC come with inherent risks of injury when used improperly or falling off one, since these PWC can reach speeds of 40-70 miles per hour. Falling off a jet ski and hitting the water at any speed is painful and can result in death or serious injury.

Knots – refers to both ropes and lines tied in a particular fashion, but also the speed across the water. "We were traveling at 2 knots per hour, and it seemed like we would never reach our destination." While it may seem like the phrase may have come from traveling "nautical miles"… and *naut* sounds like *knot*, read the knot meter explanation below, to further learn how knots in a line were used to measure a nautical mile, then decide.

Knot Meter – a meter that measures your speed across the water. In olden days a line on a spool would be thrown over the side and timed until it reached a certain length off the spool. This would tell the sailor how fast they were going. A simple device can be installed in the hull of a boat that consists of a tiny paddle wheel attached to a transducer. The transducer is hooked up to a simple meter that has a speedometer and a needle to point to the numerical speed. In modern times, a knot meter has a device inside it called a transmitter and a receiver. The transmitter sends a ping down to the ground or floor of the lake or sea and it bounces back up to the surface where it is received by a receiver. The computer translates the difference over the water into a meaningful number for the sailor.

Latitude – the angular distance of a place north or south of the equator. It is expressed in degrees of latitude or minutes of latitude and parallels of latitude. The parallel lines to the equator go from the north pole to the south pole. San Francisco is roughly 38 degrees of latitude north of the equator on planet Earth. Here are the coordinates for San Francisco as obtained from Google: 37.7749° N, 122.4194° W. See longitude and coordinate definitions.

Lazarette – a storage compartment, under a seat on a boat. The heavy lid opens on a set of hinges and has a latch, if it is meant to be locked.

Leeward – the side protected from the wind.

Line – all rope and even the anchor rope and chain tied together is called a line (or rode) once it reaches the maritime environment. Lines are used to tie off a boat, become called *sheets* when attached to the sails, are used as *halyards* to hoist sails, *shrouds* and *stays* to hold up the mast, and too many other terms to mention here. See the entry below for rope to learn when rope is called rope on a boat.

Longitude – the angular distance of a place east or west of the meridian in Greenwich, England. It is expressed in degrees and minutes. These lines are not parallel and begin at the north pole and end at the south pole. Longitude lines make the earth look like the segments of an orange, pointy at the top and bottom, wide in the middle.

Marine – relates to the sea and the practice of sailing across the sea. Mar in Latin means sea. Here are a few examples of how the word is used: marine radio, marine chart, marine life, marine biology (study of sea life), marine painter (someone who paints seascapes or ships), marines (military that supports naval operations), mariner (to describe a sailor), *mariscos* (Spanish word for seafood), and maritime law (laws that govern the sea.

Mast – any tall, vertical structure on a boat that has a light atop, or holds a sail, radio antennae or other device.

Midline – the centerline of any vessel that divides the boat in half for ease of referencing sides, direction, location and steering. "Keep your helm midline to maintain your compass heading."

Nautical – anything that pertains or relates to ships, sailors, navigation, meaning maritime. Both Greek (nautikos, from nautēs meaning sailor) and Latin (nauticus) have a common root word: naus meaning ship.

Nautical Mile (NM) – nautical miles are used to measure the distance traveled through the water. A nautical mile is slightly longer than a mile on land. If you were to use land or statute miles, it would equal 1.1508 miles (1.85km). The nautical mile is based on the Earth's longitude and latitude coordinates, with one nautical mile equaling one minute of latitude. Degrees of latitude are approximately 60 nautical miles apart. Each minute of latitude is divided into 60-seconds. This makes navigation calculations somewhat easier. 60 x Distance = Speed x Time. The 60 refers to minutes in an hour used in all (T)ime calculations. An easy way to remember this formula is the address "60 D Street" or 60D=ST also written as (60)(D)=(S)(T), which is a simple algebraic equation. Also see Knots.

Passerelle - the single or double-telescoping type passerelle is a design that increases and enhances the stowed efficiency of the plank used to walk from a yacht's stern to the dock. By doubling the plank-sections the ratio of stowed length to deployed length is increased. This allows the pocketing hydraulic passerelle to be used in a variety of boarding conditions and stowed in shorter spaces in the yacht.

Phonetic Alphabet (used by the American Military) - When conditions are poor over a two-way radio or telephone, or there is a noisy background, spelling out important words or numbers are critical to avoid confusion. The letters B, D, and P often sound the same, so using a word to explain yourself is helpful. In this case, you would use "Bravo, Delta, Papa" to distinguish the differences.

A	Alpha	L	Lima
B	Bravo	M	Mike
C	Charlie	N	November
D	Delta	O	Oscar
E	Echo	P	Papa
F	Foxtrot	Q	Quebec
G	Golf	R	Romeo
H	Hotel	S	Sierra
I	India	T	Tango
J	Juliet	U	Uniform
K	Kilo	V	Victor

W	Whiskey	Y	Yankee
X	X-ray	Z	Zulu

Port – the left side of the boat as you face forward. This is also the side of the boat that historically would be clean and could be used to approach a dock, quay, or wharf for offloading goods. The starboard side is the right side, and back in the Viking days was the side the sailors would use the bathroom. You can remember port is on the left because the words left and port both have four letters in it. (PS: Starboard and right have more letters; now you can't forget.)

Positions On Board - Each person has certain responsibilities on board a boat. Responsibilities can be equated to leadership positions meaning that each person leads the tasks for their department. Here are the most common positions found on a yacht:

> Captain - Included navigation or piloting determinations, crew leadership, boat own relationship management, budget control and full crew and guest or passenger responsibility

> First Officer/Mate - The captain's second in command of the vessel. Often this person has their captain's license and is waiting for the captain position to open up and they take the position.

> Chief Engineer Officer - All mechanical maintenance; ensuring that every piece of equipment remains operational. Also referred to as First Engineer if other engineers are aboard. Knowledge of refrigeration, air conditioning, plumbing, some electrical, engines, jet skis, and anything motorized with gas or electricity.

Chief Electrical Officer - Responsible for all electrical equipment/motors and oftentimes the internet, satellite and other computer related items.

Deckhand/Stew - crew member working on maintenance of hulls, decks, mooring and assisting superior officers as needed. Certification in PADI diving, other water sports and personal fitness is required on some vessels. Expertise in repair, carpentry, polishing and painting is always key to this role. Many times, this is a combination role to support the interior team when the passenger list is full.

Chief Steward/ess - Responsible for the interior team and the superyacht's interior. This includes linens, decor changes, table decorations, party and guest planning, and more. Often this individual acts like a concierge for the owner or guests.

Steward/ess - Responsible for interior maintenance of the yacht and offering first class (white glove) services to guests while on board. Previous hospitality experience or customer service skills are key as this role on board requires a friendly person due to the variety of requests received.

Chef - Catering or restaurant experience is a must as is a wide variety of cuisine knowledge. Responsible for all aspects of food and beverage services, budget and healthy dietary menus.

Sous Chef - This individual assists the chef and often is responsible for making the food that the crew eats. Any additional skills are a plus, such as nutrition, bartending, baking, or specializing in a cuisine.

Purser - On larger yachts where the crew is more than thirteen, there often is an individual in charge of interior operations, inventory, guest or owner activity and all accounting for the operations of the vessel. Budgets are created and tracked against expenditures.

Bosun - Often there is a person assigned the role of Bosun to be responsible for the deck team and provider leadership to the crew

Rope – is any group of natural (e.g., plant or animal), synthetic (e.g., polypropylene, nylon) or metal (e.g., steel and other alloys made into cables) yarns, plies, fibers or stands that are twisted or braided together into larger, thicker or stronger form to increase tensile strength by distributing the load to different strands. Ropes are used for lifting, dragging, tying, and weaving primarily for, but not limited to the maritime environment. On a boat rope is called a line. See the entry above for *line* to learn more.

The only time rope is called rope is when it is a **bell rope**, which your hand holds to bang the clapper to the sides of the bell to ring it; **tow rope**, which is used to tow a boat behind your boat and hopefully not the other way around; **rope ladder**, used for a swim ladder; **bolt rope**, which is attached to edge luff edge and foot of a mainsail; **tiller rope**, which is used on a sailboat to tie off the tiller when not in use so it doesn't flop around the cockpit or to tie the tiller off on a course; **foot rope**, which tall ship sailors stood on to reef, furl and stow the top sails; and the **man rope**, which are the two ropes people can hold to assist with boarding and disembarking a vessel.

Rope Trivia – "Learning the ropes" is a term that goes all the way back to becoming a sailor on a tall ship. New recruits had to learn what all the ropes were used for, how to manipulate the ropes to move the ship and how to tie knots. "Teaching someone the ropes" was done by someone with tremendous experience and knowledge of the ropes...and one would hope, patience and good humor.

Shakedown Cruise - is a nautical term in which the performance of a ship is tested near marine services whereby the ship can return if something goes wrong or needs to be adjusted after being worked on. *Maiden Voyage* is a ship's first trip of note. A shakedown cruise can occur after every haul-out where yard work may have been performed on the hull, propeller, engines and other equipment was repaired or installed. The idea is to test the vessel (or a new crew that's been installed) before taking the vessel on an extended cruise so that if anything goes wrong, the ship can turn around and return to port to correct the problem(s).

Skeg – the fin underneath the rear of a surfboard. It can also be a tapered or projecting piece of a stern section of a vessel's keel, which protects the propeller or rudder. Kayak's may have skegs that are retractable. At the bottom of an outboard engine, there is a small skeg just before the propeller. The skeg "takes the hit" so the propeller doesn't have to. Skegs also provide directional stability, lateral resistance, and steering when the engine is not running. *Skegg* in Scandinavian means "beard." Next time you see a skeg, consider if it looks somewhat like a beard!

Sous Chef – the top or highest assistant in a professional kitchen that supports the chef. This person is in charge of the production of the food. The head chef is the creative force, the boss and administrator of the kitchen, or galley.

Stern – the back of the boat. The stern can have three areas, if it is square and boxy. The port quarter, the starboard quarter and dead-astern.

Stern line – the rope or line attached to the back end of the boat that is used to secure it, so it doesn't drift away.

Steward/Stewardess – also known as a stew or stu, these are men and women (-ess) who serve the owner or guests on board the yacht, meet their needs and are often "people pleasers" making sure everyone is enjoying their time aboard the boat. They cover all duties including food and beverage service, housekeeping, laundry, and conciergerie activities such as obtaining tickets to a movie or concert. They may be part of the support staff to the galley. On occasion they are required without a moment's notice to serve as a deckhand when docking the vessel or anchoring.

Teak – teak is an oily, tropical hardwood used for centuries to build boats. It is super resilient to walking on and maintains itself in all marine conditions.

Transom – the flat part of the stern that forms the back wall of the boat. This part of the yacht may have an extended swim platform or step on to go ashore. In smaller boats, an outboard engine may be hung from it.

Transponder - A transponder is a wireless communications, monitoring, or control device that picks up and automatically responds to an incoming signal such as a satellite signal. The term is a contraction of the words *trans*mitter and res*ponder*. On a vessel, the transponder is active, and the output signal is tracked, so the position of the transponder can be constantly monitored. The input (receiver) and output (transmitter) frequencies are preassigned a unique code. Transponders of this type can operate over distances of thousands of miles and share a wide variety of information. The primary use is for location by date and time, estimated times of arrive and determining speed of a vessel. Transponders can prevent ships from colliding by reporting nearby traffic and supporting search and rescue operations.

Tyche - Pronounced Tie-kee, as the daughter of Oceanus and Tethys, she is the Greek goddess of luck or good fortune and while conducting world affairs has her hand on the rudder.

VHF (VERY HIGH FREQUENCY) VOCABULARY IN LAYMAN'S TERMS

Affirmative – Yes. (When speaking on a radio, the words yes and no can be easily misunderstood.)

Break, Break – interruption to the transmission to communicate urgently. Sometimes people listen in on conversations and have something valuable to add something to the transmission. Saying, "Break, break" allows the caller and receiver to stop talking to hear a 3rd party chime in.

Come In – Inviting someone to talk to you or acknowledge they can hear you.

Emergency/Emergency – use this only if you are in grave or imminent danger to life and immediate assistance is needed.

Figures – I'm about to say numbers. For example, "My depth here is figures one-five feet" --meaning 15 feet of water.)

Go Ahead – tells the other party you are ready to listen.

I Spell – I'm going to use the phonetic alphabet to spell out something that might be difficult to understand. Example, "I'm anchored at Mary Island. I spell, Mike, Alpha, Romeo, Yankee." Most radios have a sticker with the phonetic alphabet or find it in your radio's owner's manual. You may always post a copy of the list next to your radio.

Over – I've completed my message and am asking the other party to reply.

Over and Out – Combo of two-phrased meaning, "I'm complete with my sending and expect no reply from you."

Out – I've finished my message and expect no further reply.

Negative – No. (When speaking on a radio, the words yes and no can be misunderstood.)

Read You Loud And Clear – informs the other party that their transmission is good

Roger/Roger That – I received and understood your message. 10-4 and Copy That are also used.

Roger So Far – confirms with the speaker that part of their message has been received, especially if it is a long message.

Say Again – please repeat your last message.

Stand By – Wait for a short period and I will get back to you

Wilco – OK. I not only understood your last transmission, but I will also comply. This is a contraction of the two words will+comply.

Watch – every qualified person on board a yacht has a turn being "on watch," which means they are caring for some aspect of the boat in the capacity they are appointed. Here are some examples: steering, repair, routine maintenance, security, or normal operations. On superyachts, crew on "night watch" often clean the windows, mop floors, straighten pillows on deck chairs, and other relatively quiet duties that do not disturb the guests who are sleeping. Day watch crew may include vessel operations, such as moving the boat from one location to another, housekeeping and laundry, engine operations and more. Sometimes a crew member may say, "I'm on galley duty" rather than "galley watch." Night and day watch responsibilities always include making sure that the people are safe, the boat is safe, and the environment is safe. Phases: keeping watch, on watch, my watch is about to begin (or almost over), and even "can I swap watches with you?" –and they don't mean the timepiece on your wrist! Here are the maritime "watch standards" for keeping watch:

Middle Watch	Midnight to 4 AM (0000 – 0400)
Morning Watch	4 AM to 8 AM (0400 – 0800)
Forenoon Watch	8 AM to Noon (0800 – 1200)
Afternoon Watch	Noon to 4 PM (1200 – 1600)
First Dog Watch	4 PM to 6 PM (1600 – 1800)
Second Dog Watch	6 PM to 8 PM (1800 – 2000)
First Watch	8 PM to Midnight (2000 – 0000)

Wheelhouse – the area or room that is enclosed on a boat that includes the wheel for steering the boat. On larger boats, it is also called the bridge. It could even be called a platform if it is constructed in such a way that the officer stands on it and commands the vessel from there.

Windward – the side the wind is approaching from.

LIST OF CHARACTERS for SHAKEDOWN CRUISE

Passenger List

Mr. Abercrombie, American

Mrs. Abercrombie, American

Grace Abercrombie, American

Adrian Abercrombie, American

Mrs. Nasif, American

Braden Nasif, American

Brody Nasif, American

Mr. & Mrs. Sanchez, American

Lizzie Sanchez, American

Ship's Master & Crew List With Rank

Gunnar Johnson – Captain: Sweden; holds a 100-ton master captain's license

Jimmy Williams – First Officer: Jamaica; steward to Adrian on special assignment, holds a 100-ton master captain's license, certified in SCUBA, lifeguarding, small boats

Pete Ferguson – Chief Engineer: American; California Maritime Academy graduate

Bryce Fraser – Chief Electrical Engineer; American; computer expert, nephew to the captain, Brian Kelly – Deckhand and Bosun: Ireland, longtime friend of Jimmy

James Perkins – Deckhand: England; prefers night watch

Gabriella De Vries – Chief Stewardess: South Africa; personal stewardess to Grace

Jane Higgins – Stewardess: Australia; stewardess to Mr. and Mrs. Abercrombie

Zak Broussard – Chief Chef: American

Jean-Marie Fournier – Sous Chef: France; doubles as a bartender

Roberto Bonnano – Deckhand: Italy; doubles as bartender, occasional steward, likes night watch, cousin to Francesco

Francesco Demattei – Deckhand: Italy; cousin to Roberto

Raffaele "Raffa" Marino – Deckhand: Italy; occasional steward

Acknowledgements

Just as you cannot compress the time it takes to build a quality superyacht, a book requires time, attention to detail and a good plot to be in place that assures value to the reader before it goes to publication.

I am much richer for that process and I wish to acknowledge with great love and gratitude, my family and friends, both old and new, who contributed to the launch of The Adventures of Yacht Boy and enriched my life along the way.

From the early efforts of my sister Frances, with her first pass edits and hugely beneficial suggestions, if you, dear reader, were caught up in the fun stuff the teens got to do and explore, you have her to thank.

My mother, Mary, for her lifelong enthusiasm and persistent encouragement of my creative writing, art abilities and ongoing support in all my chosen activities. I have thrived on your enthusiasm and I love you! Thank you for living long enough to see my first book published. You are still amazing at 89!

My husband Anand, I'm grateful for your patience while listening to me troubleshooting out loud my challenges with the plot and the piloting of the yacht's destinations; your proofreading and creating endless meals for our family so I could write. Thank you for not judging my abnormal sleep hours so I could write when everyone was asleep during the infamous plandemic. I look forward to sitting at anchor with you in the future, my love.

Longtime friend, sailor and author Ian McFall offered me style coaching which made me look at my use of certain words and tendencies in my writing. I appreciate your wisdom and guidance, Ian. Your laughter and stories are priceless. I still read your motorcycle novella out loud to anyone who will listen.

Infinite love and thanks to my dear friend, fellow sailor and colleague Ashley Lee, for her patience with me as her co-author on a consciousness book project while I birthed this book first.

Art is essential to life, and we would have been stranded without the innate giftedness of fine artist Jon Tocchini, oil painter and illustrator extraordinaire from San Francisco. Bringing Yacht Boy's story to life through your powerful strokes reveal the pen is indeed mighty and perhaps the brush even mightier! Working together has been a joy and I am excited about collaborating on book two!

To children's author Bradley Steffens for his professional contributions and ideas, which opened my eyes to new potentials and opportunities. He also reacquainted me with Herman Melville through Clarel, an epic poem, and Moby Dick, which I read long ago and far away in high school while sailing in whaleboats on SF Bay. Both are great reads!

Liza Gershman, my incandescent editor who did a great job pushing me to write an even better story; You lovingly found all the shoals and reefs in my story, handed me a compass and made this book stronger for which I am super grateful. As the captain of my own ship, I yielded to the fixed position of your lightship and altered my course to prevent a disaster on the pages within. This book has sea legs because of your well-placed insistence that I steer clear of the shoals. Thank you for your vision and lighting the way.

Finally, I wish to thank Nick Bischoff of Benetti Americas, Ft. Lauderdale, FL for sharing the superyacht specifications of an Italian built 66m Benetti BNow superyacht layout, so I could guide my readers with accuracy through our fantasy aboard the *M/Y Arabella* and support your understanding of superyachts in general. *Grazie mille*!

Colophon

In publishing, a colophon is a brief statement containing information about the publication of a book such as the place of publication, the publisher, and the date of publication. A colophon may include the device of a printer or publisher. - Wikipedia

Layout for this book was conceptualized in Adobe InDesign by the author, who has a background in graphic design but was truly brought into prepress form by a modern-day knight in shining armor named Kailash Black, who made digital magic happen somewhere in Budapest, Hungary while the author was sleeping at night. These pages are engaging because of his incredible talents with InDesign.

The text of Shakedown Cruise - The Adventures of Yacht Boy is set in Marcia, licensed through the Adobe Font Library, which contains Font Bureau fonts, in the Adobe Creative Suite.

Font Bureau "Marcia" was designed by Victoria Rushton in 2015. It is a didone typeface (also referred to as Neoclassical and Modern typeface as it was born from Didot and Bondoni typefaces), which Wikipedia states is a genre of serif typeface that emerged in the late 18th century and was the standard style of general-purpose printing during the nineteenth century. This genre of fonts is characterized by extreme weight contrast between thicks and thins, vertical stress, and serifs with little or no bracketing. Marcia font has many quirks and curvy surprises, which you can observe in the title on the cover of the book.

Here is a tiny wee bio about Ms. Rushton, taken from the Adobe Font website:

"Victoria was trained as a type-designer at Font Bureau, where she spent her days lovingly kerning, plotting and snacking. She went to RISD [Rhode Island School of Design] and studied illustration because she loved to draw but turns out the main thing she wanted to draw was letters[...]."

Typenetwork.com in a news article shared:

"Marcia is based on nothing, nothing at all," says designer Victoria Rushton. "In form, the roman looks like a 19th-century modern, with its high contrast, vertical stress, and ball terminals. But when you look closely, it doesn't fit the mold at all. In fact, it seems to contradict itself. And the italic is both sturdier and simpler than most moderns. That's part of Marcia's charm."

Helvetica font is used for the name of the series. Helvetica is a mid-century font from the 20th century and attributed to a typeface designers Max Miedinger and Eduard Hoffman at the Haas Foundry in Switzerland. His goal was to create a sans-serif typeface that was completely neutral and would not contribute any additional meaning. It has become one of the most popular fonts in the world. Helvetica is Latin for Swiss. Look for very definitive vertical and horizontal strokes in this font. Look for the teardrop shape inside the lowercase "a", which is a trademark of Helvetica.

Google's Roboto font, released in 2011 for Android 4.0 "Ice Cream Sandwich" phones and re-released in 2014 for "Lollipop", is used for illustrating the text messaging between Adrian and all others. Since 2013, it has been the default font used on Android, Google

Play, YouTube, Google Maps, and Google Images. Per Wikipedia, it is also used on LCD countdown clocks and in the New York City Subway's B Division lines. It is an Open-Source font licensed from the Apache Foundation, meaning it is free to use however one desires.

Biographies

Anne Marie Peterson
Author

Annie Peterson is a 3rd generation native San Franciscan. She spent her youth sail racing SF Bay and cruising the California coast and inland waterways as a sea scout and achieved the top rank of Quartermaster (Boy Scouts of America Sea Explorer Program). An avid traveler and adventure seeker, the world provides inspiration for the many oil paintings and stories she creates from exotic destinations. When she is not writing or helping others heal their consciousness for optimal experiences, she spends her time with her husband and two young children in Los Angeles. To learn more about her work, please visit www.LeapofConsciousness.com

Jon Tocchini
Artist/Illustrator

Jon Tocchini is an artist born and raised in San Francisco, California. He received his B.F.A. degree from the Academy of Art University, Fine Art School, San Francisco, CA, USA. He is a member of the California Art Club (CAC) and Associate Member of the Oil Painters of America (OPA). To see Jon's artwork, please visit www.FineArtByJon.com

**Thank you for reading
Shakedown Cruise - The Adventures of Yacht Boy.**

Please leave an honest review of this book on Amazon. Your comments support others determining if this book is something they would enjoy, find valuable, or helpful in learning more about the world.

You may find us on multiple Social Media platforms under Young Navigator Books!

Made in the USA
Monee, IL
20 July 2023

39626487R00192